Howl
For It

Howl For It

SHELLY LAURENSTON
CYNTHIA EDEN

BRAVA

KENSINGTON PUBLISHING CORP.
www.kensingtonbooks.com

BRAVA BOOKS are published by

Kensington Publishing Corp.
119 West 40th Street
New York, NY 10018

All Kensington titles, imprints, and distributed lines are available at special quantity discounts for bulk purchases for sales promotions, premiums, fund-raising, educational, or institutional use.

Special book excerpts or customized printings can also be created to fit specific needs. For details, write or phone the office of the Kensington special sales manager: Kensington Publishing Corp., 119 West 40th Street, New York, NY 10018, attn: Special Sales Department; phone 1-800-221-2647.

Brava and the B logo are Reg. U.S. Pat. & TM Off.

ISBN-13: 978-0-7582-7344-4
ISBN-10: 0-7582-7344-4

First Kensington Trade Paperback Printing: September 2012

10 9 8 7 6 5 4 3 2 1

Printed in the United States of America

CONTENTS

LIKE A WOLF WITH A BONE
by Shelly Laurenston

WED OR DEAD
by Cynthia Eden

LIKE A WOLF WITH A BONE
Shelly Laurenston

CHAPTER ONE

He spotted her as soon as she stepped out of the house and walked around her daddy's porch to stare out into the forest surrounding the home. His brothers had called her "cute" and "kind of pretty" while simultaneously ordering him to stay away because her big sisters wouldn't have any of it. But his brothers had been wrong. She wasn't cute or kind of pretty.

She was astounding.

Leaning back against his 1971 Plymouth GTX, Egbert Ray Smith—Eggie to his Pack and those of the United States Marine Corps that knew of his existence—watched the She-wolf softly sighing and rolling her eyes. Occasionally she shook her head. He knew why, too. It was all the arguing going on inside the house behind her. All that damn arguing. If he'd known he would be coming home to this, he wouldn't have come.

As it was, Eggie hated when he was forced on what the full-humans called "a vacation," or what his military brethren called "leave." He didn't need a vacation. He didn't *want* a vacation.

He was lucky enough to be one of the few men in the world who enjoyed what he did for a living, and what he did was kill. Not just randomly, though. He wasn't some murdering scumbag. No, Eggie killed with purpose, for the protection of his kind and the other breeds and species that he really didn't like or care about, but figured deserved protection just as much as anyone else who could shift into a completely different being.

Eggie was good at killing. Some would probably say it was the only thing Eggie Ray Smith *was* good at. So then why should he be forced away from the only thing he was good at just because his fellow Marines insisted that "Eggie's startin' to make us nervous." Eggie didn't understand how he did that. He wasn't doing anything different from what he did on any given day.

But because his entire platoon—the platoon with no name, no number, that was only known about by those who could grow fangs and claws whenever they wanted—suggested he needed "a break," Eggie was now on break.

So with nothing else to do for the next month or two, depending on when his superiors would need him back, Eggie had come home.

And up to three minutes ago, he was positive it had been the most idiotic decision he'd made in a long time. What with his brothers trying so desperately to secure themselves some females. Of course, for most wolf shifters, securing females simply meant seducing them or enticing them with still-thrashing elk.

Too bad the Smith males weren't like most wolf shifters.

None of Eggie's brothers seemed to understand the words "entice" or "seduce." Instead they argued with their She-wolves. Constantly. It had been bad enough with Eggie's two older brothers, Benjamin Ray and Frankie Ray, and his youngest brother, Nicky Ray, especially since one of their little gals was a bit of a spitter when she got real angry.

Yet nothing could top Eggie's younger brother, Bubba Ray, and his She-demon from hell, Janie Mae Lewis. Their daddy liked Janie Mae because she represented the kind of She-wolf he wanted all of them to take as a mate. Strong, confident—a natural Alpha. But because Daddy liked Janie Mae so much, Bubba had to be difficult. He had to play games. Even worse, Janie Mae played those games right back. Not even properly mated yet, the pair already had two boys, the She-wolf pregnant with Bubba's third, and still they had yet to settle down. Instead they bounced between the Pack territories of Smithtown, Tennessee, and Smithville, North Carolina—arguing the entire way, it seemed.

Eggie didn't understand all that arguing. Honestly, he didn't argue with people. He never had to. He either stared until the ones arguing with him went away or he killed them. There was never an in-between, so what was the point of arguing? Unfortunately Bubba didn't seem to have the same philosophy. All he did with Janie Mae was argue. In fact, Eggie had barely stepped into his parents' Tennessee home before his brothers propelled him back to his car and he was suddenly on his way to North Carolina. And Lord knew that had been the last thing he'd wanted to do.

Until the moment he saw her.

Yeah, she was definitely the youngest Lewis sister. The one the Lewises had never talked about whenever Eggie was around. Although, in his estimation, this sister was much prettier than the other four. She had long, straight brown hair, parted right in the middle and framing just the sweetest little face with those big brown eyes and pretty full lips. Plus she had what he could only call the cutest cheeks. Although he wasn't sure cheeks should be cute. Like the other Lewises, her nose was long and refined but she was smaller than her sisters. Barely five-eight or so. For a Lewis female, that was kind of short. For a Smith female, it would be considered downright tiny.

Eggie thought about going over there, introducing himself the way men do when they see a pretty woman they'd like to meet. But then he remembered who he was. He was Eggie Ray Smith, trained killer. What would a girl like her do with a wolf like him? Would she want him to be chatty? Buy her flowers? Kill a herd of elk? And her entire family already hated him on principle. What he did for a living wasn't exactly respected among many of the shifters, although it was needed to keep them all safe.

Nah. It was best not to get all involved in . . . anything. It was best to stay right where he was. Here. On his car. Waiting for the yelling to stop so he could find a hotel in town and get some sleep.

So continuing to stare at the woman on that porch was not a good idea and he decided to study his feet instead— until he heard someone breathing.

And it wasn't him.

Of all the times for Darla Mae Smith's boss to send her home for a "visit"—a visit he'd insisted on for some unknown reason—why did it have to be now?

Honestly, only a boss with his own Pack would insist on this sort of thing. Lord knew a full-human chef never would. If they had their way, they'd never give their lowly staff any kind of break. But Darla didn't work for a full-human. No, she was an assistant pastry chef for a Van Holtz Steak House in San Francisco, and the Van Holtz wolves understood Pack life, so her boss—the executive chef and Alpha of the San Francisco Van Holtzes—had suddenly, out of the clear blue, insisted that Darla go home for a little "Pack time." Something most She-wolves who were forced away from their kin for one reason or another enjoyed. Then again, none of them had to deal with the darn arguing!

When Darla had called her daddy two weeks ago, it had just been him, Darla's momma, and her brothers. Her sisters were in Smithtown, Tennessee, dealing with the pain-in-the-butt Smith boys. So Darla had happily hitchhiked her way cross country, something she liked to do but didn't necessarily mention to her parents. But by the time she had made it to her home in North Carolina, her dang sisters were back and in the middle of their dang arguments! Not with each other, which she could barely tolerate, but with those darn Smith wolves.

And it wasn't even one argument, but several! Francie Mae, the oldest, was arguing with her mate, Benjamin Ray, about what Benji could and could not stick his big Smith nose into when it came to the Lewis family business. Roberta Mae and Frankie Ray were busy debating whether Robbie's skirt was long enough—apparently it wasn't— while Janette Mae and Nicky Ray were arguing about Nixon. Nixon, of all people!

But worse than all that was what was going on between Janie Mae and Bubba Ray Smith. The pair had been on-and-off-again for several years now. They played all sorts of games with each other, trying to make the other one jealous. When Janie had gotten pregnant with her first son, the family sort of sighed in relief, figuring the pair would *finally* become mates and end all the bickering.

That, unfortunately, did not happen. Instead, the bickering became worse. Much worse. Now, two sons later, with the third on the way, the pair traipsed back and forth between North Carolina and Tennessee, one usually following the other, stopping occasionally to argue in one of the midway rest stops that probably deserved better.

Was it really supposed to be this hard? Was love and caring supposed to be so ridiculously silly and demanding? Darla didn't think so. Neither did her friends in San Francisco—a lovely mix of shifters and full-humans that she'd met when she'd left home at eighteen to start her internship at the Baltimore Van Holtz restaurant. Lord, it was 1974! Wonderful things were happening all around them. Times were changing. There was beautiful music and people were beginning to realize that war and violence didn't answer all of life's tough questions. It was a time to travel and see the world, discover new and interesting people, religions, and species.

But Darla's kin was locked into a world Darla had no desire to be part of. One filled with jockeying for position in a Pack. Unlike their full-blood wolf counterparts, the shifters rarely settled for their position in life. They always wanted more or less or different, but never what they had. And anyone with a brain could see that what Janie wanted was to be Alpha Female of the Smithtown Pack. She couldn't and wouldn't settle for less, even if that meant booting Bubba's momma out of her current position as Alpha. Of course, that was just Janie Mae's way. And the rest of Darla's sisters, although older, were the perfect Betas. They'd fight for Janie to get her what she wanted, even if it meant going head to head with their own mates about it.

The question, Darla guessed, became what did Bubba Ray want? A few years shy of thirty and male . . . he didn't know what the hell he wanted. Especially if it meant running off his own parents. But like the true Alpha Male Bubba probably would be, he would decide what he wanted when he was dang good and ready. Something Janie Mae wasn't happy about because even though she may not need to be Alpha today, at this moment, she wanted commitments that it *would* happen.

So the fighting went on. And on. And on.

If Darla had known this was going to be happening while she was here, she would have taken a break at a commune one of her friends had told her about. Or headed off to Europe and backpacked through France again. The Lord knew there was a world of fine pastries for Darla to experience and explore and learn to make in France. But she wasn't in France, she was *here*.

Maybe, in a day or two, she could split. Head out after getting a little time in with her parents, especially her daddy, who hated this fighting as much as Darla did. Until then, though, she'd have to settle for walking away from all the unnecessary crap going on in the house.

Jumping down the stairs, Darla headed into the woods. She hadn't gotten far, though, when she caught the scent of some unknown wolf on her parents' territory, coming upwind of her.

She stopped, turned. Darla sniffed the air again, then called out, "Hello?"

A twig snapped behind her and Darla spun, her fangs instantly bursting from her gums at the sight of the gun pointed at her. The man holding that gun blinked in surprise. It was only a moment, though. Only a moment of stunned confusion at the sight of fangs on a young woman in the middle of nowhere. Then the full-human male aimed his weapon and Darla unleashed her claws, readying her body to shift and strike. Hoping the surprise at seeing her as wolf would give her the precious seconds she'd need to tear his throat out.

Darla's muscles trembled seconds before she launched herself, shifting in midair as she flew at the man. But the gun never went off. The wolf she'd scented earlier now stood behind the human. The hand holding the gun was crushed, the neck snapped.

Yanking herself away so as not to hurt the wolf, Darla somersaulted back, her wolf body slamming into a large tree. When she hit the ground, she looked up at the male wolf. She didn't recognize him as someone she personally knew, but she knew he was a Smith. Normal wolves didn't have shoulders that wide or necks that thick. He also had a full beard and dark hair that hung to his shoulders and in his face, making her wonder how he managed to see anything at all.

He stepped toward her, wolf eyes glaring down at her. At least . . . she thought he might be glaring. It was hard to tell.

Darla started to stand up but the glaring Smith wolf pulled the biggest hunting knife she'd ever seen. Positive he was about to cut her throat because he considered her weak by Smith standards, she recoiled away from him, her back pressing into the tree.

He didn't, however, kill her, but turned and threw that knife, impaling the human male who'd been coming up behind him.

That's when Darla realized that the first human hadn't

been alone. Lord. How many humans were running around her little town? Where were the town's deputies? Where were the other Smith and Lewis wolves? The bears? The lions? Was everybody at the bar just drinking? How was this acceptable?

But most importantly, why did all these human males seem to be coming to her? Honestly, Darla would be in big trouble if it weren't for this oversized Smith wolf who looked like he never smiled.

The wolf walked over to the human male, who was now on his knees, the life from him gone. Before the body dropped to the ground, the wolf yanked the knife from the human's head and snatched the gun from the human's hand. The wolf had just tucked the gun into the waistband of his jeans when another human charged.

Darla would have warned the wolf but she didn't have to. He moved so fast, yanking a second hunting knife from a sheath tied to his thick thigh. Slicing up, cutting the inside of the man's leg, then he stood and slashed the blades across, nearly taking the man's head off.

Again the wolf looked down at her, bringing one big forefinger to his lips. "Sssssh," he whispered and disappeared into the woods.

Although Darla didn't see anything, she could hear well enough. The sounds of dying men as that big wolf went about killing them. Something that would normally horrify Darla. She was a pacifist after all. And yet . . . she wasn't horrified; she just didn't know why.

Then she felt something sticky under her paw. She leaned down, sniffed. Blood. Her blood.

It must have been when she'd hit the tree. She knew she'd hit it hard but not this hard. She thought about calling out to her family. Howling. Or even calling to the wolf. But she was suddenly so weak and tired.

Maybe if she just closed her eyes for a bit . . .

★ ★ ★

Eggie finished the last human, his hand around the man's mouth, one of his favorite knives tearing open a hole from bowel to stomach. When the man stopped struggling, he dropped the body, took the weapon, and headed back toward the little Lewis girl. He briefly stopped to pull his second favorite knife from the open mouth of the other man, quickly wiping it on the man's clothes before sliding the blade back into its sheath.

He stepped out of the woods into the small clearing.

"You all right?" he softly asked the She-wolf, his gaze scanning the woods for any more skulking humans—the only species he knew that skulked, by the way. But when he didn't get an answer, he focused on her.

She looked like she was sleeping but he doubted it. Poor little thing had been too terrified for a wolf-nap. He walked over and crouched beside her, his wolf gaze instantly picking up the blood that had pooled in the leaves she'd landed in. He remembered her body hitting the tree, so he pulled her a bit away from the trunk and saw what appeared to be a low-growing branch that jutted out.

Carefully, Eggie felt around the back of the She-wolf's neck and found the wound. If she'd been human, she'd be dead, but she was wolf and that had saved her life.

Sighing, Eggie glanced back at the trail that would lead to the Lewis family house. He could still hear his and her idiot kin arguing and, to be quite honest, he was damn unimpressed with this town's idea of basic protection. An infiltration like this would never have happened in Smithtown. *Any* outsiders were caught at territorial lines and, if their presence was just an accident, and they hadn't seen anything they shouldn't have seen, then they were sent on their way with a good ol' Tennessee, "We don't like strangers 'round here" dismissal. But, if they were *trying* to get on Smithtown territory or if they did see something that couldn't be explained away—then things were handled differently. Often by the females of the town.

Smith females really didn't like strangers on their territory.

But apparently Smithville, North Carolina, handled things differently with their human witch covens and mixed species all living together in sin. Just wasn't right. Wolves belonged with wolves. Bears with bears. Cats with cats. And foxes should be put down on sight. That was the proper way of things. He honestly didn't feel right about rushing the pretty little Lewis She-wolf back to the relatives or Pack who hadn't been able to protect her in the first place.

So he didn't.

Nope. Instead, Eggie Ray Smith picked that little gal up and carried her to his car. True, he'd driven his brothers here but they could find their own way back.

Besides, Eggie knew if he hurried, he could reach the nearby Marine base and get the She-wolf's wounds tended by a proper shifter doctor and then possibly catch one of his team's standby transports back home. That way he wouldn't have to worry about driving the nine to ten hours or so back to Tennessee.

Yep. That sounded like a good plan. So he carefully placed the She-wolf into the backseat of his car and covered her with a blanket from the trunk. She was still in her wolf form and that was probably for the best. She'd most likely heal faster that way.

Once he had her all set, Eggie got into the driver's seat and started the car. It rumbled to life; his brothers made sure to maintain his vehicle, no matter how long he might be away from home. He really appreciated that as he pulled out of the woods and onto the road with a wounded wolf in his backseat and the blood of human men still on his hands.

That last part was a little unfortunate, though . . . he hated when his hands felt sticky.

Chapter Two

"Smith!" a voice bellowed behind Eggie. "What the hell are you doing here? Why aren't you somewhere other than here like you've been ordered?"

Grudgingly, Eggie looked away from his wounded charge and over his shoulder at the lion male standing behind him— and he stared until the Major cleared his throat and snapped, "Well . . . make it fast and leave. Understand?"

Looking away, the lion quickly walked off and Eggie refocused his attention on the She-wolf and the medical team taking care of her.

The doctor, a hyena, giggled a little and said, "We'll need to stitch this wound up and give her some antibiotics to stave off infection." He glanced at the jackal standing next to him. "Get her some clothes. I'll need to force a shift when I'm done."

The hyena straightened up. "Are you going to stand there and stare at me with those freaky eyes of yours?"

"Born with fangs, giggle like my youngest niece, but *I'm* the freak?"

The pair glared at each other until a black bear lumbered to the table. "Smith. Got you transport."

"Good." Eggie pointed at the She-wolf. "Fix her fast, giggler."

The hyena folded his arms over his chest. "Maybe I'm too busy. I do have other duties."

Eggie lowered his head, looking up at the hyena while he let his fangs ease out of his gums along with his signature growl.

"Okay, okay." The hyena held his hands up. "Back off, Rin Tin Tin. I said I'd take care of her."

To make sure the bastard understood that Eggie wasn't joking around, he barked once, enjoying the way the hyena stumbled back, before he turned away and stalked off. The black bear, his team leader named McMartin, followed him.

Eggie didn't like bears, but he tolerated McMartin well enough. Probably because he was a black bear and black bears were quiet like grizzlies but not as easily startled and definitely not as ludicrously large as polars.

"What else do you need me to do?" McMartin asked.

"Find out who wants her dead."

"You sure they were targeting her?"

"Yeah. I'm sure."

"Shouldn't her Pack handle this? Isn't that what wolves do for each other?"

Eggie stopped, faced the bear, and didn't say a word.

"Fine," McMartin sighed after a full minute of that. "I'll take care of it."

"Good."

"And the pilot needs to know where you're go—"

"Tennessee."

Then, without another word, Eggie walked off to get what weapons he needed.

Darla opened her eyes but immediately closed them again. The motion of the car and the bright light coming through the window made her feel a little queasy.

"What's going on?" she asked. "Where am I?"

"My car," a voice growled at her.

She forced one eye open to peek at the male driving the car. She remembered him now. The Smith male from last night. That had been last night, right? She hadn't been dreaming?

Darla cleared her throat and closed her eye again when even that small action caused quite a bit of pain. "Why am I in your car, uh . . . ?"

"Eggie."

"Eggie?" She opened that one eye again. "Your name is *Eggie*?"

"Egbert Ray. Everybody calls me Eggie."

"Oh." Well, there were some unique nicknames in her family, too, so who was she to . . . to . . .

"Wait. Egbert Ray?" Now she had both eyes open, her gaze locked on the big wolf in the driver's seat beside her. "You're . . . Egbert Ray Smith?"

"Yep."

"*The* Egbert Ray Smith?"

"Only know one." He glanced at her with eyes still shifted to wolf. "And that's me."

Darla let out a breath and she knew it was more of a shudder.

Don't panic, she told herself. *Don't panic.*

She was sure that everything was fine. That everything was just . . . fine. There was probably a very logical reason she was in a car with Egbert Ray Smith. A very logical reason.

But remembering what he'd done last night to those human men reminded Darla of all that she'd heard about Egbert Smith—Eggie—over the years. Not even thirty and the wolf was one of the most feared killers in the Smith Pack worldwide. She clearly remembered the relieved sighs of her neighbor Smiths when they'd found out, "That boy has become a Marine."

That boy. That's how they had all described him, too. As that boy. Like they were afraid of saying his name, as if doing so would bring him there. Invoke him, as her hometown witch coven would say. Although her sisters were known to cut them off mid–Eggie mention, Eggie's brothers never seemed afraid of him. But to be honest, Darla didn't put much stock in that. None of the Smithtown boys had much sense in her estimation.

Darla looked out the window, still moving only her eyes since moving her neck only brought pain, though she couldn't figure out why. "Where are we?" she asked since she didn't really recognize anything flying by.

"Tennessee."

Her fingers curled into fists. "Tennessee? Why . . . when . . . I don't understand . . ."

"You're fine."

"I am *not* fine! You've kidnapped me from the safety of my Pack and my family's home and taken me across state lines!"

"Not that safe."

"What does that mean? Not that safe?"

"You were attacked there. By full-humans."

"Oh, and that wouldn't have happened if I was in Smith County or Smithland or Smith Province or whatever dang Smith-named place you people happen to reside in at the moment?"

"Nope. Probably wouldn't."

Fed up with his attitude, her head and neck hurting badly, and being dang afraid, Darla raised her arm and pointed. "Pull over."

"Huh?"

"You heard me. Pull over!"

"Let's get to Smithtown territory first."

"Pull over *now*!"

"All right. All right." Turning the wheel, he pulled to a stop at the side of the two-lane highway, big trucks rumbling past.

"What is it?" he asked, sounding gruff and nasty. For all Darla knew, she could be in a car with a truly despicable person and she had to know. She had to know if she was truly safe or if she should try to make a run for it, sore neck or not. And the only way to do that was the way she'd been taught by her favorite great aunt.

Without moving her very sore neck, Darla raised her hands and gestured to the wolf. "Come here."

Eggie, not wanting to be out here in the open among all these full-humans, didn't quite understand what the little gal was asking.

"Pardon?"

"Come here."

He leaned over, thinking maybe she was feeling sick. Her body was still healing and he could tell she was in pain. He'd feel better when he had her tucked into a bed on properly protected territory.

"Closer. I can't turn my neck."

So he leaned in closer, moving over her so he could see her face without her having to turn. That's when she placed her small hands on his face and tugged him even closer. She gazed right into his eyes and, for a brief, wonderful second, he thought she was going to kiss him. But all she did was stare intently into his face, her gaze searching his. For what, Eggie had no idea. No one had ever looked at him for more than a few seconds at a time.

"Are you mad or something?" she asked.

"No."

"Worried? Terrified?"

"No."

"Then why are your eyes still wolf?"

"They're not."

"They're not?"

"No." He shifted his eyes to show her the difference. "See? That's shifted. That isn't."

"Huh." She blinked. "You do realize that the only difference is that your shifted eyes are slightly more dilated?"

"Never really paid attention."

"Of course," she sighed and went on staring into his eyes.

Eggie had no idea how long they sat there with him hovering over her, his arms braced on either side of her hips, her hands soft on his jaw, but he knew he liked it. And they'd barely touched.

Finally, she let out a long breath, her body relaxing back into the seat. Her hands dropping to her lap.

"Okay," she said.

"Okay?"

"Uh-huh."

Slowly, Eggie moved back to his seat, looking out the car window. "What just happened?" Because Eggie knew something had happened.

"I just needed to make sure I was safe with you."

"Safe with me?" He looked at her. "You know you're safe with me?" She was, but how could she be so sure of that fact?

She smiled, seeming relieved. "Uh-huh."

"And you know this because you . . . looked at me?"

"Basically."

"Basically?"

"Uh-huh. Basically."

She smiled and Eggie realized that she had the prettiest and deepest dimples in those cute cheeks that he'd ever seen before in his life.

"So you want me to keep going?" he asked.

"Uh-huh." Carefully she turned her head, wincing just a little from the pain. "You can take me wherever you want to, Egbert Ray Smith, because I know that I'll never be safer than I am right now . . . with you."

And she said the words with such sincerity, her dark brown eyes so trusting of him when even his own kin never looked at him that way, that Eggie knew in that moment that he'd never let anyone harm this She-wolf. Never let anyone come near her without her consent.

He'd protect Darla Mae Smith with his life.

Checking the road, Eggie pulled out onto the highway and headed home.

CHAPTER THREE

So this was the infamous Smithtown.

Darla had heard about it long before her sisters had become involved with Smith males. While Smithville, North Carolina, was the place of comfort and relaxation for all shifters, a sanctuary where they could be themselves while hunting deer and elk and freshwater seals, Smithtown was for Smith Pack members and their kin only. Even other Packs didn't venture into Smithtown without express permission unless they were looking for a fight.

So with that particular history in her head, Darla was expecting a backwoods town filled with inbred redneck wolves. But, to her surprise, it was . . . charming. The smaller houses were nicely spaced with pretty little lawns and gardens, while the bigger homes were on lovely stretches of land. There were lots of trees and hills and deer and elk roaming around free. The town they cut through had quaint storefronts, a fancy restaurant, a more casual diner, and a movie theater showing *Dirty Mary, Crazy Larry* and *The Golden Voyage of Sinbad*.

It seemed like a quiet, pleasant town and she was happy to see someplace new. She loved finding new places to visit.

Eventually, they pulled onto a dirt road. They traveled for another five minutes until they reached a small house with a wraparound porch.

"Is this your father's house?" she asked.

"No." He turned the car off and got out.

"Not real chatty, are ya?" she muttered, watching the big wolf walk around the front of the car and come to her side. He opened the door and slipped his arms under her legs and behind her back.

"I can walk," she told him.

If he heard her, she couldn't tell. He didn't respond at all. Not even a grunt. He simply lifted her out of the car, easily carrying her toward the house.

As it was in most Smith towns, whether outsiders were allowed or not, his front door wasn't locked and he walked right into his home.

And the inside of Eggie Smith's house was . . . sparse. Yes. Sparse was the word. Not bad or anything, but not exactly homey either. In the living room there was a folding card table, three folding chairs, two barrels she assumed were used for chairs, and a pretty big TV right against the wall. A color one at that with a remote sitting right on top of the set.

Yet for a man who probably hadn't been home for a very long time, it wasn't a bad place. Someone was keeping it dust free and airing it out every once in a while. Still, the way the wolf stood in the middle of it, glaring at the entire room, she had the feeling he was seeing it for the first time from an outsider's perspective.

Not wanting him to feel bad, Darla said, "You can just put me down in that chair there." She pointed at one of the folding chairs around the folding table, but he snarled a little and held her a bit tighter.

Feeling awkward because she felt quite comfortable tucked in his arms, Darla asked, "Have you been fixing up the place? I see all the tools."

"Building," he replied.

"Oh, you've been building onto it?"

"That, too."

Darla blinked, glanced around without turning her head. "Wait . . . you built this place."

He grunted.

"By yourself?"

"Mostly."

Fascinated, Darla turned her finger in a circle. "Turn, turn."

"Huh?"

"I want to see. Show me."

He stared at her a moment with that deadly frown before he slowly turned in a circle.

Impressed with what she saw, Darla grinned. "This is beautiful, Egbert Ray. Did you design it yourself?"

"No. Cousin of mine gave me the plans. I put it together. When my brothers were sober and not arguing with your sisters, they helped."

Always amazed by people who could build things with their hands, Darla looked into that scowling face. "It's beautiful."

"Really?"

"Oh, yeah. Now it's true that I can make you an éclair that would have you weeping tears of joy, but other than that, I can't build a darn thing."

"Well . . . thank you kindly." He took another look around. "Ain't got no furniture, though."

"You have chairs and a table."

"Okay. Ain't got no *real* furniture."

"I'm not spun glass, Egbert Ray. My posterior can sit anywhere it has a need to."

He grunted . . . again, and walked into the hallway. She caught a glimpse of his kitchen and it wasn't too bad from what she could see. Had all the basics anyway. Then he was taking her up a sturdy set of stairs to the second floor. He took her into the first bedroom and she guessed this was where he slept when he was home. The bed was big and also sturdy. A human king or a bear twin. Based on the thickness of the legs of the frame, she'd guess it was a bear twin.

With great care, he placed her on the bed with her back against the headboard. He stepped back, looked her over.

"Now sleep . . . or something."

Darla bit the inside of her mouth to prevent a laugh from coming out. Poor thing. He was just used to dealing with other Marines, wasn't he?

After she got control of herself, Darla said, "The stitches."

"What about them?"

"I think they need to come out."

His frown became decidedly worse and she got the feeling maybe she was annoying him.

He motioned her forward and she leaned down a bit. His fingers moved her hair aside and she felt the tips slide across her wound. She trembled a little from the feel of his fingers against her skin, but he immediately pulled his hand back and stepped away.

"I hurt you. Sorry."

"No, you didn't."

"I'll get someone to help you with that."

"I'm sure you can do—"

But he was already gone, the door closing behind him. A few seconds later she heard him howl to his Pack, although she didn't know if he was calling for assistance with Darla's wound or just complaining to the wind.

Deciding not to worry about it either way, Darla settled down onto the bed on her side so that her neck didn't have to press into the pillow. She tucked her hands under her cheek and let out a deep breath. Before she knew it, she was out cold.

Sighing in relief, Eggie got to his feet and smiled at the She-wolf walking toward him, a big axe over one shoulder, a patch over her left eye.

"Momma," Eggie said.

"Baby boy." Pauline Ann Jessop lifted the axe she'd been using to chop wood and rammed it into the stump she passed on her way to the porch steps. "Sorry I missed you when you first got here, darlin'. I was out huntin' and by the time I got back, your daddy said you were gone off with your brothers."

The She-wolf lowered her head and stared up at her son through black lashes. "Bubba called last night. He is real unhappy. Thought I told y'all not to go 'round stealin' girls."

"I didn't steal her. I rescued her."

"And left a pile of human bodies behind."

"Heard about that already, huh?" He knew that was not something his brothers would ever say over a telephone line, so the information was making it through the Smith channels like summer lightning.

"Of course I did. Now your brothers and those bitches of theirs—"

"Momma."

"—are on their way home, probably to collect your little girl."

"Ain't holding her against her will. She can leave if she wants to."

"Does she?"

"Don't know. She's recovering from a wound she got during the fight. I need you to take out the stitches."

Pauline frowned. "Darlin' boy, I know you can take out stitches."

"Yeah, but . . ." Eggie shrugged, punched his fists into the front pockets of his jeans. "She's delicate. I got these big hands."

"If she's a Lewis, she probably don't mind those big hands."

"Momma."

"Calm yourself." She walked up the steps, swinging her favorite rifle off her shoulder and handing it to Eggie. "I'll take care of your little gal. You head to the house and get the food I have for you two. It's in the pantry—the last place your father will look until he gets *real* hungry."

"You sure you'll be all right?"

Pauline stood on the same step as her six-four son, looking him right in the eyes. "What do you think, boy?"

Darla woke up while the stitches were removed from her neck, but she stayed still and quiet until the stitches were out and the bandage on.

"There ya go, darlin' girl. All done."

Surprised to hear a woman's voice, Darla turned over, but she froze at the sight of a mammoth-sized She-wolf. Honestly, one of the biggest She-wolves she'd ever seen in her dang life.

"Pauline's the name. The Smith boys' momma. And you're Darla."

Say something! Don't just sit there! It's rude!

Darla nodded, although she immediately regretted that particular move. "Yes'm. Darla Mae Lewis."

"The baby sister of those females lurking 'round my sons." She stepped away from the bed, using a towel to wipe her hands.

The She-wolf was, in a word, hearty. About her son's height, with shoulders nearly as wide, she reminded Darla more of a grizzly sow, but . . . stronger. How that was possible Darla didn't know, since all she scented from the female was wolf.

The eye not covered by a patch was like Eggie's, too. Wolf-yellow like she was about to shift, even when she wasn't. Black hair with lots of grey reached her shoulders in a shaggy mess and she wore a sleeveless plaid shirt over loose-fitting and possibly ancient jeans. Work boots were on her enormous feet and she was missing a pinky on her right hand and her middle and forefinger on her left. Darla could be wrong but they looked bitten off. She also had a scar on the side of her neck like something had once taken hold of her there, but Darla had no doubt the woman was healthy as an ox and had every intention of living another three or four thousand years.

"Yes'm, I am."

"How come I haven't met you before?"

"I've been in San Francisco."

"What the hell for?"

"Studying." When the She-wolf stared at her, she added, "To be a pastry chef."

"You have to study for that?"

"It helps."

"As ya like," she sighed, resting her hands on her hips. "You going to be sniffing 'round my boy, too?"

"I'm just on vacation to see my parents. I have no idea what happened last night or how we even got here so fast, but your son did protect me. I'm very grateful to—"

"Yeah, yeah, yeah. Grateful, right. But you going to head back to Smithville as soon as your sisters get here?"

Darla hadn't known her sisters were coming here but she shrugged. "I guess."

"Huh. I see."

Darla had the feeling she'd disappointed Eggie's mother but she had no idea how. Then again, maybe it was best not to ask.

"Anyway," Pauline went on, "that should be fine by morning. With my boys I've been puttin' in and takin' out stitches before most of them could walk. You'll be fine."

"Thank you, Miss Pauline."

The She-wolf eyed Darla before grunting, "Huh." Then she turned on her heel and walked out.

"All right then," Darla said with a little laugh. Because if nothing else, at least she wasn't the least bit bored.

CHAPTER FOUR

Eggie stared down at the She-wolf until her pretty brown eyes opened, blinking wide at the sight of him.

"Hungry?" he asked.

"Hungry? Oh. For food." Yawning, she sat up and stretched. That's when Eggie realized she'd put on one of his T-shirts . . . and not much else.

"You know," she said, her smile bright, "I *am* hungry. Starving."

"Good." He had food. Hell, he had enough food for a small army.

He reached for Darla, slipping his arms under her legs and behind her back.

"What are you doing?" she asked.

"Picking you up."

"I can walk, Egbert Ray."

"You're still recovering."

"Says who?"

He lifted her up, held her tight in his arms. "*I* do."

She stared at him for a bit until she raised her hand and pressed her forefinger against his forehead. "You know, you've got this thing so dang low, it practically touches your nose."

"I'm trying to intimidate you into doing what I want . . . but you poking at me ain't helpin'."

She giggled, a sound he didn't often hear that close to him and definitely not when he was the one causing it.

No, people didn't giggle around Eggie. Or laugh. Or breathe too hard. Or make any sudden moves that might be construed as a threat. Nope. Not around Eggie.

But Darla did.

"Well," she said, her finger stroking down to his nose, "if you're gonna insist on carrying me, you better get movin'. I'm hungry!"

"All right. All right. No need to snarl at me like a Doberman."

Eggie carried Darla down the stairs and cut through the living room to get to the dining room.

"Oh!" Darla squeaked, her hand covering her mouth. "Um . . ."

Eggie stopped. "What's wrong?"

"Uh . . . nothing." She cleared her throat. "I see you got furniture while I was asleep."

"I couldn't have you sittin' on a barrel. Just seemed wrong for a lady. Momma said you wouldn't care, but I asked one of my daddy's sisters to send over some furniture from her mate's store."

"Ahhh. Yes. That explains it."

Eggie looked at the big couch with the giant yellow and green flower pattern on it. "This doesn't really say Egbert Ray Smith, does it?"

She pressed her lips into a thin line, shook her head. He had a feeling she wasn't disapproving as much as trying not to laugh at him.

"Not really," she finally managed to answer. "I'd probably go with more solid colors for you. Darker reds and browns. Maybe a dark blue. But you know what," she added. "Ain't nothin' here we can't discreetly cover up."

"It's not like I'm ever here. Not sure it matters."

"Trust me. It matters. Think about it—on those rare times

you come home after months and months away . . . you walk through the door, throw on the light . . . and *that* couch is the first thing you see."

Eggie nodded. "You know . . . my grandmomma made me a couple of quilts few years back. They're in the upstairs closet."

"Perfect. Because it won't seem strange to your aunt that you'd put her Momma's quilt on your couch. See? You can cover up dang near anything and never have to hurt anyone's feelings."

"Why would I worry about my aunt's feelings? Actually . . . why would you? You don't even know her."

"Don't have to know her. She was kind enough to rush furniture over here to her nephew and—"

"She charged me double on the shipping for the urgent delivery and no family discount on the furniture."

"Oh, really?" Darla briefly pursed her lips. "Well, if you're gonna pay full price with your own kin, you're gettin' what you want. We'll take this crap back tomorrow and exchange it." She folded her arms across her chest, fingers tapping against her biceps. He had a feelin' if she were standing, she'd be tapping her foot right now.

"You don't have to be upset, Darla Mae."

"Who says I'm upset? Just 'cause family's not treatin' family right. It's not like I haven't gone through that or anything," she finished on a mutter. She looked up at him. "I'm still hungry, Egbert Ray."

"Okay, okay. No need to snarl."

Although Eggie did kind of like when she did.

Unlike that horrid furniture, the food was good. Of course, that food had been made by Eggie's mother, Pauline Jessop of the Jessop Pack out of Alaska, which explained the She-wolf's size. Jessop wolves were known for their size and speed, only outsized by Arctic wolves, who were descended from Vikings. The Jessops also owned the lumber empire

Jessop Mountain Timber, which meant Pauline Ann came from real money . . . and had probably trained several years as a lumberjack. It was required for all the Jessop Pack, male or female.

Sounded like a lot of work to Darla. She'd stick with managing bread dough, thank you very much.

Darla pushed the remainder of the macaroni and cheese toward Eggie.

"What?" he asked.

"You've been eyeing it. You might as well finish it."

"Have you had enough?"

"Eggie, I've had enough if I was three people. So go on." But when he didn't move fast enough for her, Darla helped him out by putting one of the steaks on his plate and followed that up with several big spoonfuls of the mac and cheese.

He studied his plate for several seconds before he looked at her. "You tryin' to tell me something?"

"Yes. Now eat."

While the wolf ate, Darla picked up her glass of sweet tea and looked around his kitchen. She had a feeling his mother had a lot to do with this room. It was nicely equipped and roomy. Maybe she used it when she needed extra space.

"So, Egbert Ray . . . what do you do in the Marines?"

He stopped eating, his fork hovering by his mouth. His eyes focused on her and narrowed a little bit. "Why are you asking?"

"Because I'm a spy."

He lowered his fork. "What?"

"Oh, yeah. I'm just sittin' here pumping you for information. That's what I do for the, um, Viet Cong."

His fork hit the plate. "Do not joke about that, Darla Mae."

"Oh, come on," she scoffed. "Who'd believe that *I* would be helping the Viet Cong?"

"Everybody. They're all paranoid right now, so I wouldn't joke about that if I were you."

"Nice Southern gals like me don't spy."

"Then why did you say it?"

"Because I'm trying to get you to talk. It's called a conversation, Egbert Ray."

"I ain't chatty."

"Fine." Darla pushed back her chair and picked up her plate and fork. She carried them to the sink and turned on the faucet. As she began to search for soap and a sponge, she realized that Eggie stood next to her, carefully placing his own dish and fork in the sink.

"I've never been to Vietnam," he told her, his gaze out the window. "Never had a tour there."

Nearly everyone that Darla knew who'd been in the military in the last ten years had spent some time in that war-torn country.

"But you've been somewhere, right?" She could tell by the scars, the way his body always seemed coiled and ready to spring into action at the slightest provocation. This was not a man untouched by battle.

Eggie scratched his forehead before facing her. "I'm in what they're about to start calling the Unit."

"Oh!" She nodded. "Uh-huh."

"You don't know what that is, do you?"

"Do I need to?" When he rolled his eyes, she quickly added, "Look, I don't believe in all this war and fightin'. As a matter of fact . . . I'm a pacifist."

Eggie stared at her. "How can you be a predator *and* a pacifist?"

"It's possible."

"Do you still hunt down your own meat?"

"I'm a pacifist, Eggie Ray. I didn't say I was a vegetarian."

"A vege-what?"

"Forget it." She motioned him away from the sink. "Go on and get the rest of the bowls and things. I'll do the dishes."

"You should be resting."

"Do not annoy me, Eggie Ray."

"Thought you were a pacifist—ow! What was that for?" he demanded while rubbing his ankle.

"Gettin' on my nerves. Now do as I tell ya and don't even think about arguing with me."

He lowered his leg. "You sure are a pushy pacifist."

Darla grinned. "Because I'm also a feminist."

Eggie's head tipped to the side, reminding her a little of a dog hearing a weird noise. "Why?"

"What do you mean why? Do you actually believe that women are treated fairly in this society?"

"No. But you're a She-wolf."

"So?"

"So no wolf is ever going to tell you that you can't do something unless he really hopes to get his throat torn out."

And what really annoyed her was that he was right, but that wasn't the point. "That's true, but I'm thinking about *all* women."

"But you're a She-wolf."

"I know what I am, Eggie."

"Then I don't see the point."

"You know what?" she snapped. "We're done talking about this."

"You were the one who said you wanted a conversation."

"Well I changed my mind!"

"No need to yell, Darla Mae. I'm standing right here."

She let out a heavy sigh and again faced the sink. "Get the rest of the dishes," she ordered.

"Sorry," he muttered. "Didn't mean to make you mad."

Startled, Darla looked at Eggie. "I'm not mad."

"You're not?"

"Lord, no, Eggie. Annoyed? A bit. But not mad. When I'm mad . . . you can really tell."

"Is it worse than . . . this?"

"This?" Darla laughed and patted Eggie on the arm. "This is nothing."

His brow lowered but he didn't look angry this time. Just confused. "Really?"

"Egbert Ray," she laughed, again focusing on the dishes, "you are just the cutest thing!"

His confused frown worsened. *"Really?"*

CHAPTER FIVE

Darla had no idea what woke her up.

She knew she was safe and her body nearly healed. She just had a little bit of a headache that started at the base of her skull. But other than that . . .

And yet, she knew she'd woken up for a reason.

Slipping out of bed, Darla made her way downstairs. As she passed the dining room, she glanced into the kitchen and she could see through the big windows and onto the porch. She stopped and spun around, staring at the wolf standing on his porch. He just stood there, staring out into the trees that surrounded his little house.

She walked to the door and eased it open, stepped outside.

"Eggie?"

He glanced at her. "You should be in bed."

"So should you."

"Just keeping watch."

She stepped closer. "Have you been out here all night?"

"Maybe."

"Maybe?" Darla sighed. "You're *such* a protector."

"I am?"

"Of course you are. But we're safe here. You said so yourself."

"Couldn't hurt to have a little extra—"

"Lord!" She grabbed his arm and yanked him toward the backdoor. "Come on."

"Where?"

"You need sleep. You've been up for hours."

"I'm used to it."

"Well, you shouldn't be. Not when you're home."

She managed to drag him through the house and up the stairs, but as soon as she got to the bedroom he was letting her use, he froze in his tracks.

Darla squealed a little when Eggie brought her up short. She realized he'd only been *letting her* drag him through the house.

"What's wrong?" she demanded. She wanted to go back to bed.

"Why am I going in there?"

"So you can get some sleep."

"But where will you sleep?"

Darla released Eggie so she could put her hands on her hips. "Tell me you are kidding."

Of course he wasn't kidding. He couldn't . . . sleep with her.

Because when she said "sleep" what she really meant was "sex," right? Because that's what he meant when he said he was sleeping with a woman. That they were fucking.

"We're both adults, Eggie," she reasoned.

"What does that have to do with anything?"

"Lord help me," she muttered. "Can we just get some sleep, please?"

"Together?"

"Yes."

"I can just sleep on—"

"That ugly couch? No. Besides, you drool even a little on that couch, something tells me your aunt is not going to let you exchange it."

"I don't drool."

"And there are no beds in the other two rooms."

"Because every time my brothers would fight with your sisters, they'd come here to sleep. If they think they'll have to sleep on the floor, they stay away."

"Then where else are we going to sleep?"

"It wouldn't be right."

She studied him for a moment. "You do understand I'm not talking about having sex with you?"

"You're not?"

Darla gasped and slapped at his arm. It kind of hurt.

"No, I am not!"

"You don't have to yell."

"Clearly I do if you think that's what I want from you."

"Wasn't trying to insult ya, Darla Mae. It's just . . . a wolf and She-wolf sharing the same bed and all—"

"Does not mean they have to have sex."

"They don't?"

"No. Now come on." She grabbed hold of his arm.

"I'm still not sure about this," he hedged.

"Why not? I've crashed with male friends before."

"You have?"

"Of course. During concerts or after a long night at the restaurant. Sometimes after a party. Eggie, it's no big deal."

"Well," he said, letting her pull him into the room behind her. "If you're sure."

"Of course I am. I mean, all those times I've *slept* with my male friends and I'm still a virgin so— "

Eggie never heard the end of Darla's sentence because he somehow ended up slamming his head into the door at her words. He stumbled back, blood starting to drip from his nose.

"Oh, Eggie! Are you all right?"

"Yeah. Sure."

And Lord, he was *such* a liar.

Thankfully he hadn't broken his nose. Although it apparently wouldn't have been a big deal because he'd already broken it seventeen times. Darla didn't know how that was even possible, but she also knew the man wasn't much for telling tall tales. It just wasn't in him.

She pulled the washcloth that she'd wrapped around ice away from his nose and took another look. "The bleeding's stopped."

"Yeah. It'll be fine. Just a bit of a headache later."

"Was it the virgin thing?"

He shrugged. "It kind of threw me off."

"Sorry. Didn't mean to."

"I know."

"Um . . ." Darla toyed with the washcloth. "You aren't going to tell my sisters, are you?"

"Why in heaven or hell would I *ever* talk about your virginity to your sisters?"

Disgusted she even had to say it, Darla rolled her eyes and admitted, "They make fun of me about it."

"Why?"

"Because they always have. Since I was fifteen or so. Anyway, about three years ago, I finally lied and told them it was done with just so they'd stop talking about it."

"But why did you tell me?"

"Because I knew you wouldn't care." Darla turned around and sat down on Eggie's leg. "I knew I could trust you not to make fun of me."

"Don't see why it's a big deal. You're only twenty."

Darla cleared her throat. "Twenty-five."

"Then that's tragic."

Darla punched his chest. "Eggie Ray!"

And, for the first time, she heard him . . . well . . . chuckle. Sort of. It was kind of a grunt-chuckle.

"Just kiddin'."

"Ha-ha."

"Won't say a word to your sisters. They don't speak to me anyway."

Darla looked at him, frowned. "Why not?"

He shrugged those massive shoulders. "Don't think they like me."

"Why wouldn't they like you? You're so sweet."

"You do know you're the only human being who's ever said that to me . . . except my mother and I'm not sure she counts."

"Of course she counts and I'm always right. Once you understand that, you'll be fine." Besides, she'd straighten out her sisters later. If they were going to live here and be part of the Smith Pack, they had to accept all the brothers, including Eggie. It wouldn't be right otherwise.

"Can we go to sleep now?" she asked, resting her head on his shoulder.

"Are you *sure* you really want to—"

"Are we *still* talking about that?"

"All right. All right. No need to get that tone."

With his arm around her waist, Eggie hoisted her off his lap and onto the bed. "Under the covers," he ordered.

Darla slipped under the covers and watched as Eggie followed behind her.

"Do you want to put up a wall between us so we don't accidentally touch in the night?" she asked sweetly.

"Don't tempt me."

Giggling, she settled into the bed. Eggie turned off the lamp she'd forgotten she'd left on and relaxed into the bed.

"Night, Darla."

"Night, Eggie."

"And, Darla . . . ?"

"Hhmmh?"

"Thank you."

"For what?"

"For not being afraid of me."

"Was I supposed to be?"

"Everybody else is."

"*I* am not everybody else, Egbert Ray Smith. You'd do well to remember that."

He chuckled—again!—and said, "Don't think I'll ever forget it."

"Good. Then I think everything will be just fine."

"Maybe."

"Don't irritate me, Eggie Ray."

"You sure are easily irritated for a pacifist."

"Quiet."

"Yes'm."

Eggie always knew as soon as someone was on his territory. Not only did he sense it, but the nearby animals told him. Then again, they often told him things he needed to know. When the weather was about to change, when danger was near, or when family was making their way to his house.

He hated waking Darla up, but he knew she wouldn't want to be found cuddled up to his chest, one arm around his waist, her head on his shoulder.

Eggie doubted he'd slept any more than he would have if he'd just stood outside the entire night, but after an hour or so of just lying here, he'd begun to do something he rarely ever did . . . relax. True, he was still ready to kill at the slightest provocation if any outsiders showed up looking for Darla Mae, but the need to pace until he fell asleep on the floor or at his kitchen table was gone.

It was nice actually sleeping in his bed. He never had before.

A crow cawed from a tree outside his window, warning nearby crows about invaders while letting Eggie know that it was his brothers. He knew this because of the panicked sound that the crow made. Crows had surprisingly long memories and after being chased by those idiots more than once, the crows always sent out warnings when the Smith boys were nearby. Only Eggie got a pass, no matter how long he might be out of the country and, in exchange, he let the crows tag along on hunts. It worked out well.

"That must be your brothers," Darla murmured, her

breath hot against his skin. He knew he should have put a T-shirt on because that felt mighty nice.

"Didn't know you were awake."

"Just for a little while. I was so comfortable; I didn't really want to move."

Eggie understood that.

"Guess we better now," he told her softly, his fingers itching to smooth her hair off her cheek. "Don't need my brothers seeing you in my T-shirt. They'll get all sorts of wrong ideas."

Darla leaned her head back a bit so she could look into his face. "You embarrassed by me, Eggie Ray?"

"No," he answered honestly. "Just figured you wouldn't want to be found in bed with *me.*"

"Why ever not?"

Before Eggie could answer, the bedroom door slammed open. Seemed excessive, though, since it had been halfway open anyway.

"You son of a bitch," Janie Mae Lewis snarled as she stormed into the room with Darla's three other sisters behind her. "You bastard, murdering son of a bitch!"

"Janie Mae!" Darla snapped, scrambling to her knees.

"Shut up, Darla Mae. Let me handle this."

"Handle what? What the hell is wrong with you?"

Ignoring Darla, Janie pointed at Eggie. "Taking advantage of *my* sister?"

"I did no such—"

"Was she even conscious when you had your dirty, disgusting way with her?"

Before Eggie even had a chance to be insulted by that—and he would have been insulted—Darla Mae roared out, *"That is enough!"*

The She-wolf took several breaths before she looked down at him. "Eggie, why don't you go deal with your brothers downstairs. I need to talk to my sisters for a minute."

If they weren't all kin, Eggie would never leave Darla

alone with a crazed She-wolf, especially a *pregnant* crazed She-wolf. But at the end of the day, they were all kin and it wasn't Eggie's place to get between them.

He slipped off the bed and walked out of his room and down the stairs. His brothers were just coming through the back door when he stepped into his kitchen.

He nodded at them. They nodded back.

It was a typical Smith boys' morning greeting.

Once Eggie had gone downstairs, Darla faced her sisters. "What is your—"

Darla's question was cut off when Janie suddenly grabbed her and hugged her tight.

"You poor, poor thing," Janie said, her hands brushing down Darla's hair. "Should we get you to a hospital?"

"Hospital?" Darla pulled away from her sister. "What are you talking about?"

"You don't have to lie to us, darlin'," Francine soothed. "Or be ashamed. This was beyond your control."

"What are y'all talking about?"

"Just tell us if he"—Roberta glanced back and forth between the others—"hurt you."

"Hurt me? Why would Eggie hurt—"

Again cutting off her sister's words, Janie yanked Darla back into her arms, pressing Darla's head to her big chest and annoyingly patting the side of Darla's head.

"Shhhh, darlin'. Shhhh. Everything is going to be all right. Let's just get her out of here," she said to the others. "We'll deal with Egbert Ray Smith later."

Darla pulled away from her sister again, this time moving out of arm's length. "You'll do no such thing."

"Darla—"

"Eggie Ray saved my life and he has been a complete gentleman."

"Yeah," Janette muttered, "he seemed real gentleman-like on his bed with you two all twined together like that."

"There's only one bed in the entire house."

"And a couch."

"Did you see that couch? I couldn't let him sleep on that thing. Might give him nightmares."

"You and your thing about ugly furniture," Roberta sighed.

"The man saved my life. I'm not about to allow him to spend the night on ugly furniture." She snapped her fingers. "That reminds me. I need to help him take that ugly furniture back to his aunt. I'm afraid if I don't help him, he'll just let her get away with it."

"Listen to yourself," Janie ordered her. "Helping him return furniture? Not telling us the truth about how he took advantage of you last night?"

"He didn't take advantage of me last night!"

"Poor thing," Roberta said sadly, patting Darla's shoulder. "You're just so innocent."

She slapped her sister's hand off. "I am not innocent."

"You mean that loss of virginity story?" Janette asked.

"Yeah," Francine sighed. "None of us really believed any of that. But it was a nice try."

Fed up, Darla asked, "Did you bring me clothes?"

"Your bag is downstairs but—where are you going?"

"Away. From *you*."

Her sisters followed behind her, Janie Mae leading the way.

Just before she reached the stairs, Janie caught Darla's arm and swung her around. "Now wait one second, little miss—"

"I don't report to you, Janie Mae."

"I'm trying to protect you."

"From who? Eggie?"

"You don't know anything about him."

"I know enough."

"Let me guess," Janie said with the tone that always set Darla's teeth on edge. "You looked into his soul and saw he was pure of heart."

Her sisters snickered and Darla took a moment to get a little bit of that Southern control she was so proud of. "I know y'all don't believe me when I say that Great Aunt Bernice taught me the way of—"

"Blah, blah, blah," Janie cut in. "We've heard this all before, Darla Mae. But you can't see people's souls, you have no fancy mystical powers, and you are not going to spend another second around that murdering hound dog!"

Darla pointed her finger in her sister's face, something she knew for a fact Janie hated. "You will not talk about him like that," Darla warned her. "Not around me."

"Y'all." Roberta stood between them. "This does not have to get nasty. Let's just go on home and talk this over with Daddy."

"I'll come home when I'm done."

"You're coming home *now*," Janie ordered.

"No, I'm not."

"I'm done with this." Janie gripped Darla's arm and pulled her toward the stairs.

Fed up with her sister's ridiculous—and downright rude!—behavior, Darla slapped her sister's hand off. And Janie pushed her back.

"You get downstairs and get your ass out of this house, Darla Mae."

"And you stay out of my business, Janie Mae."

"Y'all," Roberta warned.

But Roberta should have known better. Instead of soothing the situation, her words acted more like a starter's pistol. Darla and Janie grabbed each other's hair as soon as Roberta spoke, both screeching and stumbling down the stairs while their other sisters tried to stop them.

It was *not* what their momma would call the proper way a Southern lady acts.

They all heard the She-wolves bickering at the top of the stairs but they kept eating their cereal. Whatever the rest of the shifter world might think, Smiths weren't stupid. They lived as long as they did—and some of them lived a very long time—because they knew when to fight and when to fade into the forest. And the one thing every Smith male learned was don't get in the middle of a She-wolf fight. Especially one that involves sisters.

So they ate their cereal while standing in Eggie's kitchen and listened to all the bickering.

Eggie wasn't hurt by what he heard either. He was kind of used to it. Janie Mae had never really liked him. Eggie didn't know why, but Janie Mae must have heard enough to make up her mind and she'd never hid her feelings about . . . well, about *anything*. But definitely not about how much she didn't like or trust him.

Then again, a lot of people didn't like Eggie, but that wasn't something he allowed to keep him up at night.

Nicky Ray, the first to finish eating because he didn't really eat so much as inhale, asked, "So why did you kidnap her?"

"Didn't. Rescued."

"Not as far as everyone in Smithville is concerned."

"Don't care what everyone in Smithville thinks."

"And thanks for leaving those bodies," Bubba Ray complained.

"Sent clean up."

"Why didn't *you* clean it up?"

"Not my specialty. Sent hyenas."

"Yeah. Thanks for that."

Frankie Ray frowned. "Cleaning up bodies is considered a specialty?"

"If you want to get in and out in less than thirty minutes—yep."

Benjamin stared into his empty bowl. "Got any more cereal?"

Eggie was reaching into his cabinet for the cereal box when the bickering stopped and the screeching started. When they heard what sounded like a body—or bodies—

falling down the stairs, the brothers tossed their bowls into the sink or onto the kitchen table and ran into the hallway.

Thankfully, no one had fallen down the stairs—especially not Janie who was pregnant with Bubba's baby—but the sisters were fighting their way down, Janie and Darla right in the middle of it.

Without a thought for his own safety or the safety of his major arteries, Eggie grabbed hold of Darla and Bubba grabbed Janie. They tried to pull them apart but the She-wolves had such tight grips on each other's hair that it was damn near impossible. Thankfully, the other sisters stepped in and managed to get them free long enough that Eggie and Bubba could drag the two away from each other.

Yet now that they no longer had hold of each other, the screeching stopped and the yelling began.

"You are coming home, Darla Mae!"

"I'm not going anywhere! If I want to stay here with Eggie Ray, I'm staying!"

"That son of a bitch will kill you while you sleep!"

Insulted, Eggie snapped, "Hey!"

"Shut up, murderer!"

Darla pulled out of his arms and charged her sister. Eggie had just gotten his arm around her waist again when she pulled her hand back and slapped her sister's face. The sound of it cracked across the room and the fight turned to shock.

"How dare you," Darla hissed at her sister. "How dare you come to this man's house and insult him."

"You slapped me," Janie said, her hand resting on her now red cheek.

"Because you were rude. Now get out."

"You expect us to just leave you—"

"Get out!"

"Come on," Bubba coaxed the mother of his children, "let's go. We can talk about this when everybody calms down."

Janie Mae pulled away from Bubba and spun on him.

Eggie watched his brother lean back from his crazy mate. Lord, that woman. . . .

"I blame *you* for this, Bubba Ray! *You!*"

"Me? How is this my fault?"

But Janie was already storming away from him and out the front door. Her sisters followed right behind her. Throwing up his arms, Bubba hurried after her, with all Eggie's brothers following except for Benji.

He stopped and said, "Just keep her safe. We'll figure this out."

"Sure."

Benji gave Darla a small smile. "I'm glad you're safe and sound, Darla Mae. If you need anything, you just call Momma and Daddy. Or just howl. Someone will come."

She nodded but didn't speak.

Raising a brow at him—Benji's way of saying, "Good luck with that one, little brother"—his older brother left, finally leaving Eggie and Darla alone.

Realizing he still had his arms around her waist, Eggie released her.

He felt bad. It had never been his intention to get between the sisters.

"Darla Mae—" he began, but she cut him off.

"I need to get dressed." She looked around until her eyes settled on a red bag covered in stickers from several different countries. She walked over to it and lifted it. "Do you have a pickup truck or only that car?"

"I have a pickup." Everyone in Smithtown had a pickup.

"Good. We need to get this horrid couch out of your house and we need to go food shopping." She marched past him. "I need to bake."

Eggie didn't know if that word meant something else but he wasn't about to ask. Not when she was in this mood. So he just nodded and watched her head up the stairs. She stopped halfway up, though, and looked back at him.

"I am so sorry for what my sister said to you, Egbert Ray."

He shrugged. "She ain't my problem. She's Bubba's. Didn't mean to cause *you* any problems, though, Darla."

"You didn't do anything. But I won't let anyone talk to you like that.. I don't care who they are."

"You ready to fight the whole town then, darlin'?"

She pursed her lips and said without even a bit of hesitation, "If I have to."

CHAPTER SIX

Considering the mood Darla had been in when they left the house, Eggie expected a confrontation with his Aunt Daphne, but Darla had walked into Daphne's furniture store with a big smile and even two hours later, she'd lost it only when convenient for her to do so. How she'd managed that, though, he still didn't know.

"Look," Daphne had sighed, "I just can't be running around, taking back furniture willy-nilly."

"Oh, I know," Darla had said with what Eggie now called her deeply concerned expression. "I know." Her smile had suddenly returned and Eggie had felt like the whole store lit up. "But that's why we brought the furniture back in Eggie's truck. That way you don't have to worry about having it picked up. We've taken care of all that. It's all wrapped up nice and clean."

"I'll have to sell it at a loss."

Back to deep concern. "Oh, I know. I know," she repeated yet again. It had been her favorite phrase the entire time they were at the store. "But think of the benefit of showing how important family is to you."

Daphne's eyes had flickered over to Eggie and back to Darla. "Family?"

And that had been the first time since they'd walked into the store that Eggie had seen something other than a smile or deep concern . . . he saw anger. Real. Raw. But she had hidden it just as quick and repeated, "Family. Let me tell ya, I've been livin' 'round those Yankees in San Francisco for a while now and those people do not know about family. And it affects their business even in a big ol' city like that." She leaned in and said low, "So you could imagine how it would go over here in Smithtown. But that won't matter to you because when I start telling everybody from here to North Carolina what a wonderful store you have and how loyal a Smith you are to your kin, you won't be able to keep the wolf Packs out of here."

Daphne had sucked air between her teeth and looked back at her mate. He'd only shrugged, leaving it up to her.

"All right," Daphne had finally said, shocking Eggie because that woman didn't care if you were blood, Alpha of the Pack, or the president of the United States . . . she didn't give *nothing* away. "Fine. You know what you want to replace—"

"That set." Darla had pointed across the showroom to a dark brown couch, a couple of matching king chairs, a coffee table, three side tables in mahogany, and a matching dining set.

Normally Eggie didn't care about furniture. He spent most of his life in trees with a high-powered rifle and scope, so whether he had chairs in a house he was rarely in or not didn't really matter. But he had to admit . . . when he did come home, it would be nice to come home to this.

But now, after Benji and Frankie had helped him with the heavy lifting, Eggie sat on all that fancy furniture and felt a little . . . out of place. And anxious. Sitting like this, doing nothing, was not really his way. He'd go into his kitchen if he didn't have a still-angry She-wolf baking in there. Although he would say that whatever she was whipping up smelled delicious.

Eggie glanced at his watch again. New furniture, grocery shopping, a family fight, and not even four yet.

"What are you doing?"

Eggie dropped his arm to his lap and looked at the She-wolf glaring at him from the entryway.

"Uh—"

"Your nervous energy is making me tense."

He was making *her* tense?

"Well—"

"What would you normally do if I wasn't here, baking delicious goods?"

"Uh . . . huntin'."

"Then go hunt."

"Can't leave you alone."

"If I need you, I'll howl."

"As far as we know, you're still in dang—"

"*Out!*" She pointed at the front door. "I'll call you when dinner's ready."

"You do know this is *my* house?" When Eggie saw a flash of fang, he quickly raised his hands. "All right. All right. No need to get testy."

He stood. "But if you need me for *anything*—"

"You'll hear my howl a mile away, I promise."

Taking her at her word, Eggie walked out of his house, stripped off his clothes, and shifted to wolf. He was just trotting down the porch stairs when his brothers came out of the woods. Something told him that they'd been ordered from their homes as well. The Lewis sisters did like to bake when angry.

Bubba Ray barked and they followed him deep into the woods until they ran across an elk and chased it down. Unfortunately, they crossed into bear territory, aka Collinstown, and right into the Buck brothers. Twin polar bears that hated the Smith boys.

The fight was ugly, but nicely distracting.

Around eight, Darla walked onto the porch of Eggie's house. She wiped her hands on a rag and called out, "Eggie!"

Before she could even turn and head back inside, Eggie

charged out of the woods. He dived into the dirt in front of his porch steps and rolled around there for a few seconds, jumped up, shook the excess dirt off, and charged into the house.

Darla ran after him, yelling out, *"Don't you dare get on that couch, Egbert Ray!"*

He was in mid-jump when she yelled at him but, as Darla had done the other night, he jerked himself back, landing in the unused fireplace. At least he didn't end up with a deadly wound. Because that would definitely ruin dinner.

"Go on upstairs and get showered," she told him, unable to stop herself from turning up her nose at all the blood on his muzzle. *Messy eater. Yuck!* "Dinner can wait."

His head cocked to the side and he turned, but instead of heading to the hallway and the stairs that would lead to the only working shower in the house, he traipsed into the dining room. Putting his front paws on one of the chairs, he looked over the table she'd set up for their meal. She hadn't had much to work with, but Darla had managed to dig up a tablecloth, decent plates and glasses, and tolerable silverware. She also found some candles shoved in a drawer and some wild flowers near the house. Considering the circumstances . . . she'd done a really good job.

Eggie looked at her, turned away from the chair, and headed upstairs.

Deciding not to worry about the strange ways of Smith wolves, Darla returned to the kitchen.

One look at the little kitchen table told her how angry she'd been after the argument with her sisters. She had way too many pies and pastries for one wolf to ever eat. Even a wolf Eggie's size. Even a bear couldn't eat all this. Although a lion male could, but that was neither here nor there.

Well, she could give whatever was left over to Eggie's family. Not her sisters, though. Damn heifers.

See? Now they had her cussin'. Heifers!

No matter how far Darla went, no matter what she did

with her life, no matter her individual accomplishments, her sisters still saw her the same damn way. As a weak Omega pup they had to care for. Her parents respected her. Her brothers. But not her sisters. They couldn't just watch out for her, no. They had to make fun of her, not take her even the least bit seriously. When she'd turned eighteen, her daddy finally gave her the option of moving up north to work at one of the Van Holtz restaurants. Although the Smiths and Van Holtzes considered each other enemy Packs due to some murder rampage from ages ago, the Lewises didn't bother with all that. At the end of the day, they were business wolves and liked to make their money. They had ice-cream shops and candy stores all over the U.S., and they didn't care who bought their products just as long as their products were bought. And the Van Holtz restaurants were big buyers of the Lewis Family's Old Time Ice Cream—the grizzlies loved their Honey Nut Brittle Strawberry and the polars loved their Caramel and Sea Lion Fat Vanilla—so it had been easy for her father to get Darla a job at the restaurant.

He'd just wanted to give her a break. What no one expected was that Darla would become a really good pastry chef. Of course, because of her age, she'd had to start at the bottom, assisting the full-time pastry chefs and doing all the grunt work with bread dough. But within the year, the head of the Baltimore restaurant—Wulgar Van Holtz—offered to pay for her to go to France for some training in actual French patisseries. Always wanting to travel, Darla had jumped at the chance to go. They'd also sent her to Italy, Spain, England, and Germany—she made the best *Bienenstich* or bee-sting cake this side of Bavaria—and when she finally got back stateside, they'd put her in the San Francisco Van Holtz restaurant. A really great place for her because of the interesting people she met. As a pacifist—and no, her fight with her sisters didn't count—and feminist, 'Frisco was a good fit for her. At least for now.

Some days, though, it could be a little too hectic, a little too loud. And so big that the Van Holtzes were planning to add two more restaurants over the next few years. She'd thought about moving back to the South where she felt most comfortable and maybe opening her own little pastry shop, but the thought of dealing with her sisters every day . . .

No. Just the thought of it made her shudder. She loved them. She really did. But some days she just wanted to slap the living shi . . . tar out of 'em.

Starting to feel a little peckish—which meant her anger was beginning to drain away—Darla glanced at the clock on the wall. It seemed like ages since Eggie had gone up to take a shower.

But she could wait for him.

She looked at all the desserts she'd made. She'd need to cover most of these and wondered if Eggie had any plastic wrap. Or, more appropriately, if his mother had left him any plastic wrap.

Going into one of the cabinets she hadn't explored yet, Darla found some already seasoned cast-iron pans, which meant she could make some of her delicious cornbread for breakfast tomorrow; a couple more Mason jars of 'shine, making a total of six she'd found so far; a roll of much-needed foil; and another snub-nosed .38. Sighing, she grabbed the foil and the weapon. The foil she put on the table with the desserts for later, the gun she took to the growing pile on the kitchen counter. The wolf had hunting knives and guns all over his dang kitchen. Who needed that many weapons in a town with wolves? Well, wolves that were family anyway.

About to place the gun down, Darla sensed someone behind her and looked over her shoulder, expecting to see Eggie. But, instead, she saw a stranger, a handsome, clean-shaven young man with wet brown hair. She immediately panicked and swung the .38 still clutched in her hand at the intruder, yelling out, "Eggie! Eggie, get down here!"

The man held his hands up and growled out, "I'm standing right in front of you, woman!"

Darla blinked. "Eggie?"

"Just put the gun down, Darla. Everything's fine."

"But . . . Eggie?"

"Darla, put the gun down!"

"Oh!" She put the gun on the weapons pile and turned back to the man who *sounded* like Eggie Ray Smith.

Fascinated, she walked up to him. "Is that really you?"

"Well . . . yeah."

She leaned in closer, his wet hair smelling nice from whatever shampoo he'd used. "Really?"

"Yes, really!"

Darla took a quick step back. "Oh. You just look . . . so . . . different."

"All I did was shave."

But what a difference a shave made. Still, she had to ask, "Why?"

He shrugged. "I saw that fancy table and figured it would be nice." He looked down at the jeans and Led Zeppelin concert T-shirt he had on. "Didn't really have anything fancier than this to wear, though. So I shaved instead."

Darla smiled. "You didn't have to do that for me. I liked your beard."

"Thought a little effort couldn't hurt."

"Well, I really appreciate it." Darla went up on her toes and kissed Eggie's cheek. She heard him swallow, saw those bright wolf eyes turn toward her.

That's when she realized she was hoping he'd kiss her back. Not just on the cheek either. She might be a virgin, but she was hardly a nun. But he didn't kiss her; he simply said, "Hope I didn't ruin dinner taking so long."

"Not at all." She took his big hand in hers. "Let's go eat."

The food was good. The lemon meringue pie astounding. But it was her smile that was making him kind of a mess.

Eggie wasn't used to feeling this way about anything. He was the wolf that Packmates and the Marine Corp called on to handle dangerous situations. He could sneak in anywhere, kill anybody, and get back out again without anyone noticing. He'd been known to sit in a tree for three days straight waiting for the right moment to take his shot. Unlike others who might snap from the pressure, Eggie never snapped. He never had nightmares or woke up in a cold sweat. He never lost his temper or went up into towers so he could shoot the unsuspecting populace.

So why this pretty little gal was making him all kinds of nervous and, to be honest, a little sweaty, he didn't rightly know.

Even stranger, he didn't know why he kind of liked feeling that way. He shouldn't. It wasn't normal for a wolf to feel weak and sort of helpless because a She-wolf had dimples. Honestly, just the cutest dimples. Dimples she kept flashing at him while they ate and she talked and he occasionally grunted. The fact that he wasn't much of a talker didn't seem to bother Darla, she just kept chatting away. Normally all that chatter would annoy Eggie something awful, but he liked the sound of her voice. He found it kind of soothing.

"Pecan pie? Cherry? Boston Cream?"

"You sure did a lot of baking."

"It's what I do when my sisters get on my nerves."

"Must explain why your pies are so damn good."

That smile returned. "Thank you. Janie may think her pecan pie is better than mine, but she can choke on it."

"She's just protective of you. It's the Alpha in her. She'll make a good mate for Bubba."

"Does that bother you?"

"I don't care who he picks as a mate."

"No, no. I mean . . . everyone assuming he'll be Alpha of the Smithtown Pack one day."

Eggie picked up his glass of milk. "Why should it bother me?"

"You're older . . . stronger . . . have wider shoulders."

Eggie choked a little on his milk, and quickly grabbed a paper napkin to wipe his chin. "Uh . . . I don't really want to be in charge. Not of a Pack. Don't mind handling a team or even a squad but anything other than that is more damn people than I want to deal with. I mostly like being on my own."

She winced. "Then I'm sorry I took over your house . . . or at least your kitchen."

"Don't mind. I like having you around. You smell nice."

You smell nice? Really? You idiot!

She bit her lip, but it couldn't hide that she was laughing at him. And she should. He was pathetic!

"Well . . . thank you. I do try."

Desperate to stop looking like the biggest loser this side of the Mississippi, Eggie stood and grabbed his empty plate and milk glass. "Guess I'll get this cleaned up."

She stood as well. "We'll do it together."

"You don't have to. You did cook."

"It'll get done faster if we work together."

"Okay." Eggie piled up a few more plates and lifted them.

"Think we can sleep together again tonight?"

Eggie, who could take out a target nearly a mile away with a good scope and in a high wind, nearly dropped the plates, barely catching them in time.

He put the pile back on the table and turned. And damn the woman, she was right behind him.

"Something wrong?" she asked, having the nerve to look innocent and sweet.

"This ain't fair, Darla Mae."

"What isn't?"

"You," he accused, forcing his gaze to look at anything but her, "smelling nice and looking so damn pretty."

"You think I'm pretty?"

"Everyone thinks you're pretty."

"Not really."

"I just can't do this."

"Do what?"

He took a step away from her, ended up banging his butt into the dining table. "This. With you. Ain't right."

"Why?" She moved in closer. "Because of my sisters? Because they said horrible things to you?"

"No, of course not." Besides. He was used to her sisters.

"Because they make me look like an idiot?" she asked flatly.

"No and they don't." He swallowed. "It's just you're . . . you're . . ."

"What? I'm what?"

"You know," he shrugged. "Untouched by a man."

"I wouldn't say all that," she muttered.

Eggie frowned. "Pardon?"

"What I mean is, I'm not some innocent, Eggie. I've just been waiting for the right . . ." She grinned, nearly killing him. "The right wolf to come along."

"Well that's not me," he told her plain.

Darla didn't understand this man. Did he want her or not? He seemed to want her one second but then seemed ready to bolt the very next.

"May I ask why you're not the right wolf?"

Still not looking her in the eyes, which seemed strange since he seemed to use that stare to his benefit most of the time, Eggie said, "Because for your first time, you deserve . . . better."

"Better than what?"

"Better than a man known for his ability to kill."

"But isn't that what you're good at?"

He finally looked her in the eye. "Ow."

"There's nothing to be ashamed of," she quickly added. "We all have to be good at something."

He picked up the plates he'd just put down on the table. "I'm going to do the dishes."

And Darla watched Eggie Smith walk away. Tight butt

moving in those jeans. She knew what her momma would say. That he'd come back when he was good and ready and a proper Southern girl would wait.

Yep. She should wait because that's what nice Southern gals do. They wait.

Eggie had just made it into his kitchen when he was attacked from behind. Well, maybe "attacked" was too strong a word. But whatever the right word, he did have a She-wolf attached to his back at the moment.

Felt kinda nice, too.

"Darla, what are you doing?"

"Well, I know my momma would say nice Southern girls wait for the man to make the appropriate moves, but then I remembered I'm a Lewis and all that went out the window. I mean of five sisters, why am *I* the only one trying to be the nice one?"

"You're the nice one?"

"Why am *I* the only one not going for what I want?"

Eggie laughed.

"What's so funny . . . wait. That was a laugh, wasn't it? I'm still trying to learn your different grunts."

"It was a laugh because you actually believe you don't go for what you want."

"I don't."

"Says the girl strapped to my back."

"You were walking away. I had to do something."

Eggie walked to the sink, Darla still holding onto him. "You sure you just don't want to get even with your sister?" he asked.

"Huh?"

"Come on, Darla. In terms of gettin' even with your sister, bedding down with me would be the easiest way. Janie Mae hates me. But we can tell her whatever you want while you keep on waitin' for that perfect wolf who isn't good at killin'."

★ ★ ★

Lord, this man was *not* going to be easy. Then again, her daddy always said nothing worth having was ever easy to get . . . or something to that effect.

Darla slipped off Eggie's back and stood at his side. "Put the dishes in the sink," she ordered and, Marine that he was, he obeyed immediately.

Once the few bits of dishware were safe, Darla tugged on his arm until Eggie faced her. She didn't bother trying to haul him around. She sensed the wolf moved only when he dang well felt like it. Thankfully he felt like it.

He faced her but the man was six-four. He might as well be a darn mountain. Glancing around, Darla turned and, using a little trick only She-wolves seemed to have, she hopped up and back, her butt landing on the sink counter. She still wasn't quite at eye level but definitely close enough.

She grabbed his T-shirt and held on. If he tried to make a run for it now, he'd have to drag her along with him.

He glanced down at her hands and back to her face. "What are you doing?"

Darla took a deep breath and tightened her grip on his shirt. "Gettin' what I want."

CHAPTER SEVEN

N*o.*
No. No. No. No. No. No. No. No.

He couldn't do this.

Well, that was a lie. He *could* do this. He *wanted* to do this. But he shouldn't. Right? It would be wrong. Right? Someone tell him it would be wrong!

But it was just Eggie and Darla Mae. And she didn't seem real ready to tell him much of anything at the moment. Instead she was moving toward him, leaning into him, her gaze focused on his mouth.

Lord, her hands were so soft and her face so pretty.

Plus he just liked her. He liked when she was cranky because someone was rude. Or when she was going on about politics or going on about that damn women's libber stuff. He found her interesting and oh so sweet.

Too sweet to fuck?

Well, the way she was now kissing his jaw, he was no longer so sure. And in another few seconds, he'd no longer care.

"Darla—"

Her soft hand pressed against his mouth and she shook her head.

"No," she said, her voice low. "Don't say anything. Just kiss me. Please."

It was the "please" that did him in. That ripped away his need to be what he'd heard termed "a nice guy."

Eggie framed her face with his hands, his thumbs brushing her cheeks, his fingers lightly gripping the back of her neck. He leaned down, but stopped just before touching her mouth with his. Took a moment to revel in that feeling of anticipation. That feeling of electricity that played between them. It was just so powerful.

Her hands gripped his biceps, fingers digging into the muscle. She wanted him. This sweet, adorable She-wolf wanted *him*. In Eggie's estimation, that was pure evidence of God.

Finally, unable to wait a second longer, Eggie kissed her. And he knew in an instant that *this* had been the She-wolf he'd been waiting for his whole entire life.

Eggie kissed her, his tongue slipping between her lips. He still tasted like her lemon meringue pie, and her recipe had never tasted better.

Darla wrapped her arms around his neck and tilted her head to the side so that Eggie could easily go deeper. He did and she loved it.

Although not at all what Darla expected, this was turning out to be the softest, sweetest kiss she'd ever had. And she wanted more. Much more.

Darla grabbed hold of the bottom of Eggie's T-shirt and lifted. She pulled out of their kiss so she could draw the shirt over his head. Biting her lip, she let her gaze roam over all that hard flesh, her fingers itching to touch and explore. Noting that he was waiting for her to make the first move, she did. She pulled off her own T-shirt. Since she never bothered to wear a bra anyway—something that went against all her mother's ladylike sensibilities—she immediately reached for him, wanting to feel his body against hers.

Eggie stepped closer and Darla put her arms over his

shoulders and arched her back so her chest pressed into his. She heard him growl a little, and then he was kissing her again. This time it was a little more desperate. Okay, a lot more. And Darla loved it. She kissed him back, her body getting hot, her nipples hard.

Darla reached for Eggie's jeans and that's when he pulled back, catching hold of her hands and stopping them.

"Wait . . . um . . ." He was panting, his eyes closed. Good. This was good. Panting was good, right?

Eyes still closed, Eggie licked his lips, took a breath, then asked, "Do you wanna have my baby?"

Although it was hard, Darla decided not to panic at that question, and instead asked one of her own. "Do you mean right this second?"

Eggie's eyes opened and he peered at her. "Huh?"

She raised her brows because she really didn't know what he was trying to ask her.

"Oh." He blinked. "Oh!" Eggie shook his head. He was still panting, so that was still good, right? "I meant . . . well . . . um . . . I got some . . . upstairs . . . in my bag . . . and . . . ya know . . . um . . ."

Darla thought a moment and asked, "Are you talking about condoms?"

Lord, he looked absolutely mortified.

"Yeah. Condoms."

"It's okay to mention them. We are about to have sex."

"Yeah, but . . . you're a virgin."

"Hopefully not for much longer." Then she grinned, showing her teeth. It made him laugh and she watched him relax a little.

"I just don't want to scare you—"

"Because you have a bag full of condoms?"

"I do *not* have a bag full of condoms. Just a few. When you're stationed overseas, the military's big about making sure their Marines—"

"Have bags full of condoms?"

At that point she could see he'd given up and she laughingly pushed him, "Go get them. Now."

"Okay." He nodded. "Okay. I'll go get them." He spun away from her and quickly walked out of the kitchen. A few seconds later he came right back. "Do you see what you're doing to me?" he demanded.

And before she could answer, he picked her up and carried her out of the kitchen. "About to go all the way upstairs, get the damn condoms, and come all the way back down to get you. You're making me insane!"

Laughing, Darla put her head on his shoulder while he brought her to his bedroom. He carefully placed her on the mattress. He kissed her, stepped away, but came right back and kissed her again. Before she knew it, she was stretched out across the bed, Eggie on top of her, his tongue exploring her mouth.

He felt so good under her hands, his big body pressing her into the mattress. She couldn't believe how safe she felt with him, how comfortable. And yet she felt wild. Out of control.

Especially when he began moving down her body, kissing her jaw and throat, his mouth finally settling on her breast. He sucked her nipple between his lips, held it while his tongue teased.

Darla's back arched, her hands digging into his shoulders. He moved to her other breast and she realized she couldn't take it anymore. She pushed at him until he lifted his head and looked at her. She wiggled out from under him and got on her knees.

"Darla?"

She didn't answer him. She couldn't. She was all hot and itchy and needy and . . . and . . . she couldn't!

Slipping off her sandals, Darla then went for her jeans and her panties, lowering them until she could go on her back and kick them off. By the time she'd gotten the darn things off, Eggie was there, reaching for her. He was naked now, too, and oh, Lord. The man was perfect. Just perfect.

He began kissing her again, his hands moving down her body, the rough tips easing along her skin. Darla began to squirm. She needed him so badly. Wanted him more than she could ever hope to say. At the moment she was grateful he wasn't much for talking. She wouldn't make any sense if she had to carry on a conversation. So she didn't. She just groaned and writhed.

One of Eggie's hands stroked down her side to her leg, easing around until it settled between her thighs. Darla immediately opened herself to him. When he didn't move, she reached down and gripped his hand, tugging his fingers higher.

He chuckled against her neck and Darla smiled in spite of her frustration. Then Eggie eased a finger inside her, slowly stroking it in and out. It felt so good, Darla growled, her hips beginning to move. A second finger joined the first and Darla dug her hands into his hair. He kissed her again while his fingers moved inside her. They felt wonderful but she wanted him.

She kissed along his jaw, moving up until she was near his ear and whispered, once, "Please, Eggie."

Eggie froze, his entire body rigid. After a moment, he slowly pulled his fingers from inside her and raised his big body over hers.

"Look at me, Darla."

And she did, raising her gaze to his. He watched her with those eyes. Those beautiful eyes that told her he was more wolf than man but she didn't care because it was the wolf that made her feel safe. Protected. Cared for.

He still didn't want to hurt her. He still didn't trust himself enough. So she leaned up and nipped at his jaw, his neck, dug her fingers into his shoulders. That's when, with condom on, he entered her, pushing inside her. He was bigger than she'd thought he'd be, but after listening to her sisters over the last few years, talking about the Smith boys, maybe she should have been more prepared.

Darla bit her lip and buried her face against his neck. She didn't want him to stop but she was afraid if she showed the slightest pain, he would.

"Keep looking at me, Darla."

Damn.

Taking a breath, she leaned her head back so he could see her face.

"Don't hide from me. Okay?"

She nodded, but tightened her grip on his shoulders. She didn't want him to stop. She wasn't sure she could handle it if he stopped.

Eggie pressed forward again but Lord, he was really big, stretching her open. She swallowed but kept her eyes on him. It didn't matter, though. He read her easily and stopped.

Damn!

But he didn't pull away. Instead, he leaned down and wrapped his warm mouth around her breast again, his tongue and lips playing with first one nipple, then the other. Tugging, nipping, sucking. After a few minutes, Darla began to writhe and groan again. It felt so good what he was doing. It felt like little electric currents were shooting from her breasts to the rest of her body, even her fingers and toes.

She started to pant again, her body getting hotter, her legs opening wider. She didn't know how long Eggie went back and forth between her nipples, teasing her with his mouth. It felt so wonderful.

Eggie's hips pushed forward and she felt a sharp pain when he slid in, but it was so brief, it barely registered. Instead, she became more overwhelmed by how full she felt. It was like he'd taken over the entire area. Not that she minded. She didn't know how something could overwhelm and feel so dang wonderful all at the same time, but Eggie had managed it.

Even more amazing, he waited a bit before he moved again. Just holding himself still inside her, still enjoying her breasts with his mouth, his hands roaming her body. He stayed like that, too, until Darla's claws began to ease out and she ended up scratching his shoulders. He didn't seem to mind. She just heard a grunt, a little laugh . . . then he was moving.

And, *oh, God, please don't ever stop. Please.*

Eggie took his time, rocking into her, understanding her body wasn't used to this and seeming to feel no need to rush her. Darla clung to him then, held onto him while he brought her up and up, until that climax hit her. She gripped him tight, her mouth pressed against his neck, her startled scream lost against his skin.

When she finally settled down, with her toes still curled and her body still wrapped around Eggie, Darla realized that tears were streaking down her face. She knew because Eggie was gently wiping them away with his thumb.

"You all right?" he asked her, his voice low. Almost a whisper.

And Darla said the first thing that came to mind at that moment. "I'm so glad I waited for you."

Again, Eggie froze, his entire body rigid and when she looked into his eyes . . . she saw that small change in dilation.

She'd brought out the wolf.

Of all the things she could have said to him, it was that one thing that had him wanting to mark her there and then. He knew he couldn't. It wouldn't be right. Not for her, anyway. He'd be fine with it, but he also knew he couldn't just trap some She-wolf into being his mate. Life with him would never be easy, so it would have to be a choice that Darla made on her own. But the Lord knew she was playing with fire.

Using every bit of Marine training he'd ever had over the last ten years, Eggie reined in his wolf, leashed it, you might say. He had to. And once he leashed it, he could focus on

Darla again. She gazed up at him with wide eyes. A little bit of panic, he guessed, but he didn't see any fear. Good. He didn't want her to ever be afraid of him. The rest of the world could be, but never Darla.

He smiled down at her and she smiled back, showing him those goddamn dimples. Honestly, the woman was testing his resolve!

So he kissed her damn pretty mouth and he finished what he'd started. He stroked into her, trying to keep it together. Trying not to get too out of control. She'd just lost her virginity and he knew it had hurt her, but she'd still managed to come. So he wasn't about to ruin all that by just ramming into her like a freight train. No matter how much he might want to.

So Eggie kept going, nice and easy, simply enjoying how good she felt, how tight she was holding him, how hard she was panting. Then she whispered his name and his eyes crossed. Then she said it again and again. It suddenly hit him that she was coming again, her body tightening around his as she choked on another scream. He followed right after her, his entire body jerking against her as he came so hard he was sure he was going to burst an important blood vessel. But it felt so good. Nothing had ever felt that good. Not simply because he was coming, but because he was with Darla.

When he could finally see straight again, he quickly lifted himself off her. He was so big and she was so small, he didn't want to crush her. But as he rolled away from her, Darla rolled with him, her arms still around him, still holding him tight.

Once he was on his back, he wrapped his arms around her, kissed her sweat-soaked forehead.

They held each other like that for so long, Eggie was sure she was asleep. Until she sighed and said, "I know it's gonna sound strange . . . but I could really go for a slice of that pecan pie right about now."

Oh, yeah. He was holding onto this little She-wolf *forever.*

CHAPTER EIGHT

They'd gotten several slices of pie and returned to the bedroom. But before they could do that, Darla found an old sheet and covered the bed with it because, according to her, "I don't care what anyone says. Crumbs in a bed are *not* comfortable."

Now they sat across from each other, eating delicious pie, and talking. Well . . . Darla talked. Eggie ate, grunted a few times, and stared at her 'cause she was naked. She seemed to like being naked and he liked that she liked being naked.

"I really love making pies," she said with an amazing amount of cheer and energy. It was hard to believe, considering what they'd been doing no more than a half an hour before. "But I don't get to very often at my job."

"No?"

"Those rich shifters coming to the Van Holtz restaurant want fancy French pastries. I can make them, too, but there's just something so wonderfully self-contained about pie. Once you perfect the crust, you can put dang near anything you want in the middle. It allows me to play. Even my failures can turn out delicious."

Eggie took another bite of the Boston Cream and asked after he swallowed, "You really like living in San Francisco then?"

"Yes."

Shit. He was going to have to move to San Francisco,

wasn't he? Eggie hated big cities. Hated the thought of living in them even more. He liked the freedom he found in Smithtown being among his own. But "his own" now included his brothers' mates. And he could see that being a problem for Darla.

"But I could live anywhere," she added after another bite of her pecan pie. "I've made some great friends in San Francisco. Met all sorts of interesting people. But you can meet all sorts of interesting people anywhere if you're willing to look."

"So you want to end up somewhere with lots of different kinds of people around?"

"Sure." She leaned over and took a bit of his pie with her fork.

Okay, so maybe he could convince her to live in a smaller city. Like Raleigh or Atlanta. Maybe even someplace in Texas where Eggie had cousins who tolerated him well enough. Yeah. That could work.

"Then again—"

Oh, Lord.

"—I liked France a lot."

"France?"

"Uh-huh. Italy, Spain, and Germany, too. Went there to study under some amazing pastry chefs. You ever been to France or Italy?"

"Yeah." Of course, he'd only been there to track down and kill rich hunters using shifters as wild game, but there was no need to share that detail.

"Did you like it?"

Eggie shrugged. "Eh."

She laughed. "Yeah, I don't exactly see you on the Champs-Élysées at a café sipping wine."

"I can go anywhere I've a need to."

For some reason that made her smile and hold out her plate, offering him some of her pecan pie.

He took a forkful. "So you want to live in Europe?"

"Sure." She grabbed another small plate, this time taking a slice of the lemon meringue. "Then again—"

"All right," Eggie cut in, starting to get fed up. "If you had to choose—big city? Small city? Small town?"

She looked off, thought a moment, then replied with a grin, "Any of those!"

Sighing, Eggie picked up the plate of chocolate cream pie and focused on that.

"Today's Saturday, right?" Darla asked while she put the empty plates and forks in Eggie's hands.

"Will be in another ten minutes."

"Hmmm."

"Why?"

She carefully folded the old sheet, making sure not to get any crumbs on the bed. "I think there's a big outdoor concert today. A few great bands."

"Where?"

"Some mountains."

He closed his eyes, took a moment. "Could you be a little more specific, darlin'?"

"Ummm . . . big mountains?"

Eggie stared down at her, his bright eyes narrowing a bit. Then he carefully placed the plates down on the dresser. Giggling, Darla backed up. "Eggie . . ."

"Come here."

"No."

"Darla—"

Darla squealed and ran, still holding that stupid sheet, but she didn't even make it to the stairs. Eggie swept her up in his arms and easily carried her back to his bedroom, while she wiggled and laughed and weakly tried to get away from him.

He pulled the sheet from her hands and tossed it to the floor.

"Careful!" she squeaked. "You'll get crumbs on the floor."

"So?"

"Eggie Smith! I'm not going to spend all day cleaning up this house."

"Okay."

"It's not okay. You leave crumbs lying around, you'll attract vermin. I'm not staying in a house with vermin."

"But we can hunt 'em when we're bored. Like little treats."

Darla began to respond to that disgusting suggestion when Eggie suddenly placed her feet on the bed. He turned her around to face him, his hands resting on her hips. "So you want to go to this music thing?"

"Some good bands."

"You should be staying put here. Where it's safe."

"Why? Whoever attacked me attacked me in North Carolina. Why would they come to Tennessee?"

"Because that's what people who come after people do."

"Even wolves eventually give up on an elk if it keeps moving." She put her arms around his shoulders, crossing them at the wrists, and smiled down at him. "Besides, it'll be fun."

"I don't have fun."

Darla giggled. "It seemed like you were having fun with me not too long ago." She kissed his cheek and whispered, "Want to have some more fun?"

"Yes, but—"

"Why is there a but to that? There shouldn't be a but to that."

"You're probably a bit sore, is all. You should rest or somethin'."

Darla kissed Eggie again. She really enjoyed kissing him. "You're just the nicest, sweetest man in the whole wide world, Egbert Ray Smith."

"And you're the only person who's ever said that to me."

"They just don't understand you."

"And you do?"

"Of course!"

"And you like me anyway?"

"Very much." She placed her hands on his cheeks. "Can't you tell?"

"Wanted to be sure."

"You can be sure." She smoothed her hands down his neck, his shoulders.

"Stop looking at me like that, Darla Mae."

"What way?"

He smirked. "You know what way. And we should go to sleep."

"I'm not sleepy."

"Darla Mae."

It meant a lot to her that he never wanted to hurt her, but she was a She-wolf with needs. "How about we play inappropriate touching?"

"Inappropriate what?"

Darla dragged her hands down Eggie's chest. "Let me show you . . ."

CHAPTER NINE

Darla woke up in a great mood. It was a beautiful summer day, she had the most handsome wolf she'd ever met asleep beside her, and she'd just had the most amazing night of her life. All was wonderful.

Sticky from sweat and, well . . . *other* things, Darla eased out of bed and went to the bathroom. She showered, brushed her teeth, and came back to the bedroom. Eggie was awake now, staring up at the ceiling.

"What's wrong?"

"Nothin'."

"You sure?"

"Yep."

She accepted what he said and dug out some clean clothes from the bag her sisters had left for her. He wasn't a man she wanted to push unnecessarily. He'd tolerate it, but he shouldn't have to.

"How about breakfast?" she asked.

"I should take you out somewhere."

"Why? I have what we need for a yummy breakfast."

"I should have taken you to dinner last night. Bought ya flowers. Maybe some chocolates."

"We had pie."

She heard him grunt while she slipped on her sandals. Stretching across the bed, she rested her head on his chest and looked up at him.

"Last night was absolutely perfect. The best night of my life. We had each other and pie. Didn't need anything else." She patted his chest with her hand. "Don't let my worldly nature fool you. I'm just a small-town girl at heart."

Finally Eggie smiled and she saw the bit of stress he'd been feeling slip away from his face.

"You still up for this all day concert thing that's *somewhere* in the mountains?" he asked.

"As a matter of fact . . . I am. It's a beautiful day. We should go out and experience it."

He grunted, slowly sat up. "Then let me get in the shower."

"And I'll make us breakfast." She started to move away but Eggie caught her hand, held it.

His thumb brushed over her knuckles before he finally stated, "I'm really liking you, Darla Mae."

Her heart soared at his words but she tamped that down quickly. It was never a good idea to jump up and down and clap your hands together when a man told you that sort of thing. It was even more of a bad idea when it was a wolf.

So, when she was calm enough, she smiled and said, "I really like you, too!"

Startled those words had come out, Darla slapped her hand over her mouth. *Darn it!*

"I shouldn't have said that."

"Why not?"

"I was supposed to say something cute and enticing."

"It was cute and enticing."

"No, no." She covered her face, mortified. "I'm supposed to entice you to keep your interest. That's what my sisters would have done."

"Your sisters hate me."

"Yeah, but I am trying to keep your interest." She shrugged and just went ahead and admitted, "I don't want you to get bored."

Eggie leaned over until he could look into her face.

"Darla. I'm canine. I don't get bored when something is as entertaining as you are. Besides," he added. "Pie."

Darla laughed, and kissed him. And when she pulled away, Eggie's hand slipped behind the back of her neck and brought her toward him again. Their kiss went on and on, and she loved every second of it, but when he started to bring her down to the bed again, she pulled away from him and gave a shake of her head. "Oh, no you don't, Eggie Ray Smith. We're going out. You promised."

She heard him give a little growl and stand up. Darla forced herself not to stare—even though she wanted to. Lord, the man was just so dang perfect.

"I won't be long," he said, heading to the bathroom. She noticed he was rubbing his already returning beard.

"Eggie?"

"Huh?"

"You don't have to shave if you don't want to."

He stopped at the bathroom door and looked at her. "You sure?"

Darla shrugged. "I like your beard. I like you without it. Doesn't matter to me as long as you're comfortable. And if you're on vacation, I want you comfortable."

"Is that an order?"

"Since that's all you Marines seem to be able to handle." She winked at him and skipped down the steps. She was heading to the kitchen when she stopped by the living room. Eggie's four brothers were sitting on his couch, eating cereal and watching "Super Friends" cartoons on Eggie's color TV.

"What are y'all doing?" she asked and, like zebras at a watering hole, they all looked at her at the same time. They all looked so similar and yet Eggie was still the most handsome as far as Darla was concerned.

"Eating," Bubba Ray answered.

"My sisters don't feed you?"

"They're not talking to us."

"Why?"

The brothers all looked at each other, debating how much to tell her, she knew.

"I'm waiting," Darla pushed.

Bubba Ray put down his cereal and walked over to Darla. "They're mad because we didn't go with them last night to help you escape."

Darla frowned. "Escape?"

"They started calling you Patty Hearst," Nicky Ray volunteered with a laugh.

"*Shut. Up,*" Bubba Ray barked at the youngest brother. He looked back at Darla, shrugged. "They never went through with the plan because they didn't want to deal with Eggie without us."

"Oh, really?"

"Don't be mad, Darla. They're just worried about you. They didn't mean nothin' by it."

Darla doubted that but she asked, "Why didn't you?"

"Why didn't I what?"

"Try to rescue me?"

"I guess because you didn't look like you needed to be rescued."

"And even Bubba wasn't about to fight Eggie," Benji tossed in.

"Well, remember what happened when Nicky tried to take that deer antler from him?" Frankie Ray asked.

While the Smith boys laughed—well, except for Bubba Ray, who just looked disgusted—Darla walked in front of the TV and stood there with her arms crossed over her chest. She glared down at the brothers until their laughter slowly died and they eventually focused on the coffee table she'd picked out for Eggie.

"So I'm just a bone your brother's playin' with?" she asked.

"No, ma'am," the three brothers muttered while Bubba turned away, but not before she could see his smile.

"That's good. I don't think my daddy and brothers would appreciate that particular characterization of me."

Frankie looked up at her. "Character–what?"

Good Lord. These *wolves are the feared Smith boys*?

Because it seemed only Eggie and Bubba actually got the brains *and* the brawn. "Why don't y'all clean those bowls while I make ya some pancakes and bacon."

"Yes'm."

Darla watched them get up and walk out of the room. She stepped beside Bubba and he put his arm around her shoulders. He was a much friendlier wolf when his brothers weren't around to witness it.

"If my sisters were so dang worried about me," Darla wanted to know, "why didn't they just call? I would have answered."

"Eggie ain't got no phone. He don't like 'em."

"Oh?" She'd never noticed, but she'd been . . . distracted. "Why not?"

"We don't know. And none of us are brave enough to ask him."

He winked at her and Darla asked, "You going to make an honest mate of my sister, Bubba Ray?"

"She won't let me. Your sister is mean, Darla Mae."

"Yeah," she admitted, "but I'm sure that's what you love about her."

Eggie walked into his kitchen and found his brothers eating *his* food, which *his* She-wolf had fixed for them. Something he found unacceptable.

"Breakfast is ready," Darla said to him with that smile.

"Do you have any food left?" he growled, glowering down at his brothers. As usual, only Bubba held his gaze, the big-headed bastard smirking a little. The others went right back to their food, shoveling it in like they expected lion males to come out of the woods and steal it at any second.

Darla put his food down and tapped his chair.

"Did you eat?" he asked once he stood in front of her.

"I did. I just need to clean the kitchen and then we can go."

"No. Go get your stuff together. My brothers will clean the kitchen."

"I'm not cleaning your—" Nicky Ray began, but Eggie barked and snarled at his brother until the bastard lowered his head and went back to eating.

"We'll take care of it," Bubba said. "You go on, Darla. Have yourself a lovely day."

"Y'all are just so sweet." She stroked Eggie's hand with the tips of her fingers. "I won't be long," she murmured.

"Take your time."

He waited until Darla had gone upstairs before he focused on his idiot kin, and made everything clear in terms they could easily understand.

"I could skin ya, have you deboned, and buried in less than an hour. It's in the trainin'. So don't y'all cross me when it comes to Darla Mae."

The two eldest hunkered down more over their food, the youngest nearly choked on his pancake, but Bubba Ray leaned back in his chair and noted, "I guess this means you love her."

But Eggie wasn't about to get into discussing any of that with his kin. "Just don't get in my way, and I won't have to kill any of ya. I hate upsettin' Momma and all."

Chapter Ten

Since Eggie didn't have a phone at his house, they'd called from the road. Eggie didn't know who Darla had called, but whoever it was, they'd told her exactly where to find that outdoor concert. It was near the Smoky Mountains at a big park, and was an event run by Darla's friends. Friends Eggie didn't know, but he didn't really care. Because in the end, the music had turned out not to be bad at all, Darla was happy, and it was the perfect place to meet with his team.

Eggie had been working with the team for three years now. McMartin was their team leader; Taschen a jackal with excellent bomb-making skills; Lloyd a leopard who could blend in anywhere and was amazing at recon; and Eggie, who was really good at killing stuff.

When Eggie had gone on vacation, so had Taschen and Lloyd, but McMartin had called his teammates back in to help them figure out what had happened on Smith territory. True, as Marines, they weren't supposed to do this kind of work on American soil but this was personal and they were helping out a fellow Marine.

While the roadies and stage crew were setting up for the next band, Eggie took Darla's hand and led her away from the stage.

As they walked, Darla said, "Stop glaring at everyone, Eggie Ray."

"I'm not. I'm only glaring at the men staring at your legs."

She had on denim cutoffs, a tight Jimi Hendrix shirt, and no shoes. Her long hair was loose around her shoulders and she looked as happy and comfortable as any woman could. But Eggie could see what he was guessing Darla couldn't. The type of people who had come to this concert. Some of them were just average good ol' local boys who'd only be a problem if they drank too much 'shine in this heat, some out-of-towners looking for a good time . . . and some others. It was the "others" that Eggie kept his eyes on.

Darla leaned into Eggie, her fingers intertwined with his. Unlike her sisters, whom Eggie had watched off and on over the past few years with his brothers, Darla was openly affectionate. She held his hand, put her arm around his waist, hugged if she felt in the mood. And, to Eggie's great surprise, he liked it. He liked that she not only felt comfortable touching him whenever she wanted, but that she seemed proud to be with him. Proud to claim him as her own.

Eggie stopped and slowly turned his head, scanning the crowd. It took a moment, but he caught sight of McMartin first. The bear nodded at him and Eggie nodded back.

"Who's that?" Darla asked.

"A friend of mine."

"A Marine?"

"Yep."

"Well, go on and talk to him."

"Come with me."

"Eggie, I'll be fine." She pointed to a small group. "I think I know one of those girls over there."

"Which one?"

"The coyote. We used to work together."

"I don't like coyotes."

Darla laughed. "Go on with your Marine buddies so y'all don't have to speak in code so I won't understand what's going on."

Damn, the woman was smart.

"I wanna look around anyway." She went up on her toes

and kissed his cheek. "Go on now. I'll be fine. Maybe I'll get something to drink."

"Only unopened bottles and cans, Darla."

"Uh . . . okay." She headed off, looking over her shoulder at him and giving a little wave.

Eggie watched her for a bit until his teammates surrounded him.

"That's her?" Taschen asked.

"Yep."

"She's cute."

"She's mine."

"Told ya," McMartin said to Taschen. "Saw it in his eyes when she was being treated by the doc."

"And how does she feel about it?" Lloyd asked.

Eggie faced the three shifters. "What do I always say?"

"You hate chitchat?" McMartin guessed.

"Then why are you motherfuckers giving me goddamn chitchat?"

Darla had been right. She knew the coyote. She was a former Van Holtz restaurant sous-chef. Of course, after five minutes, Darla also remembered that she'd never liked the coyote that much. She was kind of annoying. Like now.

"Egbert *Smith*? You're involved with Egbert *Smith*?"

Darla nodded while sipping her Coca-Cola. It was wonderfully refreshing.

Barbie Klein, currently covered in body paint and a bikini, grabbed Darla's arm and nodded at her full-human friends. "I'll be back."

She pulled Darla off to the edge of the crowd and faced her. "Is there something wrong with you?" Barbie demanded.

"You're covered in pink, green, and yellow body paint, and you're asking *me* that?"

"Look, sweetie, I get it. I've been there. There is *something* about the Smith males that can be . . . enticing. Even I can admit that. But you're not me and Egbert Smith is a . . . a . . ."

"Really nice guy?"

"He is not a nice guy, Darla. He's a . . . a . . ."

"If you can't say it, maybe you shouldn't."

"Sweetie, every canine from here to Istanbul knows about Eggie Smith and avoids him."

"He's misunderstood. Besides, you just don't like Smiths."

"No one likes Smiths, Darla, except other Smiths. They're like the wolf version of the Manson family."

"I can tell you for a fact that's not funny and it's not true."

"They're not a Pack, they're a hillbilly cult filled with criminals and 'shine runners. You have to be careful."

"You don't know what you're talking about and I'm not going to stand here and listen to another word of this utter bull-crap."

Angry, Darla turned to go but stopped when she saw a full-human man standing in front of her. He wore a leather jacket with emblems and things on it.

"Sorry," she said, distracted, and took a step to walk around the man. He took a step, too, blocking her.

She looked at him again and the man smiled, which only made things worse. A smile like that never boded well for anyone. She glanced back to look at Barbie but typical coyote that she was, the little deserter had run off and left her!

Darla also realized that she'd quickly become surrounded and now had males and females in front and behind her. Most of them wearing the same leather jacket as the first. And wearing them in this heat meant they were sending a message.

No . . . this probably wasn't a good situation.

Eggie stared at Lloyd. "Are you sure?"

"Positive. And they're pushing hard to find her. Her boss knew, too. That's why he sent her home. Although I don't think he meant for her to hitchhike there."

Eggie blinked. "She *hitchhiked* from San Francisco to North Carolina?"

"Apparently she does it all the time."

Eyes crossing, Eggie realized he'd be working very hard to keep this She-wolf safe just from herself.

"All right, all right." He let out a big breath. "What I'll need you to do is . . ."

Eggie's words tapered off when he realized none of his team was paying attention to him. He looked next to him and saw why. A female coyote in a bikini and body paint stood nearby, staring at him. The one that Darla had pointed out to him earlier. But where was Darla?

"What's wrong?" he immediately asked.

"Darla needs you."

Eggie spun around, his gaze searching the area. When that didn't work fast enough, he sniffed the air, caught her scent. He motioned to his team and they vanished into the crowd. Then he went after his woman.

"Come on, baby," one of the men coaxed and Darla remembered how much she hated when men called her baby, "can't you be a little friendly to our buddy Will?"

Will must be the one standing right in front of her, staring at her in a way she found wholly inappropriate and uncomfortable.

"Move, Will," Darla suggested.

Will just smiled. She knew what they were planning. To drag her off into the surrounding woods, have what bikers liked to call "a little party" with her.

But Darla had been traveling around the States for a long time, and she had a lot of friends. Even friends she wasn't really supposed to have.

"Darla Mae," a voice called from the woods before about fifty of them walked out and slowly surrounded the full-humans.

Like the full-human bikers, the ones from the woods wore

leather jackets, but they had no colors, no emblems sewn into the leather. They didn't need them because they were not a biker club. They were a wolf Pack who just happened to like motorcycles. The Magnus Pack specifically, and the ones who'd arranged this concert and hired the bands, including, it was rumored, the surprise addition of Lynyrd Skynyrd, which was why Darla had pushed for her and Eggie to come. She knew he was a fan, as were most of the Smiths.

Although the Magnus Pack was much bigger than these fifty wolves, expanding into Europe and Asia, the Pack was run by one Alpha couple who lived in Northern California. The wolf walking toward Darla, though, was their only son, Bruce Morrighan, and he had his arm around a female Darla didn't recognize. *Must be one of his new girls.*

He smiled down at her. He was a handsome wolf. Tall, powerful. And fair. He'd make a good Alpha Male one day. "Hi, Darla."

"Hi, Bruce."

"You all right?"

"I'm fine."

He nodded at the She-wolf next to him. "This is Kylie Redwolf. My mate."

Darla grinned. "Congratulations." But when Darla focused on the She-wolf, her genuine smile faded, and she had to force a fake, safe one instead.

Darla's sisters never believed her. They never believed that, like their Great Aunt Bernice, she could look at a person and just know what she was dealing with. Now, sometimes, like with Eggie, she had to look long and deep before she was sure. With others, like Bruce, she could see it after only a bit of time getting to know the person.

Yet with this She-wolf, with Kylie, Darla had to look into those eyes for only a split second before she knew. Before she knew something was very wrong. It had happened when she met the Alpha Male of the Víga-Feilan Pack three weeks before he turned on his own adult pups. It had happened when she'd met Charles Manson, and the Lord knew she'd been right about that. And it was happening now, with Bruce's mate.

"Kylie. Nice to meet ya."

"Nice to meet you." The She-wolf looked like she belonged to one of the Indian shifter tribes Darla had met when she went to Texas to work at the Van Holtz restaurant there one winter. Kylie was a beautiful woman, but cold. So very, very cold.

"So what's going on here?"

"I was trying to leave," Darla told Bruce, her focus on him rather than his mate. "They weren't making it easy."

Bruce looked back at the head of the biker club. He'd talk to him but Darla moved her gaze on Will. Will was her problem. Amazing how Eggie's lack of conversation didn't bother her, but Will's definitely did.

Arms stretched out from his body in open challenge, the full-human leader said to Bruce, "You got something to say to me, rich boy?" He looked at Bruce's mate. "You and your red-skinned whore."

And that's when Bruce's mate swung, her fist ramming into the full-human and dropping him to the ground. He covered his face, blood pouring from between his fingers.

"You crazy bitch!"

Darla snorted a little. If he expected a lot of yelling and chest beating before a real fight, he shouldn't have said anything to Bruce's She-wolf. One look at her and Darla could tell there would never be a warning, there would never be words, there would never be anything but pain and blood and someone calling her a crazy bitch.

Watching her own back now that the two groups were going at each other, Darla looked for Will. She knew that with everyone distracted, it would be the perfect time for him to try something really stup . . .

Darla stepped away from the escalating battle and looked around. There was no Will. Nor any sign of the couple of his friends who'd been standing by him. They were gone. Darla sniffed the air.

"Oh, no!"

She charged away from the growing fight and into the woods. After about two minutes, she jumped up onto a boulder and snarled, *"Egbert Ray!"*

The wolf looked up from the bloody and battered man that he had kneeling on the ground before him. Eggie was holding onto Will's hair with one hand, his hunting knife in the other pressed against the man's throat.

The other two men who'd been with Will were being held by Eggie's friends and had also been beaten within inches of their lives. After less than five minutes. Damn. She couldn't help cussing about this. She just had to say it. Damn.

"Go on back, Darla," Eggie growled at her. "Now."

"Let them go."

He looked up at her and she saw that his wolf eyes were slightly dilated, his fangs out.

"Go back, Darla."

She crossed her arms over her chest. "I'm not gonna let you do this."

"Darla—"

"I'm not going to let you ruin our beautiful day by killing three men and burying them in the woods. I won't allow it."

Eggie stared at her and she stared back, unwilling to look away.

Look, she wasn't a saint. She really didn't mind the beating these men had taken. They'd deserved it and it would be a good lesson for them so that hopefully some other girl never had to face a similar threat. At least not from them. But Darla couldn't escape the fact that when it was all said and done, they hadn't actually done anything to her. Maybe they'd wanted to try. Or maybe they'd hoped to scare her into cooperating. Or maybe they'd planned to just harass her until she'd run off into the crowd. She'd never know and that was why she couldn't allow this. She knew for Smiths there was no question about this sort of thing, but she wasn't a Smith. Never would be. She would always be a Lewis and, more importantly, she'd always be Darla Mae.

"Come on, Eggie," she urged, softening her voice and holding out her hand to him. "I heard Lynyrd Skynyrd might be playing later tonight."

"I hate Lynyrd Skynyrd. It's my Alabama cousins who like 'em."

"Oh." She shrugged, gave him a little smile. "Ooops."

He looked away but she knew that was because he didn't want to be relieved of his anger. She understood that. She got that way about her sisters. But she kept her hand out and her eyes on his face.

"Smith?" a black bear prompted, his foot now on the back of the neck of one of those men. One push of that enormous foot and that full-human's spine would be snapped like a dry twig.

Growling, Eggie slammed his knife back into the holster on his thigh, grabbed the full-human by the throat and lifted him up. He rammed him into a tree and held him there. The full-human tried to fight him off but he might as well not have bothered. Eggie leaned in and whispered something to the male. Darla cocked her head, trying to hear him but she couldn't make out a word, the pitch too low and Eggie too far away for her wolf ears to catch anything but muttering.

When the man literally pissed himself and then, based on the smell, crapped his pants, Darla was relieved she hadn't heard anything. She didn't want to know.

Eggie stepped back and dropped the man to the ground. He glowered down at him a little longer until he turned away—she knew he didn't want to, knew how hard it was for him to do that—and walked over to Darla.

Darla still held her hand out and she wiggled her fingers at him, but Eggie shook his head. "Got blood on my hands."

But Darla realized something about Eggie . . . he'd always have blood on his hands. Whether physically or metaphorically, he would always have blood on his hands or paws for the rest of his life. She knew that now. Understood it. And, as she reached down and grasped his blood-covered hand with her own, slightly calloused and scarred from baking and cooking over the years, Darla accepted that about him.

She had to because she knew now that she was in love with him. Whether she wanted to be or not, she loved him.

Of course, her sisters would call her foolish. Not because it was Egbert Ray Smith or because he was one of the Smith boys, but because he was her first. Because for Darla, there was no separating love and sex. They were one and the same for her, always would be.

She smiled into Eggie's angry face, knowing his fury wasn't directed at her, knowing without doubt or concern that she was safe with this dangerous, deadly wolf.

"Come on," she said. "I'm starvin'."

They came out of the woods after using a rag that Lloyd had on him to wipe their hands free of blood. It didn't help with the scrapes and cuts they had from beating the men but that was all right. Maybe, if Eggie was lucky, no one would find the three and they'd die of their wounds. He knew why Darla had stopped him but he also knew men like that. Predator full-humans were, in Eggie's estimation, the worst. Because food or survival had nothing to do with why they hunted. Absolutely nothing. But if there was just one female who could rein in Eggie's love of putting down useless humans, it was Darla Mae Lewis and only Darla Mac.

As they cleared the woods, a large group of wolves suddenly stalked up to them and, going on training rather than instinct, Eggie and his teammates pulled their Smith & Wesson Model 59 semi-automatic pistols and aimed them at the wolves. The Pack skidded to a halt except for a darker-skinned She-wolf who kept coming anyway, but a tall male caught her arm and yanked her back, keeping her at his side.

"Darla?" the male demanded.

"Egbert Ray," Darla sighed. "They're my friends."

Eggie sniffed the air and growled out, "Magnus Pack *wolves* are your friends?"

"I have lots of friends. Weapons down, gentlemen," Darla ordered.

Eggie nodded at his team and he tucked his gun in the back of his jeans, under his denim jacket.

"Are you all right, Darla?" one of the Magnus Wolves asked.

"I'm fine. Just fine."

Another one of the wolves pushed through the Pack, and stepped forward. And, with one look and a nod, Eggie recognized him as one of the Navy engineers who helped his team blow up shit when necessary. "Thorpe."

"Smith."

Ezra Thorpe had been part of the Magnus Pack since he was sixteen but he'd joined the Navy when he was twenty. He was, from what Eggie could tell, one of the best demolition experts he'd known. The wolf could take down an entire block with only a couple of strategically placed sticks of weak dynamite. He wasn't real friendly but that's why Eggie tolerated him. He hated real friendly.

"Smith?" the Pack leader of the young wolves snarled. "Egbert Ray *Smith*?"

Darla smiled and nodded. "It sure is."

Eggie could be wrong, but it sounded like he heard pride in her response.

"Egbert Ray," she went on, "this is Bruce Morrighan of the Magnus Pack."

Eggie grunted at the wolf, staring until the rest of the wolf's Pack became antsy. But the wolf didn't seem ready to move until his female tried to charge Eggie again. Good thing Morrighan was fast, though, or Eggie would have had no qualms about knocking this female out. He knew crazy when he saw it and that She-wolf was crazy.

"You'll be all right?" Morrighan asked Darla while his Pack began to wander off.

"I'll be just fine. Thanks, Bruce."

"Howl if you need me," he said before he walked away, dragging the She-wolf behind him.

Thorpe grinned and began to follow after the rest of his Pack.

"Hey. Thorpe."

"Yeah?" he asked without turning around.

"You staying in Tennessee for a while?"

"Maybe."

"Good." And Eggie filed that away for later use.

When the Pack and the bikers were gone, Eggie faced Darla.

She smiled up at him. "Thanks, Eggie."

He grunted and started walking, still holding Darla's hand. As they moved through the crowd, Eggie said, "Found out why you were attacked in North Carolina."

"Oh?"

"Uh-huh."

Eggie stopped, pulling Darla up short. When she faced him, he asked, "Did you know you witnessed a murder in San Francisco two weeks ago?"

Darla blinked, frowned. "Huh?"

CHAPTER ELEVEN

"This is crazy," Darla said, stepping out of the car once Eggie had killed the motor. She closed the door. "Absolutely crazy. I think I'd notice if someone was killed right in front of me."

She walked around the front of the car but Eggie was already there, stopping her from heading into his house.

"Maybe you blocked it out or something."

"Eggie, I'm not some sensitive little flower that hasn't been on a hunt before."

"Hunting deer and seeing a man killed are two different things, darlin'."

"I saw what you did on my father's territory. Remember every bit of it, too."

He winced and Darla shook her head. "I'm sorry. I didn't . . ." She started to walk around him, but Eggie caught her hips and held her. Leaning his butt against the hood of his car, he pulled her closer, between his legs.

"Listen to me, Darla. No one is saying you did anything wrong."

"But I'm such a girl I can't handle the stress of seeing someone murdered? Eggie . . . do you really think if I'd seen something, I wouldn't have gone to the police? That I wouldn't have done something? Anything?"

He gazed at her, eventually shaking his head. "You would

have done something. No matter how stupid doin' something might have been."

"Exactly."

"That response does not make me feel better, Darla Mae."

"I know."

He tugged her closer until the grill of his car stopped her. Darla put her arms around his neck and he wrapped his around her waist.

"Look," Eggie said, "I don't want you to worry. My teammates are taking care of this for me."

"Taking care of what? They don't have any details yet. Who killed who or why. Just that the police are looking for me as a witness to a possible homicide."

"And my team will find out all the details—and then deal with it."

"You mean start killing people."

"Well, someone already tried to kill you once, so I don't see what the problem is."

"I didn't say I had a problem with it. I just wanted to see if you'd be honest with me."

"I can't promise I'll volunteer information. And sometimes I won't be able to tell you something because I just can't."

"Top secret military stuff?"

"Pretty much." Eggie hugged her close and gazed into her face. "But I ain't gonna outright lie to you. Mostly 'cause it would be wrong. But also 'cause you're smart enough to see through my bullshit."

"Only because you're not a very good liar."

"It's a flaw."

No. It really wasn't.

Darla kissed him and Eggie immediately responded. His arms tightened around her waist, his growl easing into her mouth.

When they finally pulled away from each other, they both

frowned and looked toward Eggie's front porch. His brothers stood there, watching them and eating the pie she had left in the kitchen.

She heard him snarl and Darla immediately pressed her hand to his chest. "Eggie."

When she was sure she had him calm, she focused on the scruffy wolves cluttering Eggie's porch. "Something we can help y'all with?"

"She's so much more polite than her sisters," Nicky Ray remarked. "It's such a nice change."

Eggie snarled again.

"Gentlemen?" she pushed, not sure how long she could hold him back.

"Momma wants y'all at Sunday dinner tomorrow," Bubba explained.

"Did you leave any pie that I could bring?"

While still chewing, the brothers looked back and forth among each other before shaking their heads.

Not that Darla had any intention of bringing two-day-old pie to a dinner at Eggie's Momma's house but still . . . it was the principle!

Disgusted, she stepped away from Eggie and marched toward the stairs. "Guess I'm going shopping tomorrow."

"Don't need to," Benji told Darla as she passed him on the stairs. "I think your sisters are all bringing pie."

Darla stopped at the door, faced the Smith boys, her eyes narrowing. "Oh? Are they?"

The four males backed away from her. Not that she blamed them.

With a sniff, she stormed into the house, slamming the door behind her.

Eggie's brothers shuddered after Darla slammed that door. Then they turned to leave—only to come face to face with Eggie.

"What's going on?" he asked.

"Nothing," Bubba lied. And the bastard was lying. "Why?"

"Whose idea was this dinner?"

"Momma's. It's not like she's had any time to spend with her favorite boy."

Eggie rolled his eyes. "She said that one time after drinkin' and you *still* haven't gotten over it, have you?"

"See ya tomorrow, big brother." Bubba walked by him. "Can't wait for the show."

Bubba disappeared into the trees and the rest of them followed. With a sigh, Eggie went into his house—and found Darla going through all the cabinets.

"What are you doing?" he asked her.

"Seeing what I need to buy from the store tomorrow." She faced him. "You do know what this is, don't you?"

"You being irrational?"

"No. They're challenging me."

"Really don't remember that being said."

"You don't know my sisters. This isn't over."

Eggie walked over to Darla and slipped his arm around her waist.

"Eggie . . . no."

He didn't answer, just kissed her neck.

"I've gotta make lists and . . . and things."

Kissed her jaw.

"Eggieeeee," she whined out, her arms reaching up and gripping his shoulders.

"Don't make me face that bed alone, Darla Mae." *Don't ever make me face that bed alone. Not ever again.*

Darla gazed up into his face. "But if everybody thinks that Janie Mae's pecan pie is better than mine . . ."

Eggie, smiling, picked Darla up and carried her to the stairs. "Don't worry. That'll never happen."

CHAPTER TWELVE

Darla rolled out of bed naked and stood, stretching her arms high over her head. With an allover shake, she grabbed one of Eggie's black T-shirts off a chair and pulled it on over her head while she hurried downstairs. She rubbed her stomach and gazed into the refrigerator, trying to figure out what she wanted for breakfast.

"What'cha making this morning, Darla Mae?"

Darla closed her eyes and willed herself not to jump out of her skin at the voice coming from behind her. When she felt calm enough, she glanced over her shoulder. "Hey, Nicky Ray."

"Hey."

He pointed at the wall and Darla blinked. "A phone? You put in a phone?"

"Eggie told me to." He grinned. "I'm the technically savvy one in this family."

Darla, too nice to hurt the man's feelings, smiled and nodded. "Of course you are. But Bubba said Eggie hates phones."

"He does, but he wants you to feel safe. He asked me to take care of it when we first got back from Smithville. I just didn't mention it to anybody." Nicky swiped up an apple he had lying on the counter and took a bite out of it. "So y'all coming tonight?"

"Of course."

"You sure? The whole family will be there."

"Not a problem." She yawned and grabbed the milk.

"Should you talk to Eggie first or are you speaking for both of you now?"

Darla glanced at the wolf before pouring milk into her glass. "Kind of an instigator, aren't you, Nicky Ray?"

"Don't know what'cha mean."

"I think you do."

He grinned at her and turned to go but he crashed right into his brother's chest. "Hey, Eggie."

Eggie bared his fangs and snarled. Eyes down, Nicky maneuvered around his brother and bolted out the backdoor.

Laughing, Darla shook her head and drank her milk.

"You sleep all right?" Eggie asked her.

"When I got sleep, yes." She winked and handed him her half-finished glass of milk. Eggie took it and finished the rest in one gulp.

"Now," she asked, walking to the phone, "why is this here?"

"Safety. You have any problems, you dial zero and Stacey, the town operator, will send the sheriff and deputies right over."

"You sure all this is necessary, Eggie?"

"I'm not taking any chances. Not with you."

Darla grinned and Eggie began to move toward her. But the new phone rang and Eggie's reaction was . . . surprising. He jumped back about four feet and began barking at the phone, over and over again.

Not sure how long before the dang phone was ripped from the wall, Darla quickly picked up the receiver. "Hello?"

Unable to make out any words over the continued noise, she looked at Eggie and snapped, "Egbert Ray!"

He stopped barking but then he growled at the phone like she was holding a live snake.

Good Lord.

★ ★ ★

Eggie watched Darla on that damn phone. He hated phones.

"I'm sorry," she said. "What was that? Oh, hi, Miss Pauline. Do I know who?" Darla gasped and looked down at herself. "Yes," she said into the phone. "Yes. I know him. Please send him here. Under protection please. Thank you so much, Miss Pauline."

Darla hung up the phone and looked down at herself again. "Lord! I gotta get dressed."

She darted past him and Eggie followed. "Where are you going?"

"I gotta get cleaned up." She glanced back as she jogged up the stairs. "I am just *covered* in you."

"As well you should be," he muttered, before he followed her up the stairs and to the bathroom. He stood outside while she turned on the shower.

"So who's coming here?" he asked.

"My boss."

Eggie's eyes narrowed. "Your boss? There's a Van Holtz on Smith territory?"

Darla spun around to face Eggie. "Egbert Ray, do *not* start anything with Bernhard Van Holtz."

He crossed his arms over his chest. "We got a damn Nazi coming to the house."

"He is *not* and I want you to promise me you'll be nice to him."

"To a Van Holtz? Never gonna happen. And I don't want you being around him."

"He's my boss."

Eggie stared at her. "So you're going back there?"

Darla blinked, clearly surprised by his question. "Um . . . I don't . . . I haven't really . . ." She fluttered her hands in the air. "Egbert Ray, I don't have time for all this. Now out. I need to take the quickest shower known to man and get dressed."

Eggie stepped into the hallway and Darla closed the door. It wasn't that he was surprised she was planning to go back. Planning to return to San Francisco and her life as a pastry chef for a goddamn Van Holtz. But, what did shock him was that she was planning to go back without him. At least that's how it felt when she didn't mention anything about them going back together. Not with her all distracted by some pansy wolf coming to *his* door.

Confused, pissed off, and hurt, Eggie walked downstairs, went out his front door, and sat down on his porch.

He waited.

Darla tugged on the little summer dress, slipped on her sandals, and quickly brushed out her hair.

She ran down the stairs and headed to the kitchen to get glasses and a pitcher of sweet tea together, but she saw through the windows that Mr. Van Holtz was already here, standing outside Eggie's house . . . and staring down Eggie.

"Oh, Lord!"

She charged to the door and snatched it open. Neither wolf looked away from the other as she ran out onto the porch. She stopped at the top of the stairs, getting between Eggie and her boss.

"Hello, Mr. Van Holtz."

The wolf smiled at her and she saw real concern and relief in his face.

"Darla." He came up the stairs and kissed her cheek. She heard Eggie's growl but she chose to ignore it. "I'm so glad you're okay. I heard what happened in Smithville. I'm so sorry."

"You didn't do anything wrong."

"I should have told you why I sent you home, but I didn't want to worry you."

She shook her head. "Don't even think about it, sir."

"It never occurred to me that they'd go after you there,

and I was hoping to get the situation worked out before calling you back."

"Oh. Did you get it worked out?"

"I'm sorry, no. Not yet."

Darla hated herself for feeling relieved by that, but she was . . . unsure. Did Eggie want her to stay with him? Or just stay with him for now? It was hard to tell with the man. He wasn't exactly big on expressing emotion except when he was annoyed.

"Do you think we can take a walk?"

Noting that Mr. Van Holtz wasn't looking at her when he asked the question, Darla looked over her shoulder. Eggie stood behind her now—she'd never even heard him move— his arms crossed over his chest, his wolf eyes locked on Mr. Van Holtz.

The Van Holtzes were tall but lean wolves. With less brawn, they used their brains to devastating effect when it came to a fight. And, for as long as the two Packs had existed, Smiths and Van Holtzes were sworn enemies, although Darla had no idea why. She did know that there'd been Pack wars over the centuries between the two. They'd been ugly, brutal, and something many hoped would never be repeated.

Darla gestured down the stairs and walked Van Holtz away from the porch. "Give me a minute, would you?" she asked and returned to the stairs Eggie was standing on.

"I'll be right back," she told him. "Don't follow me."

"You expect me to leave you alone with a goddamn Van Holtz?"

"Watch how you speak to me, Egbert Ray Smith. I ain't some little whore you picked up on the street somewhere. Understand me?"

He grunted and she decided to take that as a "yes" to her question.

"We won't be long, we won't leave Smith territory, just wait until I get back."

When he didn't say anything, she returned to Van Holtz's side. "Ready?" she asked, forcing a smile.

He watched Darla walk away with that smooth talkin', fancy dressed, skinny-assed rich bastard.

Eggie had grown up hating Van Holtzes. That was what every Smith was taught at birth. But now he *really* hated them. A lot.

Bubba came out of Eggie's house, his mouth full of the last slice of pie Eggie had found and hidden the night before. "You just gonna let him go off with your woman?"

"You wanna stay out of my business?"

"You can't kill him. Daddy gave his word he'd be protected and Momma would have a fit."

"I don't care. Why are you still talking to me?"

"No reason."

Eggie went back into his house, slamming the door shut, then he shifted to wolf, shook off his clothes and went out the back door. Then he tracked down Darla and Van Holtz, making sure to stay upwind of them.

Horrified, Darla sat down on a boulder, her hands on her cheeks.

"Poor Mr. Kozlow." She shook her head. "He was always so sweet to me."

Harold Kozlow was the full-human owner of the high-end jewelry store next door to the Van Holtz restaurant, and he was a smoker. Any time Darla needed a break from the kitchen, she'd go out back and that's often where she found Mr. Kozlow. Over time, even though she didn't smoke, they'd become friendly. They always ended up chatting and she would bring him pastries. It was a nice, cheerful relationship that Darla had enjoyed.

"They found him about a week ago," Mr. Van Holtz told her.

"Oh. That's horrible." Darla blinked. "But . . . what does this have to do with me? I didn't see anything happen to Mr. Kozlow."

"Two nights before I sent you on vacation . . . did you see Mr. Kozlow's sons, Alvin and Petey?"

Darla's lip curled a little. She'd never really liked those two. They made her skin crawl. "I think so. If I recall correctly. But only for a second or two."

"But they saw you?"

"I believe so."

"Well, they were picked up the next day."

"Picked up for what?"

"The police said it was because they had a witness who saw them kill their father."

Darla shook her head. "It wasn't me."

"I know but for some reason they thought it was you. At least for a while."

"What do you mean for a while?"

"They must have figured out it wasn't you because the actual witness was killed in the hotel room where the cops had put this person for his safety."

"That's awful." Darla thought a minute. "But if they found the person who saw them, why would they still be after me?"

"They still seem to think you saw something."

"I didn't. They came out the back door of their father's store and I went back inside the restaurant, like I always do when I see them."

"The last time you saw them, was their father with them?"

"No." She thought a moment. "No. I didn't see Mr. Kozlow at all. They were carrying duffel bags but . . ."

Van Holtz was staring at her, one brow raised and Darla couldn't hide her revulsion. "Eeew. Their father was in those bags, wasn't he?"

"Probably."

"Poor Mr. Kozlow!"

"The problem is, Darla, you can still place them at the scene of their father's death. You're still a threat."

"I have to talk to the police."

"To protect you?"

"No. To tell them what I saw."

Van Holtz shook his head. "Darla, I don't think you should do that."

"I know you don't, but that's what I have to do. That's the right thing to do. If Mr. Kozlow's sons killed him, they have to pay for it." She stood but Van Holtz caught her hand, keeping her from walking away.

"Don't do anything yet." He released her. "Please. Give me and my Pack a few more days to see if we can . . . fix this somehow." When she hesitated, he pushed, "Please, Darla."

She let out a sigh. "All right."

"Thanks, Darla."

"Thank you." She gave a small shrug. "I'll walk you back."

"That's all right. I can make my own way." He led her back to the boulder. "Why don't you sit here for a while? Try to relax."

"Thanks, Mr. Van Holtz."

He smiled, patted her shoulder, and walked off.

Darla pulled her legs up onto the rock and rested her chin on her knees. She wrapped her arms around her calves and let out a sigh. She had no idea what she was going to do next and for the first time that realization bothered her.

Eggie trotted through his backdoor and into his kitchen. Once there, he shifted to human and pulled on his jeans. He was reaching for his T-shirt when he caught a scent and picked up the gun he'd left sitting on his kitchen table, pointing it at the foreign wolf on his territory.

Van Holtz didn't move and he didn't panic.

"I've heard so much about the infamous Egbert Ray Smith over the last few years." He nodded. "Believe it or not, I hope what they say about you is all true. Because you're exactly what Darla needs right now."

By the time Darla made it back to the house, Mr. Van Holtz was gone and so was Eggie. She decided to believe Eggie had gone hunting for deer rather than hunting for Mr. Van Holtz.

Not knowing what else to do, she sat down at the kitchen table and wrote up the list of supplies she'd need if she was going to make all these pies to compete with her sisters. She knew those heifers would be bringing their best work and Darla wasn't about to let them win at this. Besides, it was easier to focus on something so ridiculous than it was to think about poor Mr. Kozlow stuffed in a duffel bag . . . *several* duffel bags.

She shuddered and finished her list. Once done, she ran upstairs and changed out of her dress and into more comfortable cutoff shorts and a T-shirt, then sat in the kitchen a bit longer. She didn't know how long Eggie was going to be. The man did like getting his hunting time in and he might need more of it today before they headed over to his momma's house and dealt with his family.

She glanced over at the counter where Eggie had left the keys to his car last night. She looked away, bit her lip, and looked back.

"Oh, what would it hurt?" she asked the air when she stood up and rushed over to the counter, snatching up his keys. She also went into the kitchen drawer where she'd found a box with several thousand dollars, a gun, and passports for several different people who looked just like Eggie but didn't have the same name. She took out a hundred dollars, more than what she needed but she erred on the side of caution, and put a note in the box informing Eggie of her I.O.U.

Once done, she headed outside and got into Eggie's car.

She started up the Plymouth and smiled as it purred to life.

Darla didn't have a car of her own because she didn't like having the extra baggage in her life, but like her sisters, she did love really nice cars. Especially well-maintained ones.

Easing onto the road, Darla glanced around, saw that no one was nearby, and stepped on the gas.

By the time she hit a hundred and five miles per hour, she was having a hell of a time.

CHAPTER THIRTEEN

Darla was no more than half a mile from the Collinstown neutral territory shifter grocery store Eggie had told her about when she came to a stop at a light. Letting out a breath, she sat back in the seat. Now that had felt wonderful.

To her left, she heard males yelling at her, and she looked over at a gold Mercury Cougar XR7 convertible filled with four male lions.

"Hey, beautiful!" one of them yelled over the Black Sabbath playing on their car radio. "That was some damn fine driving there, darlin'. You been runnin' 'shine?"

She laughed and gave them a little wave. The light changed and they pulled off, gold and brown lion's manes whipping in the wind.

Darla made it to the store and was just turning into the parking lot when a Chevrolet Nova SS cut her off, the back end of the Nova hitting the bumper of Eggie's car.

Darla hit the brakes and let out a whimper. Eggie's car. *Eggie's car!*

She was so mortified, she didn't notice who was driving until the driver's side door of the Nova opened and she saw a tall, blonde female step out. She looked at Darla, smirked, and said, "Sorry about that, sweetie pie. I just didn't see you."

The She-lions in the car laughed and Darla knew that these females were connected with the lion males who'd been talking to her at the light.

"Ridiculous, jealous crap," she snarled, watching as the She-lion got back into her own vehicle. Darla wasn't about to let them go, though. They were at least going to pay to fix Eggie's car!

But before Darla could do anything, a bright red Dodge Challenger rammed straight into the cats' car with so much force that it shoved their vehicle into Darla's. She squeaked and cringed.

"He's gonna kill me." Yet she didn't have time to worry about that when Darla saw Janie Mae and Francine get out of that Dodge. And Janie was definitely in a mood based on the way she slammed her driver's side door.

Darla quickly got out and ran over, getting between Janie and the She-lions before Janie could throw the first punch.

"Janie, stop!"

"Well, well, well," the She-lion sneered as the other cats got out of the car. "If it isn't Janie Mae Trash Heap. I see you're planning to bring another ass licker into the world."

Darla turned on the She-lion. "Shut up!"

The She-lion eyed Darla. "Who are you?"

"None of your business."

One of the other cats whispered in the She-lion's ear and she eyed Darla again.

"You? And that freak of nature Eggie Smith?"

And before Darla could stop herself, she'd slapped the little sow across the face. Unlike Janie Mae, though, this sow slapped her back.

Of course that only unleashed the wrath of Janie and Francine. And by now, Roberta and Janette had also shown up. They scrambled out of the Pontiac GTO they were driving and came at the rest of the She-lions like the wrath of God.

It was not pretty.

Darla did try her best to get them all to stop but none of it did any good or mattered once the Collinstown Sheriff's Deputies showed up. And those bears were none too happy about any of it.

★ ★ ★

Eggie's father put a beer in his hand and sat down in the chair beside him. They sat in the front yard while Eggie's mother and aunts arranged furniture in the backyard for dinner later that evening.

"She really wants to testify?"

"I don't think she wants to, Daddy. But she will. I know her."

"She's one of them moral types?"

"Yep."

"Then you know what you gotta do, boy."

"She won't want me to."

His father frowned at him. "Why do you have to tell her anything?"

"She'll know. She always knows."

Daddy chuckled. "Yeah. Your mother's got that skill, too. Only woman alive who's ever caught me in a lie." He glanced at Eggie. "You love this one, boy?"

"I do."

"Even though your momma says she's a little frail?"

"Daddy."

"I'm just saying . . . it's something to be aware of."

"I'm fully aware, and she's not frail."

"All right, all right. If it'll make you feel better, your brothers are jealous."

"No, they ain't. They love their mates."

"Sure they do. But your mate is actually nice to you."

"She's not my mate, Daddy."

"Don't know what you're waitin' for, boy. I marked your momma the first weekend we were together. Knew I had to hold onto her or I would lose her."

"I can't worry about that right now. My first concern is keeping her safe."

"So she can't take care of herself?"

"Daddy, you're making me crazy. One second you're asking me why I haven't marked her yet and the next, you're talking about how weak she is."

"Just making sure you're thinking with the head on your shoulders."

Why did Eggie bother? Some days he really didn't know.

"Maybe I should look into it," his father suggested.

"No, Daddy," Eggie quickly said.

"But I just want to—"

"No." Because Eggie knew his daddy would only make everything worse. "I don't want you to do anything."

"Then what did you come to me for?"

"I don't know. Talk to my father, maybe?" His father frowned. "You know . . . father-son chats." The frown got worse, and Eggie sighed. "Forget it."

"I will."

Eggie was about to get up and head home when his brothers came charging out of their parents' house.

"What the hell's going on?" Daddy demanded.

"The girls are in Collinstown jail again," Bubba told them while he headed for his truck.

Eggie and his father laughed until Benji walked by and said, "Don't know what you're laughin' about, Egbert Ray. Your girl is there, too."

Darla rubbed her head in a desperate attempt to make her headache go away, but it wasn't working.

Although that probably had a lot to do with the arguing going on between the bars. The bears had put Darla and her sisters in one cell and the She-lions—sisters from the local Barron Pride—in the other. And none of them had shut up since.

"What did you do to my car?"

Darla opened her eyes and let out a huge sigh. She was so relieved to see Eggie. Then she pointed an accusing finger at the other cell. "That heifer hit your car!"

"Your whore was hittin' on our males!"

Eggie looked at Darla, raised a brow. "Really?"

"I was not!"

The deputies walked in and began to open the cells. "Y'all can pay your fines out front."

"The usual?" Bubba asked as he waited for Janie to come out. He didn't look happy and Darla didn't blame him. She was five-months pregnant with his child but she was still getting into fistfights with cats. Just . . . no.

"What's the usual?" Eggie asked as he took Darla's hand when she stepped out of the cell.

"This one's not in here for the fight," the deputy explained.

"She's not?"

"She was trying to stop it."

"Then why—"

"She's in here for doing a hundred and ten in a thirty mile per hour zone."

The entire jail fell silent, all eyes focusing on Darla.

"I was just . . ." She cleared her throat, tried again. "Seeing what your car could do."

"And it can do a hundred and ten?" Eggie asked.

"Apparently."

"Our deputies lost her on Miller's Road but they'd logged the make and model. Then they got to the fight and saw the vehicle there."

"Right," Eggie said. "Got it."

Eggie glanced at her, shook his head, and started to walk off.

"Uh . . . Eggie?"

He stopped, focused on her.

Darla shrugged and admitted, "We still need to go to the grocery store."

He growled and walked out . . . not that she blamed him, though.

CHAPTER FOURTEEN

The sisters all ended up baking at Eggie's house and once they were finished with the pies, they brought them over to Miss Pauline's.

By the time the Lewis sisters arrived, the "family dinner" was well under way and Darla would call it more of a party than a dinner. To her, dinners involved sitting at one table inside the dining room, but to the Smiths, it apparently involved many tables set up in rows in the backyard, music, and 'shine. Lots of 'shine. Not surprising, though. For decades, the Smiths had made their Pack money with moonshine.

Darla hadn't seen Eggie since he'd paid her rather large fine at the Collinstown jail and handed her his truck keys. "Keep it under sixty," he'd ordered her, and because she'd promised that's exactly what she did. Much to the annoyance of her sisters.

Oh, what could she say? It was the one thing the Lewis sisters had in common. Their love of fast cars. Even Darla. Nothing was more freeing to her than hitting the gas and making a tight turn without losing control. Very few things in life really beat that feeling as far as she was concerned.

She helped her sisters put out the pies on the dessert table and she had to admit, their food looked *amazing*. As opposed to each one doing her own thing, they'd all worked together to get the pies done in a short amount of time, and she was really proud of her sisters. Then again, how could she still be mad at any of them when they'd gone after those cats like . . . well . . . like dogs after cats when they'd seen the Barrons hit Eggie's car? So, for the first time in a very long time, they'd worked together and had done a great job.

"I'm gonna find Eggie," she told Janie.

Her sister didn't argue, just nodded and smiled. It wasn't that Janie liked Eggie any more than she had the day before, but Darla had the distinct feeling that the fact that Eggie had paid Darla's fine without a word of complaint somehow meant something important to her sister. Like he'd passed some test neither of them had known existed.

She walked through the crowd, smiling at people who greeted her. Relatives of Eggie's that she'd never met but who somehow knew her name. It was strange.

She sniffed the air and walked off into the woods, following Eggie's scent. She found him sitting on a tree stump, staring off. He looked pensive. Or angry. Or pensive and angry. She really didn't know.

Standing next to him, Darla started off, "I am *so* sorry about your car."

Eggie blinked, gazed at her. "My car?"

"Remember?"

"Oh. Yeah." He shook his head, looked off again. "Can fix that, no problem."

"You can?"

"Can fix anything with a motor. So can my brothers. Frankie does nice body work, too. He'll bang that little dent out."

"Well, I'm sorry I didn't ask."

He gazed at her again. "Ask what?"

"About borrowing your car."

He shrugged. "That don't matter."

Really? "But I just took it. I didn't ask."

"Wouldn't have left the keys out if I didn't want you driving the car."

"Oh. Well, I'm definitely sorry about the fine."

Still gazing at her, he asked, "What fine?"

Darla was beginning to get a little frustrated. "The fine you had to pay . . . because I was speeding . . . in your car . . . that I took without your permission?"

"Eh. Don't really care about that."

Throwing up her hands, Darla demanded, "Then what do you care about?"

"You."

His simple response had Darla blushing from her face right down to her dang toes. "Oh."

"Besides," he added, "those cops were so impressed." Eggie grinned. "Where did you learn to drive like that?"

She laughed a little. "Daddy. When we were young, he used to let us take turns sitting in his lap and driving the car around the parking lot of the store. Our feet couldn't even touch the pedals."

"And once they could?"

She shrugged. "Then there was no stopping us." They both laughed and Darla added, "Lord, Momma has never forgiven Daddy for that either. She said it was his fault we were out-of-control heathens."

His arm reached out and wrapped around her waist, pulling her close. "Look at me, Darla Mae." She did. "If you need my car, you take my car. You need money, you take it. You don't need to leave any notes. You need my gun, dammit, woman, you use my gun."

"I'm a pacifist, Eggie," she sniffed. "I don't like guns." But when Eggie kept staring at her, she added, "I may know how to *use* guns, but I just don't like them."

"You know how to use them?"

"Momma insisted. She said every Southern lady should know how to use a gun in case we have any more problems from Yankee soldiers."

"Lot of Yankee soldiers coming around Smithville?"

"Momma likes to be prepared."

"Smart lady, which is why I trust her daughter to do what she needs to do. You don't need to ask."

"I appreciate that, but . . ."

"But what?"

"If you trust me so much, why did you follow me and Mr. Van Holtz earlier today?"

Damn this woman! He honestly couldn't get anything past her.

Eggie let out a sigh. "I followed because I don't trust Van Holtz wolves."

"Don't trust Van Holtz or don't trust me?"

"Just told you I trust you, Darla. But, ya know . . ."

"No. I don't know. What am I supposed to know?"

He shrugged. "Fancy rich wolf with his tea-and-cakes lifestyle."

"I think he's more of a coffee man."

"How am I supposed to compete with that?"

"It's just coffee."

Eggie rolled his eyes. "What I mean, Darla Mae, is that he's rich and charmin' and can buy you the kind of life you deserve."

"You think I'd only be with someone who's rich?"

"No. I think you deserve to only be with someone who's rich—and the Smiths will never be rich."

"I didn't know I was so shallow."

"I never said—"

"If you think money matters to me, of all people, then I've been making a big mistake."

She tried to pull away but Eggie tightened his arms and pulled her closer. "I know that money doesn't mean anything to you, Darla. But I also know you deserve to be comfortable."

Now she looked really disgusted. "Comfortable? You think I want to be *comfortable*?"

Uh-oh.

"Well—"

"You just think I'm some little vapid princess who wants to be pampered?"

Eggie squinted at her and said, "Not if what you just said is considered . . . bad."

She crossed her arms over her chest. "So I guess you heard what he said to me."

"Yeah."

"And?"

"And I think he was undressing you with his big, dumb dog eyes. He's not to be trusted. Plus I heard the Van Holtzes have a real problem with mange."

"First off, Egbert Ray Smith, Mr. Van Holtz has a mate he's devoted to. And secondly, the Van Holtzes haven't had a breakout of mange for at least a decade."

"That makes me feel better. I also heard they spread distemper. They're dirty, nasty distemper dogs, runnin' around, spreading disease to unsuspecting pretty She-wolves like yourself."

"Eggie Ray!"

"It's true. The males of that Pack are known for having Canine Transmitted Diseases. CTD."

"I'll only say this once to you: The Van Holtzes do not—" Darla stopped talking abruptly and leaned back a bit, eyes narrowing on Eggie's face. "Egbert Ray Smith . . . are you jealous?"

Eggie snorted. "A Smith jealous of a Van Holtz? Why do you ask? Did hell freeze over?"

"So you're not jealous?"

"No. I'm not jealous. That's what the Smiths would call crazy talk."

"Huh. I see."

"I have no reason to be jealous of a goddamn—"

"Blaspheme!"

"—Van Holtz, and I'm not about to start now. For any-body. I was just giving you a friendly word of warning."

"About the Van Holtzes and their CDT?"

"Exactly."

Darla turned in his arms and sat down on his lap. "Unlike your brothers . . . you're kind of *quietly* stupid."

"Sometimes." Eggie scratched his head. "It's not my fault, though. It's *your* fault!"

"My fault?"

"You're confusing me and making me do stupid and ridiculous things. Things I would never do!"

"Such as?"

"Instead of doing what I do well, which is hunt down these murdering friends of yours—"

"They're not my friends!"

"—and killing them so you can't be hurt or at risk ever again, I'm *not* doing that because I know you wouldn't want me to. So, instead I'm sitting here, about to go have dinner with my *family*. Which is also your fault, 'cause they wouldn't have invited me if it weren't for you."

"Of course they would have."

"Darla, no one likes having me around."

"I do."

Eggie studied her. "You do?"

"I'm here, arguing about dog mange and other ridicu-lousness, Eggie Ray. And the only reason for that must be because I like being around you. You're so cute and charm-ing . . . in your own terrifying, predatory way, which works fine for me because, you know . . . She-wolf."

His arms still around Darla, Eggie hugged her tight, bury-ing his face against the side of her neck. "That's the nicest thing anyone's ever said to me, Darla Mae."

"I know, darlin', but with some effort, I'm sure we can make that better for you."

Eggie chuckled and gripped Darla's waist, lifting her up. She squealed a little and laughed and he loved the sound of it. Turning her around, he brought her down on his lap facing him, her legs straddling his waist.

Once settled, Darla pushed Eggie's hair off his face and, without fear, looked into his eyes. "Your beard's growing back."

"Yep."

"Will you have to shave it when you go back on duty? And cut your hair?"

"Depends on what they have me doing. I'm not like other Marines, Darla. My training was different, where I'm stationed is different, I rarely wear my uniform, even the job I do is different."

"Were you drafted?"

He snorted, smiled a little. "Smiths don't get drafted."

"No, I mean when there was a draft."

"Smiths don't get drafted," he repeated. "Not after what happened with us during World War I."

"What happened during World War I?"

Eggie stared at her and finally answered, "Nothing." When her eyes narrowed, he decided to keep talking. "Anyway, we were told we were no longer allowed in the military except on a case-by-case basis. I actually had six weeks of evaluation before I ever went into Basic Training."

"Because of the nothing that happened during World War I?"

"Uh-huh."

"You are the *worst* liar."

Eggie sighed and admitted, "It ain't my strong suit."

Darla started to say something but his momma yelling from the backyard beat her to it. "Eggie! Darla Mae! Come on, you two. We're about to eat."

"Be right there," Darla called back.

"You hungry?" he asked her.

"Starving." She pressed her hands to his shoulders. "Can I ask you something first, though?"

"Sure."

"Something you said earlier . . . about not going after Mr. Kozlow's sons . . ." Eggie nodded. "You said you didn't because you knew I wouldn't want you to."

"Yeah. I knew huntin' somebody down and getting them before they can get you wouldn't sit right with you."

"It wouldn't. I mean, I know my sisters won't ever agree with my philosophy on this sort of thing, and I can't say I'd feel the same way if it was one of my nieces or nephews, but for me . . . personally . . . it would just bother me."

"I know. That's why I'm sitting here with you on my lap and my momma screaming for us to come get something to eat and not in San Francisco doing what I do best."

"Well, it means a lot to me that you take what I say seriously. That you respect me enough."

"Darla, if they're standing right in front of us, trying to hurt you, I'll do whatever I have to. But I know that what Smiths normally do is not what you'd do. I understand that." He gave a small shrug. "My daddy doesn't, though."

"Your father?"

"Yeah, I went and talked to him before I had to break you and your wild-ass sisters out of prison."

"We were not in prison. And what did he say?"

"He doesn't agree, but I should have known he wouldn't. He thinks we're making a big mistake, but I told him to back off. That we'd be handling this our way. He didn't like that, but I think he listened. For once. Maybe." Studying her face, Eggie frowned and asked, "Darla . . . are you crying?"

She sniffed, wiped the corners of her eyes with her knuckles. "It just means a lot to me that you listen to me. That you *hear* me."

"How can I not? You're the only one who talks to me."

"Oh, Eggie!" Darla exclaimed as she suddenly burst into tears and wrapped her arms around his neck.

Eggie stroked her back and tried to reassure her. "It's all right. I don't really like talking to anyone but you. I don't find your voice irritating. I find most people's voices irritating. Now that I think about it . . . I find most *people* irritating. Whether they're talking to me or not."

She pulled back and he realized that now she was laughing. "Well, I'm glad you cleared that up for me."

"Good." He framed her face with his hands and wiped the tears from her cheeks with his thumbs. "Now let's go get you something to eat before everyone assumes we're doing something that we're tragically not."

They stood together and Eggie waited until Darla finished wiping nonexistent dirt off her perfect ass before he took her hand and they headed back to dinner.

"Eggie?"

"Huh?"

"Can I tell everyone that you were jealous of a Van Holtz?"

"Not if you want to be able to sit for the next week."

"Egbert Ray!"

CHAPTER FIFTEEN

Dinner went well, with everyone relaxed and enjoying themselves and the food really delicious, especially Miss Pauline's fried chicken.

But the hit of the evening was definitely the pies Darla and her sisters had made.

She knew they'd done a good job with their pies, they usually did, but she was really surprised by the enthusiasm with which everyone downed their pie and then the requests for recipes. Recipes that none of the Lewis sisters would ever give out. In fact, the more requests Darla got for her recipes or to just make a pie for someone, the more she started to get an idea that she—to her surprise—really liked.

Still, it was too soon to think about it now. Instead, she helped Miss Pauline clean up.

"So, Darla," Miss Pauline began, "how are you doing?"

Darla nodded. "Fine, Miss Pauline."

"You sure?" She leaned in a bit, a trash bag filled with paper plates and plastic cups in her hand. "Earlier it looked like you'd been crying."

"Oh, that was nothing. Just me being an emotional mess."

"Darla Mae . . . is it true you're one of those polygamists?"

Darla froze but before she panicked, she asked, "Polygamists?"

"Yeah. You know, you don't fight or whatever? Like that Indian fella from a million years ago."

Darla let out a relieved breath. "Gandhi," she clarified, although she didn't bother with explaining timelines. "And yes, I consider myself a *pacifist*."

"So you don't fight?"

"Well—" she began but she heard her sisters laugh and glared at them. They quickly pretended to find something else interesting and Darla refocused on Miss Pauline. "I prefer not to fight. I prefer to discuss things in a reasonable and objective manner."

"You been in any of those sit-downs?"

"Sit-*ins* and yes. I've been to a few. Also done some marches."

"What for?"

Darla shrugged, thinking back. "Uh . . . for women's rights, for racial equality, to end the war."

Miss Pauline folded massive arms under her massive breasts and studied Darla. "What the hell for?"

"Pardon?"

"What does any of that have to do with you?"

Darla glanced at her sisters, but they appeared as confused as she; Janie Mae gave her a huge "got me" shrug. "Uh, I guess I don't really—"

"What I mean is you're a She-wolf. You get out of life whatever the hell you put in. You'd never let some male hold you back. And who cares about race? Species are the real problem. Like idiot cats and hyenas. Don't much like bears either, but I couldn't care less what color they are or what god they pray to as long as they stop talking about that damn honey. And war's just a chance for our males to hone their hunting skills. So why should you go around marching for what sound like full-human problems?"

This was one of those arguments that Darla had heard before from her own kin and it had annoyed her then, too. "Because everything affects everyone, Miss Pauline. We can't just sit back and let full-humans do this to each other and think we won't be affected. That we can pretend none of their problems matter. And I, personally, think we have a moral obligation as shifters and more powerful beings to help protect the weaker full-humans who are being mistreated or abused simply because of their gender or race or religion."

Miss Pauline stared at Darla, wearing a frown that looked exactly like Eggie's when he was annoyed. Only Darla found Miss Pauline's frown a little more terrifying.

Darla cleared her throat. "Not that you, personally, are obligated to do anything, of course. I just meant . . . me. My personal belief system."

Miss Pauline grunted and walked around Darla, heading back into her house.

What was that? she mouthed to her sisters.

I don't know! they all mouthed back.

Someone touched Darla's shoulder and she jumped, spinning around to find Eggie standing behind her.

"I'm sorry," he said. "I didn't mean to—"

Darla didn't even let him finish, just threw herself into his arms. "Thank God you're here!"

"Uh . . . okay."

"What did you say to her?"

Eggie's mother turned away from the sink full of dirty pots and pans and faced her son. "Just chattin'."

"Momma—"

"I didn't know I couldn't talk to her."

"Not if you're going to interrogate her."

"Is that what I was doing?"

"I'm guessing it was."

"Did she say that?"

"She didn't have to. I know the signs."

She crossed her arms over her chest. "Are you accusing your momma of something, boy?"

"I'm just asking you not to be hard on her."

"I haven't been. In fact, I've been extremely nice."

Eggie didn't like the sound of that either. "Why?"

"What do you mean why?"

Taking his mother's hand, Eggie pulled her out of the busy kitchen, down the hall, and into the living room.

"What's going on?" he asked her plain.

"I don't know what you mean."

"*Momma.*"

"Look, you don't think I see? That I don't know my own son?"

"What are you talking about?"

"I see how you look at her, Eggie. You love her."

"What if I do?"

"Then I had to check her out."

"Why? Darla is—"

"Very pretty and very smart and very well bred. So's a purebred German Shepherd."

"*Momma.*"

"But is she also strong enough to be the mate of my boy?"

"She's not my mate."

"Not yet."

"But she's not now, so don't do what you always feel you need to do."

"And what's that?"

"Put her through the gauntlet."

"Now, darlin' boy—"

"No, Momma. Whatever you're thinking, whatever you've got planned . . . you leave Darla Mae out of it." He headed back to the hallway.

"But we both know," his mother said behind him, "that if she's going to stay here, be with you, she needs to be more than just a smooth-talking polygamist."

Eggie stopped, sighed. "It's *pacifist,* Momma." He looked back at her. "And who says she's staying here?"

"You'll let her go?"

"Who says I have to stay either?" He shrugged when he saw his mother frown. "A wolf needs his mate, Momma."

★ ★ ★

"There's not even a slice left," Roberta whispered to Darla. "All those pies we brought and not even one slice left."

"There were some leftovers," Darla whispered back. "But they're like coyotes. They scavenged everything! Took a bunch of stuff home."

"I got ten bucks from Frankie's Aunt Jen."

"For what?"

"She wants me to make her some pies."

"Which ones?"

"Pecan and apple."

Darla reached into the back pocket of her cutoffs and handed her sister a twenty dollar bill. "From Eggie's Aunt Beulah for the blueberry, cream cheese, and lemon meringue."

"Shee-et. Thirty bucks just for some pies?"

"Thirty bucks for *our* pies, darlin'. You need to keep that in mind."

"You want to meet tomorrow and make them together?"

"Yeah. Sure." She saw Eggie come down the back porch stairs. He looked at her, his eyes reflecting the lights put up around the yard, and jerked his head toward his truck.

"I gotta go. Tomorrow at noon?"

"Okay. I'll see if the others are up for it."

"See if the others got money, too, but don't let Janie try and hold out any money on us. You know how she is."

Darla quickly walked through the backyard and around the house. As she stepped into the front yard, she met up with Eggie's father. He stood by a tree, smoking a cigarette and drinking from a Mason jar she assumed was filled with 'shine.

She waved and he asked, "You have a good time tonight, darlin'?"

"I did. Thank you, Mr. Smith."

"Thank you for coming. I know you're the only reason my boy came here tonight."

"Oh, no. I'm sure—"

He waved that jar around, dismissing what she was about

to say. "Let's not play with each other, pretty girl. You're here, so my boy's here. And that's all right. It's good to see him happy."

Feeling uncomfortable, but not knowing why, Darla nodded. "Well, thank you so much, Mr. Smith. Have a good night."

"You, too. And take care of yourself tomorrow."

Darla glanced back at the wolf. He watched her from under the branches of the trees and she had no idea what to make of the look he was giving her—and not sure if she wanted to make anything of it.

Eggie stood with his butt resting against the passenger door of his car. He smiled when he saw her and that made Darla smile back.

"You ready?"

"Yes." She walked to him and went up on her toes, kissing him lightly on the mouth. "Let's go home."

And as Darla turned from him and reached for her door handle, she quickly edited her statement to, "I mean, let's go to your house." She opened the door. "I mean, let's go to *your* home." She cleared her throat, knew her face was red from blushing.

So awkward. Poor guy probably thought she'd bought that furniture just for herself. Horrified, Darla sat in the passenger side and closed the door. Eggie got in the driver's side a few seconds later. He closed the door and looked at her.

"You done babblin'?" he asked.

Darla nodded. "Uh-huh."

"Good." He kissed her. "Now let's go home."

CHAPTER SIXTEEN

"The problem is," Eggie explained as he closed the front door of his house, "that you have two Alpha Females in the same town. Momma ain't ready to give up her position yet."

Darla stopped in the middle of the living room and faced him. "Will Janie have to fight to the death against your mother?" Because she really didn't know *who* would win that one.

"An Alpha fight to the death hasn't happened in about half a century. Doubt my momma plans to start all that up again." When Darla only stared at him, he asked, "Does Janie Mae plan to start all that up again?"

Darla forced a laugh and headed into the kitchen.

Eggie followed her. "Any more sweet tea?"

"In the fridge. I'll get it."

"Nah. I've got two hands. You want some?"

"Sure." She picked up a pad and pen and walked to the corner of the kitchen.

"What are you doing?"

"Need a list. A few of your aunts and cousins asked for pies. I'm getting together with my sisters tomorrow to bake."

"Hope you ain't doing all that for free."

"Nope. We have cold, hard cash." She looked at him over her shoulder. "It feels so decadent making money from my wares."

Eggie chuckled, took two glasses down from one of the overhead cabinets and poured the sweet tea. He placed one glass on the counter beside Darla and walked to the other side of the kitchen so she could have some space.

While he sipped his sweet tea, he watched Darla work on whatever she was working on. She had her bare foot pressed against the opposite knee so that she was balanced only on one leg, and she used the pen to occasionally scratch the back of her neck. There was just something so beautiful and perfect about the whole thing. Something that Eggie didn't understand but knew he had to have in his life for as long as the Lord allowed it. He couldn't imagine not coming home to her. To find her in his house. In *their* house.

"I love you, Darla."

She froze, the pen resting against her neck, her body still being held up by that one leg.

"You don't have to say anything," Eggie went on. "Just listen." He put his glass down and shoved his hands into the front pockets of his jeans. "I feel like I've been waitin' my whole life for you. Not someone like you, but *you*. And I know being with me for the long term won't be easy. I know I'm not real chatty. Not real friendly. I find almost everyone but you, the full-wolves in the forest, and that Columbo guy on TV real annoying. And I don't really have any intention of changing. I'm not even sure I could if I wanted to." Eggie cleared his throat. "But I promise to always be faithful. Never to argue with you over ridiculous bullshit. To keep my blaspheming to a minimum. And to never take you for granted. I will do whatever I can to make you happy. If that means living in San Francisco or Timbuktu, I'll do it. I just never want you to feel trapped. But, if being with me isn't what you want . . . you just say the word. I'll still protect you, Darla Mae. I won't let anything happen to you, but I don't want you to feel like you *have* to be with me. I want you to be with me because you want to be with me."

Eggie took a breath. "Anyway, that's it. Just felt the need

to get that off my chest. Hope I didn't make the night uncomfortable for ya."

Darla dropped her raised leg, her bare foot slapping against the ground. She placed the pen on the counter and took a step back.

She slowly faced him, eyes downcast. "Eggie Ray . . ."

Eggie steeled himself, waiting for her to "bring down the hammer" as McMartin liked to call it.

She sighed, deep and long, then walked across the kitchen. "There's just so much going on right now. People trying to kill me," she said as she went through one of the brown paper grocery bags she'd brought from the store earlier in the day. "Poor Mr. Kozlow. A sudden influx of pie requests. Your mother calling me a polygamist. Suddenly getting along with my sisters. It's just all too much, Eggie." She walked over and stood in front of him.

"I understand."

"You do? Really?

He wasn't happy about it, but he understood. "Yeah. Of course."

"Good. Because for the first time in years, since I left my daddy's house when I was eighteen, I feel like I'm home. And I'm happy. And I'm safe. And that, Egbert Ray Smith, is because of you."

Darla placed a white paper bag from the Smithtown Pharmacy on the table. "Picked that up when I was out with the girls."

She walked back to the counter, faced him, and said, "I love you, Eggie Ray."

Eggie nodded and waited for more—because there was always more when it came to Darla Mae and that's where he was expecting that damn hammer—but after nearly a minute she shrugged and said, "That's it. I love you. I'll always love you."

Darla looked off and suddenly added, "And I like pie."

Relief washing over him, Eggie grinned and asked, "You like pie?"

"Yes. I think pie will end up making me a decent amount of money. So I like pie. I'm a big fan of pie."

"That's good. It's good to be a big fan of something."

"I think so." She nervously combed her hair behind her ears. "So . . . am I supposed to make a run for it and then you catch me? Or just put up a fight?"

"Do you feel like making a run for it?"

"Not particularly."

"Putting up a fight?"

"Pacifist."

"And I fight all day. It's my job. So I'd rather not start off fighting my mate unless you want me to."

"Well, it's just the two of us here. I mean, can't we do this however we want to?"

"As far as I'm concerned, Darla Mae, we can do whatever we want whatever way we want and however many times we want to."

She smiled, appearing relieved. "Good." Then she pulled off her T-shirt, tossed it aside, and shimmied out of her cut-offs. She kicked those and her panties away, turned from Eggie to face the counter, and pulled her long hair over to her left shoulder, leaving her right bare. She rested her hands on the counter, bent one knee, and leaned forward a bit.

Darla looked at Eggie over her exposed shoulder, her smile so unbelievably sultry that he became instantly hard—so hard it hurt.

"What are you waitin' for, Egbert Ray? Come on over here and make me yours."

Eggie's growl was so low, Darla didn't hear it but she felt it. It was like it rumbled through the kitchen, through the floor, up her legs, shooting through her body.

When Eggie reached for his jeans, Darla faced forward,

her hands gripping the counter. It took Eggie only seconds to strip off his clothes and find the condoms she'd purchased from the Smithtown pharmacy. Of course when she'd picked them up—much to her sisters' giggles and the disapproval of the maned wolf pharmacist who clearly hadn't attended the feminist seminar Darla had gone to about women owning their own sexuality—Darla had thought of them only for emergency purposes in case Eggie ran out. Now she was relieved because she didn't think she could wait until he went upstairs and got his own.

When Eggie moved up behind her, she felt the heat pouring from his body. His arms reached around her, his hands bracing on either side of her own. His chest pressed against her back and his mouth against her neck.

Darla closed her eyes, leaned back against the wolf behind her.

"I love you, Darla," he growled against her throat, making her smile.

Eggie gently dragged his right hand across Darla's hand and up her arm. Then he reached under her arm and pressed his hand against her stomach. Her breath caught when his fingers eased down, the tips caressing her. Her toes curled against the floor, her hands gripping the counter tighter.

She trembled as his fingers became more insistent. Eggie's other arm went around her chest, the hand gripping the opposite shoulder. He kissed her beneath the ear and moved down her neck to her shoulder.

While his fingers stroked her and her body trembled, her knees weakening, Eggie pressed his mouth against a muscle on her shoulder blade. He kissed the area, licked it. Darla began to pant, her entire body shuddering. And when she cried out, Eggie bit down hard, and the feel of his fangs sliding past skin and muscle, scraping against bone, had the power of her orgasm doubling, tearing through her. It felt like she exploded from the inside out.

When the roaring in her head stopped, she heard Eggie's voice. He spoke to her in between kissing her neck.

"Darla? Are you all right?"

She really couldn't imagine anyone taking such care with her the way Eggie did. It always seemed as if her happiness meant everything to him.

Maybe that Arctic fox yogi she'd met in France—who'd turned out to be not from India but from Queens, New York—had been right when he'd said karma would take good care of her. Because how else did she get so lucky?

"Finish it, Eggie," she told him, breathless, desperate. "Finish it now."

Eggie tried not to scare her. But her desperate plea, the way she leaned against him, the scent of her lust, all conspired to rip away his control. To bring out the wolf that he barely kept reined in as it was.

Gripping her hips, Eggie pulled her back a bit and pressed his condom-covered cock against her pussy. She was already wet and open, her muscles relaxed.

"I love you, Darla," he whispered against her ear. "I'll always love you."

"I love you," she replied, her ass pressing into him. "I love you."

Unable to wait, Eggie pushed his cock inside her and both of them groaned. Darla's arms stretched across the counter, her body lengthening as she bent forward to give him better access to her body. He took her then, his cock stroking inside her.

Every time Eggie pushed in, her pussy tightened, the muscles rippling around him. Without much effort, this one little She-wolf was effectively sucking his brains out. He couldn't think. He couldn't reason. The Lord himself could walk into the room and Eggie wouldn't be able to stop.

He reached around Darla, his fingers, still wet from her

pussy, gripped her nipples. He played with them, teased them, until Darla's body was shaking as she writhed beneath him. It was all too much.

Eggie came, a growl torn from him, his body tightening around Darla's. His hands holding her breasts, his face pressed against her neck.

Darla cried out with him, surprising Eggie because he didn't think he'd manage to get her to come again. Not so soon and not with him being completely lost in his own pleasure. Of course, he would have taken care of her as soon as he could think straight again, but he was glad he hadn't left her behind. The human male in him was proud of that.

He carefully pulled out of her, stroked his hand down her back. "Don't move," he told her.

Eyes closed, the top half of her body resting against the counter, Darla weakly raised her hand and sighed, "Oooookay."

They sat on the kitchen floor, Darla between Eggie's incredibly long legs, and he cleaned off her wound. It had already started to heal but would still leave a scar, letting any shifter know that she'd been marked and mated.

"You sure you're all right?" he asked again.

Darla smiled, patted his knee. "I'm fine. Stop worrying."

"You're very quiet."

"Just happy. Nothing to say when you're just happy."

Eggie put aside the first aid kit and wrapped his arms around her, held her tight. Darla never felt trapped in his arms. Never felt scared or worried or annoyed. She just felt . . . safe. And loved. Very loved.

They sat like that for a very long time, just holding onto each other. Until Eggie asked, "Any chance you hid one of those pies away before you headed over to Momma's?"

Darla looked up at her mate, raised a brow. "Pecan work for you?"

CHAPTER SEVENTEEN

Francine and Roberta showed up with a list of requests for pie and a list of supplies they'd need for all the baking. They decided to wait for their other sisters before going shopping and got out what few supplies they had left to get started on some prep work.

Darla took them into the kitchen and while they chatted and got to work, Eggie trotted down the stairs in his wolf form. He came into the kitchen, circled around Darla's legs, his body pushing against her, his tail curling around her knees. Francine opened the back door and he went out, leaving them alone.

"Where's he off to?" Francine asked.

"Got me."

"When will he be back?"

"No idea."

"And you're okay with that?"

"Yeah. He always comes back with half a deer or something, so he's clearly thinking of me."

Roberta giggled but when she saw Francine glaring at her, she stopped and went back to cutting up butter.

"He marked you last night, little sister," Francine said. "I can smell it."

"Even though I showered this morning?"

Roberta giggled again.

"Are you sure about this, Darla?" Francine pushed. "I

don't have a real problem with Eggie—other than the fact his nickname is Eggie—but still . . . he's not like his brothers."

Thank the Lord for small favors.

"No. He's not. But I'm willing to make that sacrifice." And Darla was sure she almost sounded serious rather than sarcastic.

"Daddy and the boys won't be happy." The "boys" being their brothers, but Darla had already known that. But once she talked to her father, she'd be able to smooth things over. She always had before.

"I love him, Francine."

"I know you do. But does he love you?"

"He told me he did last night."

Francine blinked and looked over at Roberta. "He *said* that to you? Actually spoke the words?"

"More than once." In fact, all night long, but that wasn't her sisters' business, just hers. Always hers.

Suddenly tears rolled down Francine's face. "Oh, baby sister!" Then she was hugging a very confused Darla. "He does love you!"

"I know."

"You *think* you know," Francine explained when she pulled back. "But you don't really. But if Eggie Ray Smith actually said the words . . . he must have meant them. Benji says Eggie never says anything he doesn't mean. Ever."

"Oh. So my sense about it is meaningless."

"You're the same woman who thinks she can look into people's souls. I mean . . ." She shook her head.

"You know, if you opened your mind and allowed yourself to experience things, you might actually learn to read people just like I do."

"Did you learn to read people before or after you ended up with the Manson Family?"

Darla stomped her foot hard. "I did not end up with the Manson Family! I was there for less than an hour! And I knew he was a nut even then!"

The backdoor opened and Janette and Janie Mae walked in. Janie looked between Francine and Darla. "What's going on?"

"Eggie marked Darla last night and she's still trying to pretend she didn't join the Manson Family."

"You lying sow!"

"We don't have time for this," Janie cut in. "I've got a list of pies and a chance to make some real cash."

Darla's eyes grew wide. "I was thinking the same thing!"

"You were?"

"Yeah. It's brilliant. We open a pie store or a bakery here and sell pies to the entire town."

Her sisters stared at Darla and Janie said, "Actually, that's not what I was talking about. But it is brilliant."

"Then what are you talking about?"

Janie grinned. "Racing against those Barron sluts."

"I am not racing a cat. And neither are you, Janie Mae. You're five months pregnant."

"Only three of you need to race. Three of our best against three of theirs. I figure you, Roberta, and Janette. Francine's out because she drives like Grandpa Lewis."

"Gee . . . thanks."

"And how are we supposed to make money from that?" Darla asked.

"Both the bears and the cats have been taking bets. The cats are favored to win."

"So you bet on us?"

"It was easy. I had the money from every damn Smith wanting a pie."

Darla glared at Roberta. "I thought I told you to get her gosh darn money!"

Roberta shrugged. "Ooops."

Eggie wandered into the back door of his oldest brother's house. He knocked over the trash can and went through it. He was always amazed at the stuff his kin was willing to toss out. He usually found all sorts of stuff he could fix up later, you know, when he had time.

Not finding anything interesting today, he went to the refrigerator and with his muzzle grabbed hold of the towel someone had left hanging from the handle. He pulled it open and studied the contents. Francine was usually pretty good about having plenty of food available for her mate and pups.

"Hey, Uncle Eggie." Two of his brother's older sons walked through the kitchen, patting Eggie's side as they did. He gave them a welcoming bark and went back to finding something to eat. There was a raw roast, so he pulled that out and went to work on devouring it.

"Does your female not feed you, little brother?" Benji asked from the doorway. "And make sure you clean up when you're done. I don't want to hear from Francine about it."

Yawning, Benji made his way into the kitchen and hauled himself up on the counter. "Hand me the milk, would you?"

Eggie stared at his brother.

Benji rolled his eyes. "You can't just shift to human for two seconds? You ain't no full wolf, Egbert Ray." Benji wiped the piece of raw roast from his face that Eggie had tossed at him. "Bastard."

Eggie had just finished the rest of the roast when Bubba Ray walked in. "You cooling off the whole neighborhood, Egbert Ray?"

"Don't start with him," Benji warned. "He's in a mood and throwin' meat."

"I think that's him being playful, big brother. Word on Main is that Egbert Ray marked little Darla Mae as his own last night."

"She agreed to that?"

Eggie growled and bared his fangs and Benji quickly held his hands up. "It was just a question, no need to get nasty. She just seemed a little . . . hippy-dippy to be comfortable as the mate of the most—what was that word Aunt Ju-Ju used?" he asked Bubba.

"Reviled."

"Yeah. The most *reviled* Smith in the Northern Hemisphere since our ancestor Milton 'Gut Eater' Smith was terrorizing England."

"Boiling all those pretty little girls."

"I thought he liked 'em raw."

"No, no. He liked 'em boiled up in stew or barbequed over an open spit for the fine flavor and tenderness of the meat."

Eggie shifted and bellowed, *"All right, that is enough!"*

His brothers burst out laughing and Eggie stormed over to the sink so he could wash the blood off his face.

"Every last one of you are bastards," he muttered around the running water.

"Look," Bubba pointed out. "Darla marked him back. How cute."

Normally Eggie didn't get involved in this kind of verbal sibling squabbles, but for once . . . he actually had a little ammunition.

"At least mine let me mark her." He slowly faced his brother, saw Bubba's eyes narrow while Benji snorted. "Didn't even have to argue with her. She just told me she loved me and offered the back of her neck." He crossed his arms over his chest. "How many pups you got with Janic Mae now, Bubba Ray . . . and still she's as unmarked as a newborn babe. So which Smith has control of his female now, *boy?*"

His younger brother's nostrils flared out, a sure sign that he was pissed off. Good. But before Eggie could really revel in his moment of triumph a soft, "Eggie?" from the backdoor had him cringing.

Darla walked in, her gaze glancing at the three males before she walked over to Eggie. She gazed up at him and he waited for it. Lord, she must be mad. Her being a feminist and all. Not that he blamed her. He deserved it.

"Why are you standing here naked, with your brothers, and smelling like blood?"

"I'm not sure explaining it would make it any better."

"Okay. I need your car," she said, surprising him.

"Sure. Told you to take it whenever you need it."

"Yeah, I know. But I thought I should let you know I'm not just taking it out. I need to race it."

"Race it? Against who?"

"Cats."

"You need to race cats?"

"Yeah. I don't have a choice. Janie Mae bet on us winning and if we lose, we can't get what we need to make the pies we promised everyone because that's the money she used. So we race the cats, we win, we make pie."

"You live a complicated life, Darla Mae."

"I know. Anyway, you know how races go. Your car might get damaged and—"

"Frankie can fix it. He works the mechanic shop with our uncles. Now give me a couple of minutes to get dressed and I'll go with—"

"Lord, no," she quickly cut in. "That cats will have a fit if you come. Your name was mentioned specifically as a do not attend." She glanced at Bubba. "And Janie Mae doesn't want you there at all."

"What did I do now?"

"Breathe?" Eggie asked, grinning when Bubba snarled at him.

Darla started to move away, but she stopped, looked back at him. Eggie girded his loins, preparing for what she was about to say to him.

"So it's okay then, Eggie?" she asked sweetly, fluttering her eyes up at him. "If I take your car? I didn't want to do it without your permission."

Eggie twisted his mouth to look like he was thinking

about it, but it was really so he didn't laugh. "I give you permission." He nodded. "Take the car. Enjoy yourself. But be careful. Can't trust cats."

"I know. Thank you, Eggie." She winked at him and walked out.

Bubba, his mouth open, stared at him, and Eggie shrugged. "What?"

Darla got into Eggie's car.

"What took you so long?" Janie Mae asked as Darla closed the door.

"I was torturing your mate." She grinned at her sister. "It was surprisingly fun!"

"It is, isn't it?"

"Although I can see why you're waiting to let him mark you."

"Yeah. I love him but he needs to realize I'm his partner, not his Beta." Janie studied her for a moment, then asked, "Are you going to stay here, Darla Mae?"

"Mostly."

"What does that mean?"

"It means when I'm home, so to speak, I'll be here. But if I need to go, I'll go."

"This is a Pack town, Darla."

"Meaning?"

"There's a way things are done here—"

"You mean when you're Alpha. When you run the Smithtown Pack by Bubba's side."

"Maybe I do."

"Well, if you need me, I'll be there. But if you're asking me if I'm going to be one of your Beta females, following you around town every day, then the answer is no."

"Still think you're a lone wolf?"

"I never thought that. I know I'm not. I need my friends, my family, my Pack, Eggie. But I do need my freedom. I need to be able to roam free. For Eggie that means spending hours exploring the hills and forests of this entire town. For me that means exploring everything whenever I feel like it."

"You think you'll feel that way forever?"

"I know if I stop feeling that way it'll be because of me. Not you. Not Eggie. Not anyone." Darla started the car. "Can I suggest something to you, Janie?"

"I guess."

"Eggie's daddy could have put his foot down and told Eggie he had to stay here, that he couldn't be a Marine, he couldn't leave town, he had to stay and be part of the Pack. But he let his son go and be what he wanted. And now Eggie always comes home, and he's always here for his family. You gotta know when to let go, big sister, and when to hold on. You learn that . . . you'll be an amazing Alpha."

Janie Mae smiled at her. "Look at you, teaching your big sister something." But unable to let that sweet moment just be, Janie added, "Did you learn that from Charlie Manson, too?"

Darla growled. "I can't believe you heifers keep bringing that up! I went one time and didn't even stay!"

"Look, Patty Hearst—"

"Stop calling me that!"

"—you're the one who keeps involving herself with these cult types."

"Gee, I wonder what in my background"—Darla hit the gas and tore away from Francine's house—"would attract me to large groups who have nothing in common but hanging around each other constantly, sleeping on the floor in large people piles, and hunting innocent strangers? Really, I have no idea how I could be comfortable around that sort of thing!"

Eggie waited on top of the hill while his brothers stripped off their clothes. They were going hunting on orders from their daddy. He wanted venison for dinner. Fresh venison, not a frozen slab from the shifter-friendly grocery store. It had been a while since he'd sent them out to do that for him, but it gave the brothers something to do while their females were out racing and baking.

If they could get the venison quick enough, then Eggie could track down some wild boar for Darla. She'd told him she loved fresh boar. He could barbeque it for her the way he'd learned when he was in Korea for a while.

He snapped at his brothers, trying to get them to hurry up rather than stand around chatting like a bunch of old She-wolves.

His brothers shifted to wolf and ran off down the hill. Eggie looked out over Smithtown territory—the one place on earth he loved more than any other.

Truly happy, Eggie charged after his brothers.

The rules had been set when they'd first arrived. A clean, fair race in this open land where wolf, bear, cat, and hyena territories all butted up against each other.

It was a Monday so most folks were at work or being responsible in some other way. Plus, this was Lewis sisters against cats in this race, not Smith She-wolves, so there'd be no audience for this event because no one really cared beyond whether they won money or not. In the end, it was just the Barron sisters, the Lewis sisters, and two grizzlies from Collinstown who would be the refs. They'd decide who was the winner if it was a tight race and they'd be able to keep the maulings down to a minimum if it came to that—which it probably would.

Now here Darla was, making a tight turn, far ahead of the pack. The Barron sisters were getting cranky about her lead, too. Getting more and more aggressive as the number of laps wound down.

When they hit the last two laps, Darla knew that the Barrons were gunning for her. Since any of the three Lewis sisters winning meant they all won, Darla made a split-second decision to pull back and let Roberta fly past her. She did.

Of course, it was just as one of the Barrons shot across the makeshift track—and took out the tail end of Roberta's car.

Darla watched her sister's car spin toward the center of the track, almost taking out one of the grizzlies, who dived for cover.

Janette, the family hot head, rocketed past Darla and rammed into the side of one of the other Barron sisters, sending that one airborne.

"Shit!" Darla burst out, not caring she was cussing because she knew this was about to get damn ugly. She downshifted and quickly pulled up next to Roberta's wreck. Lord, Frankie Ray was going to lose his mind when he saw his car.

Darla jumped out of Eggie's car and ran over to her sister's. She went to pull the driver's side door open but the handle was missing. So she ran around the other side just as Janie Mae got there. She pulled open the door and reached in, dragging her sister out. When she had most of her head and shoulders free, Janie Mae grabbed hold too and together they laid Roberta out on the grass.

"Those bitches," Roberta snarled from her spot on the ground. "What happened to clean and fair?"

Darla put her hands on her sister's shoulders to stop her from getting up. "Just rest a minute, darlin'."

Janette drove her car up and jumped out. "Are you all right?" she asked two seconds before one of the Barron sisters tackled her to the ground.

Janie Mae started to go over there, but Darla grabbed her arm and yanked her back. "Don't you dare, Janie Mae."

"She's outnumbered!"

"You're pregnant!" Darla took a breath. "Just stay here. I'll deal with it."

Darla rushed over to the three She-lions on one wolf fight. She tried to pull one of the She-lions off but they were on her sister like ticks on a hound dog.

As she tried to reach in again to get a good grip, one of the grizzlies was there. He caught Darla's arm. As he lifted her up and away, Darla heard a popping sound and the grizzly stumbled back. He dropped her and Darla landed hard on her knees.

"What the hell . . ." she heard the grizzly gasp.

Darla looked up and saw blood pouring from two holes in the bear's shoulder. He'd been shot.

Moving fast, she caught hold of his arm and using all her strength, yanked him down just as seven or eight more shots rang out.

"Down!" Janie Mae screamed out. "Now!"

Everyone who wasn't already down, dove to the ground.

Eggie and three of his brothers had a good grip on the buck's body while Bubba Ray had him by the throat. Bubba pushed the animal to the ground, trying to suffocate him before the rest of them lost their grip.

But instead of finishing him off, Bubba suddenly stopped, his head lifting, his nose casting for a scent.

Since Bubba was never one to go off a kill, Eggie released the buck and backed away. He turned, lifted his head. That's when he heard it. Rapid-fire shots. No one used automatic weapons inside Smith territory or in any of the nearby shifter towns. Not even the hyenas used them.

Which meant only one thing . . .

Eggie took off, instinctually knowing that his brothers were right behind him.

Darla hid behind Janette's car with the bear as more shots hit the vehicle.

"What's going on?" the bear demanded.

Darla lifted up his T-shirt, trying to see the wound. "They're here for me," she admitted. "They're trying to kill me."

"Using guns?" It was the unspoken rule among their kind that in a physical fight, shifter challenged shifter with claws and fangs only.

"They're full-human," Darla admitted.

The bear chuffed and Darla stared down at him.

"Move," he told her.

Still crouching and keeping her head down, Darla moved back and he shifted to his bear form. Roaring, he turned, slipped his front paws under the car and tossed it like a toy.

Darla charged back over to Janie and Roberta, hiding behind Roberta's car. "You two, shift and go."

"Are you kidding?"

"Janie, you've gotta protect your baby. Go."

"She's right." This came from one of the Barron sisters. "Protect your pup and get help. We'll handle—"

Shots from another part of the nearby woods came at them, Darla barely moving in time as bullets riddled the ground.

At that point, they all shifted. Janie and Roberta charged off and Darla ran after the wounded grizzly. Bears had the best noses and he was so pissed off, she knew he'd go right to one of the shooters.

Eggie heard more shots and changed his direction, heading straight for Darla. But Bubba ran into his side, pushing him off course. Eggie snarled, snapped at his kin, but Bubba didn't back down. While they all kept running, Bubba kept pushing.

Thankfully during that little bit of time, Eggie's years of military training kicked in. Although he wanted to run right to Darla's side and swoop her up, his battle-ready side knew he couldn't. He had to be smart; Darla was depending on that. So Eggie ran beside his brother, quickly figuring out that Bubba was going wide around to where the shots were coming from.

The firing continued but now they were hearing screams. Eggie decided to believe all that noise was from the full-humans. It made it easier to keep doing what he needed to do.

Suddenly Bubba made a hard left and charged forward. He was fast and Eggie had to race to catch up. His brother leaped onto a big rock and launched himself off. He caught hold of the leg dangling from a tree branch and yanked. The full-human flipped forward, landing hard on the ground. An M-16 flew out of his hands, but he was already reaching for another weapon attached to his ankle. Frankie ran up, opened his muzzle, and wrapped his jaws around the man's throat. Ignoring the screaming, Frankie snapped the full-human's neck and went off looking for more.

Eggie was about to follow when bullets riddled the ground at his feet and he took three steps back. When Eggie stopped, he looked up into the face of a human male—and the automatic weapon he held locked on him.

Darla followed the bear to one of the big trees. The shooter sat on a branch, busy reloading his gun while he made a panicked whimpering sound, his eyes constantly straying to the grizzly charging toward him. The full-human hadn't been expecting shifters. Then how the hell had he found them? Smithtown, like most shifter-only locations, wasn't on any maps and was protected by shifters involved in different divisions of the government, military, and National Guard. So the attackers hadn't just tracked Darla down here.

The grizzly went up on his hind legs and pressed his front paws against the tree trunk. At his full shifted height, this bear was ten feet long but he still couldn't quite reach the human on the branch. So Darla ran up the bear's back, launched herself from his hump, and crashed into the human as he was raising the gun to shoot her. She hit him with her full weight, knocking him backward off the branch. He screamed, the rifle knocked from his hand and his arms pinwheeling. Darla went down with him, the ground rushing up. She waited until the last second to jump from his chest and flip forward. She rolled across the forest floor until she landed flat on her stomach, her front and hind legs spread out. She knew she looked ridiculous but she was alive and unhurt. That's all she cared about.

Darla heard more shots, more screams, and she knew this had to be stopped. She got to her feet and shifted back to her human form. The bear was busy tearing the now-dead full-human to pieces, which seemed kind of a waste.

She rushed up to him. "Hey. Hey!" Unfortunately the bear was still focused on the man at his feet. So Darla tapped the bear on his shoulder.

As grizzlies were wont to do, he was startled and swung his big forearm at her. Darla squealed and ducked, her arms over her head. Her shifter body could withstand a lot, but she'd rather not spend the next week recovering from a bear mauling.

"Wait, wait, wait!" she yelped.

She heard chuffing, felt bear-breath on her raised arms. She peeked up and saw the bear inches away from her.

"I was just going to suggest," she squeaked out, "that maybe you and your friend could push the full-humans to the center of the track. That way we could just finish them off all at once."

The bear gave one more big chuff, making Darla yip, before he lumbered off. She let out a relieved breath.

It was official, grizzlies were the worst!

Darla shifted back to wolf and headed toward the track. It was time to end this.

The human's gun had jammed. Eggie wasn't surprised. He knew the weapon and refused to use it because of the jamming issues. Eggie also knew how long it would take the full-human to clear the weapon to make it useable again. So he charged forward, but he never reached the man. A grizzly barreled out of nowhere and ran over the male, then came back and picked the screaming man up by his head, giving a good shake while crushing the human's skull.

Eggie ran toward the clearing where he guessed the race

had taken place. There were two cars in the middle of a rough-hewn track and another car . . . perched in a tree.

Assuming one of the grizzlies had something to do with that, he saw the Barron sisters run down two men and tear them to pieces. He stopped, his gaze searched the track, looking for Darla.

"Run!"

Eggie watched five human males run toward him. Two were taken out by Eggie's brothers, another blindsided by a She-lion. But the last two ran past, bears hot on their asses.

Too bad they were heading toward a half-circle made up of a few of Eggie's aunts, uncles, and cousins, in their shifted forms, who had come out of the woods next to Smith territory. Someone must have gone for help.

Eggie scanned the area one more time, then headed after the last two men.

Eggie's family ran past Darla and she knew that Janie and Roberta had sent them. Once they were past the trees, they fanned out into an arc and they waited. A few seconds later, she heard screams and shots and saw men running from the other side of the clearing. They were so busy looking back at the bears—who could have easily overtaken them by now but hadn't bothered—they had yet to notice the ones waiting for them.

They'd passed the cars in the middle of the track when one of them finally looked forward and saw the wolves waiting. He slid to a stop, grabbing the other one's arm, and yanking him back.

Hands shaking, they raised their weapons. Not wanting them to hurt anyone else, Darla walked out. When she knew the men saw her, she shifted from wolf to human as she walked.

"You," one of them said when she moved close enough.

"Hello, Alvin. Petey."

"But you're . . . you're . . ."

Petey shook his head. "What are you?"

"Something you'd never really understand."

"Get back," Alvin ordered.

"Stop," Darla said. "Please. You have to know you're out-numbered." She looked between the two men. "Let's just stop this violence now."

"You want us to believe you'll let us go?"

"I don't want anyone else hurt because of me. I want this to stop. Please." Darla stood right in front of the men now. "Let's just end this. Okay?" She placed her hands on their weapons, carefully lowering them. "What you tried to do to me today . . . I'm just going to forget it. You tried, you failed. It's over." She tugged once on the guns. "It's over."

They finally released the weapons so that Darla held one in each hand. "I forgive you for what you tried to do to me," she said. "I forgive you." And Darla truly meant it.

She stepped back from the men as Eggie walked up behind them in his human form. He was reaching for them when she turned away.

"Shame," she sighed, "that I can't feel the same forgiveness for what you did to nice Mr. Kozlow."

Darla walked toward the trees where Janette and Francine waited. She threw down the guns she hated and walked past her sisters. "Come on," she said over the full-human screams coming from behind her. "We've gotta track down Janie and Roberta, get our money from the Barrons, and make those pies."

"Wait," Janette asked. "Did we actually win?"

CHAPTER EIGHTEEN

Eggie, his brothers, and the two grizzlies who'd been refs at the race had dumped the human remains onto hyena territory. By the time they were heading back to their own property, the hyenas were easing out, sniffing the bodies. Then when territorial lines were crossed, the hyenas' laughing howl could be heard for miles as those bodies were torn apart and fought over.

Eggie's brothers and those bears had stared at him with clear disgust and fear. Disgust because it had been his idea to again use the hyenas for clean up. But the fear . . . that came from what they'd seen him do to those two fucks who'd come on his territory to get *his* She-wolf.

He'd been confused when Darla had walked away like that. She, of everyone, knew what he'd do. She was also the only one who could have stopped him—but she hadn't. Yet when he'd seen the other shifters watching him, when he'd seen their fear, he'd understood what she was doing—securing his position as the one Smith not to be fucked with even though he was and never would be Alpha of the Pack. Darla was, in her infinite brilliance, also securing her safety and the safety of any pups they might have in the future. After what he'd done with his bare hands and the full-humans' own edge weapons, all while in front of those bears, cats, and wolves, no one would be going near Darla to harm her whether Eggie was home or not.

Absolutely no one.

And that message would spread to every Pack, Pride, Clan, and shifter family throughout the States.

Knowing that, he headed toward his house, only slowing to a stop when he saw his father leaning against one of the nearby trees, waiting for him.

Eggie walked up to him and shifted. "What?"

His father raised his hands. "I know, I know. You're pissed."

"You let the full-humans know she was here, didn't you? You wanted them to kill her."

"Not to kill her. To prove whether she was worthy. To prove she had some backbone."

"So you brought full-*humans* to Smithtown territory? You put my mate and her sisters at risk? And Bubba's unborn pup? Just to prove Darla was *worthy*? Of what?"

His father smirked, took off the New York Yankees cap that he wore as a joke, and rubbed his black and grey hair. "You ain't an easy boy, Egbert Ray. You're handsome enough, I guess. At least that's what I hear from your young cousins." He put the cap back on. "But none of our strong She-wolves came out of the woodwork to be with you."

"Your point?"

"I put up with Janie Mae and them sisters of hers because there's real strength there. They'll keep the Smith bloodline strong and going long after you and I are nothin' but dust. Already those two boys of hers—"

"You mean your grandsons?" he asked flatly.

"—are real scrappers."

"You mean violent idiots?"

"They're strong. Just like their momma and daddy. That's what I want for you. Now your little gal is sweet as all get out but I didn't see no strength in her."

"You weren't looking very close then."

"Yeah." He grudgingly agreed, Eggie's daddy never one to enjoy anyone proving him wrong. "I guess."

"And? What does putting my mate's life at risk mean to you? That she can stay now? That she can be part of the Pack?"

"That's exactly what it means."

"Well that's good, Daddy." Eggie walked up to his father until he was only inches away from him. And, for the first time in his life, Eggie saw fear in those eyes. And Eggie realized he'd gotten his true strength from his momma. He'd gotten her sense, too. "Darla's a forgiving woman. Hell, she'll pretend it never happened. Because you're family. Because you're my daddy." Eggie leaned his face in a bit closer, their noses almost touching, and he whispered, "But I won't forgive anything. Ever. You remember that, old man."

Eggie turned from his father then and headed to his house and his woman.

As soon as Eggie walked into the house and tried to put on that smile for her, she knew something was wrong. If it was something that needed to be dealt with right now, she knew he'd tell her. But the fact that he wasn't telling her anything meant it was personal. He'd been hurt and he didn't want to bother her with it.

Darla set down the spatula she was using to put the meringue on yet another lemon meringue pie and wiped her hands off on a towel. As Eggie stood there watching her, she grabbed a kitchen chair and pulled it over to him. She climbed onto it, pressed her hands to Eggie's face, stroked his jaw, his neck. She wrapped her arms around him and rested her head on his shoulder.

"I'm so glad you're home," she told him.

His arms tightened around her waist and he held her close. "Yeah. Me, too."

Early the next morning, Eggie woke up in Darla's arms. Woke up because some cruel bastard was knocking on his backdoor.

Not wanting Darla bothered, Eggie slipped out of bed and

went downstairs. He opened the door to his Aunt Gertrude. He knew he was standing there naked in front of one of his relatives but he didn't care. It was too early for this mess.

"Yeah?"

"Oh. Eggie. Mornin'."

"Mornin'."

Gertie cleared her throat. "Darla around?"

"Asleep."

"Right. It's just . . . she said she'd make a pie for me."

Disgusted that someone would bother him this early in the morning over a goddamn pie, Eggie closed the door in his blood relative's face.

"Who was that?"

"Gertie."

"Did she want her pie?"

"No one needs pie at six in the morning, Darla. And Gertie don't need pie at all."

"Eggie Ray!" Darla, wearing one of his T-shirts, pushed past him and went to the door. "I can't believe you didn't put on pants before you answered the door," she snarled.

She snatched the door open. "Mornin', Miss Gertie."

"Mornin', Darla dear. Sorry to bother you so early."

"No problem. Hold on a sec. I've got your pies right here."

Darla went to retrieve several pies and when Eggie looked at his aunt, she sneered at him. He replied by baring a fang. The She-wolf's eyes grew wide in fear but Darla rushed back before Gertie could make a run for it.

"Here you go, Miss Gertie."

"Thank you, dear. Have a nice morning." She nodded at Eggie. "Egbert Ray."

"Aunt Gertie."

Darla waved at his aunt and closed the door.

"Egbert Ray!"

"Too early to yell."

"It was more of a bellow. You can't snarl at everyone who comes to the house."

"Wanna bet?"

"Why do I bother?" she sighed, trying to walk around him. But Eggie caught her around the waist and pulled her close.

"You're not wearing panties," he growled.

"No time to put any on. I knew you'd scare off all my business."

Eggie dragged his mouth against her throat. "I'm taking you back to bed."

"More people will be coming to get their pies."

"They can wait," Eggie told her, carrying her to the stairs, loving the sound of her giggles. So he was really annoyed when that damn phone rang. So annoyed, he started barking and didn't stop.

Darla slapped at his arms until he released her. "Honestly! The barking!" She stomped over to the phone, not realizing his T-shirt was now riding high on her hips so that he could see her perfect ass sway as she walked. It was entertaining.

Darla answered the phone and Eggie watched her face fall. She turned to him and held the phone out. "It's for you."

Without her even telling him who was on the other end, Eggie already knew. He walked over and took the receiver from her. With one arm around her, pulling her close, he brought the receiver to his ear. "Yeah?"

"It's McMartin. Be ready to move out in an hour."

"Yeah."

McMartin disconnected and Eggie dropped the phone back in the cradle. He wrapped both arms around Darla, holding her tight.

"When will I hear from you?" she asked.

"Don't know. Sad to say, no news is good news in my business."

She let out a breath. "I understand." Darla took his hand and led him toward the stairs. "Come on, darlin'. Let's get you packed."

CHAPTER NINETEEN

Eggie didn't return home again for four months. He'd been worried it would be five, but they had finally cut him loose for at least a month of leave. More likely two, though he didn't know if they'd been planning that or if it was because Eggie had mauled a full-human superior officer the other day when the man had gotten on his nerves. The human was still alive and believed himself to have been attacked by someone's loose attack dog, but still . . . it was a definite sign to the shifter officers who ran his platoon that Eggie needed to go home.

The problem was, though, that when Eggie walked into his little house, he found it empty. He didn't expect a note or anything because Darla'd had no idea when he'd be home. But it had been four months with only a few calls between them. He needed to see his mate.

Eggie went upstairs, showered, and changed his clothes. He stopped first at his momma's and checked in with her, barely spoke to his daddy, and then had headed over to Frankie and Roberta's house—he would have gone to Bubba and Janie Mae's but he had no idea if they were together this week or broken up—and asked about Darla.

It turned out she'd gone back to her father's house for a few weeks. The pie business had taken off and while Francine and Roberta were arranging a storefront in town right on Main Street, Darla had headed off to get them seed money. Apparently his father had offered her money but she'd very sweetly but firmly turned him down. Eggie had never told Darla what his father had done but maybe she'd done that thing of hers . . . looking deep into his soul or whatever it was. No matter the reason, though, she'd said no and now was trying to raise funds on her own. Of course if anyone could do it, it was Darla Mae.

Using his recently repaired Plymouth GTX—Eggie guessed Darla and her sisters were still racing against those She-lions since that probably brought in some cash—he headed to Smithville, North Carolina. He went right to Darla's father's house but Mr. Lewis and his sons ordered Eggie off their territory, saying that Darla didn't want to see Eggie.

Eggie didn't really believe them, but he left anyway, not wanting to fight Darla's kin. Yet he came back every night as wolf, stood outside the house, and he howled. He howled and howled until her father and brothers came out and ran him off again.

Well, his nights could be worse.

Darla had slept the afternoon away after arriving from San Francisco on the late flight she'd caught. It hadn't been as hard as she'd thought it would be: Darla had raised the money for the shop she and her sisters were going to open in Smithtown. She'd had a list of people to ask but it had been Mr. Van Holtz who'd given her the majority of the money. It was a loan and she expected to be able to pay him back in the next couple of years if everything went as well as it had been going the last few months. Plus she got a little extra cash from other contacts she'd made over the years.

Mr. Van Holtz had been very happy about all this for Darla, but he'd also been disappointed that she'd never be coming back to work at the restaurant. Apparently the newest pastry chef assistant was not working out and was the fifth one in five months. Darla had felt bad for him but when she saw the head pastry chef yelling at the new assistant, she remembered what she wouldn't miss about this job . . . dealing with a talented but mean chef on a daily basis.

Grinning, she came into her father's living room and kissed him on the top of the head. "Hello, Daddy."

"Hello, sweetheart. You sleep all right?"

"Yes, I did."

"I'm glad you're home."

"Yeah, me, too." Darla knew she could have gone straight back to Smithtown after her meetings in San Francisco, but go home to what? An empty house and a list of pie orders to fill? No. That didn't sound like fun. So she'd headed to her family's territory first. But she wouldn't be able to stay too long. Janie would be having her baby any day and Darla felt she should be there to help out. At the moment, her sister wasn't making any friends who'd be willing to help except the newest mate of one of the Smithtown-local Reed boys. But Lord that particular She-wolf was annoying, so yeah, Darla should be there.

"Where's Momma?"

"Over at her sister's house."

"Okay." She felt bad that she was relieved at the news, but her mother had been riding Darla since she'd found out that Eggie had marked her youngest, and it didn't seem to be something that would end soon. Her mother thought Darla could have done better—and that she should still try.

Yet Darla knew she'd done better than she could have hoped for.

Besides, life with Eggie would be hard enough with him being gone for such long periods of time that the last thing she needed to hear was her mother going on and on about all the other eligible bachelors around town. But Eggie's time away was a price Darla was willing to pay to have Eggie Smith as her mate. He was worth it. *And,* she reminded herself yet again, *it wouldn't be forever. He has to retire from the Marines eventually.*

"Want me to make dinner, Daddy?"

"I thought I'd take y'all out tonight," her father offered. "Your mother will meet us at the restaurant."

"Okay. That sounds really ni—"

The howl cut into Darla's words and she gasped in surprise. "Eggie."

She started to run to the door, but one of her brothers caught her arm and held her back. "You just gonna run out there to him?"

"Of course I am. It's my . . ." Darla stopped talking and faced her male kin. "How do y'all know Eggie's howl?"

"Well," her father admitted, "he's been here a few nights now . . . howling for you."

"You told him I wasn't home, though, right?" When her kin only stared at her . . . *You didn't tell him?*"

"No need to bellow, sweetheart."

"Oh, Daddy!"

"Don't think he's earned the right to know a damn thing," her brother said. "Gotta make him work for it."

"Make him . . . ? He saved my life. He loves me. We're mated."

"Eh." Her father shrugged. "He could put in a little more effort."

"Daddy!"

Darla snatched her arm away from her brother and sprinted to the front door. She snatched it open and ran outside. By the time she made it across the lawn, the wolf had shifted to Eggie and she threw herself into his arms.

Hugging him tight, Darla whispered, "I'm so glad you're home."

"Me, too." He kissed her neck and held her close. "Me, too."

Darla leaned back a bit so she could look him in the face. "I didn't know you were here, Eggie. I haven't been at the house for days."

"I know."

Darla blinked. "You know?"

"Yeah. I knew after the first hour I got here. Your scent had faded. Then when I went into town for breakfast the next day, my cousins told me you'd gone to San Francisco on a business trip."

"But then . . . why did you keep coming here every night? Daddy said you were here, but that he kept running you off."

"Yeah. He did."

"Eggie—"

"It's a male thing. I had to work for you. That's all."

"Are you serious?"

"Of course. You don't think if we have a daughter, I won't do the same thing to the lowlife slug that tries to make her his mate?"

"You don't even know this boy yet and already he's a lowlife slug?"

"If he's messin' with my little girl."

"A little girl you don't have yet."

"We will." He started walking toward the house. "But later. Now you'll introduce me to your daddy proper-like."

"Wait, Eggie."

He stopped. "Uh-huh?"

"Suggestion. For first impressions with my daddy and all . . . may wanna put on pants."

"Oh." They both looked down to see Eggie deliciously naked. "Guess you have a point." He smiled and Darla grinned back. She kissed him, hugged him tight.

"Come out with us," she told him. "Daddy's taking everyone to dinner."

"I don't think he wants me going."

Darla snorted. "Daddy!" she called out, startling Eggie.

"Yes, Darla?"

"I'm going with Eggie to get his pants. Then we're *all* going to dinner tonight. The whole family, so Momma can meet him, too."

"I didn't invite him."

"Daddy!"

"Oh, all right!" he snapped from still inside the house. "But hurry up. Ain't got all night."

"See?" she told Eggie. "You can always get what you want. You just need to be nice about it."

"Is that what I'm missing? Just being nice?"

"Darlin'," she teased, "let's not ask for the world." She kissed him again, her arms around his shoulders, her legs around his waist. "Now let's go get your pants."

"Will I have to put them on right away?" he asked, gently nipping the tip of her nose.

Darla gave the wolf she loved a wide smile. "Not if I have any say in it."

EPILOGUE

More than thirty years later . . .

Eggie came out of the woods and walked toward his house. He knew the car sitting in front of it and the tall, beautiful She-wolf leaning against the overpriced piece of Eurotrash vehicle. But Eggie didn't mind too much because he knew it wasn't a car she would buy. No. Not her. She still had that '78 Camaro sitting in his barn that she used every time she came to town to visit.

Too bad she wasn't alone this time. She was with *him*. The boy.

Eggie walked up to a nearby tree where he'd left his jeans, shifted to human and pulled the jeans on. Yet even before he'd done that, she'd sensed Eggie's presence. He could tell. She had his sense of things. His skills. In fact, Eggie would say she was better at what she did than he'd been. Her skill had been inborn. Part of her DNA.

The boy, however . . . was blissfully unaware of the danger lurking right behind him. Smooth and charming? Sure he was. But that was it as far as Eggie was concerned.

Eggie stood behind the boy, wondering how long before he'd notice Eggie was there.

About thirty seconds, it turned out.

Slowly, the boy turned and faced him, eyes wide. A Van Holtz. On Eggie's territory—with permission. The thought made him feel like sneering. So he did. At the boy.

The boy swallowed at that sneer and took a step back. But the woman with him stepped around and threw herself into Eggie's arms. "Daddy."

"Hey, Sugar Bug."

Eggie hugged his only daughter tight while he eyed the Van Holtz wolf standing on the other side of her.

Dee-Ann pulled away from Eggie and looked at the boy, waiting for him to say something.

Clearing his throat, the boy stepped forward, held out his hand. "Mr. Smith. It's good to see you again."

Eggie looked down at that hand and then, slowly, looked back at the boy. He saw the color drain from his already pale face. Yankee who never saw the sun was the problem there.

A squeal from the porch and Darla Mae came rushing down. She'd filled out a bit over the years, but it worked for her. Gave Eggie even more to love—although she claimed she hated when he said that.

Arms wide, Darla reached up and hugged their daughter. She favored her mother in the face, but she had Eggie's eyes. Whether wolf or human, her eyes were cold and yellow and deadly. Sometimes, when she'd come to visit, the two of them would go to the mall, get a couple of chocolate shakes, sit around, and just stare at people. Taking bets on who they could get to piss their pants with nothing more than a look. It was something they'd been doing since his little girl was about five or so. It was also something they never told her momma about.

"Oh, my baby girl," Darla cheered. "I'm so glad you're home!"

"Me, too, Momma. You all right?"

"I'm just fine, Sugar Bug. Even better now that you're home." She stepped back and Darla, as always when first seeing her daughter, had to wipe tears away.

"Momma, don't cry."

"I'll cry if I want to, Dee-Ann Smith." She lightly tapped Dee-Ann aside and smiled at the boy.

"Ulrich Van Holtz." Darla threw her arms open. "Come on over here, darlin' boy."

Smiling—probably because he was relieved—the boy willingly went to Darla and hugged her.

Eggie's eyes narrowed and he started to bare his fangs. But he stopped when Dee-Ann's elbow tapped his ribs.

"Daddy." And she sounded just like her momma when she said it that way.

Darla *finally* pulled away from what Eggie still considered an enemy wolf and smiled happily at the pair. "I'm so glad you're both here."

"Sorry we're late, Miss Darla," the boy said. "We stopped by the store to pick up a few things."

"Ulrich Van Holtz, are you going to make me one of your fancy dinners?"

"I sure am. Especially if you make me that pecan pie of yours."

"Already baking in the oven." She motioned to the house. "You go in there and get comfortable. Your room is all ready, so if you want to rest first—"

"Oh, no, ma'am. I'm ready to cook."

"Great. Then get going."

The boy turned to grab the bags out of the backseat of the car but he stopped and stared at Eggie since Eggie was standing in front of the door.

"Uh . . . excuse me, sir."

Eggie stared a little longer, just a few seconds, before he stepped out of the way. The boy grabbed several bags and Dee-Ann grabbed the last two. Before she stepped away, she kissed her father on the cheek.

"Lord, I missed you, Daddy." She lowered her voice to a whisper. "You never fail to entertain."

Eggie winked at his little girl—all six feet and two inches of her—and watched her and that worthless Van Holtz head into their house. Tomorrow Eggie would go hunting with his little girl. They'd spend the day roaming the hills of the town he loved while Darla entertained the boy with food shopping and visiting with the rest of the Lewis sisters at the pie shop.

Once the young pair were inside the house, Darla slapped his arm. "I thought I told you to be nice to him!"

"I didn't shoot at him this time."

Her eyes narrowed. "Thought that was an accident."

"Oh. Yeah. Sure."

Darla rolled her eyes and started to walk away, but Eggie pulled her back. "Mange."

She gasped and whispered, "That boy does not have mange! Stop saying that."

"Distemper, then. He's got that Van Holtz Distemper Strain. CDT."

"Egbert Ray Smith, the only temper you need to worry about right now is *mine*."

"You gettin' cranky, Darla Mae?"

"Egbert Ray."

He walked her back until he had her pinned against the car, and he kept her there by putting his arms on either side of her. "You're not really mad at me, are you, Darla Mae?"

"Furious."

"Guess I'll have to make it up to you then."

"Not here you won't!" she giggled, putting her hands on his chest and trying to push him back. Although she wasn't trying very hard. "Just stop picking on poor Ulrich."

"He's with my Sugar Bug—"

"Ridiculous nickname." That she used just as much as Eggie.

"—and I can't let him off easy."

"But he likes you so much."

"Darla Mae."

"All right. I *think* he wants to like you, but you make it impossible."

"Not sure he's right for my little girl is all."

Darla pressed her hand against Eggie's cheek. "Trust me

when I say . . . there is no wolf on this planet more perfect for your daughter. At least not one that can actually shift to human."

"All right, all right. I'll keep the snarling to a minimum this time. But not the glaring."

She sighed. "Fine."

"Now kiss me and tell me you love me."

"Who says I do?"

"You did . . . last night."

She blushed, her grin wide, probably remembering how he'd woken her up in the middle of the night with kisses and nuzzles. "Egbert Ray Smith, stop it."

"Stop what? Loving you? 'Cause that ain't never gonna happen, Darla Mae."

"I know, Eggie," she said, her pretty eyes warm and, as always with him, welcoming. And damn it all, she still had those dimples, too. "That's what makes everything perfect for me. Always has. Now come on." She took his hand, led him toward the house. "Let's go see our beautiful baby girl and her mate."

Wed or Dead
Cynthia Eden

For Megan, editor extraordinaire.
Thanks for all of your insight and assistance.

CHAPTER ONE

The bride almost left her groom at the altar. The temptation was pretty damn strong.

Normally, Kayla Kincaid wasn't afraid of anyone or anything, but when she put one foot down on that too-red carpet at the Forever Chapel, her heart raced so fast that her chest hurt. She gripped the flowers in her hand, a small bouquet of daisies that the groom had grabbed from God knew where. There was music playing. Some sweet little old lady was nearby, stroking an organ and smiling, and Kayla realized that she had frozen after taking that single step.

This was her wedding day? How the hell had this happened? She wasn't supposed to be getting married. She should be hightailing it out of Vegas, and not getting all sweaty-palmed around the daisies as she got ready to say *I do.*

How? *How had this happened?* Her death grip tightened on the slumping bouquet.

Then the groom turned toward her and flashed that megawatt smile of his. The smile that revealed all of his perfect, white teeth.

Oh, right. *That was how.*

Gage Riley waited for her at the end of that narrow aisle. The groom. She swallowed. He wasn't dressed in a fancy tux. He wore jeans that clung to his lean hips and a black T-shirt that stretched taut over his muscled chest and those wonderful big and broad shoulders that had probably made plenty of women drool over the years.

With his perfect, sculpted face, that rock-hard jaw, his wild mane of midnight black hair, and those sky blue eyes, he was the sexiest man she'd ever seen.

She managed to unfreeze herself and take another step toward him. *Gage.* Sexy, but dangerous. Oh, she knew he was dangerous.

He was also a job. Her assignment. And Kayla had her orders.

Get close to him. By any means necessary. In this case, any means included marriage.

But . . .

But this didn't *feel* like an assignment.

The little old lady playing the organ began to frown at her. Gage just kept smiling. He looked confident. Strong. He had no doubt that they were about to be joined as man and wife. Kayla couldn't help glancing over her shoulder. There were about five feet between her and the front door. Maybe . . . maybe she should just make a run for it. Before things went past the point of no return.

She tried to swallow again. The lump in her throat was getting worse.

Warm, strong fingers curled around her arm, just below her elbow. Kayla didn't jump because she'd grown used to the silent way that Gage could move. Despite the guy's big size, he was eerily quiet when he walked, and, jeez, the guy was *fast.*

"Going somewhere?" He asked in that deep, dark voice that sounded like sin in the night.

Very slowly, Kayla turned her head back so that she faced him. The smile had slipped from his face. Such a handsome face. He always looked so open and almost carefree.

But there was more to Gage than met the eye. Much, much more. Her gaze dropped to his lips. Sensual. She'd felt those lips on hers plenty of times. That had been the plan, right? Get close? Make him trust her?

Only marriage hadn't been on *her* agenda. It had been on his. He'd pushed for this, and she'd realized that if she didn't take this step, she'd lose her connection to him. Then the assignment would go to hell.

"It's too late to run," he told her. His hand lifted and brushed against her cheek. The caress was gentle. So at odds with fierce strength that she knew he could wield. "I'd just follow you, sweetheart."

She was killing the daisies. The little old lady had stopped playing and was now glaring at her in a not-so-sweet way. The minister—wait, was he a minister or a justice of the peace—or something else? Whatever. The guy peered suspiciously at them from his perch near the front of the chapel.

Gage leaned toward her and his lips pressed lightly against hers. "It's just a few simple words. Nothing for you to be afraid of."

Kayla stiffened. "I'm not afraid." Admitting fear to herself was one thing. Confessing it out loud, to someone else? *No way.*

Besides, she wasn't *really* afraid. Nervous. That was all. A wee bit nervous. Gage was the one who should be afraid. The guy didn't know just what he was setting himself up for here.

He didn't know her. Not really.

If he did, he would be the one running.

Her groom-to-be had no idea that she'd stashed a gun in her purse. Or that she kept a knife—*silver*—strapped to her ankle. He didn't know that she'd spent most of her adult life becoming a perfect predator, and he damn sure didn't know that he was her current prey.

Gage's lips caressed hers once more in a light kiss even as he pulled the damaged daisies from her hand. When his head lifted, his blue eyes seemed even brighter. "Good. If you're not afraid, then come marry me." A thread of demand underscored the words.

Gage wasn't usually the demanding sort. He was more easygoing, more—

He tossed the daisies on a nearby chair and threaded his fingers through hers. "Want me to carry you?" His smile flashed again.

That smile of his was like her freaking kryptonite. No man should have a smile that melted panties. His did.

The organ began to play again. *One foot in front of the other.* Kayla took a deep breath and began to walk. *One foot.*

Gage was right by her side.

In front of the other.

Before she knew it, they were standing in front of the minister. He was smiling and the light reflected off the top of his bald head. He was talking. Nodding. Looking all pleased and happy.

Kayla couldn't hear a word he said. Her heart raced too fast and too loud for that.

Gage kept a tight hold on her hand. Probably because he was afraid she'd make a break for it.

But Kayla wasn't leaving. She'd never left a job before, and she wouldn't start now. From the corner of her eye, she glanced at Gage. Poor guy. He had no idea what was coming for him. Did he think this was some kind of epic romance?

Think again.

She was the predator. He was the prey. And, soon enough, he'd grow to hate her.

Gage nudged her. When she glanced up and found the minister staring at her, Kayla realized she was supposed to speak. "Uh, I do." That was what folks always said, right? *Promise to love, honor, and cherish.*

But what she'd really do . . . *Lie, betray, hurt.*

Her chest began to ache. This wasn't what she wanted. Why couldn't things have been simpler for her? For him?

The minister beamed. Gage's strong voice rumbled beside her as he made his vow.

And she hated her life. Just once, she wished she could be normal. A woman in love—a woman actually marrying the man of her dreams.

Instead of just being a woman who was using herself as bait to set up her groom.

Gage turned her toward him. Even over the thud of her heartbeat, Kayla heard the minister say that Gage could kiss his wife.

"Hello, wife," Gage murmured, and finally—*finally*—the wild thud of her heartbeat quieted, because it stopped for a few seconds. "You're mine, now. Forever." The words held a hard edge that she'd never heard before in his voice.

Then Gage kissed her. Not the light, teasing kisses that he'd given her before. An openmouthed, hot, I-want-you-naked kiss that sent a shudder through her whole body.

She kissed him back just as wildly. Because despite all the other madness that was happening, Kayla did want her husband. And, before he found out the truth about her and this little fantasy came to a crashing end, she'd have him.

The hotel room was one of those ridiculous pink explosions that you found in Vegas. A romance-ready room. Heart-shaped Jacuzzi. Rose petals scattered on the floor and on the massive bed. Pink champagne chilling next to a box of chocolates on the bedside table.

But when Gage carried Kayla inside the decked out room, his bride didn't so much as give the surroundings a glance. Her eyes, big, gold, fuck-me eyes, were on him. Her hands curled around his neck. "I want you." Her soft confession.

Did she actually sound a little surprised by that fact?

Damn, sometimes, she was so adorable . . . he could just eat her. Actually, he would.

He couldn't believe that he'd gotten her to marry him.

The lady had sure surprised him on that one. He'd been expecting her to run as fast as she could.

But she'd straightened her slim shoulders. Lifted her slightly pointed chin. And let him drag her down the aisle.

A surprise, but he wouldn't question fate. Not then.

Gage kicked the hotel room door closed and carried Kayla to the bed. He'd been wanting to get her naked and beneath him since the first night they met. Now that he had her in that room with him, nothing was going to stop him from claiming her.

Except . . .

Kayla put her hand on his chest when he closed in on her. Gage was leaning over the bed, more than ready to taste her, when her small hand slammed into his chest.

"I . . . ah . . . need a minute."

Seriously? She'd put him off for weeks. Tempting him with that sweet ass and those curving breasts, and now that she was legally *his,* the woman was still putting the brakes on things?

He barely bit back a growl. A man's control could last only so long.

But he pulled away. Stood. Began to strip.

Her eyes widened as she looked at his chest, and her pink tongue slipped out to lick along her plump lower lip. He had plans for that tongue. And for her.

Sexy little Kayla Kincaid. The first time he'd seen her, he'd gotten hard and territorial. One look, and he'd thought . . . *mine.*

Sometimes, you knew what you wanted with one glance.

She eased onto her feet. Stood beside him a moment. The top of her head barely skimmed his shoulders. Her dark hair, silky, curling lightly, drifted down her back as she tilted her head to stare up at him. "I'll be right back," she promised.

His gaze dropped to her lips. Full, red. Bitable. Just like the rest of her.

He did like to bite.

Kayla turned away and darted into the bathroom. *Hurry back, sweetheart.*

His control wasn't lasting much longer.

He wanted her in that bed. Wanted her spread wide. And he wanted to hear her scream his name.

For almost two months, he'd played her game. Done the whirlwind courtship bit. Acted like the gentleman for her. Wore a mask to hide the real way he felt. The real way he *was.*

Playtime was over.

Kayla had her secrets. So did he. The time for a big reveal would come later. The time for fucking—yeah, that was *now.*

The bathroom door squeaked open. Gage turned to face her, still clad in his jeans. His eyes went to her face first. Heart-shaped, delicate—deceptively so. Her eyes were shining, her high cheeks flushed, and she looked . . .

Excited. Gorgeous.

And naked.

His gaze swept down her body and the cock that was already up for her hardened even more against the zipper of his jeans.

Her breasts were small, but rounded perfectly with light pink nipples that he couldn't wait to have against his tongue. Her hips curved, flaring, and the bare V of her sex had his mouth going dry.

Take her.

He'd waited long enough.

"Why are you still dressed?" Kayla wanted to know. He managed to drag his gaze away—okay, on the third attempt, he dragged it away from that V—and back up to her face. "I thought you were supposed to be stripping."

He nearly ripped his jeans off. Then in one lunge, he was at her side. Gage lifted her up, holding her easily, and he thrust his tongue into her mouth. Her arms wrapped around him—and so did her legs. The soft flesh of her sex brushed against his cock even as her tight nipples pushed against his chest.

He was gonna go freaking insane. Gage wasn't a man accustomed to waiting, but for her, he'd tried. *Can't wait longer.* Because he could smell the lush scent of her arousal. She wanted him. He was on fire for her.

His tongue met hers. Tasted. She was always a blend of sweet and spicy on his tongue. Innocence and sin. Such a mixed combination. One that fit her too well.

He pulled his mouth from hers and began to kiss a path down her neck. He was strong. Gage doubted that she understood just how powerful he really was, and he easily kept her lifted against him.

When his tongue licked over her skin, down low where her shoulder curved into her neck, Kayla shivered.

He'd make her do more than that.

His teeth scored her flesh. Bit lightly. Marked her. That was the way of his kind.

Her nails dug into his shoulders. Her breath came in ragged pants, and Gage could feel the slick wetness of her sex against him. *More.*

He'd known she'd be like this. White-hot to the touch. Able to burn a man straight to the soul.

He lifted her higher and her soft gasp would have made him smile, if he hadn't been so damn hungry for her. But there were no smiles now. No soft touches or kisses. There was only lust, blazing out of control.

He held her in the perfect position for his mouth, and he took her breast between his lips. He licked, sucked, and her breaths came even faster. His cock was so swollen it hurt, and he wanted to drive into her more than he'd ever wanted anything else.

"*Gage . . .*"

No, actually, he did want something else. He wanted her to come for him.

Still holding her, he headed for the bed. He lowered her onto the covers and rose petals slid beneath her. Their light fragrance mixed with the sweet scent that was just . . . *Kayla.*

She was making him crazy.

Gage took his time licking and tasting her other breast. Her hands were on him. Her fingers slid over his back and urged him closer.

Not yet.

Kayla's legs were parted, and he stood between them at the side of the bed. The perfect position to thrust deep, if he'd wanted to thrust.

Not yet.

He wanted another taste. A far more intimate one.

His gaze dipped to her sex and her legs widened even more. "Do you know . . ."—his voice was so dark he knew it sounded more like a growl than anything else—"how long I've wanted to put my mouth on you?"

Her lashes lifted. She stared back at him with glinting eyes and flushed cheeks. Then Kayla shook her head. He saw the flash of hesitation in her gaze, the innocence that he'd learned could appear and vanish in an instant. She tried to come off so tough and assured, but that innocence kept slipping out.

His knees brushed the carpet as he lowered his body between her splayed legs. Gage wrapped his hands around her hips and pulled her to the edge of the mattress so that her thighs brushed against either side of his shoulders. "Since the first night, you came into the bar"—*his* bar—"wearing that short black skirt, and I kept wondering what you were wearing underneath it." He'd looked at her and gotten hard. Wanted. Craved. "And I wanted to shove that skirt up . . ."—he put his hands between her thighs and loved her gasp—"and find out."

Her eyes were on him. So wide. So deep.

He'd been insane for her. The need always pulsing in his body, but Kayla hadn't let him get close enough to fuck. Not that first night. Not all the nights since. They'd danced around each other for weeks, becoming closer and closer, but deep kisses and heavy petting had been all that he'd gotten from her.

Until tonight. Until they'd drank until one a.m. at his bar, then slipped out to find a chapel.

Now he had her. There'd be no escape for her. Or him.

His fingers slid into her. She was wet and tight. Perfect.

But he didn't just want to touch with his fingers. He licked his lips, then Gage put his mouth on her. Her hips bucked up against him as she gasped out his name, but his left hand just rose again and locked around her hips, holding her easily in place.

He let his tongue slide over her sex. Sweet, slick flesh. Hot. He used the fingers of his right hand to open her to him. To press lightly into her even as his tongue slid over her clit.

She wasn't trying to pull away anymore. Kayla was pushing against him and her body was eager for more. Fair enough, he was more than eager, too.

He devoured her. Gage's mouth took and tasted even as his fingers thrust. She moaned and shivered and her body tightened beneath him.

He wanted her to come against his mouth. Then she'd be ready for him. He didn't want to hurt her the first time, so he *had* to make sure she was ready for him.

And her taste . . . *sweet and rich*. Better than chocolate. And chocolate had always been his vice.

One of them, anyway. He had quite a few.

He pulled his fingers back and thrust his tongue into her. His thumb pushed down on the center of her need and she came, jerking beneath him.

Gage pulled back, savored her taste on his tongue, and knew that he now had a new vice. *Her.* The lady was at the top of his list.

He'd have more of her. All of her. *Now.* He reached over and yanked out one of the condoms that waited inside the nightstand. Part of the romance package. The hotel knew how to please its guests. He was about to be pretty fucking pleased.

Because he was finally having her.

He donned the condom, and two seconds later, his cock pushed against the entrance to her body. Her eyes were on him. He couldn't go easy anymore. He'd used the last of his control. But she was ready now. She had to be—

Kayla arched against him, and Gage thrust balls-deep into her core. A ragged groan ripped from him because she felt so good. Tight. Wet. Hot.

He pulled back, but her sex clamped around him, gripping like a fist along the length of his cock.

So good.

Her eyes were open and on him. "Give me more," she whispered.

And he did. Gage drove into her, deep and hard, and the bed squeaked beneath them. Rose petals were going everywhere, and he didn't give a damn. All that mattered was taking her. Claiming her.

In and out. He thrust again and again. Her legs wrapped round him, holding him tightly. Her nipples stabbed up into the air, and he just had to taste one again. He leaned forward and took one pebbled nipple into his mouth.

Her fingers sank into his hair. "Gage!" Her sex tightened even more around him as her body stiffened. Her second climax was close. Hell, *yes.*

His head lifted because he wanted to watch her come. One thrust. Another. Then her lips parted as she called out his name. Pleasure flooded over her features. Her eyes lit with golden fire. Her cheeks flushed an even darker pink.

And she came around his cock.

Gage exploded inside of her, letting his own release pump through him. The pleasure damn near ripped him apart, pulsing in his blood and giving him a heady rush that had Gage clenching his teeth and holding her even tighter.

This, this was beyond just sex. Beyond the fleeting pleasure he'd known with other women. This was fucking fantastic.

Gage leaned forward and pressed a soft kiss to her lips.

Kayla jumped, as if she was startled by that gentle touch, and her eyes widened as she looked at him. "That was . . ." She licked her lips. "It—"

"It was the start," he told her, smiling, and getting hard within her again. *Need another condom.* Good thing that box in the drawer was full. "And, sweetheart, the pleasure is only gonna get better." He'd guarantee it.

He'd finally gotten Kayla exactly where he wanted her— and Gage wasn't going to let her go.

So he put his mouth back on her. This time, he skimmed his lips over the raised scars that slid over her shoulder, and he knew that the night was going to be incredible.

The faint light of dawn slipped through the curtains when Kayla eased from the bed. Gage still lay tangled amid the covers, and his dark lashes cast shadows on his cheeks. Unable to help herself, she paused and just stared down at him for a moment.

He looked so . . . peaceful. The lines were smoothed from his face. The wild power of his eyes was shielded by his lowered lids.

Just a man. That was what he looked like then. With his tanned flesh appearing even darker against the crisp, white sheets, with a rose petal in his hair—he just looked like a man.

Not a monster.

She turned away and crept toward the bathroom.

He was a man, and she was supposed to just be a woman. If only. Life sure had a way of sucking.

Kayla shut the door behind herself. After taking a deep breath, she glanced up and stared at the reflection in the mirror. Her lips were swollen. Her eyes glittering. Her hair was an insane tangle around her face. She didn't know how many times she'd climaxed, but she did know that Gage was the best lover she'd ever had.

Yep, he was at the top of her big list of four men. She figured he'd be staying there a while.

She straightened her shoulders. There were some faint red marks on her neck. Marks Gage had left. She'd left her own share of marks, too. They'd been wild. Fierce.

Happy.

Just like a real honeymooning couple.

She glanced away from the mirror, almost hating the sight of her own reflection. *Why couldn't it have all been true?*

Because her life wasn't a fairy tale. She wasn't some princess who got to live happily freaking after in a castle.

I've always been more the wicked queen type.

And Gage wasn't Prince Charming, no matter how tempting he appeared to be.

Kayla reached for the handbag she'd put in the bathroom hours before. The bag, her clothes, and her weapons. It was almost six a.m. Just minutes away. That meant her call would be coming in three, two, one—

Kayla answered the phone before it could even ring. "The job is done," she told her boss. The job. Her marriage. Getting close to Gage Riley. She'd done everything she was supposed to—

"Not quite," came the rumble of Lyle McKennis's voice. "But you're real close, Kincaid."

Her hands tightened around the phone. Close wasn't good enough. Close wasn't—

"Actually, you're killing close," he continued, voice cold and flat in her ear. "You're the only hunter who's ever been able to slide under Riley's radar."

Because when Gage Riley saw her, he saw just a woman. Not a hunter.

"You know what he's done," Lyle said. "You know what he is."

Yes. She looked up and forced herself to stare into the mirror again. She stared past her own reflection. Gazed at those marks on her neck.

"He's sleeping now, isn't he?" Lyle murmured.

"Yes." Why was her body starting to feel so cold? Numb?

"Then it's time." Satisfaction purred through Lyle's words. "Make sure you use silver."

What other weapon would she use? Nothing else would work, not on Gage.

"Go kill your new husband," Lyle ordered, "and give the world one less monster to fear."

CHAPTER TWO

The knife was a light weight in her hand. She'd killed before with a weapon like this one, and Kayla had no doubt that she'd do so again. But . . .

Killing Gage? Ice seemed to fill her veins.

Yes, she knew that had been Lyle's plan all along. From the first moment, when he'd told her to head into Gage's bar and to seduce, but not touch. She'd known Lyle wanted her to take out Gage. Another target. Another mission.

She'd always been such a good soldier. No, *hunter.*

Only the plan had changed for her. Gage was supposed to be a monster, she *knew* that. Lyle had told her all about Gage's crimes. She'd read his file. Read it over a dozen times.

But when she looked at him, she didn't see the monster. She just saw the man.

A man who'd wanted to marry her.

So on her thirty-fourth birthday, she'd headed to the chapel with him. And now, with dawn coming, the game was supposed to be over.

She was killing close. Lyle had that bit right. Gage trusted her. This was the time her group had been waiting for. They'd planned this attack for months.

Carefully, she opened the bathroom door. The door made just the softest of creaks as it slid over the carpet. Gage still slept in bed, but he'd rolled so that his back was to her. Such a strong, muscled back. There were faint scars on his back.

She'd touched them in the dark. Just as he'd touched her scars.

He'd kissed her scars. The lines that sliced over her flesh. He hadn't asked her about them. Hadn't questioned like her other lovers had done. He'd just stroked them with his fingers and his tongue and made her feel perfect.

She'd never been that.

Kayla glanced at the knife. Was she really supposed to just shove it into his heart? Then walk away while he bled out?

You know what he is. Don't be fooled. Gage's kind was so good at deception. She had to remember that. He'd been born to lie. To deceive.

She'd met others like him before. So many over the years. More than most people realized.

Her own family had been attacked by someone like Gage. A man, hiding a beast inside. One dark night, he'd killed her mother and father. Left her brother in a pool of blood, struggling to breathe. Attacked her.

Monsters lived and breathed in this world. Most folks didn't know that truth. They thought the world was all happy and shiny and full of birthday parties, play dates, and football games.

She knew better. *Monsters are real.* And her handsome husband, with his slow smile and strong hands—he was a monster.

Kayla took a step forward. *One foot in front of the other.* The mantra was the same one she'd used when she'd walked down the aisle. Only no minister waited for her this time.

The robe she wore rustled around her feet as she took another slow step. Another.

When she felt something wet on her cheek, Kayla stopped. What the hell? Her left hand lifted and swiped across her face. Was she crying? She *never* cried. She hadn't, not since the men at the cemetery had put her parents in the ground.

"Come back to bed," Gage said, his voice rumbling out

and making her jump. He faced the window, not her as he added, "I miss you."

He wouldn't miss her for long.

Kayla took a deep breath and forced herself to keep walking. A few more steps, and her legs brushed against the edge of the bed. "Th-there's something you should know about me . . ." His back was still to her. Why did he have to make such an easy target?

This should be better for you. You don't have to look him in the eyes when you attack.

But stabbing a man in the back had never been her style.

Liar. The insidious whisper came from deep within. Her secret shame.

Her hand clenched around the knife's handle. Gage was supposed to be dangerous. Lethal. The strongest paranormal badass to claim Vegas in years.

Because he *was* a paranormal. The supernaturals were real and breathing . . . and many were hiding in the shadows of Sin City.

He was the perfect target right then. Tousled hair. Sated male. Defenseless. It would be so easy. Just lift the knife. Drive the blade into his flesh.

"Oh, I think I already know all the secrets you have, sweetheart," he murmured, his voice a low and sexy growl.

Kayla shook her head. Damn tears. "No, you don't—"

In a flash, he rolled toward her. He leapt up and came at her with claws ripping from his fingers.

Not defenseless.

Claws . . . because Gage Riley wasn't human.

Shifter.

His blue eyes shined at her with the light of the beast and he put those too-sharp and too-long claws of his at her throat.

The move actually seemed only fair, considering that she had her knife pressed over his heart.

"Hello, hunter," Gage whispered.

Her own heart shoved hard against her chest. "How long . . ." Kayla licked her lips. Why was her mouth so dry? "How long have you known?"

He brought his head in close to hers. Inhaled her scent. Pressed a light kiss to her cheek. Did he taste the salt of her tears? "Since the first time you walked into my bar."

What? Kayla shook her head, lost, confused. He'd known since then, and he'd still—

His claws skated lightly over her throat. He didn't break the skin. Didn't hurt her. But she knew one slice would cut open her jugular.

"Are you really going to kill me now?" Gage asked as he pulled back to study her with a cocked head. "Just hours after our wedding?"

She was supposed to.

That was her *job*. As a hunter, she was the one sent out to keep the humans safe in this world. When a supernatural crossed the line and started killing, her team was sent in. They delivered justice. They were the heroes.

Only she didn't feel like any kind of hero right then.

Killer.

"Was screwing me part of the deal?" Gage demanded as his voice roughened.

Her eyes slit at that. Maybe it was deserved, and maybe it damn well wasn't. Instead of stabbing him, she wanted to punch him right then.

"If so," Gage continued with a shake of his head, "that was a rather fatal mistake."

They were at a supernatural standoff. Claws versus silver. If he'd just sheathe his claws . . .

"Cause now that I've had you . . ." Gage smiled at her, and revealed his growing canines. *Sharp.* "I think I want another bite."

He'd kept his fangs from her. Kept the claws away last night. But it looked like he was done playing nice.

So was she.

The bed was rumpled. The air smelled of sex. He was naked.

She stared into his eyes. If he knew what she was, then Kayla had no idea why he'd married her. Sure, she'd been ordered to say the "I do" bit. She'd been told to do anything necessary in order to get past his defenses.

Gage Riley ran the wolf pack in Vegas. Since the wolves had moved to town just eight months ago, hell had hit the city. Supernatural madness. Attacks. Killings.

The pack had to be stopped. *By any means necessary.*

But sex wasn't a means. Making love was more. Far more.

"Lower your claws," she told him and managed to keep her voice totally calm. Rather impressive under the circumstances, but she'd been trained to be cold. Passionless. *I'm not that way with him.* "You aren't going to kill me." Those words were the truth because she'd learned a few things about Gage during their time together.

More than a few.

He wasn't a heartless bastard. Not a cold-blooded killer.

I won't be wrong about him.

His eyes narrowed as he studied her. Then that half-smile that had always charmed her curled his lips. "Killing you isn't what I have planned at all."

He dropped his claws and there still wasn't so much as a scratch on her skin.

Gage glanced down at his chest. She'd nicked him with the blade, and drops of blood slid down his flesh. Blood—and the faintest plume of smoke.

The old legend was true. Werewolves—or, in this case, wolf shifters—and silver just didn't mix.

"Now are you gonna cut my heart out?" he asked and his smile hardened. "Though to confess, sweetheart, it sure feels like you already have."

Her lips parted in surprise. Wait, what? Did he mean—

But then Gage's head jerked up. His nostrils flared and she

knew the wolf was pulling in scents. *"Company."* A snarl. His eyes had never looked so cold before. A chill skated over her. "Guess that's your backup, huh?" Gage charged.

No. She wasn't supposed to have any backup. Not yet. And she couldn't hear anything. But . . .

But Gage had a shifter's sense of smell and hearing. Far, far more advanced than a human's. That was why it was so hard to take out shifters. They always saw their enemies coming, or smelled 'em. You couldn't sneak up on prey that could hear you from a mile away.

"I won't go down easy," he promised, and she believed him. It would be a bloodbath for whoever came in that door.

Kayla shook her head and dropped the knife. It fell to the carpet without making a sound. "You won't go down at all." She'd be punished for this. No question. But . . .

I won't kill him.

Sometimes, even a hunter had to break the rules. Especially when she'd started to go soft for her prey.

Kayla turned away from him. If more of her team members really were heading down that hallway—*and why hadn't Lyle told her that he was sending in a team so soon?*—then Gage would have to act fast. "We're three floors up, but that shouldn't be an issue for you." Shifters could easily survive a fall from that height. He could jump out of the window and vanish. Simple. With dawn just breaking, there wouldn't be too many folks out to see him, and if any did, they'd just think they were having some kind of hung-over delusion in Vegas. "Go now, before they arrive."

She dropped her robe. Jerked on her own clothes. She wouldn't be naked when her team swarmed. Swarmed—and took her into custody because she'd sided with the enemy.

An enemy who attacked your own family.

Kayla yanked on her boots. She could hear the careful tread of footsteps in the hallway now, and her gut clenched.

What would happen to her? Those who disobeyed Lyle

didn't exactly get the chance to hang around the unit for long and make amends. There weren't any second chances for hunters. Lyle sure didn't believe in them.

If Lyle cast her out of the unit, what would happen to her brother?

Kayla glanced around the room with its trampled rose petals. She needed to get the knife and strap it back to her ankle. She had to have her weapon close by in case—

"Looking for this?" he drawled and the faint hint of Texas she'd heard a few times before slipped into his voice again.

Gage had dressed, but the guy hadn't fled yet. The window waited behind him, just begging for the man to leap through it and get the hell out of there. But, no, he was just standing near the wrecked bed and waving her knife between his claws.

"Go," she gritted out. In about thirty seconds, maybe less, the team would be breaking down the door. She knew their MO. They would have already cleared the third floor. Gotten all the nearby guests relocated during the night.

While I was making love to Gage.

Oh, hell, had the team heard them?

She hoped the walls were thicker than they looked. She hadn't exactly been playing it quiet last night. Gage had made her scream.

She'd made him growl. Maybe roar.

The silver knife was blistering his fingers. She could see the smoke from across the room. The more powerful a wolf shifter was, the more the silver was supposed to burn. If that old legend was true, Gage had to be very, very powerful indeed.

"You think I'm gonna leave you?" Gage asked, and he threw the knife. It flashed, tumbling end over end, before embedding hilt-deep in the headboard. Her gaze darted to the shaking knife handle, then back to him. Gage lifted one brow at her. "Think again."

"It will be your funeral," she whispered. Why couldn't he leave? She was trying to *help* him. Didn't he get that? She didn't want him hurt. Kayla wanted him to have a chance.

A chance the guy wasn't taking. Dammit. Fine. Whatever. Maybe she could buy him some more time so that he could get his sanity back and flee like a smart shifter.

She turned and headed for the door. Took two fast steps.

And was jerked back against her husband's hard, muscled body. "You're not leaving me," he told her, his words whispered right into her ear. "You promised forever, remember?"

He'd obviously gone insane. Kayla jerked against him, but there was no give to the guy at all. She'd always known he was much stronger than he looked, but Gage's arms wouldn't budge no matter how much she twisted and shoved against him.

Then the hotel room door flew inward, driven by a powerful kick, and three men dressed in black, from toe to ski mask covered heads, burst into the room. They were all armed, and their weapons were pointed right at—

Me.

Shit. Kayla gulped and stopped struggling.

Gage had pulled her in front of him and he was using her as a human shield. His claws were back at her neck. *Again with that?* And a growl rumbled from his throat. Her husband was definitely showing the beast-like tendencies that he'd kept so carefully hidden for weeks.

He sure wasn't so easygoing right then.

"Stand the hell down," Gage ordered, voice cold and deadly, "or watch her die."

The guy in front lifted his left hand immediately in a signal she knew meant the others should freeze. She couldn't see the guy's face, but she didn't have to. She'd know Jonah anyplace. The tall build, the wiry strength. He was the lead on this mission, and the others would do whatever he commanded.

"Let her go," Jonah said, and his own voice matched

Gage's in arctic chill. The perfect hunter. Cold and emotionless. Jonah hadn't always been like that.

But then again, she hadn't always been a killer, either. They'd both been more, before.

Before a night of blood and screams. Death and hell. And monsters.

"Let her go?" Gage repeated, sounding surprised. He actually laughed, then said, "I don't think so," as he began to back up—with her still clutched tightly against him. His slow, deliberate steps eased them across the room.

Oh, so *now* he was heading toward the window? Kayla kept her movements timed with his and made sure to use her body to shield him. At least he was fleeing now. Better late than never. He'd drop her before he made his exit. He'd be safe. She'd be—

Um, well, something.

Jonah took a step forward.

Gage's hold tightened on her. "Move again," he told the men in black, "and you'll find yourself walking in her blood."

Kayla's breath froze in her lungs. Were the vicious words an idle threat or the real deal? In that moment, she wasn't sure. Claws were at her throat. A shifter at her back. And guns waited in front of her.

Hardly the perfect morning-after that most brides experienced.

Jonah holstered his weapon. He gave a quick hand-motion to the two silent men behind him. They lowered their weapons.

"Why isn't he dead?" Jonah asked her.

Did he really want her to go into that *now*?

Gage stopped the backward walk they were doing. He lifted his hand and slammed it into the window. Glass shattered and rained down around their feet.

"Because she loves me," Gage told him, voice clear and loud. And definitely with a *duh* edge. "And that's why she's leaving you assholes behind and joining *me.*"

Kayla's jaw dropped, but before she could speak, Gage spun her around and pulled her flush against his body.

"Put your arms around me," he ordered with glinting eyes and a locked jaw. "And hold the hell on."

She put her arms around him but shook her head. No, he couldn't mean to take her with him. Not *through* the window. While he'd easily survive the fall and quickly heal from any broken bones, as a human, she didn't have that luxury. A fall from the third floor could kill her.

Probably *would* kill her.

He brought his head in close to hers. His lips feathered over her cheek and he whispered, "Trust me, I'll keep you safe."

On a three-story fall? The hell, no, he—

Gage leapt through the window, holding her tight, and Kayla screamed.

Wind whipped past her. *I'm dying.* So this was the way she was going out. Better than getting slashed apart by a vamp or incinerated by a demon but—

They were on the ground. Gage's knees had barely buckled. And . . . she was fine. Still held tightly in his arms.

No bruises. No cuts. Nothing.

Holy hell. They'd made it.

"Come on," he muttered and put her on her feet. His hand still had a tight grip on her arm, and as he rushed forward, he pulled her behind him. Her boots crunched over the glass that had fallen from their window.

Cat shifters were supposed to be pretty freaking awesome at landing on their feet after jumps like that, but the wolf had shown her just how agile his beast could be.

"Kayla!" Jonah's scream had her turning back. He was leaning out of the window, and he'd jerked off his ski mask. His face was white. His eyes wild.

"I'm okay!" She yelled back to him. "I'm—"

Gage grabbed her and threw her over his shoulder. Really,

that was too much. No, the jump through the window had been *too* much. In a minute, she was gonna get pissed.

But she didn't have a minute. Before she could do more than pound her fist into Gage's back—*hard, leaving lots of bruises*—he tossed her inside an SUV.

Kayla could have jumped out. When he ran around to the driver's side, she could have leapt for safety. If she'd wanted safety. But . . .

But she didn't move.

And, technically, she *could* have gotten away from the guy when he tossed her over his shoulder. Her body was a lethal weapon, after all. Not much could subdue her.

But she hadn't fought back too hard then.

She wasn't fighting now, either.

Gage jumped behind the driver's seat. He bent low and hot-wired the ride. *Sneaky and impressive.* She liked a man with skills. Then he gunned the engine as he shot that SUV out of the parking lot fast enough to make her head whip back.

They'd be pursued, she knew that. Lyle wouldn't just let them vanish into the night.

No way would he do that. The real hunt . . . well, it was only getting started.

CHAPTER THREE

Gage was good at losing any tails who thought they were dumb enough to be able to track him.

This wasn't his first life-or-death ball game. Not even close. So he raced through the city, cutting down streets, twisting the SUV through tight alleys, and taking all the shortcuts that most wouldn't know about in Vegas.

He switched vehicles at a run-down gas station. When they ditched the SUV for a pickup, Kayla didn't even try to run from him. Huh. She wasn't talking, but she wasn't running either. Was that a good sign?

He wasn't sure quite what to make of it. Or her.

So he just kept heading toward the desert. Dust trailed behind them, and in his rearview mirror, he saw nothing but an open road.

No tail. No more hunters.

It looked as if they'd gotten away clean. For the moment.

Gage exhaled slowly and some of the battle-ready tension started to ease from him. The beast who'd wanted to claw his way to freedom stopped fighting the leash Gage had wrapped around the wolf's neck.

"You're not just gonna . . . dump me in the desert, are you?" Ah, his wife finally spoke. Pity her words just pissed him off.

Is that who she thinks I am? What I am? A killer. His hands clenched around the wheel. "I've got other plans for you."

She took that in silence and the anger churned higher in him. He wanted Kayla to strike back at him. To yell. To explode. But she didn't.

Kayla just sat there, looking too sexy and fuckable, with her hair mussed and her head turned away as she glanced out at the blurring terrain. Her profile gave no hint of her emotions, but she had to be feeling something. He was about to rip apart inside.

Stick to the plan. Stick. To. It.

He'd known all along that she had secrets. The fact that was she was a hunter—

"I let you escape."

He laughed at her confession. Such bullshit. Did she even see it? "Sweetheart, I let myself escape." That was why he'd booked a room on the third floor. That kind of jump was nothing to him. Always have an exit strategy—that was his motto.

Always.

He jerked the wheel to the right and barreled down the thin strip of road that most folks would never even notice, not the way it was nestled behind an old, run-down highway billboard.

From the corner of his eye, he saw Kayla stiffen. "Where are we going?" Now there was suspicion in her tone.

Because she realized that he wasn't just blindly fleeing the city, scared of the big, old tough hunters.

Fuck that. No, fuck them. He'd never been afraid of hunters, and he wouldn't start now. He'd left Vegas for a reason.

In less time than it took to shift, he could have taken out every man in that hotel room. He hadn't, though, because that wouldn't have been part of his plan—and he did have a plan.

So now it was his turn to play the silent game. But the game didn't last long. All too soon, they were pulling up next to the small, wooden cabin that lay nestled in the middle of freaking nowhere.

Before he'd even parked, two men strode toward them. One was tall, fair, with light hair. The other, darker, leaner, shadowed the blond's movements. Neither man looked particularly happy.

What else was new?

Gage almost smiled. He would have, if he hadn't still been so pissed off. *She'd betrayed him.*

He jumped from the truck and slammed the door shut behind him.

The blond approached. "Thought you'd be here sooner," Davis Black said, rubbing his chin as he surveyed the pack alpha.

"Um . . ." This came from the dark wolf. A grin lifted his lips as William "Billy" Tanner glanced over Gage's shoulder and back at the truck. "Trouble with the missus?" The light hint of his native Mississippi drawl rolled beneath the shifter's voice.

Gage slit his eyes. "Nothing I can't handle." The other members of the pack wouldn't be making an appearance. That was the plan. Only his top two enforcers were supposed to meet him here.

The others would wait, until he needed them.

"Is everything set up?" Gage asked as his gaze swept the area. The place looked deserted. With its sagging roof and busted windows, the cabin seemed damn near uninhabitable. But appearances could be deceiving.

Why didn't humans ever seem to truly understand that fact?

The truck door squeaked behind him. So Kayla was coming after him now?

Control. He just had to hold on for a little longer. A few more minutes, and he'd have her in the cabin. They'd be alone. Just a few more—

He saw Billy's nostrils flare. "Oh, man, she smells *good.* Like sex and—"

His control snapped and Gage slammed his fist into Billy's

jaw. Though he was stronger than a human, Billy wasn't an alpha, and that blow had him stumbling back.

"Billy," Gage barked out as the wolf howled inside of him, "don't push me right now." The thread of his control had been stripped raw.

The easygoing façade he'd worn for Kayla was gone. All that remained right then was animal instinct. He hadn't realized just how wild he'd be after claiming Kayla.

A little matter of betrayal could break a guy.

But he didn't want Billy sniffing around her. Pity he needed the guy, for the moment. A moment that wouldn't last much longer if Billy kept pushing and eyeing Kayla like she was some kind of tasty meal.

Kayla's feet crunched over the graveled drive. Gage turned and took in her wide eyes as she gazed down at Billy. What? Like this was the first time she'd seen a guy get decked? In her line of work, not likely. She'd probably decked more than her share of assholes. The lady packed a pretty good punch. She'd sure hit him a few good times back at the hotel.

"She doesn't look like much of a hunter," Davis said and he was still rubbing his chin. The guy always did that. His eyes swept over her. "Kinda small, don't you think? A little weak."

That whipped her gaze off Billy and got it locked on the other wolf.

"Looks can be deceiving," Gage said. Who knew that fact better than shifters?

Most folks—those who knew the truth about supernaturals, anyway—thought that shifters were born to deceive. A beast, wearing the skin of a man or woman. How did you get more deceptive than that?

They were good at lying. Tricking. And killing.

Kayla's head turned toward him. Her eyes weren't flashing her emotions. No, she had whatever emotions she was feeling masked too tightly.

Humans were good at deceit, too.

She kept walking until she was by his side. "You didn't make any calls once we left the hotel."

There hadn't been a need. Gage shrugged and knew the gesture would say, *yeah, so?*

He saw the understanding in her eyes and the flush of fury on her cheeks. *Her mask was fading.*

"You really did know what I was," Kayla snapped. "The whole time, you knew."

Ah, but knowing was just the first part. Knowing and actually springing his trap—two whole different things.

But Gage let a cold smile lift his lips. He had to do the show right. "Hunters have been after my pack ever since the moment we took over this town." And that's what he'd done—taken over. Every paranormal in the city knew that Gage's pack were the alpha dogs. They'd kicked demon butt, terrorized the vamps, and made sure that the fools knew who was dominating Sin City. It had been perfect.

Then the hunters had come along and started their dumb-ass little cat and mouse game. Supernaturals had been dying. Going missing.

He'd lost two wolves.

No more.

When members of his pack had fallen under the gun, Gage had known it was time to attack.

He just hadn't realized part of his attack plan would be so sweet. At least, not until he'd met Kayla.

Now she was bound to him, body and soul, just as he was bound to her.

A shifter and a hunter. How insane.

He caught her hand and led her toward the cabin. For the first time, the lady dug in her heels and his jaw almost dropped. *Now?* Now she was gonna start fighting?

Not when they'd jumped from the window.

Not when they'd been in the hotel parking lot and she could have escaped.

Not even when they'd been at that one-stop gas station.

Now?

The timing was so perfect, he almost smiled.

Instead, he tightened his hold on her and hauled her closer. "You need me to carry you in?" He injected a note of menace in the words. He was rather proud of that low growl.

Her breath huffed out. "Maybe you're forgetting, I *dropped* that knife, I—"

He heaved her over his shoulder. The lady was in one serious fighting mood now and she kicked and punched and, *ouch,* hell, yeah, he'd have bruises from that one.

Luckily, he healed fast.

She didn't though, so he made sure his hold didn't hurt her. Unbreakable, yes, but painful? Not to her.

Hurting her wasn't part of the plan he'd crafted.

But he knew some pain couldn't be avoided, no matter how hard he tried.

As they headed for the cabin, Billy rose from the ground and swiped away the blood that dripped from his nose.

Gage spared him one glance. "We gonna have a problem?" If they were, he was more than ready to kick ass. This, too, was part of the plan.

Kayla dug her nails into his back, and he almost shuddered. Did she know he liked that?

Later.

Billy shook his head. "No."

"Good," Gage almost purred the words. "Now go stand guard." *Cause company will be coming.* Soon.

Davis dogged Gage's steps as he made for the cabin. Kayla was yelling now, at the top of her very powerful lungs. Yells wouldn't do her any good. The folks close enough to hear her weren't exactly the helping sort.

"You sure this is a good idea?" Davis's voice was low. "Maybe you should just kill her and dump her—"

Gage knew his lethal gaze had stopped the tumble of the guy's words. Davis had always been too quick to kill. Gage had recognized that weakness, but he'd still taken the guy into the pack. He'd needed Davis's strength, and he'd thought that the pack bond might temper the beast's savagery.

Maybe I thought wrong.

Kayla stopped struggling. Even over her own screams, she would have heard the guy's dark words. Figured.

"I'm not done with her yet," Gage said, and that was all that he'd say to the enforcer. "Now guard the fucking perimeter, and make sure we don't have any uninvited guests."

A muscle jerked in Davis's jaw, but he didn't argue. Good. Gage took Kayla up the cabin steps and inside. He kicked the door closed and dropped her on the floor. Not too hard, but, she *had* pulled a knife on him.

Drop. Her sweet ass slammed into the old, hard wood.

"This makes two times, wife . . ."—he said deliberately as he leaned his shoulders back against the doorframe—"that I've carried you over the threshold."

She shoved the hair out of her eyes. Oh, yes, those golden eyes blazed with fury. "I'm not a sack of fucking potatoes!"

No, she wasn't. He didn't want to fuck potatoes.

Kayla leapt to her feet. "I *protected* you! Dumbass wolf! I. Protected. You!"

The anger in his own gut burned. Gage lunged forward, making sure he towered over her. "You set me up."

"I—" She snapped her lips closed then gave a curt nod. "Fine, I did."

He blinked at the easy admission. He hadn't quite been expecting things to move so . . . fast.

"But . . ." Her chin tipped up. Every time she did that, he wanted to kiss her right on that stubborn, sexy chin. "But I didn't go for your heart when I had the chance."

Didn't she? Why the hell did she think they were in this mess? "I saw the knife. Most wives don't exactly go around bringing silver knives into bed with them."

Her arms crossed over her chest. Did she huff? Sounded like it, and then she said, "I'm not most wives."

No, she wasn't. Gage stepped away from her and paced around the room. The place was pretty bare as far as furniture was concerned. An old, sagging bed. A wooden table. Two chairs. A dark brown refrigerator that hummed.

The cabin wasn't a place of comforts. He used this area for only one reason—interrogation.

It was the perfect place to learn the truth from his enemies. And the desert was perfect for making unwanted bodies disappear.

He'd buried his share of enemies out there. Vegas could be vicious. Only the strong survived. The weak . . .

They fed the animals in the desert.

He circled around her and headed toward the fridge. Gage grabbed a small bottle of water and drained it in just a few gulps.

The wooden floor creaked beneath Kayla's feet. "So . . . you really knew who I was, the whole time?"

He sat the bottle aside and turned back to her. "Yeah, I did."

Her chin was still up, but he saw the move for the defense that it was more than anything else. "Then why marry me?" Kayla asked.

Wasn't that the big old million dollar freaking question? "I didn't do it because my *boss* told me to." The jab burst from him. He didn't have a boss. Others jumped when he crooked his finger.

Kayla flinched. "That wasn't why I married you."

Did he look stupid? Was he supposed to buy her BS because she was good in bed? *Very good.* "How many?" He gritted and his claws were ripping from his fingertips. Faint lines of red bled into his vision. The wolf inside wanted *out.*

"How many what?" She fired right back as her brows rose and her small fists went to her hips.

"How many men have you screwed for the sake of your cause?" He'd like to kill them all. Every single one. Slowly. Painfully. The wolf was good at giving pain. "In order to get close, how many times did you strip and—"

She moved fast for a human. No wonder she was such a good hunter. In two seconds, she was across the room. Her index finger jabbed into his chest. "Watch it, wolf, or you'll make me lose my temper."

Right. Cause that was scary. Last week, he'd beheaded a four-hundred-year-old Born vampire. So compared to him, a curvy brunette was oh-so-terrifying.

He lifted his claws and let them skate down her cheek. "Don't make me lose mine." His threat was lethal. Or it should have been, but it was complete bullshit. He'd never use his claws on her. He'd already seen the marks on her beautiful skin. When they'd made love, he'd felt her scars.

Other wolves had sliced her sweet flesh. He never would.

Her breath stilled on a rasp, but she met his gaze. No fear showed on her face. She should have been terrified. Instead, her lips tightened, and she gritted out, "None, okay? There haven't been any others."

Wait . . . *none?*

"Despite what you think . . ." She jabbed him again with that finger. "I'm not a whore. I don't sleep with men just because of my job." Then she whirled away.

I hurt her. Her shoulders were up, her back straight, and Gage felt like shit. But he still asked, "So what made me different?" As a hunter, she should have been repulsed by him. All the other hunters he'd met sure had been.

Hunters. Humans who'd learned the supernatural secrets and were out to keep the world safe—by getting rid of said supernaturals.

They were as vicious as any shifter, as ruthless as the vamps, and as conniving as the demons. In short, hunters could be damn near perfect at killing.

Unless you found their weak spot.

His gaze drifted over Kayla's body. *Hello, weak spot.*

"Maybe I wanted you," she said, not glancing back at him, but striding nice and slow toward the opposite wall.

Good thing she wasn't looking or she would have seen his shock.

"Sometimes, you want something so badly . . ."—her voice dropped now, but because of his enhanced hearing, he had no trouble making out her words—"that you'll do *anything* to get what you want."

He knew that feeling. Hell, he was *looking* at the thing he wanted most.

Enough to risk the pack.

She turned to face him and her features were a blank mask. "So, no," she said, "I didn't *screw* you for the job. I did that part all for myself. Because I wanted to be with you." Kayla shook her head. "Sometimes, I make dumb choices. Sue me."

He'd rather screw her again. And again. But they'd get to that fun task soon enough.

"What's your excuse?" Kayla wanted to know as one dark eyebrow rose. "So you tagged me as a hunter day one, fine, I get that. Go you. But why keep pretending? Why do the whole courting bit? Why marry me?"

Was she really that blind? Had to be. Otherwise she'd realize she was the one who held all the real power. "Poor little hunter." He shook his head and tried to look like he felt sorry for her. "What happened to make you this way?"

Her other eyebrow arched, and a faint line appeared between her brows.

"So untrusting . . ." He continued slowly, softly, and the memory of her scars beneath his mouth flashed through him. *Poor little hunter . . .*

"You're a *werewolf,* of course, I don't trust—"

"Wolf shifter," Gage corrected as he cleared his throat. She knew the distinction. Calling him a werewolf was just insulting. "The moon doesn't make me howl. I do that, whenever I want." Nothing controlled him. No one. Werewolves were monsters made up by Hollywood. He was the real deal.

"And you do whatever you want, right?" she snapped. Her hands were fisted. Someone was feeling all feisty. Good. He didn't like her emotionless mask.

"Yes," he told her clearly, "I do." That was the benefit of being alpha.

"No matter who you hurt."

Ah, now she was getting personal. "I've never physically hurt you." Wouldn't. He protected those who fell under his charge and he'd *never* attacked an innocent. No matter what the supernatural rumor mill might say.

But other wolf shifters weren't like him. There were some psychotic bastards running around loose in the world. He knew it, and the scars on Kayla's body said she knew it, too. Of all the shifters, the wolves were the ones who danced the closest to the edge of insanity. Their beasts were just too strong to always be controlled by the men and women who carried them.

Wolf shifters needed a pack to hold them in check. To provide them with security. *That* was why he'd started the Vegas pack. Someone strong had needed to come in and take over, and the wolves—hell, yes, they'd needed to band together. No one wanted to start a bloodbath. No one wanted to turn feral.

But sometimes, no matter what you wanted, the beast could still take over. He thought of Kayla's scars again. The lightly raised flesh on the curve of her hip and on her shoulder. The narrow lines that slid down beside her spine. Someone had hurt her badly. From the looks of those scars, the wounds had occurred long ago.

When she'd just been a kid.

"In the dark . . ." he said, and tried to keep his voice emotionless. A hard task, when so many emotions wanted to break free. "All monsters aren't the same." She should know that. Good and evil didn't really exist. The lines were too blurred for that vague distinction in the paranormal world.

Her lashes lowered to shield her gaze. "I know. That's why you don't have a silver knife in your heart."

Bloodthirsty little vixen. He'd known she'd make the perfect alpha female. You had to be willing to fight to the end in order to be an alpha.

Kayla was a fighter.

"You were the wrong bait," he said simply. The words were the truth. "Your bastard of a boss should have been brave enough to come after me himself." Instead of hiding in the shadows and slowly picking off the paranormals who crossed his path.

Instead of taking my wolves. Two wolves gone. He'd better get them back.

Now that he had Kayla with him . . . it was gonna be his turn to use her as bait. He sighed, and with a genuine trace of regret, told her, "I'm sorry."

Her lashes lifted and she frowned at him. "For what? Kidnapping me? Bringing me to this rundown shack?"

Hardly. Those were just the start of his sins. Gage waved them away with a negligent flick of his fingers. "For what's coming." Then he took her chin in his hand, and kept his touch featherlight. He could already hear the approach of vehicles outside. The others had come much faster than he'd anticipated.

Gage had thought that he'd have at least another hour. But, no, the guests had arrived too soon.

They shouldn't have gotten to the scene so quickly, not unless . . .

His hands swept down Kayla's body. *Idiot.* He should have realized the truth sooner. She'd come far too willingly. He'd thought she was just changing her mind about him. That she wanted to escape with him.

But she'd still been setting him up.

His hand slid under her shirt.

She slapped at him. *"Now* isn't the time to—"

"You've got a tracker on you." Shit. Shit, *shit.* And all those scars that pissed him off—one of them could easily have been left on her flesh when a tracking device was implanted. Hunters often used those devices, he knew that. But he'd been thinking with his dick, not his head. *Should have checked her.* He should have sliced beneath her skin and checked like he would have with any other hunter.

Only she wasn't any other hunter. She was . . . Kayla. *Mine.*

As he patted her down, her eyes widened, then she gave a slow, negative shake of her head. "Stop the frisking routine, okay? I don't have a tracker." Her words rushed out quickly.

But would she even know if she'd been tagged? Or would her boss want to keep his secret watch on her and all his other hunters? "You chose the wrong side for this fight."

She swallowed. Her lips trembled a bit but she said, "I chose the only side I could."

Those cars were coming closer. He could hear the crunch of gravel beneath the tires. Either she was tagged for tracking . . . or the dark suspicion that he'd had for weeks was true.

If Kayla didn't have a tracker on her, then he could have a traitor in the pack. Because he had *not* been followed from Vegas. He'd made sure of that fact.

"When your team comes, what will you do?" His claws were pushing through his fingertips. "Go running back to them?"

Her gaze stayed locked on his. "I'm not going back."

Well, well . . . Exactly what he wanted to hear, but Gage didn't let his expression alter. "Good." Then, since she deserved to know, he added, "Because I wasn't giving you up." Just so they were clear.

Her lips parted in surprise.

Time was running out. Those vehicles would be braking

any minute. Before the hunters came storming in, he wanted his taste to be on her, wanted her taste on *his* lips. So Gage stepped forward and pulled her close. His head dipped toward her, and he kissed her with the wild need that pounded through him.

What they had, it wasn't about hunter and prey. It was man and woman. Lust. Need. A desire that couldn't be satisfied, not with just one night.

Maybe not even with a thousand nights.

"We're just getting started," he promised against her lips. *His.* His wife, his for-fucking-ever.

Just let the hunters try to take her. He was more than ready to rip them apart.

And they *were* coming. So big. So tough. So stupidly sure of themselves.

Pity. This time, he'd used the bait—and they were the ones running into a trap.

Another kiss. Another slow lick of his lips over hers. Then Gage pushed her back. Away from the cabin's door and windows. "Scream for me," he said.

She didn't speak.

She liked to make things hard. That was his Kayla.

"Scream," he said again and lifted his claws. He had to transform before the hunters entered the cabin. During those few moments that it took to shift, he was vulnerable. Open for their attack. He wouldn't be vulnerable before them.

But once he was in his full wolf form . . .

Ready for hell, hunters?

He smiled and knew that his growing fangs would show. "Your scream will distract them when they rush inside. They'll want to help you." While he had the chance to attack them. "Time to pick your side, wife."

Then the fire of the change swept through him. A white-hot explosion of pain as his bones broke, reshaped, as his muscles stretched and his body contorted. Fur burst along his flesh. His hands became paws. His body hit the floor, and when he opened his mouth again, the growl of a beast broke from his lips.

His gaze found Kayla's. She stood where he'd left her, against the wall. Her eyes were on his. Wide. Deep. Afraid?

Another growl came from him as he took a step toward her. He could smell her fear. A hunter, afraid of the prey she'd deliberately sought out. What the hell?

She could handle him as a man, but his beast made her shake.

A normal reaction for most humans, but Kayla was far from normal. He'd find out the rest of her secrets. He had to.

But right then he leapt for the shadows on the other side of the room. The hunters were closing in now. Three, two—

The cabin's door burst open. The men rushed inside. Still wearing their dark clothes and with ski masks over their heads. The muzzles of their guns swept the room—and froze on Kayla.

Bait.

"I told you she didn't go willingly," one of the men said. The leader. The leader always talked first and stormed onto the scene like he was some big deal. Gage had learned that lesson long ago. He watched, still and silent, as the guy pushed past the others and hurried to Kayla's side. "Where the hell is he?" The masked guy demanded as he reached for Kayla's arm. "Where—"

Gage's snarl seemed to echo in the small cabin.

Three men. One wolf. Perfect odds.

Gage leapt forward. Clawed the weapon from the first dumbass. Used his teeth on the second. They screamed and yelled, and their blood flowed.

Too easy.

The wounded men tried to slip back out the door. Fleeing. He guessed the humans couldn't handle a little pain. Hunters weren't big on courage.

Except for Kayla.

His head swung back toward her. That jerk with her was aiming his gun. The muzzle pointed right at Gage. Was that supposed to scare him? His hind legs shoved down, and he leapt into the air. He wasn't faster than a bullet, so he'd take the hit, but then he'd take out the fool who—

"*No!*" Kayla shoved the guy's weapon away.

Choose your side. It looked like she just had.

"Kayla, what the hell—" The human began, but that was all he had the chance to say. Gage's paws drove onto his chest as he took the hunter down. They hit the floor and the human tried to jerk away.

Gage wasn't letting him go. The leader was the one he wanted. The one that he'd use to break the group targeting his pack.

Gage brought his mouth to the guy's throat. He could rip the man wide open in less time than it took to breathe.

"*Don't!*" But, suddenly, Kayla was there. Coming right up next to the beast. "Don't hurt him. Please." A ragged breath slipped from her. "He's my brother."

Gage felt an ice-cold pain in his chest. So cold. But . . . since when did the cold burn?

As the cold spread through him, the wolf slumped away from the hunter on the ground, and he knew he'd made a fatal mistake. He'd been distracted. He'd heard Kayla's cry and his attention had slipped away from the hunter.

Second weapon. He should have known the guy would have one. All damn hunters did.

The asshole in the ski mask still had his gun up. When he'd fired, the weapon hadn't made a sound, but its bullet had torn straight into Gage's chest.

Kayla's presence should have distracted her team.

Not me.

Gage's form convulsed, and he shuddered as pain lanced through him. The pain—that was coming from the shift. His body was transforming rapidly—too rapidly—back into the body of a man. Gage stared down at his chest. That wasn't a normal bullet.

Something was hanging out of the back of that bullet. Like a—feather?

Then he knew. *Fuck me.*

Tranq.

"Bastard . . ." He managed to wheeze the word. Speech was near damn impossible.

He couldn't control his body. Couldn't stop the shift. Couldn't do anything but hit the floor as the tranquilizer poured through his veins.

"What have you done?" Kayla's voice came from a distance. She sounded afraid. Angry. Then she was there, touching him, holding him. "Gage?"

He couldn't speak.

The hunter could. "So it's true . . ." Disgust flowed through the man's words. "The others told me . . . they said you were getting too close to him."

Why couldn't he feel Kayla's fingers against his flesh?

"I didn't want to believe it." The floor creaked as the hunter came closer to her. "Not *you.* You couldn't be working with a dirty animal like him."

Things were starting to dim. Just how much of a dose had the guy emptied into him?

"Help us, Jonah," Kayla said. She was pleading with the guy. "Help me get him out of here before the others—"

Too late.

More footsteps raced from outside. More humans coming in, when the wolves should have been there to have his back.

Understanding hit him even as he fought to hold on to consciousness. Kayla had been telling him the truth.

No tracker. Even through the daze, he realized the significance of what was happening. Kayla hadn't led anyone to them but—

Betrayed.

The wolves who should have been there to protect him . . . one or both of those assholes had turned on him.

"I can't help you," Jonah said. "I'm sorry."

There was a whoosh of sound. A gasp. Gage managed to turn his head—it took his last bit of strength but he turned his head—and he saw the feather sticking from Kayla's chest.

The tranq worked faster on her. She fell immediately, slumping back on the floor.

The hunter's feet padded closer. The guy bent down. Put his fingers to Kayla's throat.

He still had on his ski mask, but Gage didn't need to see the man's face. He had the bastard's scent now, and he'd be able to track him any place. Brother or not . . . "Y-you're . . . dead . . ."

Through the ski mask, the one she'd called Jonah stared back at him with golden eyes an exact shade to match Kayla's. "No, wolf, you are."

The darkness swept over Gage, but he still smiled as the drugs pumped through him. Smiled because he knew the hunter was wrong. And when Gage woke again . . .

He'd make sure the hunter got just what he deserved.

CHAPTER FOUR

She was in a cage.

Kayla's head hurt, pounded like a freaking bitch, and she was *caged*.

The cage was the first thing she noticed when she opened her eyes. Rather hard to miss it since the bars were over her head where a ceiling should be.

Holding prison. Yeah, dammit, she knew this place. She'd seen a unit like this plenty of times before.

A cage to hold shifters.

I'm not a shifter.

"Hello, sweetheart."

She was just married to one.

Her head turned slowly to the left as she followed the sound of that deep voice, and that was when she noticed the second big important fact of the moment. She wasn't alone in that cage. Gage. A big, half-naked, *pissed* Gage was beside her. And . . . and he was chained to her.

A silver handcuff circled his right wrist. A chain extended from that cuff . . . extended about five feet . . . then ended in the matching silver cuff that locked around her left wrist.

"What the hell?" She jerked off the small bed. More of a cot than anything else. The bars of their cage were silver, she knew that. The better to keep the wolves in place. Because every time they touched silver . . .

They could burn.

She grabbed Gage's wrist. The flesh was an angry red. Blistered.

"Don't worry," he told her, with a flash of that crooked, half-smile, "you can kiss it later and make it all better."

She dropped his hand.

He grabbed hers right back as the smile vanished from his face. "I'm killing him."

The cold knot in her stomach told her exactly who he was taking about. "Don't." How had things gotten so screwed to hell and back? "He's all I have left."

"Then he shouldn't have fucking *shot* you."

She had nothing to say to that. The chain hung between them. With her free hand, she reached up and rubbed her chest. It hurt, ached, and she knew there'd be one shiner of a bruise on her flesh where she'd taken the tranq.

How could she explain this? Right then, she was more than ready to tear off Jonah's head, but . . . he really was all that she had left. "He's had a hard time with wolves."

"Yeah, cry me a bleeding river." Gage's eyes blazed at her. "The dick shot his own sister, so I don't care what kind of sob story you spin. He's a dead man."

She glanced over her shoulder because she didn't want to look in his eyes anymore. She wasn't going to let him go after her brother, but she wasn't about to argue right then, not with cameras on them.

And she was sure they were being watched. Her gaze went to the left. The right. Ah . . . there. Nestled in the far corner of the room. The slowly rotating camera had to be recording their every move.

Rats in a cage. No, wolves in a cage.

But . . . just why were they still alive? Her, okay, sure, she was human, so they wouldn't just bury a silver bullet in her heart and dump her body. But Gage? He was at the top of Lyle's most wanted list.

So why was he caged and not killed?

"Is this the MO?" He wanted to know and he tugged on

her wrist to pull her attention back to him. "You catch the wolves, then you lock them up here?"

She licked her lips. "Sometimes."

"And sometimes you just kill them."

Her gaze snapped back to his. "The only shifters we hunt are those who've been preying on humans. *Killing* humans. What are we supposed to do? Let human cops go after them?" Her laugh was bitter. She'd learned the brutal truth about the way that worked when she'd been sixteen. "Human cops wouldn't be able to handle the monsters." That was why her team was called in.

"But you can," he said flatly.

"I can." Whispered. Her team could. Lyle's group was contracted by Uncle Sam. The government knew all about supernaturals, and they paid a good penny to make sure that the right people—the right hunters—went after their vicious prey.

They weren't just randomly picking up supernaturals. Not all the supernaturals out there were even dangerous. But some . . . some were real-life nightmares that couldn't be stopped by normal means. Lyle's team was hunting the cases that no one else could manage.

Stopping the killers. Taking out the nightmares.

Gage's brows lifted as he glanced around the cage. "You're doing a real top job of handling things now."

"Screw you, wolf." She spun away. Paced as far as the chain would let her. Kayla was in this whole messed up situation because she'd lusted after the wolf. She should've known better. Actually, she *had* known better.

"I don't prey on humans," Gage said, his voice quiet. "I never have."

Her fingers wrapped around the bars. The cage was built to keep supernaturals in. Would a human be able to find a way out? "Tell that to Slater Hawk." Hawk's case had been the one to pull her in on the hunt for Gage Riley. Slater Hawk had been sliced apart and then dumped in the desert.

"Since he's burning with the devil, I won't tell Hawk anything." How could a man's voice sound so careless when he was talking about death? "But believe me, that torturing SOB got exactly what he deserved."

Her heart raced faster. This was what she'd suspected, the reason she hadn't driven her knife into Gage's chest. "Why? Why'd you kill him?"

"Because he was a twisted bastard who carved up four showgirls in the city. I don't like it when women get hurt."

She'd heard about the attacks on those ladies only . . . Lyle had told her that the wolves had been behind them. And he'd had proof, not just some BS story. She glanced back at Gage. "Why kill a human . . . when your own pack was really slaughtering those women?" Had Hawk just found out the truth? "I saw the pictures," she told him. The poor women. Brutalized. Tortured. "I know the difference between claw marks and stab wounds." This wasn't amateur hour. She knew the difference, far better than most.

She'd carry claw marks on her body until the day she died. The chain clinked against the floor as Gage moved toward her. "If you cut off a shifter's hand while he's in animal form, that limb never shifts back. Certain hunters take shifter body parts like that . . . as trophies." His hands closed over her shoulders and he leaned in close to her. "But you knew that, sweetheart." His breath feathered over her ear. "Didn't you?"

Her eyes closed. He was too close to her. And she was too weak where he was concerned. "You-you're saying . . . Hawk killed a shifter and used—"

"No." Snapped out. "I'm saying someone gave Hawk that claw, someone set the pit bull out, and got him to carve up those girls so that my pack would look guilty."

Her eyes opened as she faced him. Dread was a cold knot in her stomach. "Why?"

Metal screeched behind her. She didn't look back. She knew that sound. The heavy metal entrance door was being shoved across the stone floor . . . screeching and groaning like an old man in pain.

Gage smiled at her, and the sight was grim. "Ask your boss."

Slowly, Kayla glanced back over her shoulder. Sure enough, her boss, Lyle McKennis, was stalking toward them. As usual, he was perfectly styled. His dark hair was slicked back. His suit was wrinkle free. And his handsome face even sported a wide grin.

Her heart beat faster. Whenever Lyle smiled like that, it was a bad sign.

Very, *very* bad.

The door slammed closed behind him.

Jonah stared down at the small video monitor. The wolf was touching Kayla again. That jerk was *always* touching her—and she didn't seem to mind at all.

What the hell was wrong with her? After all they'd been through together. *Why?* Why would she side with a beast now?

She had to hate the shifters as much as he did. They were all monsters. They destroyed everyone and everything they touched.

And she'd married one of those freaks?

He'd thought it was just cover. Just her following orders. Until he'd seen the way she touched the guy back at that cabin. When the wolf had fallen, she'd rushed to his side. Her fingers had trembled. There'd been fear in her voice.

Then when she'd looked at Jonah, he'd seen the anger in her eyes. His big sis had been furious at him for taking down her wolf.

"Great job," one of the other hunters said, as he slapped Jonah on his back. "Another pelt for you."

Jonah didn't respond. Did the guy even realize that Jonah's sister was in that cage on the screen? Lyle was walking toward her now. The boss had better get her out of there.

Sure, Kayla had made the wrong choice, but Jonah wasn't gonna let her be caged.

I shouldn't have shot her.

His stomach twisted and bile rose in his throat as he remembered that desperate moment. The others on his team had all been convinced that Kayla had turned traitor. He hadn't believed it—not until he'd seen the truth with his own eyes.

Bring her in or take her out.

Those had been his orders, and he sure hadn't planned to let the trigger-happy hunters with him get a shot at her. Max and Bryan tended to shoot first and celebrate immediately. Of course, right then, they weren't celebrating anything.

They were being stitched back together, courtesy of Kayla's wolf and his killer claws.

"Sorry about your sister," the hunter next to him said. Travis. One of the new guys that Lyle had brought in recently. So he *did* realize that Kayla was the one being held like an animal.

Only she's not.

"The boss will clear this up," Jonah said. Lyle had to fix this mess. Kayla was the one thing that mattered to Jonah, and he wouldn't watch as—

Lyle wasn't heading toward the cage. He walked right up to the video camera. Smiled into the lens. Then Jonah heard the boss say, "I got this," right before the lead hunter reached up—and yanked out the video and audio surveillance system.

The screen immediately went blank. What the hell? This wasn't protocol. All interrogations were to be monitored. Those were orders that came straight down from the federal government. *All* of 'em had to be recorded. And with his sister involved . . .

Jonah spun on his heel, but Travis grabbed him and pulled him back. "Sorry, man," Travis said, with a shake of his blond head. "But I've got orders—and you're not leaving this room."

The door opened. Two more hunters entered the surveillance area.

"When family's involved, hell, it's just a bitch." Travis exhaled as he shook his head again. "You just sit tight, and this will all be over soon."

The hell it would.

"What are you doing, Lyle?" Kayla demanded, grabbing at the bars with white-knuckled fists. "You can't—that camera is always supposed to stay on!"

Gage realized that his little hunter sounded furious.

She didn't realize what was happening.

Gage stood in the middle of the cage—*he hated cages*—and watched silently as the one she'd called Lyle turned to face them. What the guy was doing was pretty obvious.

He was making sure he didn't have an audience for this little party.

And Gage knew exactly *why*.

Laughter pulled from him. Deep. Mocking. Did the hunters even realize what was happening?

Lyle smiled, flashing white and very sharp teeth.

"You know . . . for a hunter . . ." Gage kept his voice bland. "You sure as shit smell like a shifter."

Because there was no mistaking that scent. Wild. Woodsy. *Animal.*

It was a little bonus that Mother Nature had given the supernaturals. They could always recognize their own kind. Demons could always see right through the glamour and find their brethren. Witches could feel the pull of magic exerted by others like them.

As for shifters . . . one smell was all it took to recognize another animal.

Kayla's shoulders stiffened. She was still staring at Lyle, but the tension in her body was screaming right then.

Only she *wasn't* screaming. When she spoke, her words

were soft. "You're wrong. Lyle McKennis is the lead hunter in the area. He can't be a shifter."

"Why?" Gage asked as Lyle kept the smile on his face. "Because he's the big, bad boss who's sent you out to kill the shifters in this town? Sorry, sweetheart, but our kind has a long and vicious history of turning on each other."

Only Lyle had gotten smart. The jerk didn't have a pack of his own, so he'd tricked humans into killing for him.

Shifters truly were very good at lying.

Lyle was almost at the cage now.

"That's not true," Kayla said and gave a fast, negative shake of her head. "He's the one who found me and Lyle after—after our parents were killed. He saved us, got us help—"

Fast as a striking snake, Lyle's hand shot through the cage bars. His claws were out, and they shoved right against Kayla's throat. "And I'm the one who's gonna kill you, too, if you don't do exactly what I say."

He was a dead man.

Gage rolled his shoulders. He let his own claws break from his fingertips. "I'm guessing you don't want to die easily," he said in a considering way as he studied the other shifter. "You want me to take my time with things. Strip away your flesh. Make you beg and scream before I give you that fucking sweet release of death." The guy had to want that—or else he wouldn't be touching Kayla.

Lyle's green eyes narrowed. He was staring at Kayla, not Gage. And the bastard *needed* to move those damn claws away from her.

Gage's nostrils widened. A new scent had hit the air. Blood. Kayla's blood.

A snarl sprang from his lips, and he leapt those few feet that would take him to the side of the cage. He slashed out with his own claws, and if Lyle had moved even one second slower, he would have cut the guy's hand off.

"Don't fucking touch her." Gage's lethal order was the growl of a beast. His wolf wanted out.

Sure, wolves liked the scent of blood just as much as any shifter, but not when that scent belonged to a mate.

And Kayla was most definitely *his*.

When the blood scent came from a mate, the wolf within just wanted to destroy any threat near her.

Lyle had backed up and made sure to get clear of the cage. His cocky smile was back. "I thought it might be like that. I mean . . . I knew the truth about her for years. I figured if I just put her in the right wolf's path . . ."

Gage pulled Kayla away from the bars. He looked at her throat and lightly touched the flesh. Just scratches, but he understood the point Lyle had wanted to make.

I can kill her. You can watch.

Screw that.

This Lyle asshole could watch while Gage cut *him* open.

"What truth?" Kayla demanded as he pushed Gage's hands away.

It was Lyle's turn to laugh now. "Why, exactly, do you think your wolf married you? Because he took one look at you—and fell in love?" His voice mocked her.

How could they get out of the cage? How could he shut that jerk's mouth?

Kayla's breath heaved. "I don't—"

"You're a potential mate for a wolf shifter. Your scent is different, at least it always was to me." Lyle's gaze darted to Gage. "And I'm betting it is to him, too. One scent, just one deep breath, and I could tell you were . . . ripe."

"Bastard!" Kayla screamed. "I don't—"

"Of course you were only sixteen when we met, so I decided to give you some growing time. I knew you'd be the perfect lure that I needed." He gave a little shrug. "It's so hard to find potential mates for wolves these days . . . so hard, but in that bloodbath, I found *you*."

Gage barely managed to hold his wolf back. The beast was clawing him from the inside. Ripping and tearing with his fury to break loose. "What do you want?" Because the jerk had to want something. Otherwise, Gage wouldn't have woken in the cage.

He wouldn't have woken at all.

"I want your pack—and you're gonna give them to me."

"Keep wishing, asshole." He'd never turn on his pack. Pack was sacred. Pack was life.

Lyle's green eyes narrowed. "This city's mine now. I'm taking over."

It would feel so good to smash the jerk's face. He could already imagine the bones crushing beneath his fist. "Is that why you sent that human to carve up the showgirls? Cause you were taking over?" And using Hawk to do his dirty work for him.

Some humans didn't mind getting their hands bloody. Some liked the blood—some, like Hawk.

Lyle just smiled and his canines lengthened. "I've always found humans to be very accommodating."

"I'm gonna kill you." The snarled threat wasn't Gage's this time—it was Kayla's. Now she'd broken through the shock and was going right for the rage. Good.

They'd need her rage.

"Doubtful." Lyle didn't look worried at all. The guy just shrugged and rocked back on his heels. "You've always rather lacked what I think of as the killer instinct. Some humans have it . . ."

Hawk came to mind. That bastard had refused to turn on Lyle all the way to the end. No matter how much pain Gage had given to him. *I gave him plenty. Payback for the women's pain.*

"Some don't," Lyle finished. His gaze hardened on Kayla. "But if you don't do exactly as I say . . . I promise, I'll bring your brother to you in pieces."

Kayla sucked in a sharp breath. Hell. The brother was gonna be a problem for them. Gage hadn't counted on that attachment when he'd been doing all his grand planning.

Lyle obviously had.

When Lyle's gaze turned back to him, Gage knew the other shifter had planned for all sorts of fucking situations. "Your pack . . ." Lyle said, almost snarling. "I know you got them to pull from the city. To *hide*. That's not gonna work. They aren't gonna stay in the shadows and then jump out and try to take me down."

Actually, they were. That was *his* plan.

"So you'll take me to them." Lyle crossed his arms over his chest, stretching his fancy suit. "And I'll take them out."

So there'd be only one top dog in Sin City.

"Not happening." Gage hadn't built that pack from the ground up just to watch the wolves get destroyed.

Lyle pointed to Kayla. "Then she'll be the one in pieces." He turned away. Strolled toward the door like he didn't have a care in the world. "You've got an hour. So I'd suggest you start rethinking that position of yours." He reached for the heavy door handle, then glanced back. "Because it's so hard to find a good mate these days."

Then he was gone. The metal clang of the shutting door echoed through the room, and Gage swore in disgust and fury.

That son of a bitch wasn't going to push him into a corner. Lyle wasn't destroying the pack that Gage had built, and Lyle damn well wasn't hurting Kayla.

Not while I'm still breathing.

Kayla glanced over at him. For a tough hunter, she sure looked vulnerable. No, *broken*.

Especially with the faint drops of blood on her neck.

"He was . . . he was the only person who kept me going after my parents died." Her voice was softer, huskier, than he'd ever heard before. "Lyle found me, alone in that house with their bodies. I was holding Jonah, trying to stop the bleeding and *save* him—"

Gage didn't speak when she broke off and inhaled on a deep, shuddering breath. He just waited. She needed to put these pieces together faster. Didn't she realize yet what had happened? As soon as he'd seen Lyle—as soon as he'd caught the bastard's scent, Gage had known the truth.

"He—he said he was a hunter." Her shoulders hunched even as she wrapped her arms around her stomach, as if she were trying to hug herself. Or to guard herself. "Th-that he'd tracked the wolf shifter. That he was there to help us . . ."

Only Gage bet that if Kayla hadn't been so wild with her grief at the time, she would have seen the blood on the man's fingers. Wild with grief . . . and too young.

You were only sixteen when we met, so I decided to give you some growing up time.

The bastard's words rang through his mind. "You were just a kid. You didn't realize—"

Her savior was the monster who'd been at the door. The monster who'd destroyed her life.

Her hands fell to her sides as she lifted her chin. The gesture almost broke his heart. "He . . . killed them? My parents?" Her fingers rose to rub against her shoulder. He knew a line of scars was beneath her shirt. Right in that exact spot. He'd kissed those scars during that too short night at the hotel. "Lyle was the wolf who tried to kill me?" she asked, but he knew the words weren't a question, not really.

Kayla had realized the truth. After all Lyle had said, she had to know it now.

Dammit, he hated this. She shouldn't look broken. Broken wasn't his Kayla. Strong. Fierce. *That* was her. Not this lost shell. She looked like she'd just lost everything. She hadn't. Didn't she see that?

Gage caught her arms. Pulled her close. "When he cut

you, he knew." Sometimes, wolves could recognize potential mates from a scent, just like the bastard had said. But if blood was involved, oh, yeah, that recognition level amped way the hell up.

Blood always tells.

"Knew what?" A faint line was between her brows. "That I'm some predestined wolf mate? That's bull—"

Now a little spark was coming back. He didn't want a spark. He wanted a raging inferno. "There's nothing predestined about it. Certain people are genetic matches for shifters. It's DNA, not a merging of the souls." Some human females could carry a hybrid shifter. Some couldn't. Science.

But women like her were getting more rare each day. Had that been the reason Lyle first attacked her? Maybe he'd thought her mother was a match, but then he'd found an easier target just waiting there in the house for him.

"He won't kill you." Gage said it with certainty. His fingers flexed against her skin. Soft. Weak. Human.

"He won't get the chance," Kayla snarled right back and even though it looked like tears might be glistening in her eyes, her voice cut better than any shifter's claws. Good. "I'll take his heart first, then shove it right down that bastard's throat."

Ah . . . inferno. There was the woman he wanted.

"Only if you beat me to the attack," Gage said. She wouldn't. "Now, sweetheart, it's time for us to get the hell out of here." Because while Lyle might not actually carry through on his threat to kill Kayla, the guy would no doubt get off on hurting her.

Won't happen.

Or maybe Lyle would just kill her brother.

And she'll break then.

Gage wouldn't let her break.

There were whispers about wolves in the paranormal circles. Of all the supernaturals out there, the wolf shifters were the most unstable. The most given to insanity. Unless they had the security and the strength of a pack, their primal natures could take over with dangerous consequences.

Wolves weren't meant to be alone.

But Lyle was.

And from what Gage had seen, Lyle was most definitely psychotic. The sooner he was dead, the better.

Lyle walked slowly down the hallway. He didn't glance back at the holding cell. There was no point in looking back.

There never was.

Kayla knew the truth about him now. Good. He was getting rather tired of hiding himself.

A hunter passed and nodded his head toward Lyle. Lyle's back teeth clenched. They were all getting on his nerves.

Years . . . *years* he'd spent playing attack dog for Uncle Sam. Being the federal government's bitch.

At first, he'd hunted alone. So much darkness. So much blood.

"Sir." Another hunter slid by him. This one even gave him some dumbass salute. A new recruit sent up from some boot camp in the South. Did this look like the fucking military?

Lyle turned a corner and stalked into his office. He slammed the door, and realized his hands were shaking.

The wolf inside wanted out. He'd denied the beast for too long. He needed to hunt. To kill.

Not to hide in some dank hole in the ground. Not to stand back while the blood flowed.

He liked the blood too much to just stand back. Liked the kills. The screams . . .

Kayla's mother had screamed. So sweetly. She'd screamed and begged, and so had Kayla. The beast had loved their cries.

The beast had wanted to rip Kayla open, and he'd slashed with his claws. That night, he'd known only blind rage and bloodlust, until he'd caught the sweet scent in the air. Until the beast had realized that Kayla Kincaid wasn't just prey. She was something more.

Something far more precious.

The man had pulled back the beast. Stopped the slaughter. Of course, it had been too late then. Her parents had been dead. Her brother barely breathing. And Kayla—she'd been terrified.

Lyle paced to his desk. Sat down heavily in the chair, then looked down at the claws that had burst from his fingertips.

A slip. He was having more and more of them lately. If he wasn't careful, the hunters would all learn the truth about him.

He clenched his hands into fists and his claws cut right through his skin.

The beast wanted out.

And the man was just tired of fighting him. Lyle knew he was . . . different. Too savage. Too twisted. He'd always known. But he'd tried to channel that bloodlust, to use it— he'd hunted his own kind. Tracked the deadliest paranormals.

But they weren't enough.

Sometimes, innocent blood just tasted sweeter.

His teeth were lengthening. His bones starting to pop.

No, no, he couldn't shift now. He had to hold on just a bit longer. He had a job to do.

A pack to destroy.

The wolves in Vegas thought they were so smart. Banding together. Growing stronger. Wolves didn't face the risk of insanity when they were in a pack.

The pack is strength. A stupid wolf mantra his parents had told him long ago . . . before they'd been killed by the government. The same government that had taken Lyle in and made him into the monster he was.

The pack is life. Did Gage recite that same bullshit?

Blood smeared on his jeans. He barely felt the pain in his palms. When his claws cut him, he almost liked the flow of blood.

Almost?

If he'd had a pack, maybe things would have been different for him. Maybe he would have controlled his beast.

Maybe not.

But the wolves in Vegas weren't any more damn special than he was. If he had to face the fury of the beast alone—day in and day out—then they should have to face it, too.

They should all know what it was like to feel sanity slipping away, moment by moment, until nothing remained.

Until there was only fury. Instinct. Death.

They should *all* know.

He'd make sure they knew.

Because he was gonna rip that pack apart, even if he had to sacrifice every single hunter in his compound in order to do the job.

After all, what were human lives worth? Humans were weak, meaningless . . .

And only the strong survived in this world.

He was the strong. He was the alpha, and he'd prove that truth to everyone.

CHAPTER FIVE

"So how the hell do we get out of this cage?" Gage demanded, as he paced the small perimeter of their prison, and since he was pacing and they were chained, she pretty much had to pace, too.

Kayla hated the chain that bound them. And hated that she had to tell him, "We don't get out."

Those words stopped him. Gage glanced back at her. The faint lines on his face seemed deeper than before. "There's always a way out."

Such an optimistic shifter. She shook her head. "Not this time. The cell was designed for the maximum containment of a shifter. Even with your strength, you won't be able to break the bars. And when you try"—because she suspected he was already thinking about that—"the silver will just burn you. It's highly concentrated . . . the purest form I've ever seen." Guaranteed to make a shifter scream.

"So you're just what—giving up?"

Her eyes narrowed. Who did the guy think he was talking to? Sure, yeah, she'd had a sob worthy moment; wasn't a girl entitled to that when she found out her whole life was a lie? But she was pushing forward, and she wasn't gonna fall apart again. Kayla straightened her shoulders. "I'm picking my moment," she said, "and when the right moment comes, I'll get us out of here." The moment wasn't happening then. Sure, no cameras were on them. No other hunters listening in. But this *wasn't* the moment to escape. "In an hour, Lyle will be back."

"And you want to wait for him?" He looked at her like she was crazy.

No, what she really wanted was to slam her fist into Lyle's face. But waiting was all she could do . . . then. "When he opens that cage door, that's when we'll get our freedom." They just had to move fast enough and be strong enough.

They wouldn't have long, but that door *would* open. Lyle—lying, conniving bastard—would be the one to unlock the cage.

Then it would be their turn to attack.

Gage was back to pacing. "And what if they just drug us again? Instead of opening that door wide, what if they shoot us, then drag us out of here one at a time?"

He would point out that option. She shrugged and tried to appear careless. Such an act. "Then we're screwed." Because her plan—the only plan that she could think of right then—involved Lyle opening the door for her. He opened it, then she killed him.

End of story.

The guy had always underestimated her. She'd pushed for the more dangerous missions. He'd held her back, saying she wasn't ready.

I'll show you killer instinct, asshole.

The chain rattled. Her gaze lifted. Gage was closing in on her and his eyes were glowing with the light of his beast.

She held her ground. Her heart raced in her chest, drumming fast enough to almost hurt, and she wondered just how acute his shifter senses really were.

Could he smell her fear?

If we don't get out, I die.

Because she knew that when it came down to a choice between Gage's pack and her, well, there wasn't a choice at all.

Gage might think that Lyle wouldn't actually kill her, but Kayla knew better.

Did he really kill my parents? The suspicion was in her gut, knotting deep. For years, she'd been following his orders. He'd given her a home. Given her protection.

And now he wanted to carve her up.

Like he had carved up her mother and father? He'd been there that night, but not as the rescuer she'd thought. As the monster she'd feared.

Gage's fingers rose to touch her throat. She flinched, then realized that his claws weren't out. Her breath whispered from between her lips.

"I don't like that scent from you," Gage said, his voice a dark rumble of sound.

Uh, come again?

"Fear usually smells good . . ."

So he *could* smell it.

"But coming from you, the scent just makes me want to kill." Then he leaned forward. His arms wrapped around her and he lifted her up against him. Gage's lips pressed against her throat. "I swear, I'll kill him."

He was kissing her wounds. His mouth was gentle, but the hands holding her were hard with strength and power.

She trembled against him as his lips moved toward the curve of her ear, and that tremble—it wasn't from fear.

I should've had more time with him.

Gage hadn't married her for love, yeah, she got that part. But why couldn't they have just enjoyed a few days together? Had death really needed to come calling hours after she said "I do"?

Would it have been so wrong to take more pleasure? Before the pain that was promised?

I'll carve her up.

Her eyes closed. Her hands curled around his shoulders. She knew what she wanted.

They had an hour.

No cameras. No audio recordings.

An hour.

She rubbed her body lightly against his. *Take more pleasure.* Because if the escape plan forming in her mind didn't work, she'd know only pain in the time to come.

No, I want pleasure.

"I don't . . . I don't care why you married me." Her voice came out soft and husky.

His head lifted. She couldn't read the emotion behind the strong lines and angles of his face. And she'd always thought he seemed open? What a lie.

Shifters are born to lie. Lyle's words. She just hadn't realized—*he* was the one with the best skills at deception.

"I don't care why," she said again. She didn't even want to talk about that genetic match bull right then. She just wanted . . . him.

Maybe he had been playing her, the way she'd intended to play him.

Catch a hunter. Spring your trap.

They were both trapped then, and they had only each other. So she simply said what she felt. "Before he comes back, I want to be with you again."

His pupils expanded until only black seemed to fill his gaze. No more bright blue.

Slowly, he lowered her to the floor. Her feet touched the stone. Okay, right, she got that this wasn't exactly the honeymoon suite. The cage bars weren't sexy. The cot was narrow. The—

"Your timing is shit," he told her, voice roughening with arousal.

Um, yeah, true, but it wasn't like she had a rain check option going on then.

Gage pulled in a deep breath. "Don't cry out," he told her in that hard rasp that sent shivers skating over her body. "He'll hear, and I don't want him hearing a single sound that you make for me."

Kayla licked her lips. No screaming this time. Check. She could do that.

Could he? The guy had been pretty loud last time...

Then his hands were on her jeans. Yanking at the snap and jerking down the zipper. She kicked out of her boots and—

His fingers slid between her legs. Pushed up into her sex, and she gasped at the sensual touch.

Kayla rose onto her toes, trying to adjust to the feel of those long, hard fingers inside of her. She wasn't ready, not yet, but—

His thumb pushed over her clit. His fingers withdrew. Thrust again.

Her knees did a little jiggle even as her sex tightened around his thrusting fingers. Just that fast, Kayla knew she was getting wet for him. Adrenaline and need fired her blood and her nails scratched over his arms as she pulled him closer.

When they kissed, there was nothing soft or gentle about it. Wild. Heat. Hunger.

Craving.

If this was her last time with him, she'd take everything he had. There was no control. No holding part of herself back.

Only lust. Only him.

He lifted her up into his arms. She loved his strength . . . when she'd feared that same strength in others. Her legs wrapped around his hips, and she held on to him as tightly as she could.

He positioned his cock at the entrance of her body. The broad head pushed past the sensitive flesh of her sex. He wasn't thrusting deep yet. Gage still had his control.

She wanted that control to break. No, to shatter into a million pieces. She wanted him wild and desperate for her— the way she was for him.

Kayla's mouth broke from his. Wolves liked to bite, almost as much as vampires. They liked their sex rough. Hard. Consuming.

Just the way she did.

Kayla pressed her mouth to his neck. Licked his flesh. Gage shuddered. Good, but . . . she wanted more. She opened her mouth. Put her teeth against him, right where the curve of his shoulder met his neck. Then she nipped him.

"*Kayla . . .*"

She knew that wolves marked their mates this way. A bite to claim. Was she claiming him?

She wasn't a wolf but . . .

Kayla let him feel the press of her teeth once more, and she could almost hear the rip of his control.

Better.

His hands hardened on her, digging into her hips, and he thrust deep. Gage drove into her with one fierce plunge. And it was exactly what she needed. What she wanted. Each withdrawal and thrust had his cock sliding right over her clit, and the sensual strokes made her whole body tighten. Pleasure. So close. So—

He took two steps, kept his tight hold on her, and Kayla found her back slammed against the cage bars. He was still thrusting into her and she loved it. But this position, sweet hell, it made him go in even deeper.

After living the last eighteen years only feeling rage and pain, this was what she'd hoped for.

Wild and hot.

Her breath panted out. She wanted to scream as the pleasure built, but she bit her lower lip to hold back the sound. He was swelling even bigger inside of her. Going even deeper. *Yes.* She'd never felt more connected to another person. Never felt as if she belonged to another, the way she belonged to him.

His eyes were on hers. So intense and deep. She could see the edge of his canines. Lengthening, because the beast was close.

Then he put those canines on *her.* In nearly the exact spot that she'd bit him. Kayla arched toward him. She wasn't afraid of the beast that lurked just beneath the surface of the man. She wanted him to bite her.

But—

Gage yanked his head back. Thrust faster. One strong hand lifted and wrapped around the bar near her and she wanted to call out a warning to him. He'd be burned. It would hurt—

Her climax hit her on a wave of pleasure so intense that every muscle in her body seemed to clench. She lost her breath, and when she opened her mouth to cry out because she couldn't hold the sound in any longer, Gage kissed her. He drove his tongue past her lips even as his cock thrust into her core.

Then he seemed to erupt within her. She could feel the jet of his release inside of her. Her sex contracted around him, greedy for that pleasure to continue. Why did it have to end? She'd just found him.

Why did everything have to be so twisted for them?

Why couldn't she just be a woman . . . and he just be a man?

Gage's mouth slowly lifted from hers. He stared at her with the hungry, lustful eyes of a beast.

Never just a man.

He was so much more.

Her heart raced in her chest. Pounded so fast. Gage withdrew from her—dammit—and carefully lowered her to the stone floor. When her unsteady knees finally regained their strength, she remembered—his hand. In the heat of the moment, the guy had actually reached out for the silver bars.

She caught his hand and winced at the angry blisters lining his palm. "Gage . . ." His name whispered from her.

His fingers clenched into a fist. "I didn't even feel the pain."

Her gaze rose to find him watching her.

That half-smile flashed across his face. "Fucking you felt too good."

She wanted to smile back at him because that grin had always gotten beneath her skin. That grin—from the first sight, it had told her he *couldn't* be a monster, even when she knew otherwise. But Kayla couldn't smile in return. She knew what future was coming for them.

And it wasn't going to be easy or pretty or *good*. In order to escape, she'd have to turn on the men she'd worked side by side with for years.

She might even have to kill them.

Or else she and Gage would be the ones to wind up dead.

"I want to see my sister," Jonah demanded as he marched into Lyle's office. He didn't know what the hell was going on at the compound, but he sure didn't like it. He'd been forcibly held in that surveillance room by the other hunters—*so much for friendship*—and then, twenty minutes later, when they'd finally let him go, he'd discovered that more hunters were stationed in front of Kayla's holding cell.

When he'd tried to go inside and talk to his sister, the hunters—jerks who he'd counted as friends before—had lifted their weapons toward him.

What the hell was happening? Things couldn't have gotten this screwed, this fast. It was like a nightmare. One that he just couldn't wake up from, no matter how hard he tried.

He'd been trying pretty damn hard.

"I *want* to see her," Jonah said again. He had to make sure she was all right. It was his fault she was in containment. *His fault.*

Lyle leaned forward in his chair and gave a sad shake of his head. "I'm afraid that's just not possible."

"Make it possible." Lyle could do anything he wanted. The man was the head honcho at the compound. He just answered to the government guys in their fancy suits—and those guys came around only when it was prison transfer time. "Give me clearance to see her. Now." Anger had him seething. He still had his weapon. The others hadn't taken that, and if he didn't get to see his sister soon—

Lyle exhaled on a slow breath. "You know she betrayed us."

The boss's words scraped right over Jonah's soul. His jaw

clenched, and he straightened to his full height. "There's been a mistake." That was what he kept telling himself. A mistake could be fixed. "If you'd just let me talk to her . . ."

There was sympathy in Lyle's gaze, but he said, "She'll try to bring you over to her side, too."

"I'm not goin' on the side of a freaking wolf!" Not after what that shifter had done to him so long ago. *Three months.* He'd been trapped in a hospital for three months because of the beast that had come after his family. He'd nearly lost his arm. Had been clawed open.

And his sister was siding with those monsters now?

"No." Lyle pushed to his feet and walked around his desk. "No, I never thought you'd join up with a wolf."

Jonah's breath heaved out. Right. Lyle trusted him. Lyle *knew* him.

"But then," Lyle's assessing gaze swept over him, "I never thought Kayla would either."

Her betrayal didn't make any sense. "Why?" Why would his sister turn on the hunters, on him, for a wolf?

"Because they're fucking."

Jonah's teeth ground together so hard that it hurt. *I'll kill that wolf.* "I can—I can get her to come back to us." If he could just talk to her—

"The others know that she can't be trusted now." Lyle walked toward him with slow, measured steps. His green gaze was watchful. Always so watchful. "What we do in this world, it's life or death, and if you can't count on the hunter who's supposed to be watching your back . . ." He shook his head sadly. "Then just what good is that backup?"

No good. Worthless. But Kayla wasn't worthless. She was everything to him. Jonah fought to keep his voice calm. So much was happening. So much he still didn't fully understand. "Why—why'd you turn off the surveillance camera?" That hadn't been protocol. Not even close. And with Kayla there—

"Because you're already in enough pain." Lyle's hand came

up and clasped his shoulder. "I didn't want you to see just how far your sister has fallen. I didn't want any of the other hunters to see just how twisted she's become. They thought she was a friend, but the truth is, she's been working with Gage Riley. She's been planning—" His hand tightened on Jonah's shoulder and his words broke away.

Jonah frowned at him and knocked that comforting hand away. "Just what has she been planning?"

"She was selling us out to her wolf. Telling him where our compound was located. You want to know the real reason all of Gage Riley's pack mates vanished from the city?" The faint lines around Lyle's mouth deepened. "They're planning to attack us, and Kayla was going to help them destroy every hunter here." The briefest of pauses, then, "Every hunter, including you."

Bullshit. Kayla would never turn on him. No matter what else had happened, he wouldn't believe that. Kayla wouldn't hurt him, wouldn't turn on him—

Not the way I turned on her. He could still see her eyes. When she'd realized that he'd shot her . . . *betrayal.*

She was the only family he had. When he'd been in that hospital, wired to those constantly beeping machines and drugged out of his mind, Kayla had been there. Every day. Bandaged and bruised herself, she'd held his hand.

"Everything's gonna be all right, Jonah, I promise . . ." Kayla's young voice. A voice that he still heard late at night, when the memory of pain and death came to him.

Jonah cleared his throat. "What's gonna happen to her?"

Lyle turned away and headed for the door. "Come now, Jonah. Do you really think I'd kill a human? *Her?*"

Yes. Because Lyle could be the coldest SOB that Jonah had ever seen.

And as his boss walked out of the room, Jonah knew . . . nothing would ever be *all right* again.

I'm sorry, Kayla.

★ ★ ★

"He'll be back early," Kayla said as she adjusted her clothes. "No way is he going to give us an hour. The guy will be coming back—"

"Now," Gage told her because he could hear the tread of footsteps in the hallway. Lyle had a hard step. Pushing forward with too much eagerness. The guy was hurrying down the hallway in his rush to return.

Cause you want to watch us bleed.

Kayla spun back to face him. Her lips were still swollen from his mouth, but her face was so controlled, so determined. She was a brave one. "Once we're out of the cage, that's when we have to attack."

As long as they didn't get tranquilized or shot first, yes, that was the plan. Not a very good plan, but all they had for the moment.

She pulled on the chain. "They think this will keep us in check."

Because silver could be such a bitch to his kind.

"But you can stand the pain."

Yes, he could.

"So the silver's not a weakness. It's our advantage." She lifted the chain and met his eyes. "It's our weapon."

Hell, yes, it was. Because Lyle might not be so good at handling the pain. The bastard wasn't an alpha, no matter what he might be telling himself.

Gage smiled at her. "Anyone ever told you . . . you're beautiful when you're planning to kill?"

Her lips seemed to curl, just a little. "Only you."

The metal screeched as the holding room door opened.

More footsteps. Lyle came in, wearing that smug grin of his. He inhaled, then laughed, "I knew you'd just have to take that one last chance to fuck her."

And Gage had known that the guy would catch the scent of sex on Kayla. A human wouldn't have known, but a shifter's nose . . . no fooling it.

Kayla's shoulders stiffened. "You've got it wrong. I'm the one who wanted the chance to fuck him."

Now Lyle's grin slipped.

Good.

But then Lyle pulled a gun out from the holster on his hip. "This isn't loaded with tranqs, Kayla, my dear. And you know I'm one damn good shot. After all, I taught you, didn't I?"

The chain hung between Kayla and Gage.

"So this is what's gonna happen," Lyle said as he came closer to the cage. "I'm gonna open the cage and Kayla, you're gonna come out. I'll unchain you, and if either you or your wolf try to come at me . . ." He lifted the gun. Aimed it at her. "You'll get a shot right to the head. Between those pretty gold eyes of yours. Then Gage can howl over your cold, dead body."

Fury and fear swept through Gage. He'd been worried the guy would try some shit like this—

"So you'll free me from this cage, and then do what?" Kayla demanded. No fear from her. Just anger. "Let me waltz out of this place?"

Lyle laughed. "No, of course not. I'm gonna torture you until you break." His gaze met Gage's through the bars. "Or until he does."

"I'm not the breaking type!" Kayla snapped.

"Everyone is, after a while." Lyle punched in a key code on the cage's lock, then scanned his left thumb. A soft click and whir sounded. Lyle stepped back and aimed his gun at Kayla's head once more. "Now push open the door and come on out. Then I'll un-cuff you."

So the torturing fun could begin.

Kayla glanced back at Gage. "I'm not afraid of pain."

"That's what they all say," Lyle told her, "at first."

Gage's claws were out. He wanted to rip into that bastard. He *would*.

As soon as that gun wasn't pointed at Kayla's head.

Kayla walked from the cage. Because of the chain that bound them, Gage had to step forward, too. Slowly, carefully.

"Stop right there, Gage, that's far enough," Lyle commanded and Gage caught the scent of the guy's sweat. Good. Lyle was afraid. He should be.

As Gage stared at him, Lyle's left hand lowered and came back up with a set of keys. But his right hand—the bastard lifted his right hand and pressed the barrel of the gun between Kayla's eyes. "Now be a good girl," he said, "and unlock your handcuff. Then drop the chain."

Kayla's fingers were rock steady as she reached for the keys. Gage couldn't see her face, just the perfectly straight line of her back.

He hated the sight of that gun barrel pressed against her head. Hated—

Lyle pulled the trigger.

CHAPTER SIX

The shift hit Gage instantly. A wild burst of fiery pain ignited within him as the wolf inside erupted in fury.

He fell to the ground, landing on all fours, as his hands began to twist into claws. The man couldn't control the beast this time.

Gun. Kayla. Shot.

There was too much fury. Too much pain and rage. Too—

Lyle's laughter echoed in his ears. "Don't worry, the first chamber was empty."

Gage managed to lift his head. The man he'd been was slipping away. Too much hate burned inside of him.

Lyle could have killed her.

"The second one, though . . . it's not empty," Lyle promised. "So stay in the cage, wolf, or you really will watch me blow her brains out."

The silver chain burned against his flesh. Burned even hotter now that the wolf was coming out, but the shift was exactly what he needed to lose the cuff that circled his wrist. Because he didn't have a human wrist anymore. The bones snapped. Elongated. Became narrow enough to slide from that silver cuff, and, sure enough, the cuff fell from his paw a few seconds later. The lock on Kayla's cuffs clicked open. She caught the chain, not letting it fall to the stone floor.

Lyle looked back at him. "I knew the beast wanted her."

More than he wanted breath.

"So I figured I'd see just how much control the man had over—*Ah!*" Lyle's words ended in a scream. Kayla had jerked the chain back toward her. Since it wasn't anchored to Gage anymore, it flew easily into her grip. Then she slammed that silver right at Lyle. Right into the bastard's face. The gun fell from Lyle's hands. A bullet fired out, slamming into the side of the cage's bars.

The scent of smoking flesh filled Gage's nostrils.

And since the cage door was conveniently open . . .

The wolf just leapt right out of the prison.

Kayla kicked out with her foot and sent Lyle stumbling to the floor. Then she jumped on top of him and wrapped the silver chain around his neck. Once, twice. "You're gonna play Russian roulette with me?" She snarled. "I don't think—"

Lyle tossed her away. She flew back and her body crashed into the side of the cage.

Lyle grabbed at the chain and the silver burned his flesh. *Your turn to enjoy the pain, asshole.* Before the guy could get free, Gage was on him. His claws dug into Lyle's chest as he penned the bastard to the floor.

Then he lowered his head for the kill.

Lyle started laughing again. "D-do it . . ." He dared and Lyle's face was showing the pressure of his own impending shift. The guy's wolf wanted out. It was there to see, in the bright eyes, the hollowed cheeks, the lengthening canines. "Do it . . . and her—her brother's dead . . ."

Like a human was really supposed to matter to him. A human who'd *shot* Kayla.

Gage's teeth sank into Lyle's throat.

And Kayla's hands closed around the back of Gage's head. She yanked on him, trying to pull him up. What? Was the woman crazy? You didn't grab a wolf by the head. She jumped back when he came up snarling.

Then she grabbed him by the tail.

The fuck, *no.*

"Please," she begged him, voice strained and desperate. "Let's just make sure my brother's safe first, then we can kill him, okay?"

No, that was not *okay.* He wanted Lyle dead then.

Kayla hurriedly backed away. He'd expected her to keep fighting. Blood dripped down Lyle's face. "Y-you're so . . . fucked . . ."

Said the man who was about to lose his throat.

"I'm . . . already in . . . your pack . . ."

Yeah, Gage knew that shit. Betrayal was a bitter, burning pill to swallow. But he'd suspected the truth, ever since the first wolf had gone missing. A wolf, one of his own, had sold him and the pack out to the hunters.

To this wolf in a damn hunter's guise.

Who is it? The demand of the man inside the beast. But the beast couldn't speak. He had to shift back to manage that. But . . .

But he heard the sound of racing footsteps just outside the door. The holding room might not have audio surveillance, but the hunters patrolling the area hadn't missed the sound of a gunshot. They weren't that clueless.

And speaking of that gun . . .

Kayla was back at his side. *Now her retreat made sense.* She'd gone for the weapon. Kayla aimed the gun at Lyle's head. Payback. She was a sexy bitch.

"Where's my brother?" Kayla demanded.

Gage kept Lyle penned. Kept that bastard bleeding as he let his claws sink even deeper into his flesh.

Lyle spat blood. "Gettin' . . . sliced open—"

She fired the gun. The bullet sank into Lyle's right shoulder. The shifter howled in pain and rage.

"My bad," Kayla murmured. "I thought that chamber would be empty."

Before Lyle could do more than growl in pain, the door of the holding room flew open.

Gage glanced up. Huh. *Guess we found her brother.*

Because Gage was staring straight into eyes the same golden shade as Kayla's. The man's hair was curly and dark, just like hers, but his face was harder, all lines and stark angles.

The guy was wearing black, shoulder to damn toe, and he was armed.

More men rushed in after Jonah. All wearing black like it was some sort of hunter uniform—probably because it was. All of 'em were holding weapons—weapons they aimed at him and Kayla.

"Shoot them!" Lyle screamed as he bucked beneath Gage's hold. "The bitch is . . . helping him! They're . . . trying to escape!"

And that was why Kayla should have let him kill the prick when he'd had the chance.

Now at least six weapons were pointed at him and Kayla. Not the best odds.

But he'd had worse.

"Don't anyone fucking fire!" That was Kayla's brother screaming that order. Would the others actually listen? Right then, they all looked confused. A little scared, too. Maybe they hadn't faced off against too many shifted wolves before.

Sometimes, the hunting was easier to do from a distance. When you got up close and personal with a wolf, the fear could slip past any man's guard.

"Jonah!" Kayla cried out her brother's name and tried to rush toward the hunter.

Gage leapt forward and put his body between her and the armed men. Had the woman missed the guns? He opened up his mouth and snarled a warning at her—and them. *Stay the hell back.*

"Shoot the bastard!" Lyle yelled. It sounded like the prick was getting stronger. Shifters always healed fast.

"My pleasure," Jonah said with a slow, mean grin.

WED OR DEAD 241

"No! Dammit, *don't!*" Kayla was screaming now. The woman's voice shook with fury. "If you shoot him, I'll put a bullet in Lyle's head!" Then she scrambled back.

Scrambled back—and pressed the gun barrel to Lyle's head. If the hunters had just arrived five minutes sooner, they would have seen their boss toying with her. Getting off on her fear.

But now . . . they just saw Kayla. Threatening to kill the guy they all probably idolized. Dumbasses.

"Kayla . . ." Sorrow whispered through her name as Jonah spoke. "You can't do this." The faint lines around his eyes deepened. "You can't—"

"He's a shifter!" She snapped back at him. "Lyle's a wolf! He's been lying to us all for years! Haven't you ever wondered why he didn't go into any of the interrogations with the other shifters? It's because they would have known what he was! They would have—"

"She's crazy," Lyle tossed right back as spittle flew from his mouth. "She's screwing that shifter, and she's lying to-to try and save . . . his ass! They broke . . . out of the cage and tried to . . . kill me!"

Right . . . who were the hunters going to believe? Their boss? Or the woman who'd just shot him, right in front of their eyes? Gage didn't wait for their reaction. He attacked.

The first swipe of his claws went toward her brother. *Shouldn't have shot her.* He sliced deep into the guy's arm, and Jonah stumbled back.

Kayla's scream grated in his ears. He hated the sound of her pain. But he couldn't stop, not now.

A bullet sank into his side. Asshole hunters. He clawed the nearest one. Slammed his head into the legs of another. Used his teeth to take down a third.

"Told you!" Lyle shouted. The guy's voice was *definitely* stronger now. "I told you he was a killer! Twisted, sick son of a bitch. Take him out—"

A gun blast destroyed the last of his words.

Gage whirled around. He saw Lyle groaning. Grabbing his leg.

This time, Kayla had shot Lyle in the upper thigh.

"That'll slow you down," she whispered. Then she looked up at Gage. Her gaze burned with fury. So much rage. *Directed at me.* So he'd made her brother bleed. The guy had deserved it.

An alarm sounded somewhere down the hall. No doubt, more hunters would be there soon in response to that shrill cry. Over-eager men and women who couldn't wait to pump his body full of silver.

They had to get out of there before the back-up arrived.

Kayla hurried to her brother's side while Lyle continued to scream.

"Jonah?"

Her brother's head had slammed into the stone wall— courtesy of Gage. He vaguely remembered shoving the guy back after he'd clawed into him. Jonah's right hand bled, the muscles near his wrist slashed deep.

The guy was trying to stop the blood flow, but his shirt was already stained red. "Why?" Jonah rasped. "Why . . . for him?"

She put her hands over his wound. "It's going to be all right. I promise, everything will—"

"It will never be okay, sis . . . *never.*"

Gage rushed toward her. They had to leave, *now.* Still in wolf form, his head pushed against her shoulder.

She shoved him back. "Get out of here, Gage."

That screeching alarm hurt his ears. And it must have messed up his hearing because there was no way she'd just said—

She yanked at her shirt, ripping the material, and wrapped it around her brother's wrist. "He's going to bleed out if I can't get this stopped!"

Were those tears in her eyes? The wound wasn't that bad.

She just needed to take a breath and see that. If he'd wanted, he could have made the dumbass lose that whole arm.

I just gave him something to remember me by.

He closed his teeth around her wrist. Pulled lightly.

She shook her head. "*Go!* I'm not leaving. I *can't* leave him."

But he was supposed to just turn tail and leave his mate behind?

"Stop them!" Lyle was shouting again. Hell. Could this shit get any more screwed?

"Go," she told him again, and dammit, those *were* tears. He hated the sight of them.

More hunters were coming. Gage could smell their sweat. Excitement and fear. They'd come in, and he'd attack.

They'd shoot.

Who would survive?

Get to the pack. There was a traitor in their midst. As alpha, it was his job to keep them safe.

Even if it meant leaving her behind?

Kayla's gaze held his.

No more time.

The wolf turned away from her and leapt through the doorway. He raced down the hallway, using his enhanced senses to guide him. Fresh air and freedom to the left. More containment rooms and prisoners to the right. Guards coming—

He dodged, leapt—and flew straight through the window. Glass rained around him and when he landed outside on the dank earth, Gage didn't look back.

Even though he knew the hunters were giving chase.

Fools. Didn't they know that in this hunt, they'd be the prey?

No one listened to her. She tried to tell Jonah the truth about Lyle. She tried to tell the other hunters.

They'd ignored her.

Cuffed her.

Tossed her into another cell.

Dammit.

Jonah had been taken away. Rushed to the med unit. He'd be okay. *He'd be okay.*

They'd stop the bleeding and her brother would survive. There just wasn't an alternative for him—or her.

Gage had attacked Jonah. She should have expected that move. You weren't supposed to trust wolves. Everyone knew they had a tendency to bite the hand that fed them.

Like he'd nearly bitten off her brother's hand.

A guard came inside. Curtis Latham. She knew him. The guy was new but she'd worked with him in the field once. Saved his ass that day, too. The guy had *better* remember that. Kayla ran toward the cell door. "I'm telling the truth!" Telling it to anyone who'd listen, only no one would believe her. "Go check Lyle's wounds. He's *burned* because I used silver on him."

Curtis narrowed his gaze on her. "You shot him. Twice."

True. Was she supposed to be sorry for that? "He put his gun to my head and pulled the trigger. He's a sick SOB that needs to be put down."

Curtis glanced away. "He's the reason I'm still alive."

Yeah, well, she'd thought the same thing, just days before. "He's lying to you. To us all! Please, Curtis, just go and check his wounds." Before Lyle healed himself.

Curtis glanced back at her. His eyes were confused, angry. "He said for me to guard you."

She grabbed the bars and jerked on them. "Where am I supposed to go?" Kayla all but screamed at him. "Just go look at him. His neck and his hands. The silver burned him. He's a wolf, I swear!"

A muscle jerked in Curtis's jaw. Then he slowly shook his head. "Lyle's the one who gave the order—he wants you to stay alive. If he'd really tried to kill you, then why would he do that?"

So that he could use her later. But that wasn't going to happen. Her time being bait was over. Didn't the guy get that? Gage was gone. He knew the full deal about her—about all the hunters. He'd escaped the grounds, and the guy wasn't coming back. Not for her.

Not for anything.

"I've fought with you," she told Curtis and knew that desperation threaded through her words. "Stood by your side. Covered your back. And I've never lied to you." She just had to make him listen. "Please . . . check his wounds. All you have to do is—"

The door opened. Lyle walked in, limping heavily Her gaze immediately went to his neck and—*healed*. No burns.

Bastard. Damn quick-healing wolf.

Lyle smiled at her, then winced, lifting his hand to his shoulder. She could see the bandages clearly. What a load of bull. If his burns had healed, then that bullet wound had healed, too. He was just playing a game in front of Curtis and the other hunters.

"Boss—you okay?" Curtis asked at once.

Kayla rolled her eyes. "Of course, he is. The guy's a wolf, he can heal—"

"Is she still screaming that story about me being an animal?" Lyle's steps were slow, as if he were hurt. He kept dragging his "injured" leg. Now that she knew the truth about him, the guy's acting skills were pretty impressive. He'd sure fooled her for years.

Why can't anyone see through the lies? Why couldn't I?

Maybe people just saw what they wanted to see. What they needed to see?

A hero. A man who'd saved her from the wolves. A friend who wanted to protect her and make her stronger.

Not a lying killer who'd just wanted to use her.

"Someone had to see your wounds," she told him. "Not just the bullet wounds—the burn wounds from the silver." There'd been too many other hunters in that holding room.

Someone would have noticed his burns. "All your lies are about to come out."

Curtis glanced nervously between them. "Boss . . . I, uh, I thought I saw some blisters on you—"

"She'd been punching me. The flesh was red from her attack." Lyle gave a little shrug with his "uninjured" shoulder. "I'll probably bruise later."

"Bullshit," Kayla called.

Curtis shifted from one foot to the other. "I . . . I know the difference between blisters and punch marks." He peered at Lyle's neck again. *Yes. He was getting suspicious.*

"Pull back his bandage!" Kayla urged. This would do it. "Check out the bullet wound at his shoulder, because I bet it's already healed, too." Curtis was starting to believe her. This would work. She'd get out of there and together, she and Curtis could take Lyle down.

"You're so desperate," Lyle said, sighing, as a frown pulled down his mouth. "When did you become like this? Did Gage make you this way?"

If Lyle had been just a few feet closer to the cell, she would have attacked. But he wasn't heading toward her. Lyle was closing the distance between him and Curtis.

"I don't want you to doubt me," Lyle told the hunter. He wasn't wearing a shirt. Just a heavy white bandage around his shoulder. A loose pair of sweat pants. "If this is what it takes to prove the truth to you . . ." His hands rose to the bandage.

Curtis nodded. He leaned forward. "I just need to know—Kayla's always been so—"

Lyle grabbed him by the head.

Kayla screamed.

And Lyle broke Curtis's neck in one powerful swipe of his hand. The hunter never even had a chance to cry out.

Lyle let Curtis's body drop to the floor. Curtis hit with a thud. Shaking his head, Lyle stared down at the hunter's twisted body. "You shouldn't have doubted me, kid."

Ice filled Kayla's veins. Horror and nausea spun in her gut, and she could taste bile rising in her throat. *Dead.* "You bastard—*why?*"

He looked up at her. Frowned. "It's your fault that he's dead. You should have just kept your damn mouth shut, and he'd still be breathing."

Only Curtis wasn't breathing. He was dead. And how many more would fall before Lyle was done?

How many had he killed over the years? When she'd thought that the hunters had been protecting humans, fighting the monsters . . .

Oh, God, we were the monsters.

Lyle grabbed the body and dragged Curtis's limp form over to the cell. Lyle dropped him near the bars. "There. When the body's discovered, everyone will just think you killed him. Curtis got too close, and you attacked him. We all know how lethal you can be."

Her hands wouldn't stop shaking. *She* couldn't stop shaking. Tears burned her eyes.

"He got too close, trusted the wrong person, and you snapped his neck." Lyle snapped his fingers. "Just like that."

Her knees wanted to give way. She stood only because of her desperate grip on the bars. "What do you want from me?" *Curtis. Dead.*

"I want your wolf."

She shook her head. "He's gone. Gage isn't coming back."

Lyle smiled. "We'll see about that." Then he turned away and headed back toward the door. Was that psycho actually whistling as he walked away and left her with a dead body?

"Gage chose his pack!" She cried after him. "Not me. That's why he left! He went to keep them safe."

Gage wasn't coming back.

Lyle glanced over his shoulder. "Then I guess you'll be the next one to die."

When he left, the metal clang of the door seemed to echo

through the whole room, through her. She looked over at Curtis. So still. His eyes were closed, his head turned toward her.

He'd been a good man. He hadn't deserved this . . .

She let go of the bars and her knees buckled. She slipped to the floor and her fingers, still stained with her brother's blood, rose to cover her eyes.

We're the monsters.

Why hadn't she seen the truth sooner?

Gage tracked silently through the compound. He knew where Kayla was, of course. Her scent was one he'd never forget. So he eased through the hallways, slipped around the corners, and tracked back to her as quickly as he could.

Outside of her new holding room, he paused. Inhaled. Kayla wasn't alone in there. But the one with her . . .

Shit.

Gage used the key card he'd "borrowed" from the guard station and swiped it across the electronic lock. The lights flashed green, and he shoved open the heavy, metal door.

Kayla was in the cell, on the floor. Her hair fell in a curtain around her. A hunter was slumped close to her. His neck was twisted, and his hands were stretched out on either side of his body.

"I didn't do it," she said, without looking up. "I swear, I didn't kill Curtis."

"Sweetheart, you don't have to tell me that."

Her head whipped up. Her eyes widened. "You—you shouldn't be—"

He glanced back down at Curtis. "There's something you should realize, though . . ." He made sure the door was shut behind him. "Curtis isn't dead."

CHAPTER SEVEN

Gage advanced slowly, letting his claws rip from his fingertips. The guy smelled human. Well, mostly. But he didn't have the stench of death about him, and usually, that scent came quickly once the heart stopped beating.

He put his hand out on the guy's chest. No heartbeat. That *should* have meant the fellow was dead. But with the supernaturals, *should* didn't really apply so much.

Then the one she'd called Curtis sucked in a sharp breath. His eyes flew open, and beneath Gage's hand, his heart started to beat once more.

Son of a bitch.

Gage had never seen anything quite like that.

Then the guy's head and neck snapped back in place.

"Oh, my God." Kayla's whisper.

"Not quite," the guy said, and his eyes—the eyes that still held Gage's, changed. The blue color faded until only black remained. "But I have heard that demons are distantly related to angels, so who the hell really knows?"

Demons.

And that's exactly what Gage was staring at.

Curtis glanced at Gage's hands. "I really hope you aren't planning to use those claws on me. Especially since I was gonna help you out."

"You're a demon?" Kayla asked. She was back on her feet now. "What the hell? A demon hunter at my side and a shifter for a boss? Are there any humans other than me and Jonah in this place?"

Curtis shrugged. "Probably." He lifted a brow at Gage. "Uh, those claws?"

Gage backed off, for the moment.

Curtis took another deep breath. "Thanks. I'd prefer to die only once today."

"Only you didn't die!" Kayla snapped back. "Dammit, I was *crying* over you."

"And that was really sweet," Curtis said instantly. "I was touched that you cared—"

She tried to grab him through the cage bars.

He leapt away and jumped quickly to his feet. "I *had* to play dead. Okay? What? You think I was gonna take him on? I'm a low-level demon. He's a shifter. If he'd found out what I actually was, the guy would have just sliced off my head."

That was a fast way to kill a demon.

"Broken bones . . ." Curtis sighed. "I've always had a special knack for healing them. Guess that's my talent. But there's no coming back once you actually lose your head."

Not for any supernatural. Beheading would pretty much kill them all.

"I was just waiting for Lyle to clear out," Curtis said, voice reeking of sincerity as he faced Kayla. "I had to be sure he was gone, then I was going to let you know I was all right. I was just about to move when *he* pushed open the door."

"Get. Me. Out." Kayla gritted. Her cheeks were flushed. Her eyes sharp, golden glass.

Curtis yanked his keys from his pocket and fumbled to free her. The second that door opened, the guy tried to scurry back. Too late.

Kayla slugged him. Damn. That was a powerful right hook. Good thing the guy could heal so fast. "Don't ever make me think you're dead again!"

"Ow! Shit, I was trying to help!" Curtis rubbed his jaw. "I

was waitin' for the coast to clear, then I was gonna help you get out."

"And you still will," Gage told him. He didn't know what the demon was doing working there as a hunter, and right then, he didn't give a shit. He just wanted to get Kayla out of that place.

He had to hurry up and go check in on his pack. Once they were secure, and once he'd destroyed the fool who'd betrayed him to Lyle, then he could come back and bring this compound to the ground.

Curtis nodded. "Right. I-I still will."

"We need transportation," Gage said. Number one priority. They were in the middle of the desert. They needed a fast ride, one that wouldn't be traced.

"Got one." Curtis nodded and rocked forward on his heels. "But I'm going with you."

Like he wanted another hunter riding shotgun.

Before he could refuse, Kayla nodded. Her eyes met Gage's. "If he stays, he really will be dead."

She kept acting like he was supposed to care about the hunters. But . . . *fine.* Gage pointed at the guy. "Demon, I don't trust you."

"Fair enough," Curtis said instantly. The demon was sweating. "I don't trust wolves either. One just tried to kill me."

The demon was a dick.

Curtis grinned. "Want to know why I'm a hunter?"

"Because you're a screwed up demon?" Gage tossed back as he scanned the area. No cameras in the room. No audio surveillance. Good. They were clear. *Let's haul ass.*

"Because two years ago, a wolf shifter killed my mother. A shifter I've spent months tracking."

The guy was staring at him a little too intently. "I didn't kill your mother." He hadn't killed a demon in at least three years, not two. And he sure hadn't killed any women.

He had a rule about that.

"She wasn't a demon. She was human." Sadness whispered through Curtis's words.

So the guy wasn't a full demon. A hybrid. That explained the human scent that clung to him—and that had to be the reason why he'd managed to fool Lyle.

Gage had an enhanced sense of smell, even among wolves. But Lyle—that guy might not have been able to pick up on the slight difference in Curtis's scent.

Lucky for the demon or else he would have gotten a broken neck much, much sooner.

Or maybe that beheading . . .

Curtis told him, "Lyle found her body, so he said. And he promised that he'd help me find her killer."

Only Gage figured that Lyle *had* been the killer.

"He promised me that, too," Kayla whispered. "He swore we'd stop the wolf who'd hurt my family."

"I can't forget her," Curtis said and the pain hardened his voice. "Her throat was sliced open. He'd . . . clawed her. Torn her open. I-I just wanted to find the shifter and *make him pay.*"

Rage was something Gage could understand. So was vengeance.

Kayla's glittering stare told him that she understood just as well.

"Don't worry," Gage promised as they headed for the door. *Get out. Get the pack safe. Then destroy.* "We'll make the bastard suffer." They'd make him burn.

Kayla knew they couldn't leave. The SUV was there, just about twenty feet away. The perfect escape. But . . .

But she couldn't do it.

Jonah. Dammit, there had been so much blood pouring from his wound. Was her brother okay?

Did Gage really think that she was just gonna race out of the compound and leave him behind?

Leave Jonah . . . and the others?

Can't get to Jonah while he's in the med unit. There'd be too many eyes and ears on him then. But while Jonah and the other hunters were getting stitched up . . .

We can save the wolves.

"They're in containment," she softly revealed to Gage. She wasn't looking at him yet because she was still plenty furious. *He'd hurt her brother.*

The guy would pay for that, but now wasn't the time to go at him for her pound of flesh. Now was the time for fast action.

Curtis wasn't with them. He was off getting ready to steal that sweet ride of an SUV that seemed to just wait for them.

Crouching, staying low behind a line of boxes, Gage turned to look at her. "What? Who's in containment?"

The breath she sucked in felt cold in her lungs. *We're the monsters.* Time to be something else. Better. "Your wolves aren't dead." She wasn't a cold-blooded killer. Neither were the other hunters. They were doing their jobs. Or what they *thought* had been their jobs. "They're in containment at this facility. I don't—I don't think they've been transferred out yet."

Shipped out to a far more secure location—one that no one had escaped from since she'd been in Vegas. The hunters weren't just attacking supernaturals blindly. They had a . . . hit list. Of sorts.

Most of their orders came from Lyle, but he was on a leash, too. Or at least, she'd always thought he had been. The hunters were tied to good old Uncle Sam—or maybe not-so-good. The government sent them out on missions that normal channels just couldn't cover.

When they caught their prey, they turned them over to the federal agents for holding. Or for extermination.

So the story went. Only now she wondered just how many "exterminations" had truly been necessary?

Her gut clenched. How much blood was on her hands? And could she ever get it the hell off? She was afraid that no matter how hard she scrubbed, the stain would always remain.

"We can get them out," Kayla said. They had to get them out. Now that she knew the truth about Lyle, leaving the two wolves behind wasn't an option for her. "We just have to move fast."

Before Lyle realized that Curtis wasn't dead and that she wasn't still locked in her own cage.

Gage's eyes hardened. "When were you gonna tell me they were still alive?"

"Uh, now?" Okay, yes, she should have mentioned it earlier. Would have if it hadn't been for the whole drugging and gun-in-her face thing. Jeez. She was doing her best.

"Both of them?" He gritted out. "Shamus and Faye?"

"Yes." And, well, they'd been mostly all right when she last saw them.

Before she'd headed out to say her "I dos" with Gage, Lyle had told her that the wolves weren't due for transport for another two days. So as long as those plans hadn't changed, "They'll be in Block B." Sequestered. Monitored. Getting inside that area would be tricky, but they could do it.

She wanted this blood off her hands.

Curtis hadn't returned yet. If they were going, they needed to move, *now*. They'd get the shifters, then haul ass back for that SUV. If luck was on her side—*yeah, right, since when?*—they'd bust out of this place before any trigger-happy hunters could spot them.

"Come on." She barely breathed the words. She had her hair shoved under a black cap and she'd donned the black uniform of a hunter, just like Gage. The better to try and blend in with everyone else. That blending would last only for so long.

But most of the hunters were in the infirmary or out on a mission. Only a skeleton staff walked the hallways and with Gage's enhanced senses, they would be able to dodge those guys easily enough.

He always knew when someone was coming. From what she could tell, Gage seemed to smell the hunters long before she heard them. Such a handy talent.

He nodded, and the hunt started.

Adrenaline raced through her blood, keeping her tense and edgy. But this wasn't her first op, and she knew how to hold on to her control. They crept soundlessly down the stairs that led to Block B. The transport area. The prisoners housed here were all due to ship off for continued confinement.

The only ones housed there now were the wolves. Category H—for Hostile Holding. "We have to take out the surveillance first," Kayla whispered. Her hands were sweating. Her heart beating so quickly. Escape had been at hand, but now they were in the belly of the beast again. All by her choice.

You owe the shifters. Do this.

The door to the surveillance room was shut. Her fingers lifted and punched in the access code. Lyle wouldn't have been able to reprogram all the access codes, not yet. At least, she *hoped* he hadn't.

The lights flashed green. *Yes.* She shoved open the door.

The hunter watching the monitors for Block B spun toward her in surprise. "Kayla? Why are you—"

Gage lifted his gun. "Don't move," he ordered as he stalked toward the blond male.

The hunter froze. "K-Kayla? What's going on?"

"I'm sorry, Thomas, but those prisoners aren't being transferred."

Gage was less than a foot from him now. Could Thomas see the flash of fang? Probably. The guy was sweating. Trying to back up and—

Gage grabbed him and rammed the guy's head into the wall. One hard rap, and Thomas fell.

Hell. Kayla raced across the room. "You weren't supposed to hurt him!"

"And he wasn't supposed to have shifter blood beneath his nails." Gage's nostrils flared and she knew he was pulling in the scent. His jaw tight, he growled, "The bastard's lucky that he's still breathing."

He *was* still breathing. But Thomas was definitely out.

Gage's gaze rose to the monitors. "Shamus."

She stood slowly and followed his stare. He was looking at the redheaded male wolf shifter who had been brought in first for containment. She still didn't know how an Irish wolf had wound up in the new Vegas pack, and from what she'd gathered, Shamus hadn't exactly been the sharing sort.

Blood dripped from the redhead's side. He stood just a foot away from the silver bars, and he glared straight up at the camera.

Shamus had put two hunters in the infirmary when he'd been brought in.

An animal. Lyle's words drifted through her mind. *See how wild? How vicious? This one will have to be put down before he can kill again.*

"Has he killed?" Kayla asked quietly.

Gage nodded.

So have I. When had the line between good and evil become so blurry? Maybe it had just always been that way. "Has he killed innocents?" she pressed.

Gage's stare slowly turned to her. "I'm getting him out of there."

Okay, so that wasn't the answer she'd been hoping to hear. Kayla grabbed his arm and stopped him. "If that guy is gonna get loose, then turn on humans . . ." She couldn't let that happen. That would just be more death on her. Kayla swallowed. "I've seen what wolf shifters can do to humans. I won't let him hurt innocent people like that."

Gage stared down at her. "When will you stop judging us all, based on what happened to you?"

She felt that hit all the way to her soul. But Kayla didn't

let him go. "Is he a threat to the humans?" Lyle had said so, but now she knew Lyle was a lying sack of shit.

That I trusted for years. That I freaking loved. He'd been a second father to her, only the increasing icy certainty in her gut told her that the guy had quite possibly killed her real father.

No, not quite possibly. *You did it. I know you did.* Her blinders had been smashed to pieces now.

And I was with Lyle. I fought side by side with him for years and didn't realize the truth.

She had to clench her teeth to hold back the scream that wanted to break free. She'd been so blind. So driven by rage and anger. Lyle had given her targets, and she'd been only too eager to attack.

"I trust Shamus." Gage spoke softly to her. His body was tense beneath her hand. "Things . . . haven't been easy for him. But he isn't psychotic."

As wolves were prone to be. *Like you, Lyle?*

"He's in control, and as far as I know, Shamus never killed a human in his life, not even those who deserved death."

Her breath rushed out. Okay, that was something.

"And the woman?" The female wolf. The one with the short, close-cropped black hair, the coffee cream skin, and the dark eyes that looked like she'd seen hell a time or twenty.

"Faye can't shift."

That surprised her. "She's a hybrid?" She had heard about another wolf like that, once, but that wolf shifter had lived way down south.

"No. She's full-blooded." His gaze darted to the screen that showed Faye's image. "But when she was thirteen, a sick prick got hold of her. A doctor who said he could cure wolves. Faye's parents wanted her cured."

"Why?" She'd thought wolves loved their beasts.

"Because they didn't want to be monsters. Didn't want her to be one."

Kayla flinched.

"The doctor pumped liquid silver in her veins. Burned her from the inside out. She's never been able to change."

Her eyes squeezed shut. She couldn't even guess the agony a procedure like that would bring to a child. "Wh-what happened to the doctor?"

"The human who got off on torturing wolves?" Fury burned in his voice. "Don't worry. He's not 'curing' anyone. Not anymore."

No. She bet he wasn't.

Not good. Not evil.

Where did Gage really fall on that scale? Where did she?

Her eyes opened. Determination fueled her blood. "Let's get them out of there," she said. "Before the next guard shift comes to check on Thomas."

She grabbed the key cards. Headed for the woman first. Faye stood in the middle of her prison. Her head was down. Her body held perfectly still.

But when Kayla and Gage entered the narrow corridor that led toward the caged wolf, the woman's body tensed. Her head snapped back. *"Alpha."* Hope and fear twisted the one word.

Gage hurried toward her. "We're getting you out, Faye."

Faye's dark gaze—her eyes almost looked pitch black—locked on Kayla. "The hunter? She . . . smells of you."

Great. Shifter noses. Kayla swiped the key card and jerked open the cell door. "Come on."

One wolf down.

One to go.

But Faye didn't move. Her gaze stayed locked on Kayla. "Is this . . . a trick?" she asked. Her eyes narrowed. "You hate me. Why would you help us?" That gaze slid back to Gage. "Even if you're fucking the alpha . . ."

Yeah, I am. And with shifter senses, well, hell, she might as well be wearing a giant neon sign that said, *Hi, I'm Kayla, and I just screwed the alpha.*

"Why go against your own kind?" Faye demanded and her soft voice was laced with steely anger.

"Cause they're not my kind." Lyle wasn't. He wasn't Gage's kind, either. He was just a murdering sick bastard. *That* kind.

He'd told them all that Faye was psychotic. That she'd sliced open five men in Vegas. Kayla had seen the pictures, but hadn't talked to the men. Lyle had told her interviews weren't necessary. Now she wanted to know . . . "Why'd you do it?"

Faye held up her hand. Claws broke from her fingertips. "The bastard doctor didn't totally kill my wolf."

Were the claws supposed to scare her? *Think again.* "Five men are now walking the streets of Vegas with your mark on their faces. *Why.*"

Because Kayla had to make sure she was doing the right thing. She was going against years of training. Everything she'd ever believed.

Faye's delicate face hardened. "Those men," the word was a curse, "got off on hurting women, and they made the mistake of thinking they'd hurt me, too." Faye's lips thinned. "No one hurts me and just walks away. Those days are long gone."

There was no missing Faye's intensity. Or the pain that echoed in her voice. Kayla stared at her—and believed.

Not evil. Not good.

Was the whole world a shade of gray these days? Everything had seemed to be in such big, bold colors just days before.

Kayla turned away from Faye. Staring into the she-wolf's eyes, it was a little too much like . . . *looking in a mirror.*

Same rage. Same pain.

"Alpha?" She heard Faye ask. "Shamus . . . I heard him yelling . . . is he . . . ?"

"He's next," Gage said, voice flat. "You're both coming home."

Home. The word caused an ache to lodge in Kayla's heart. Did she even have one anymore?

Don't think about it. Not now. She just needed to do the job. Get them all out of there with minimum bloodshed, yeah, that was priority number one for her. She slipped around the corner, punched in the code for the next holding room, and tried like hell to keep her control in place.

Time to face the big beast. Shamus would hear her coming, no doubt, but it wasn't him she was worried about. Well, not *too* worried. Not with Gage having her back.

We just have to hurry.

Lyle was too confident. He thought the silver was all he needed to contain his captured prey.

Guess you never thought one of your own would turn on you.

Time for Lyle to think again.

"Come near me . . ." Shamus bellowed and she flinched. *Hell, did he have to yell?* Did he want to bring all the other guards his way? "And I'll cut you open!"

Actually, that was pretty likely. So she'd better stay far away from those razor-sharp claws.

"I'm trying to help you," she muttered as she rounded one more turn and came face-to-face with his cage—and him.

Big Red was freaking huge. Had to be at least six-foot-three, maybe six-foot-four. His shoulders were like dang mountains.

"If you so much as scratch her, Shamus," Gage snarled from directly behind her. *Soft moving wolf.* "You'll answer to me."

Silence. Shamus's stare drifted between them. "A hunter?" Disgust dripped from the words.

"I'm the hunter who's here to save your ass." She used the key card and his cell door swung open.

Shamus didn't move. "Is this a trick?" His claws were up. Before Kayla could answer, he lunged forward—and those claws came right at her neck.

She jumped back, but Gage was already there. He leapt in

front of her and locked his hand around Shamus's thick throat and slammed him back against the silver bars.

Faye cried out as the scent of burning flesh filled the air.

"I *warned* you," Gage growled. Then he yanked Shamus away from the bars and dropped him on the floor. "She's mine, and you *don't* ever go at her with your claws. Got it?"

Shamus lifted his head. "G-got . . . it, alpha."

Right. When a lesson was burned into you, it was kinda hard to misunderstand.

Psychotic tendencies. That had been in Shamus's file. His gaze cut to her. Oh, yeah, white-hot fury and—

"Faye," Shamus whispered the woman's name like a prayer. The fury vanished from his eyes and was replaced by a look of longing so intense that Kayla felt damn . . . uncomfortable.

Faye had crept near her. Then the smaller woman paused, and moved nervously from one foot to the other.

"I caught your scent on the hunter," Shamus said. He rose to his feet in an instant and didn't even seem to be aware that his back was still smoking. "I-I thought he'd done something to you, that—"

"*Later.*" Gage's snarl. "We're getting the hell out of here now."

Kayla got the picture. Big Red was sweet on not-so-delicate Faye. But Faye wasn't even looking at him. She was looking *everywhere* else. The cage. The ceiling. The floor. The floor had to be real fascinating the way she was staring so hard at it.

Shamus had been captured when he'd charged at the hunters—coming straight in for a direct attack against them.

"You came at us because we had her," Kayla said, understanding now. That was almost sweet.

Shamus threw her a fast glance. Wow, wait, his cheeks had just heated. He didn't look quite so fierce then.

Gage caught her hand. "There's movement two hallways over. Guards."

Crap. Okay, the weird love thing between the wolves could wait.

She pulled out her weapon. She'd taken the liberty of snagging it when she'd taken the uniform from the locker room. "I'll get us back to Curtis." Then she'd leave Gage because her work wasn't done. Not yet. "You just stop me if you hear guards, or if you smell 'em."

No way would she walk into an ambush. Not with her wolf by her side.

Her wolf? Now she was definitely getting all possessive on him.

She was in such trouble.

Gage stopped her twice as they headed back to the garage. She knew he could have just killed the guards they passed. Knew that Shamus wanted to slice them open, but Faye's light touch on his arm seemed to calm the wolf. Right then, they were all focused on escape. But judging by the glint in Gage's eyes, the fight would come soon enough.

She just wondered how many lives would be lost when the hunters faced off against the whole Vegas wolf pack.

Not Jonah. She'd have to make sure he didn't get caught in the crossfire.

Though it seemed to take forever, they were soon back in the shadows of the garage. When it came to stealth, no one beat the wolves. Just get them away from that silver, and they were good to go.

Lethally good.

"How the hell are we getting out of here?" Shamus wanted to know. "There's a fortified fence out there, patrolled with half a dozen armed guards."

Once you got in, you weren't supposed to get out. Unless you were a hunter.

Curtis stood next to one of the SUVs. The guy was rocking back and forth on his heels.

Could the wolves smell him sweating?

"You're just gonna drive out," Kayla told Shamus and saw Gage's head snap toward her. "Easy as pie." Not exactly.

She glanced at Gage and found herself caught in his stare. "*We're* gonna drive out," he corrected. Right, ahem, he would have caught that bit.

But now wasn't the time to hash this mess out. Curtis had seen her and he lifted his hand, indicating the coast was clear. They hauled ass, staying low and in the shadows, as they headed for the vehicle. Shamus and Faye jumped in the backseat, and kept their bodies near the floorboard. For such a big guy, Shamus could sure cram in tight. If anyone looked over, they wouldn't even see those two in the back.

Since she and Gage were dressed like hunters about to head out on a mission . . . no one would give them a second look, either. Everything was working as she'd hoped. Now if her racing heart would just settle down.

"They'll track us once we leave," Curtis said. His voice broke at the end. Fear was definitely getting to him. He must have gotten too nervous waiting alone in the garage. "As soon as they figure out what's—"

She shoved him out of the way and ducked her head under the dash. It took her less than sixty seconds to disable the GPS tracker. Piece of freaking cake. "They won't track you now."

She popped her head up, and found Gage staring down at her.

And didn't the wolf look all solemn and determined?

"We'll come back for him," Gage promised her. "We'll get Jonah out, too."

She blinked. Okay, she hadn't been expecting that.

"Your brother's safe. He doesn't realize what Lyle is yet, so the shifter isn't going after him."

Curtis had run off and was punching in security codes, trying to get the gates open. And since no one knew he was supposed to be dead, he was schmoozing his way past the other hunters who'd just appeared. Feeding them some BS line about how he was off on another mission. The hunters were buying every word he fed them, and they were all just seconds away from a clean escape.

An escape that didn't include Jonah.

No.

"When Lyle finds out that I've escaped, he'll turn on my brother." She knew it. "I can't leave him behind." She wouldn't. She'd freed Gage's wolves. Done her part. Now they could get out of there. She and Jonah, well, they'd find a way out, too.

I won't leave my brother. Not even for Gage.

Gage lowered his head. "Yes, I figured you'd say something like that." His voice was calm. Weird. She'd thought he would fight with her. Do . . . something. The wolves in the back were dead quiet.

She stepped away from the SUV. "Go." She cleared her throat. "When this is over . . ."

What? She'd find her hubby and they could live happily ever after? That wasn't the way things worked. A hunter and a wolf didn't have a shot at forever. Besides, she wasn't even sure he wanted to stay bound to her.

Kayla pulled in a deep breath. So maybe she wouldn't offer any lines about what would happen when this mess was over. She could just say, "Go take care of your pack." Then Kayla turned her back on him. Dammit, was she actually tearing up? What in the hell was happening to her? She was a fountain these days.

She took one step, then found her body hauled back against Gage's rock-hard chest. "Before I found you in that cage"—his breath whispered over her ear—"I made a side trip by the infirmary."

Kayla tried to jerk free. *No give.* "Gage?" Now she was afraid because his low voice had been so angry. So . . . determined.

"While all the medics were busy stitching up the wounded

hunters, I borrowed a few supplies from their office," he growled the words.

Her heart seemed to stop even as a dark suspicion grew in her mind.

The heavy garage door was opening with a groan and shriek of metal. Curtis was rushing back toward them.

"Sorry, sweetheart, but I'm not risking you," Gage told her and shoved something sharp—a needle!—in her arm.

No. *Jonah!* She opened her mouth, but Gage put his hand over her lips, smothering her instinctive cry. Her feet kicked back at him. Landed a hit. Another. But he didn't let her go.

And she could already feel the drug slipping through her system. First her brother, now Gage? Why was everyone drugging her?

"When you wake up, you'll be safe."

And he'd be a dead man.

Jonah. Her eyelids fell closed and a tear slipped down her cheek.

CHAPTER EIGHT

S he was still out.

Gage paced beside the bed, shooting frowns at Kayla's unconscious form. Just how long was the woman gonna stay that way? They'd gotten away from the compound. Made it back to the safe houses he'd set up for the wolves.

He'd met with his aides. Gotten extra guards to start patrolling.

And she was still out.

Had he drugged her too much? He put a knee on the bed and leaned over her. She was breathing okay. His hand lowered to her chest. Her heartbeat was good. Steady. No, um, actually, it was picking up now and—

Her eyelids flew open. She kicked out at him and landed an attack right to his groin.

Son of a bitch.

"Tell me you weren't groping me while I slept!" she yelled.

He sucked in a breath. Well, at least she was awake, and she seemed very, very aware. No gradual waking for her. Just slam-bam, wake-up, ma'am. "No, I was . . . just . . . checking your heartbeat." He'd been too worried for a grope. But now that she was awake—

Her eyes narrowed. "Where the hell am I?"

Awake and enraged. He'd try to play things cool, for a while. "You're in a shifter safe house."

"Oh, hell, no." She jumped from the bed and rushed to the door. "This place might be safe for you, but I'm not a shifter. I'm a hunter. That puts me at the top of any shifter-kill list."

He caught her arm. Stopped her before she could race into the hallway. "You're my wife. None of my wolves would dare to hurt you."

Or he'd tear them apart. Simple fact of pack life.

Her breath huffed out. "Yeah, well, what about me hurting them?"

"You won't." Because she wasn't a cold-blooded hunter, out to destroy every shifter she saw. She'd never been like that.

Her shoulders fell. "I am so mad at you."

His aching cock attested to that fact.

"And I *am* going back for my brother."

Yes, he'd been rather afraid she'd say that.

"Those hunters—they all have to learn the truth, Gage. When they realize what Lyle is, they'll fight him. I know they will."

She had an optimistic side. He hadn't noticed it before. The optimism was cute. Kind of.

He freed her hand. Stared down at her and had to tell her, "Your brother's gone."

Her face drained of color. "Wh-what do you mean?"

"When Curtis came back to the SUV, he told me the guards had already reported your brother as missing. Even before we left the compound, he'd already broken out." He kept his voice flat as he delivered the news she had to hear.

She'd been so worried about leaving her brother, but . . .

He left you.

He didn't say the words. There was no need. She'd understand.

Now Kayla was the one who grabbed his hand. Her nails dug into his flesh. "Find him for me."

Uh, he had enough problems of his own right then. A pack to protect. A traitor to smoke out. A wife to woo.

Her dumbass of a brother could wait a bit.

"You *owe* me, wolf," she said and her voice rose a notch. "You drugged me, you clawed my brother . . . now you *find* him." She licked her lips, then whispered, "Please."

Hell. Like he could resist when she stared at him with those big, lost, golden eyes. She looked so sweet and innocent right then, but she'd shot a man less than six hours before.

"Wolves are the best trackers out there," Kayla said. Damned straight they were. "You can get his scent. You can find Jonah for me."

She seemed to be missing the point. So he had to say, "What if he doesn't want to be found?"

Her lashes lowered. "I need to make sure . . . Lyle is so good at lying . . . what if Jonah didn't leave? What if he—"

Died?

Gage nodded, then realized she couldn't see the movement. "I'll find him." He had to be careful. If he didn't watch it, the woman would realize just how much control she had over him.

Too much.

"But you have to help me find someone else first." Because he needed her just as much as she needed him.

A small furrow appeared between her brows as she glanced back up at him. "Who?"

"The mangy wolf who sold out my pack." He'd rounded up all the men and women in the Vegas pack. A pack he'd assembled.

Wolves on their own didn't survive. They needed the strength of a family. The security of a pack. Without it . . .

Hello, insanity.

There was a reason most serial killers were actually wolf shifters. They couldn't control their beasts. Not when they were on their own.

Hell, just look at what had happened to Lyle. The guy was grade-A psychotic, with no pack in sight.

The wolves needed the bond of a pack. Or the bonds of a mate.

Mated wolves never lost their minds. They never went down that slippery slope that led to the total darkness of the beast.

I won't go now, thanks to her.

Hell, yeah, he owed her. She had no idea how much. When this battle was all over, he'd make sure he paid his debt.

"I didn't even know there was a wolf giving Intel to Lyle—" Kayla began, but he cut through her words.

"You know now," he said simply. They both knew for certain now. "You can help me find the SOB. And stop him."

"Uh, yeah, I do have my awesome days," she said with a roll of her eyes. "But I'm not psychic. I can't just magically tell you which wolf has been selling you out."

"Sweetheart, we don't need magic." Because he'd already narrowed the field down to two wolves. The two that he'd trusted the most in the pack.

Those two wolves were being held in lockdown. Contained, away from the others.

His two closest friends.

One would be dying soon.

"Come with me," he told her and offered his hand. "Because I don't want to kill the wrong wolf."

She stared at his hand, hesitated.

Come with me. He wanted her at his side.

"Fine," she growled, almost sounding like a wolf, "but if I'm gonna be in a den of shifters, you'd better give me my gun back."

He almost smiled.

Such a bloodthirsty little hunter.

Lyle stared out at the desert. It just stretched as far as he could see. Appearing empty. Almost never-ending.

The hunters were scrambling behind him. Trying to secure the facility.

The facility could burn for all he cared.

He was tired of it all. He just wanted to shift. To run. To kill.

The quiet kills in secret weren't good enough anymore. Why should he have to hide? Act like he was something else?

The power was growing within him. The beast wanted *out.*

He'd come to this city, planning to take over. The place had been ripe. He'd been ready. No longer just taking orders from dicks in suits, he'd been set to change the game. To show them the real face of the paranormals they needed to fear.

Sin City had been meant to become his. He'd set his little dominoes up, then gotten ready to watch them fall.

Only Gage Riley was in his way.

He'll fall.

Lyle would make sure of it.

His weapon in this world was his gift at deceit. His mother had been right. He really had been born to lie. He'd fooled the hunters so easily. Would keep fooling them. They were his tools, and he'd bleed them until they were dry.

Then, once the other wolves were gone from Vegas, once the city was his, he'd let his wolf out. He'd let his beast rage, and he'd tear and claw his way through any hunters who were still left standing.

He wasn't a fucking lap dog. Not anymore. He was alpha.

Time the rest of the world bowed to him.

Psychotic? Insane? Those words had been tossed around plenty by his parents. They'd seen him for what he was long before anyone else did.

So he'd stopped them from seeing. From hearing. From breathing.

Wolf shifters were supposed to maintain their control and balance if they lived in a pack. If they took a mate.

He'd thought about living in a pack once.

Even almost taken a mate . . .

But he'd had more fun killing her than anything else. Kayla's mother had sure been blessed with one sweet scream.

Mates and packs weren't for him. He didn't want the rigid bonds of control that would hold his wolf in check.

He liked the blood. He liked the violence.

The desert stared back at him.

He liked the kill.

The wolves were chained to the wall. Chained with silver. Oh, jeez—who'd been the unlucky shifter who'd drawn that duty?

Kayla walked silently into the darkened room with Gage. Her gun was tucked into the waistband of her jeans. Hell, yes, she'd gotten it back. Like she was gonna just walk into this room unarmed?

She didn't really know how Gage thought he'd be able to use her, but—damn, that one guy was smoking. Smoke literally rose from the blisters on the blond man's wrist where he was bound.

Two shifters. One blond and fair. One dark, dangerous.

They'd been at the cabin. When Gage had first brought her to the desert, these wolves had been there. Like she would have forgotten them so soon.

I've narrowed it down to two. Now she knew what Gage had meant.

"Since you said there was no tracking device on you," Gage said as he crossed his arms and stared down at the wolves, "that means the hunters found us in the desert by . . . another means."

A traitor.

"I didn't sell you out!" The blond wolf yelled as he jerked against his chains. More smoke plumed in the air. The guy should know, the more he struggled, the more he'd burn. "Dammit, trust me, Gage!"

"That's the problem, Davis," Gage said quietly, "I did trust you."

Kayla's gaze darted between the wolf shifters.

"Just as I trusted you, Billy," Gage said and his gaze swung to the silent, glaring wolf. "I trusted you both. With my life and the lives of the pack."

Only his pack members were under attack. Two had been taken.

Where were Shamus and Faye now?

Gage crossed his arms over his chest as he studied the two chained shifters. "Only two wolves knew that Kayla and I took shelter at that cabin. *Just you fucking two.*" Rage snapped through the words.

The dark wolf, Billy, still wasn't talking. He just sat there, the silver chaining him, and glared back up at Gage with narrowed eyes.

"I've been with you for five years," Davis shouted, spittle flying from his mouth. "Do you really think I'd betray you to a human?"

"No." Gage spoke so instantly that Davis relaxed. Started to look confident.

But Billy quickly shook his head, obviously thinking the blame was coming his way. "No way, alpha, it wasn't—"

"I think," Gage said, cutting through Billy's words and still staring right at Davis, "that you'd betray me to a wolf."

Had Davis tensed at that? Yes, he had. His hands were straining against the cuffs. The guy was desperate to break free. Not that Kayla blamed him. If she were burning, she'd be feeling pretty desperate right then, too.

But . . . just how strong were the bonds on him? If another one of his pack mates had chained him, would that person have felt some sympathy for the shifter? Maybe not tightened the silver chains enough?

"A wolf?" Billy asked, frowning. "What the hell are you talking about?"

Kayla stepped forward. Gage had brought her in there, so

she figured it was time she did her part. "The leader of the hunters, Lyle McKennis . . . He's actually a wolf shifter."

Billy started to laugh. "You're shitting me."

"No, I'm not." Carefully, she studied the chained wolves. Davis had widened his eyes and the guy *looked* surprised. But his hands were still twisting within the bonds.

"And you knew?" Billy threw at her. "You knew what he was and you were still—"

"I didn't know. I thought he was human." She'd been blind. Only seeing what she wanted to see.

And was that why Gage had brought her in? Did he think he was blind where these two wolves were concerned?

She could understand the fear. When you trusted someone so much, it was easy for the person to mislead you. To lie right to your face.

But this time, things were different. It wasn't just about blind faith. Because this time, Kayla had a way to help Gage. After all, this really was her area of expertise. "Lyle's sent other folks undercover in packs before." He liked to do that. Divide and conquer, that was his strategy.

"Like he sent you?" Davis demanded. His hands stilled as he looked up at her. "He just tossed you right at the big boss."

"I've been working with Lyle for years, so he didn't track me." No, when Gage had first asked her about a tracking device, she'd immediately denied having one. But, actually, years before, Lyle had implanted one just under her right shoulder.

She'd dug it out. She wasn't a dog to be tracked. Not even by the man she'd put up on a stupid pedestal.

And he sure did fall.

So Lyle checked in with her via regular calls. He didn't use the calls with his other hunters. That would have been too risky. Or so he said. He'd given her special privileges, because she'd been his top hunter.

So he'd said. *Lying asshole.*

"They all have trackers," she whispered. "All the other

hunters. In case they're ever captured or for when they find a target . . ." The better to apprehend them. The better to send in the team.

Just like the team had come for her and Gage.

The chained men frowned at her. The silence in the room seemed heavy. Too thick.

"And you *don't* have a tracker, Kayla?" Gage asked, voice deep and rumbling as he broke through that silence.

She shook her head. But, hell, maybe that wasn't good enough. She pulled over the neck of her shirt, revealing the thin scar that sliced around her shoulder. "I took it out two years ago."

She'd thought it would be hard to figure out which member of the pack was betraying Gage. Checking all the pack for trackers? Yeah, she'd see that going over real well. Like they'd all be willing to strip for a hunter and let her search their bodies.

But with just two men . . . finding the tracking device would be a piece of cake.

"Who has it?" Kayla whispered as her gaze darted between Davis and Billy.

"Search me all you want, sweet thing," Billy invited, his slight accent thickening. "Strip me. Feel me up. I don't have—"

Davis lunged away from the wall —and his hands were free. Tricky wolf, he *had* been breaking out of his bonds.

But she'd suspected that. She dodged when he came at her, slicing with his claws. Kayla hit the floor and missed the claws that could have cut her open. Davis twisted, trying to come at her again.

But Gage had him. He caught the other shifter's hands and held them above Davis's head.

"You sold us out!" Gage snarled.

But Davis just laughed. "So the fuck did you. You're the one screwing a hunter."

Kayla grabbed the silver chain that had fallen behind

Davis. "No, he's not just screwing me." She wanted to set that record straight. "He *married* me." She slammed the chain into Davis's side and watched him fall, howling. "So don't forget that!"

Then she turned to the other wolf. Billy. The guy was watching her with a slight grin on his face.

The silver.

Okay, if he was innocent, then it was time to free him. She rushed to him and started jerking on the chains.

"If Gage hadn't married you," Billy said as his grin widened a bit more, "then I would've. I love it when a woman kicks ass. There's nothing sexier."

The door opened. More wolves came rushing in. Wolves and that enhanced hearing of theirs. She guessed the guards outside had heard everything.

One shifter, a woman with short red hair, tossed Kayla a pair of keys. While she went to work on Billy's chains, the other wolves closed in around Davis.

This wasn't gonna be pretty. Shifter battles never were.

"Why?" She heard Gage demand. "Why would you turn on your pack? You let them take Shamus and Faye. You let them take our own damn family."

Because to the wolves, pack was family. A bond that went even deeper than blood.

"They're not my family. They're strays. Strays that didn't belong in *my* pack."

Shamus shoved through the crowd of wolves. His claws were out and his face twisted with his fury. It took three other wolves to hold the guy back when he went for Davis's throat.

Free now, Billy stalked to Gage's side. Good. He was showing that he stood with the alpha. Even if the alpha had ordered him chained.

"You were a stray, too," Gage said, voice lethal. "We all were. That's why we came together. To be more. To be stronger."

"With you at the lead." Davis's lips turned up in a sneer. "Cause you think you're the only damn alpha around."

"And you thought you could take me?"

"When the time was right, I fucking was!"

The right time . . . "When was that gonna be?" Kayla asked, her own body tight with fury. "When you'd let the hunters take out all the other wolves? When you thought no one would come to Gage's aid? When you thought he was gonna be weak—"

"And I would be strong!" Davis yelled.

More growls from the wolves.

Kayla caught sight of Faye. Faye's claws were out. She wanted her pound of flesh, too. From the look on the shifters' faces, they all did.

Did Davis realize just how screwed he was?

"You think you're strong?" Gage challenged as he yanked off his shirt and tossed it to the ground. "Then come and see if you can take me out. Fight *me.*"

Oh, damn. She'd heard of this before. When one wolf turned on the others in his group, the guy would have to face—

"Trial by pack," Billy said grimly.

Gage nodded. "Damn straight." Gage stared at the wolf who'd betrayed him. "And I'm going to rip you apart."

Kayla felt a shiver go down her spine. These men and women . . . right then, they were all barely human. She could feel the rage and wildness in the air. The wolves wanted out. They wanted to rip and tear and kill.

The line between human and beast was blurring.

"Here. Fucking now," Gage said.

The other wolves stepped back. Formed a circle around Gage and Davis.

Um, here? *Now?*

Gage began to shift. No wonder he'd tossed his shirt aside.

"I *should've* been alpha," Davis shouted. His eyes were

wild. Shining too brightly. "I'm stronger, smarter. You've been in my way for years." His bones popped.

Broke.

She hated the sound of shifting wolves. The growls. The pain.

The fury.

"It'll be over soon," Billy told her. His shoulder brushed against hers. The guy seemed to be trying to comfort her, when he'd been the one caged moments before. "Gage doesn't play with his prey."

That was supposed to make her feel better?

Kayla glanced around the room. She saw claws and lengthening canines everywhere she turned. It looked like every wolf there—except Faye—was about to shift.

She remembered another time. Another place. *A big black wolf, one that came at her with his fangs bared.*

Gage had finished his shift. He stood in the middle of that snarling circle. Big, strong, dark. His body vibrated with fury as he bared his fangs.

Her mother had still been alive. Broken, bloody, but breathing.

Davis had shifted. His coat was white. His eyes burning so brightly. He pushed down with his hind legs, then leapt at Gage.

She'd shaken her mother. Begged her to get up. Then Kayla had heard the growl.

A growl broke from Gage's beast. He swiped out with his claws, and blood spilled on Davis's white coat.

"First blood," Billy said, excitement thick in his voice. "Alpha always gets—"

The wolf had sprung at her from the shadows. She'd tried to run, and his claws had raked down her back. She'd slammed into the floor, and he'd been on top of her. His mouth had gone for her throat.

The white wolf leapt up and sank his teeth into Gage's throat.

Then the door had opened. She'd told Jonah to wait outside. When they'd first arrived back at the house, something had been wrong. She'd known it. Because she'd heard her mother cry out for help. And she'd smelled the blood when she'd stepped onto the back porch.

Jonah had said that he'd wait outside for her. Jonah had promised. She'd made him promise.

Gage shook off the other beast. More blood flowed. The shifters in the room were shouting. Lifting their clawed fingers up as they cheered.

Cheering for death?

He'd broken his promise. Jonah had come in. Had she screamed? She couldn't remember. Would never remember, but she thought . . . she thought she had. She'd screamed and he'd come to help her.

Gage slammed his body into Davis's. They both hit the floor. Didn't get up.

The wolf had attacked her brother. Biting and clawing and Jonah had screamed. She'd been crying. Begging the wolf to stop.

"Stop," Kayla whispered.

The black wolf's head jerked toward her. In that wild stare, was there any of Gage actually left? *Only the beast.*

But when he turned to look at her, Davis used that moment to attack. His claws sank into Gage's shoulder.

Gage howled and the memories blurred in her mind.

"You can't distract him," Billy growled to her as his arms wrapped around her and he pulled her back. She didn't even remember stepping forward. "He needs to kill the bastard."

Killing . . . that's all she'd known since that long ago night.

She'd managed to get to the drawers near the kitchen sink. She'd crawled her way there. Kayla had yanked open the drawer and grabbed one of the knives inside. "Get away from him!" Her yell had distracted the wolf. He'd let go of Jonah.

Gage knocked the other beast away. Attacked again. Again. More blood. More howls. Gage was definitely stronger, but Davis was a dirtier fighter. And Davis wasn't giving up, no matter how much blood soaked his white coat.

The wolf came at her. She screamed and thrust the knife out. The silver handle glinted in the light before it sank into the beast's thick fur. The wolf stared at her, eyes burning bright, then leapt away.

With that knife still in him, he'd run through the open door.

Gage had his teeth at Davis's throat now. No more cheering calls came from the wolves. Only silence filled the room.

Like the kind of silence she'd known when the wolf left her alone in the house that reeked of death.

Her mother hadn't been moving. Her brother—he'd been so broken. Eyes shut, barely breathing. All because of a wolf.

"Stay with me, Jonah! Stay!" Her hands had grabbed him. Shook him. "It's gonna be all right . . ."

Her father was due home soon. He'd get there. He'd take care of them all. Everything would be all right.

Gage wasn't ripping the guy's throat out. Why not?

Her breath burned in her lungs. She didn't want to watch this anymore. She'd never wanted to watch.

Couldn't she have more than blood and death? Just once?

She turned away and pulled from Billy's arms.

She'd managed to drag and stumble her way into the living room. She'd grabbed the phone so that she could dial nine-one-one, then, there, in the corner, she'd seen—

Her father had already made it home.

"What the hell is the alpha doing?" Billy asked, voice whisper soft. "He can't let him live, the pack won't let—"

Kayla glanced back. Gage was shifting. Muscles and bones reshaping. The fur seemed to melt from his flesh. Golden, strong flesh.

Davis was on the floor. Bleeding. Chest heaving. But not fighting, not anymore.

The shifters—at least a dozen, maybe two—were muttering. Glancing around uneasily. But they weren't attacking. For the moment, no one was.

"You wanted to join Lyle," Gage snarled and his voice was still closer to that of a beast's than a man's. "Then you fucking will. I'll deliver you to him and the hunters." His hands clenched. Hands now, not the paws of a beast. "From this moment on, you're out of this pack. Banished. If any one of us ever sees you again, *you're dead.*"

Gage wasn't killing Davis? He wasn't going to rip the other shifter open right then?

"You're Lyle's bitch, so he can cut you up himself. And I'm sure he will." Gage turned away from the wolf. "You're not worth my claws."

Billy whistled. "That is cold."

Gage's eyes were on her now. He was stalking toward her. Naked. Powerful. He . . . hadn't killed. Wolves killed. It was what they did.

She knew all about the pack trials. Two wolves. They fought until death. Only . . .

Neither wolf was dead.

"I'm more than you think," Gage gritted out, and she barely could hear the words. Barely—because her attention wasn't on him then.

It was on the beast behind him. The wolf that was now up, not looking nearly so injured. Up—and launching at Gage's back.

Kayla didn't waste time on a scream or a warning. Billy was already charging for Gage. He slammed into Gage, knocking the alpha out of the way.

But Davis wasn't stopping. He charged for both men.

Enough.

Kayla yanked out her gun. Aimed in an instant, and fired.

CHAPTER NINE

B ecause he'd jumped into the air, the bullet slammed into the middle of the wolf's chest. He fell to the ground, and landed with a thud.

Gage tossed Billy aside. No one spoke. No one moved. No one, but Kayla.

"I guess that ends the trial." She lowered her weapon. Gage heard no emotion in her voice. And she was so pale.

Her gaze swept the room. "Any other pack problems we need to solve?" Her tone implied there'd damn well better not be any.

The wolves glanced his way. They had a dead wolf on the floor, one who'd died by a hunter's hand. Not exactly the way a trial by pack was supposed to end.

Gage looked back at Davis's body. Such a waste. And why? Power? Why hadn't the guy understood? Being alpha was a pain in the ass most days.

You had to put the pack first, when you wanted something for yourself.

I want her. A hunter, mated to a wolf.

You had to turn on your friends . . .

Billy wasn't meeting his gaze. How was he supposed to soothe that one over? A little, "Oh, sorry, man, I thought you were setting me up to die," wasn't gonna cut it.

And you had to lie to the woman you'd claimed as your wife.

Your brother's missing. No. Jonah wasn't. That line had been pure bull. Jonah was right where he was supposed to be—at Lyle's side. But Gage had to keep her away from that compound. He couldn't let her race back there. So he'd lied.

I'll save her brother. I'll make everything okay.

Davis's eyes were closed. The silver bullet had lodged in his heart.

The bastard had been his friend. "See you in hell," he whispered. Funny. He'd always thought he'd get there long before Davis.

"Get rid of the body," he told Shamus. The redheaded wolf was glaring down at Davis's form. Yeah, after all that had happened to him, Shamus sure as hell wasn't taking betrayal well.

I don't take it well, either.

Neither did Kayla. So he was gonna have to be real careful how he played this.

Except . . . she was turning away. She kept her grip on her gun and she walked toward the door. The other wolves eased back for her, clearing the path.

Alpha.

They might not like her, but they respected her. Bullets and death had a way of showing a woman's spirit. No wolf within, but the lady was one hell of a fighter.

She killed to keep me safe.

And he hadn't killed . . . because he wanted her to see him as more than a beast. More than a monster.

Could she?

"Kayla!" He hadn't meant to roar her name so much as just say it, but the beast was too close to the surface for much control.

She stilled and looked back at him. She had a "don't-try-me" expression tightening her face.

He held out his hand to her. Some things had to be done.

For the pack.

For me.

Just in case something happened . . .

"My wife." Now these words were softer, but still growled. It was time to claim his mate in front of the pack. She wasn't a hunter anymore. She was one of them.

Forever.

Confusion swept over her features. She glanced at the other wolves. Then back at him.

Gage kept his hand up. The pack needed to see them as unified.

Kayla licked her lips and took a step toward him. "Uh, Gage?"

Shamus hauled the body out of the room. Left a trail of blood in his wake.

Yeah, wolf pack life wasn't exactly sunshine and paradise, but his Kayla wasn't the sunshine type.

He didn't speak, just waited for her to come to him.

And she did. With slow, uncertain steps, when she wasn't the type for uncertainty, either. Her hand lifted and, hesitantly, her fingers curled around his. "What, ah, what am I supposed to be doing?"

She'd taken his hand. And he'd take her. "This," he said simply, then pulled her against him. His lips found hers in a hot, hard, openmouthed kiss.

The pack cheered around him. Blood, sex, and violence— yes, they all understood those three things.

He kissed her harder. His tongue tasted her. So good. The best he'd ever had.

Never let go. No matter what happened. No matter what he had to give up, Gage wasn't letting Kayla go.

And that was why he'd married her. Not for the pack. Not to get Intel on her boss. Not even because she *might* be able to give him children since her scent marked her as a genetic match for a shifter.

He'd just wanted her. So he'd taken her.

His head lifted. Her lips were swollen. Red. "Mine," he said simply.

No one spoke.

Kayla glanced around. "Um . . . mine?" She said and pointed at Gage's chest.

The shifters roared their approval.

She winced.

Damn but she was cute.

Gage lifted her into his arms. She was all that mattered right then. She might not realize it, but he'd pledged his life to her with that one simple word.

Mine.

Mine to protect. To care for.

Mine to put above all others.

Some of the pack might be pissed over Davis's death. Some wouldn't think that a human should have been involved in the trial.

Some might even be wanting her blood.

Not anymore.

With that one word, he'd given a warning. Any who touched her would regret it because . . .

Mine.

No one hurt what was his.

He carried her from the room that smelled of death and blood, and he didn't look back.

When the bedroom door closed behind them, Kayla knew just what Gage had planned.

Not like it would take a genius to figure this one out.

"Gage, I need to find—"

He kissed her. Lowered her feet to the floor, then pushed her back against the wall. Her wolf was aroused, no doubt about it. And, okay, maybe she was, too. The guy knew how to kiss.

Hell, yes, he did. Adrenaline still spiked in her blood, making her heart beat faster and letting that wild heat inside of her surge ever hotter but . . .

She pulled her mouth from his and sucked in a fortifying breath. "We have to—"

"Fuck," Gage said, voice guttural. "I *need* you." His eyes blazed down at her. So bright. She loved the blue of his eyes. "Not about the pack. Not about hunters. I just *need you.*"

Her breath seemed to freeze in her lungs. Wasn't that what she'd always longed for? Someone who needed her? Someone who just wanted her, exactly as she was?

Darkness, scars, and all?

His hands tightened around her arms. "I didn't marry you . . . because you might be able to give me children."

That whole mate thing again. It could make a girl tense.

"I married you because I couldn't breathe without tasting you."

Oh, well. She wasn't even sure what to say to that, but the words sure made her feel good.

Besides, it didn't matter that she couldn't toss out a ready comeback. Gage didn't give her a chance to respond. He kissed her again. His aroused flesh pressed into her. Long, full, so thick.

Why did I marry him?

Not for the mission. Not because he was a job.

Because I wanted him.

She still did. Always would.

So she didn't push him away. Why couldn't she have what she wanted? Couldn't she just take it? Take him?

Her hands wrapped around Gage's powerful, broad shoulders, and she pulled him closer.

She loved the way he kissed. The slow thrust of his tongue, the sensual press of his lips. She got wet just from his kiss.

His hands slid down her body. Curved around her ass. Lifted her up against his cock.

Yes.

Her body was already eager for him. She rubbed against

him and liked it when he tensed against her. Power. It could come in so many forms.

His mouth lifted from hers. He stared into her eyes. "I'm not letting you go."

He wasn't talking about that moment. She got that part. But she didn't want to think about the future then. About what could happen—or who could tear them apart.

Then he was kissing her neck and she could just moan and shudder because, oh, *yes,* that part of her body was sensitive. When he used the edge of his teeth in the lightest of caresses, her eyes closed and her tight nipples pushed into his chest.

"Bed," he muttered against her. "I want—"

Her eyes opened. "No." Because this was also about what she wanted. Her hand pushed against his chest. That wonderful, naked chest and all those fabulous muscles.

Her sex clenched in eager anticipation. Soon he'd be thrusting deep and hard into her, but first . . .

He was naked. His thick cock pushing up toward her. So she wrapped her hands around the aroused flesh that she craved. Stroked him. Pumped once. Twice. He swelled even more beneath her fingers.

Her mouth had gone dry. She wanted to taste him.

Kayla eased onto her knees.

"Sweetheart, you don't have—"

She put her mouth on him. That move shut up her wolf. The guy's eyes seemed to roll back into his head. She licked him. Sucked him. Loved his taste.

Her hands wrapped around the base of his cock as she took his aroused flesh into her mouth. Deeper. *Deeper.* She tasted him with each caress of her lips and tongue. Salty, wild. He tasted just the way she'd thought he would.

His hands were slammed against the wall now. Not on her. Gage wasn't trying to guide her movements or force her to take more of him. No. He was staring down at her with feral eyes. His claws were out—*in* that wall. And a ragged groan that was her name tore from his lips.

She smiled up at him—then took him deeper.

"Kayla."

She wanted him to come and—

His claws ripped from the wood. He grabbed her. She started to flinch away. His claws . . .

"Never . . . hurt you." His voice was barely human.

But he wasn't hurting her. He was yanking her clothes off, tossing them aside, and pretty much shredding the material with his claws, but he *wasn't* hurting her.

Then he was lifting her against the wall. The claws never even skimmed her skin. He lifted her up and parted her legs.

Kayla guided his cock to the entrance of her sex. When he thrust, she arched toward him so that his flesh sank deep within her.

Yes.

Their eyes locked. She couldn't look away from him. There was so much intensity in his stare.

Her sex clenched around his cock. Thrust. Withdraw. Thrust.

Kayla's hands locked around his shoulders as she rose up and then slid down, pushing back against him. She wasn't going to be able to hold back for long. She was too aroused. Slick, sensitive, her sex parted easily for the driving thrust of his cock. Again and again and—

She opened her mouth, *screamed* his name. Kayla didn't care who heard her right then.

Then he came inside of her. A hot rush of release that just sent the pleasure crashing over her again. She held onto Gage, digging her nails into his flesh. Marking him because no matter what the hell else happened between them, there was one thing that she was sure of. One absolute thing.

Mine.

Gage belonged to her.

New clothes were brought to them. A good thing, because the ripped look wouldn't have worked so well for

Kayla. She dressed quickly and tried to peek at Gage's ass only three times.

Four.

Clearing her throat, she turned away. "I need to talk with the demon." Curtis might be able to tell her more about what had happened to her brother. She'd drill him, then start a search plan.

If her brother had left the compound, that meant he'd realized the truth about Lyle. He'd known she wasn't lying.

He believed her.

"I'm afraid that's not gonna be possible."

Frowning, she glanced back over her shoulder. Gage was dressed now. No more sexy peeks at his ass. Pity. "Why not?"

"Because I had two of my pack . . . escort Curtis to a safe location."

Her eyebrows rose. She'd thought they were already in a safe house. "Then escort me to this same location." Seemed simple enough to her.

But Gage didn't exactly look agreeable as he said, "I didn't want the demon knowing where I'd hidden the rest of the pack, so I didn't let him get close."

Right, okay, sounded fine to her. "He probably had a tracker on him anyway." Unless he'd dug it out. Without Lyle knowing? Maybe . . . the demon seemed to have plenty of secrets. "I would have mentioned that tracker bit to you," she muttered and some nice, remembered fury spiked her blood. "But you know, you *drugged* me first."

His lips tightened.

Speaking of trackers . . . "We need to check Davis's body. If he was tagged, then Lyle could already be on his way here."

Gage didn't look particularly worried about that. "Yes," he said slowly, with a faint nod. "He could be."

Just like that, the light finally dawned. "You . . . want him here." Gage wanted Lyle to come after them.

Gage held her gaze. "I dug the tracker out of the demon before I let him go to the safe house."

So he *hadn't* been so clueless after all. Tricky wolf.

"And I brought it here with me."

What? Her breath expelled in a rush.

"So I figure with Curtis and Lyle both giving off a signal to this place, we'll be having company soon."

The killing kind of company. "Why?" Why would he want to bring the hunters to him?

"I brought in reinforcements," he said with a shrug and didn't even look a little bit concerned about the coming attack. "Wolves from other packs. Wolves who are tired of being hunted."

She couldn't read his expression. Nothing showed past the stoic wall of determination that hardened his strong features. "You're setting your own trap."

"It was my turn."

Or had it been his plan all along? Suspicion slipped through her.

"Shamus will be coming soon. He's going to make sure you're taken away from this place during the battle."

Was the guy saying she couldn't handle a fight? What? Did she *look* like a piece of fluff? "I've been battling since I was sixteen years old," she pointed out.

"So aren't you due for a break?"

She blinked at him, then forced her clenched jaw to relax. They'd gone from hot sex straight to him kicking her out? That was too fast of a onc-eighty for her. "I'm not going to leave you when you need me." That was *not* who she was.

His lips tightened. "And I don't want you to see what I do to the men you once considered friends."

Her heart was about to slam through her chest. "You're not killing them all." That wasn't an option. "They think they're making the world a better place! That they're out there fighting monsters—"

"Then they should be prepared for when the monsters fight back."

She shook her head. No, no, she wouldn't let a bloodbath happen on her watch. "They only thought they were taking out killers. We had files, reports! We didn't attack innocents!"

But he just stared back at her, and her words seemed so hollow to her own ears. Nausea rolled through her.

So many lies. Lyle had fooled them too well.

They'd let themselves be fooled.

"He's the one who should be stopped," she muttered and refused to back down. "The others—give them a chance, Gage."

"So they can fill my heart with silver? Cut off my head?" His smile held a cruel edge. "Sorry, sweetheart, that's not happening, not even for you."

A light rap sounded at the door.

Gage's nostrils flared. "Shamus."

"I don't want you to lose your damn head." She didn't move. She could still *feel* the guy inside her. She wasn't walking away and leaving him to a bloody battle. This was more than sex. The guy had better realize that.

"I won't. I'm rather attached to my head."

He was driving her crazy. "This isn't a joke!" She tried to keep her voice calm and make the wolf see reason. "The hunters . . . they'll come in expecting a trap. Lyle will be ready to use and lose them all, if he can take you out." Because she'd seen the fury in Lyle's eyes. He wasn't stopping, not until he'd taken over this town.

And if he had to kill a few dozen humans and wolves? So what? He could always recruit more hunters, and he sure didn't care about the wolves.

"There's another way," she said, desperate. "There's always another way."

Gage shook his head. "There's no time." His steps were slow as he stalked toward her. His hand lifted and the back of his fingers slid down her cheek. "The wolf's at the door, and I'm gonna tear him apart."

Or he'd get torn apart. The humans would die.

This didn't have to happen. "My brother . . ."

Gage looked at the door. "We'll find him when the fight's over." Then his hand fell away. He slipped around her. Opened the door.

The redheaded wolf waited, with his arms loose at his sides.

"Take her back home, Shamus," Gage said.

Home?

The thought was so foreign to her that Kayla blinked at first. But . . . she did have a home. An apartment in the city. One that gave her a night-time view of the strip that took her breath away.

So why didn't that place feel like *home*?

She took a deep breath and squared her shoulders. "Sorry, Shamus," she said—and then she slammed the door in the shifter's face.

Gage blinked. He looked . . . surprised. Really? He should know her better than that.

Kayla jabbed her finger in his chest. "I don't walk away from fights. Not ever. I don't tuck my tail between my legs and run—"

His brows shot up. Whoops, okay, wolf reference. Her bad.

Kayla cleared her throat. "I don't run because things get tough, got it?"

"This isn't—"

She jabbed him harder. "You don't get to spout 'mine' bullshit one minute and then toss me out the next." And it . . . hurt. To go from the best sex ever to a cold toss out the door, yeah, that was tough. But she wasn't about to let him see her pain. She'd never let anyone see.

Only Jonah.

Where are you?

"Those men don't deserve death, and I'm not letting you claw your way through humans because a psychotic wolf has been jerking us all around." Kayla took another deep breath. Weren't deep breaths supposed to calm down fury? She wasn't feeling calm. "I'm working with you, and we'll make sure we take out the real monster."

There was still no emotion showing on his handsome face. "Just how are we gonna do that?" Gage asked.

Yeah, how the hell were they gonna do that? Plans and options spun through her mind. *Think.* "When the hunters come, don't send any wolves out. Not a single one." This was crazy, she knew it but . . . "I'm the only one who will face them. I'll make them see reason."

"Uh, sweetheart, no one believed you before."

Good point.

"You broke out of your cell. You ran from them." His lips tightened. "Those assholes will just shoot first and dump your body later. No dice."

He reached for the door handle again. Yanked open the door.

Shamus was still there. One red brow was up. With his shifter hearing, like a closed door would really stop him from eavesdropping on their little conversation.

There had to be a way of stopping this hell. She just had to show the others what Lyle really was.

But Lyle . . . he wouldn't be in that first wild rush of hunters who came to storm the place. He always held back. Gave the orders from a distance. Moved in when the targets were secure.

When the hunters attacked, they'd be out for blood. *Mine.* Dammit, yes. And Gage's. So to save all their sorry asses . . . "We have to attack first."

Shamus whistled. "Bloodthirsty. I like that."

Gage punched him.

"They're coming after us. Getting ready. Moving out." Kayla was talking faster now because she *had this.* "So this is

the time when we go for them. We attack while they're en
route. We close in on Lyle, we take him out of the caravan."
When heading into new territory, the hunters swept in on a
straight line. "The last SUV." That was his. *Always.* "We take
him out, and we make the others see what he is."

They'd drag his sorry ass out of that SUV. Tie him in silver. When he started to burn, the other hunters would be
forced to see him for what he truly was.

"And you think that's gonna stop them?" Gage demanded,
his voice full of doubt. "They'll just shoot him and then keep
coming after my pack."

Because hunters hated wolves. They thought shifters were
monsters that needed to be put down.

It was Kayla's turn to shake her head. "We're not all like
that." *I'm not.* She needed him to recognize that truth in her
eyes. "Give us a chance to show you that we can be more."
Better. I can be better.

Not just a lost soul seeking justice for crimes long ago. A
woman now, wanting to fight for the man she was craving
more than life.

Slowly, very slowly, Gage nodded. "But if this doesn't
work . . . if they keep attacking . . ." He lifted his claw-
tipped hands. "They will be stopped."

And she knew that he really meant . . . they will be dead.

Gage paced down the hallway with Shamus. Kayla was
arming herself. Getting bullets. The silver that the pack handled only with reinforced gloves.

She was hot when she got battle ready.

She was also dangerous.

"Hunt for me," Gage told Shamus, because no one in the
pack hunted like the red wolf.

Shamus gave a slight nod. "The prey?"

"Her brother."

Surprise flickered briefly over Shamus's face. "You want
me to kill him?"

"No." If he did that, he'd lose her. "I want you to make sure his fool ass stays alive." Gage yanked out a scrap of cloth he'd taken from the compound. Cloth that had once been Kayla's shirt. "His blood's on this." When it came to humans, Shamus could track a scent with deadly accuracy. "Take him out of the fight."

Because Jonah would be coming, Gage had no doubt about that. Coming for his sister and coming for vengeance.

Shamus took the cloth. Turned. Walked quickly away.

"You can't lie to her."

Billy's voice. Coming from a few feet behind him. But then, he'd known Billy was there, watching.

Slowly, Gage turned to face the wolf he'd considered his friend. The burns from the silver had faded. Mostly. "I'm sorry." For the pain Billy suffered.

Billy lifted one shoulder in a shrug. "You're alpha. You do what the hell you want."

Not when it meant that he hurt the ones he cared about.

So he tried to explain, even though an alpha wasn't supposed to justify. *Just act. Rule. Dominate.* There was more to Gage than that, there always had been. "Only you and Davis knew Kayla and I were at that cabin. And you two were both close with the other wolves who went missing." It was easier to be lured out into the open, easier to be attacked, when the one luring you wore the guise of a friend.

Shamus had told him that both Davis and Billy were near the site when he was taken. He'd broken away from them and attacked the hunters. Gotten trapped, but the other two had both gotten away.

And when Faye had gone missing, they'd been there, too. Been there, but hadn't managed to save her.

"So you shackled me in silver." Billy exhaled and glanced away. "Damn painful, hoss. Damn painful."

For the pack. "The silver wasn't about pain. It was to make sure neither of you ran before I could find the real traitor."

Billy glanced back up at him. "You could have *asked* me first."

Asked him. Asked Davis. One wolf would have lied, and no matter what the stories said, Gage wasn't the sort of wolf who could actually smell a lie.

He didn't think those guys existed.

So Gage just stared back at Billy. "Davis wanted you to look guilty." He'd been setting the other wolf up all along. Timing their guard duty together, even tossing seeds of suspicion out among the pack. "He planned to let you take the fall."

"Yes, I figured that. The guy probably thought he'd kill me." Billy's claws flashed out. "But I'm tough to kill."

So others had discovered. There was far more to the shifter than met the eye. He'd run from his home in the South because he'd wanted a fresh start.

But Gage knew what he'd left behind. That death and hell that waited in the South, that was one of the reasons he'd suspected Billy.

"We can't run forever," Gage said. It was a lesson they all needed to learn. Maybe it was time for Billy to face his own demons.

Time for them all to face that darkness.

Gage kept his hands by his side. "You want to run at me, come the fuck on." Billy deserved his pound of flesh. The first slice would be free. After that, Gage would slice back.

Billy shook his head. His claws were out, but he made no move to attack. "I don't like fuckin' silver." He turned away. "But I like this pack. Pack first. *Always.*"

Gage knew that Billy understood. The pain, it didn't matter. Not when there was a pack to protect.

"Next time, *ask,*" Billy snarled over his shoulder.

Before the wolf could storm away, Gage grabbed his arm. "I will." He exhaled a rough breath. "And for now, right now, I'm *asking* you to help me."

Billy's brows shot up as he glanced back at Gage.

"We're goin' after Lyle. Taking out the last SUV that comes onto our land because Kayla says he'll be in that one." Minimum bloodshed. Right. He knew that was what she wanted. Wolves—well, they liked the blood.

A lot.

But for her . . .

"I want a scent blocker." It would be the only way they could sneak up on Lyle. Lyle couldn't know they were closing in if he couldn't smell them. "I know you've got a stash." Another reason he'd suspected Billy. "Get it."

The shifter nodded and rushed away.

Gage watched him go. He'd try it Kayla's way, for a time. He'd give the orders for all of the other wolves to stand down. But if her plan didn't work, if one of those hunters fired at them first . . .

The wolves would be the ones to finish the battle that the humans had started.

CHAPTER TEN

The SUVs slid onto the old, broken road just after midnight. The vehicles crept forward in a long, snaking line, with their headlights off and their engines barely growling, just as Kayla had predicted.

"Now I know why you picked this place," Kayla whispered from beside him. "One way in, one way out."

Damn straight. He'd laid his trap so carefully. The hunters had miles to go before they were even close to the safe houses he'd set up for the pack. And they didn't know it, but the hunters were already surrounded by the wolves.

Easy kills.

"That's him." Kayla pointed to the last SUV. One a bit bigger than the others. "That's the one Lyle always uses."

Because he liked to send the others in first. Gage knew the bastard was a coward at heart. Why else would he send humans to do the dirty work for him?

"Come on." He grabbed her hand and headed into the darkness. The goal was to separate that SUV from the others, but they wouldn't have much time. The hunters were the shoot-first variety, and he'd already told Kayla what would happen if some trigger-happy dick fired back at him or her.

Death.

He had a wolf stationed nearby, one who knew to take out the SUV as soon as Gage gave the signal. The guy wasn't just a shifter, he was one grade A, first-class sniper. Gage waited, wanting that SUV closer. *Closer.*

He lifted his hand. In the dark, humans couldn't see so well.

Wolves could.

There was no thunder when the weapon fired, but the SUV's front left tire blew out. Then the right tire exploded. The SUV swerved, flipped, and thudded into the earth.

And Gage and Kayla were already moving. Racing toward the wreckage even as the other SUV drivers slammed onto their brakes.

Hurry. Hurry.

Gage punched his fist through the already broken passenger side. He yanked open the door, nearly ripping it away from the vehicle.

Lyle hadn't been driving or waiting in the passenger seat, but the bleeding bastard was slumped in the back of the vehicle. Gage pushed past the two groaning men in the front and grabbed his prey.

"Judgment time, asshole," he snarled. Then he kicked out at the back doors of the SUV, knocking them wide open, and he dragged out that sorry excuse for a wolf.

Blood poured from a gash on Lyle's forehead. He was bleeding . . . and laughing. "Y-you're . . . dead," Lyle gasped out. *"Dead!"*

"No," Kayla said, voice clear in the night. Footsteps thudded, coming close. The other hunters were swarming. "You are," Kayla told him.

Then Gage heard the snick of a gun. *One shot.* That was all it would take.

The pack would attack.

Kayla whirled around and used her body as a shield to block Gage and Lyle. *"Stand down!"* she screamed. "Or we'll all die!"

Not her. The others, yes, but Kayla wasn't leaving him. He wouldn't let her go.

He could see the hunters now. Three were already close enough for him to kill easily. Gage could leap forward and slice their throats in seconds. Did they honestly think the guns in their hands made them stronger? Fools.

"Let him go," one of the hunters ordered from behind his black ski mask. Masks. These bastards were always hiding. And they said shifters were the ones who pretended to be something they weren't.

"He's been lying to you all," Kayla said. Wait, hold the hell up . . . had she just put her weapon down?

Kayla lifted her empty hands in the air.

She fucking did.

Gage growled.

Lyle shouted, "Shoot her!"

Gage slapped his hand over the bastard's mouth. "No matter what else happens here tonight," he whispered into Lyle's ear. "I'm cutting you open."

Lyle heaved in his hold, but Gage was stronger. He just tightened his grip around the jerk.

"No one has to die tonight," Kayla said, proving, quite clearly, that a human's hearing was nothing compared to a shifter's. "I've worked with you all—so many times—just give me a chance to prove that what I'm saying is true!"

They weren't lowering their weapons. "Move back, Kayla," he ordered. Because his wolves were going to spring up soon, and he wanted her away from the coming bloodbath.

"Let him go," the guy at the front of the growing pile of hunters said. "Let Lyle go, then we can talk."

Such a lie. Once Lyle was clear, the hunters would open fire. They were holding back only because Gage was a claw away from killing their precious leader.

"If Gage lets him go," Kayla said, "Lyle will kill me." After the briefest of pauses, she told them, "Then he'll watch while you all die, too."

The men shifted restlessly, from one foot to the other.

"Don't you wonder why he's never touched silver?" she

questioned them. "Why he always uses his black gloves when he's near the silver cells?" Kayla shook her head. "You've seen all this, just as I have. Only . . . I didn't put the pieces together. I didn't want to believe he was the real monster."

The tension in the air thickened.

He didn't like this. Every muscle in Gage's body was battle ready. The hunters hadn't fired yet, but Kayla's small body had no cover if the bullets were to start raining on her.

Too vulnerable. Standing in front of him, offering herself up to the hunters. Hell, no, this wasn't acceptable.

He heard the faint snap of a twig. To his left. Gage inhaled and pulled in the scents around him.

"I can prove what he really is," Kayla said, her voice loud for all to hear. "I can—"

Gage leapt toward her. Lyle broke from him as he moved, rolling to the ground. Gage didn't even look back at that prick. He grabbed Kayla even as the thunder of a gun echoed around them.

First shot.

Now it would be his turn to attack, and all the bastards would die.

The bullet blasted near him, scraping over his arm and ripping open the skin. Gage didn't cry out. He was too long acquainted with pain for that. He twisted his body and took the impact when he and Kayla slammed into the earth.

Then he opened his mouth and roared the order, "Kill!"

The wolves had already shifted. They were ready. Eager for the fight to come.

The foolish hunters . . . they wouldn't have a chance.

"No!" Kayla cried out, but it was too late. He'd given the order.

Streaks of black, gray, and white burst from the darkness and lunged for the hunters. The humans were trying to fire, but they couldn't aim well at their targets. Not in the dark. Not with so many wolves rushing around them and moving so quickly.

"It doesn't have to be like this," Kayla whispered, then she shoved away from Gage. "It *won't* be like this."

She ran right into the battle.

Dammit, *no.*

His claws burst out of his fingers as he took off after her.

Lyle had raced to a nearby SUV. Big surprise, he was trying to jump inside and make a run for it. Coward to the core.

"Going someplace?" Kayla demanded, then she grabbed a gun right out of the hand of a nearby hunter. She slugged the guy, and he fell to the ground with a thud.

Nice punch. That right hook was really killer.

Kayla aimed the gun at Lyle. "Get away from the vehicle. Get your ass out here right now, shifter!"

Two hunters jumped in front of Gage. He could have just slit their throats with one long swipe of his claws.

He knocked them out instead. Just slammed their heads together and stepped over them when they fell.

Another hunter was rushing up behind Kayla. Why were they all in their damn ski masks? Why—

Too close.

Gage leapt to take out the man sneaking up to attack Kayla but a gun blasted and, in the next breath, a bullet slammed into Gage's upper back.

Son of a bitch.

The bullet went through right under his shoulder, and blasted out the front of his body. Snarling at the pain, Gage whirled around. Saw the hunter just steps away. The guy giving off the heavy scent of fear and sweat. The guy with the shaking hands. And the gun that was about to fire again.

"Bad mistake," Gage told him. Then he attacked. His claws cut deep into the fool's wrist. The gun clattered to the ground—and the hunter fell, too, crying and begging for mercy.

Mercy? What the fuck did he look like?

Kayla screamed.

Gage whirled back around. A hunter had her in his arms. Held tight against his chest. The masked man had a gun.

No. Not her. *"Kayla!"* His roar thundered across the gunshots and the howls of the beasts around him.

"Shoot her!" Lyle screamed. He was hanging with his body half-in, half-out of the SUV. Lyle's hand was rising. He'd gone into that SUV to get something . . .

A weapon?

Kayla slammed her head into the hunter's ski mask-covered face. Then she jabbed her elbow into his side and kicked down hard on his foot.

The guy's hold eased on her. She moved, spinning around, and knocked the gun from his grip even as she put that hunter down on his ass.

Gage had never seen a better alpha female. *Never.*

He ran toward her, grabbed her, and pulled her close. "I fucking love you."

Her gasp filled his ears.

Then, because Gage knew what was coming and he didn't have time to do anything but protect the woman he loved, Gage twisted his body to shield her.

And when the bullet hit him—the bullet that had been fired from the gun clutched in Lyle's white-knuckled fist, Gage felt the burn of the silver in every inch of his body.

"Gage!" Kayla's scream. Her hands were on him, nails digging into his chest.

He tried to fight through the burning agony. Kayla wasn't safe. Lyle would shoot at her again. The bastard had to be stopped.

The beast was coming out.

Gage lifted his hand and saw that the shift had already started. He hadn't even felt the break and snap of his bones, but his hand—*not the hand of a man.*

Kayla lifted up her gun and fired at Lyle. Again and again. "Shift," she whispered to Gage. *"Shift!"*

The hunter she'd pounded was trying to lift himself off the ground.

And the shift was too damn slow. Kayla was battling Lyle on her own, and Gage tried to force his body to transform faster. But the silver was in his blood and every breath hurt.

Her bullets slammed into Lyle, but they weren't silver. She'd grabbed a hunter's weapon, but the idiot hadn't packed silver. Why? Lyle's order? Had he *wanted* the humans to die?

When her bullets hit Lyle, the bastard just laughed as his blood flowed. And he took aim at Kayla again.

"No!" Not Gage's scream, because he couldn't scream right then. He could roar and howl, but speech was lost to him.

The desperate cry came from the hunter that Kayla had attacked and knocked down. He was lunging for her now, but Lyle had already fired his weapon.

Kayla leapt to the side. The bullet tore across her hip and the scent of her blood broke Gage and his wolf.

The shift finished in a white-hot burst of agony. The pain didn't matter. Kayla did. Gage leapt up and charged at Lyle. Lyle took aim on him then. Lyle's finger tightened around the trigger. His total focus was on Gage.

You want me, asshole?

Gage snarled.

Lyle just kept smiling. Completely out of the SUV now, the sick freak stalked forward. Smiling, watching Gage, and aiming his gun.

The fool never saw the wolf closing in behind him. The wolf with a coat tinted red. The wolf who would want his own justice.

Shamus leapt at Lyle before he could fire again. His claws dug into Lyle's back as the red wolf took him down.

Lyle screamed.

The chaos around them seemed too quiet for a moment. Hunters spun around. They'd ignored gunshots, too immune

to the sound, but Lyle's echoing scream of pain and rage—
they hadn't ignored that.

Two men immediately fired at Shamus.

He jumped away from Lyle's bleeding body.

Lyle rolled clear of Shamus, then he managed to stagger to
his feet. "K-kill—" Lyle began.

"No." It was the other hunter again. The one who kept
going after Kayla. The one who was now holding her arm.
Holding *her*.

Gage tensed. That scent . . .

The hunter jerked off his ski mask. *Jonah.* "Everyone
just—stop!" Jonah shouted.

The wolves weren't stopping. They were attacking.
Killing.

The hunters fought back. No one was listening.

Shamus was transforming slowly back into the form of a
human. Lyle was trying to grab another weapon.

And more asshole hunters were attempting to get at Gage
and Kayla.

Kill them all. They could end this now.

"Screw this!" Kayla's voice. So sweet and vicious. That
was his lady. His head jerked around and he saw her bend
down. She grabbed a gun from the holster on Jonah's ankle.
"Silver?" He heard her ask.

Jonah nodded.

Kayla lifted the weapon. Aimed it at Lyle. *"Silver!"* she
screamed.

But even as she fired, two hunters pointed their weapons
at her.

Gage took one of the assholes out with a slash of his claws
across the guy's legs.

The other hunter—Jonah shot him in the arm.

And Kayla shot Lyle. Her bullet ripped into his chest. Lyle
flew back and fell onto the earth. Smoke drifted up from his
wound. Smoke . . . as the silver burned his flesh.

And the hunters were watching him. Every. Second . . .

"What the hell . . ."

"How the fuck . . ."

Many stood now, lost, confused. It was the perfect time for the wolves to take out the humans. So easy. Like slaughtering sheep.

"He's a wolf!" Kayla shouted. "He's been lying to us, tricking us all along!" Her voice seemed to echo in the night.

The men and women in their ski masks still had their weapons. But they weren't fighting. Not yet.

Some were too injured to fight. The scent of blood was strong in the air.

Some were too scared. A wolf always knew the scent of fear.

"Gage and his pack . . . they aren't evil." Kayla's voice was clear and strong. "They haven't done anything to the humans in this city."

Well, nothing that the humans hadn't asked for. The wolves weren't exactly perfect.

No one was.

"We don't have to destroy each other!" Kayla's eyes burned with intensity, just like her voice. "We can just . . . walk away."

If the hunters didn't start walking in less than five seconds, they wouldn't have a choice in the matter.

The wolves were standing back, for the moment, but it would just take one roar from Gage to send them into action. *Just one roar . . .*

Then Jonah strode forward. "We aren't killers." His words carried easily. There was a heavy edge of command in his words. "We protect. This *isn't* us."

Lyle was digging the silver out of his chest.

A few of the hunters lowered their weapons.

"A *damn shifter? All along . . .*"

A woman yanked off her ski mask. Her face was pale. Shaken. "What . . . what have we been doing?"

"Following the wrong path," Kayla said with a sad shake

of her head. "And it's time to change that. It's time for all of us to change and to make this right." She was at her brother's side. "Walk away from the wolves. These shifters aren't the ones who are evil." She swallowed, exhaled, and said, "To them, *we're* the evil ones. We're the ones who came after them when all they were doing was trying to live."

Silence.

The wolves were straining forward. So eager to finish the fight.

Gage didn't give the order to attack. Not yet.

"Put up your weapons. Clear out of here," Jonah said. His words held the unmistakable whip of an order. "This fight isn't ours." His gaze slanted back to Lyle. Still on the ground. Still clawing at his chest as he tried to dig out the silver. Disgust tightened his face. "And you sure as hell aren't our leader."

The rest of the hunters lowered their weapons. Then they slowly headed back to their vehicles.

No more fighting. Just . . . walking away?

Well, fuck me.

Kayla had been right. They weren't out to kill blindly. They weren't killing at all.

"I'm sorry," Gage heard Jonah say to Kayla. "I should have trusted you sooner. Hell, you're the only one I *should* ever trust."

Her hands reached for his.

Gage's eyes narrowed. *Get to her.* He raced toward them, his claws tearing over the earth.

Faster, faster . . .

"Everything's gonna be okay now," Jonah told her, and he pulled her close for a hug.

Gage opened his mouth and roared.

Jonah jerked away from Kayla and saw Lyle—charging right for them. Bleeding, but with the silver gone, the guy wasn't done yet.

Not even close.

"This isn't how it ends!" Lyle screamed as spittle flew from his mouth. "Not for me!" His claws lifted. "Not for you!" He went for Jonah's throat.

Gage locked his teeth around Lyle's leg and jerked him back. He'd wanted his pound of flesh, and he *had* made a promise to the other wolf.

You're dying. A promise was a promise.

"This *is* how it ends," Kayla said as she backed up, pulling her brother with her. "So have fun in hell, asshole."

Lyle was shifting. Fighting. Clawing. "Your father—you know he begged to live!"

Kayla flinched.

"Begged!" Lyle spat. His face was elongating, his eyes burning bright. "So did your bitch of a—"

Gage slashed his throat.

The bastard stopped screaming.

You won't hurt her anymore.

The other wolves closed in.

And Lyle didn't scream again.

"Come back with me," Jonah said. The other hunters were long gone—headed back to base or to who the hell knew where.

Maybe some of them would just keep driving. Keep running.

Kayla didn't blame them. Everything they knew had all just changed. They had to figure out what they were going to do . . . who they were going to become.

Lyle was dead. The wolves were shifting back to their human forms. Turning to their alpha for guidance.

"You don't belong with them," Jonah told her. Her brother was standing strong and steady beside her. His hand rested on her shoulder. "Come back with me. We can go forward."

"Forward to what?" she whispered. When you were lost, how the hell did you know which direction to take?

His hand tightened on her. "Not everything was a lie. Lyle

was working for the government. He was a contractor, yeah, but he was being sent out after real killers. Those cases were real."

"Not all of them." And that knowledge would keep tearing her apart. "Some of those people that we captured, they were innocents, Jonah. Supernaturals that Lyle just framed because he wanted them under his control." Or because he'd just wanted to take them out.

"Then we free them," he said simply. With such determination. When had her kid brother grown up on her? "We find the containment areas that are housing them, and we make sure that they get their freedom."

She nodded. Yes, yes, that was what they had to do. No matter what it took, she had to give the ones she'd taken justice.

"We can do it," Jonah said, voice rough, eyes deep, "together."

Her gaze slipped away and found Gage. Surrounded by his wolves. Standing tall. Powerful. "He told me that you were . . . missing. That you'd disappeared from the compound."

Silence.

She didn't need Jonah to confirm the lie. She'd already figured it out on her own.

"He didn't want me to go back for you." Her shoulders sagged a bit. It had been one hell of a day. Week—*year.*

"It doesn't matter," Jonah said instantly. "I was coming for *you.* I saw Lyle burn in that holding cell, I knew the truth, and I was coming to make sure you were safe."

No wonder he'd been stationed so close to Lyle.

"I figured it was my turn to stand guard," her brother told her softly.

She glanced back at him. Found his gaze on hers. He looked so worried. So . . .

"I'm sorry." His voice held a ragged edge. "Oh, damn, Kay, I'm so sorry for everything that happened. I *shot* you."

"With a tranq."

He looked away. "You're the only thing I care about in this world. The only thing that *kept* me in this world, when I was sure ready to leave it."

She'd known that. She'd seen his eyes. All those long days in the hospital. All the surgeries. All the pain.

It was her turn to reach out to him. "You'll make it up to me."

"Following orders . . ." He muttered and shook his head. "I'm not a damn robot, and it was *you*. I should have trusted you. Not listened to the lies about you falling for a wolf."

Gage's head snapped their way.

Ah . . . shifter hearing. His eyes narrowed on Jonah. Yep, that was a flash of fury in his gaze.

I fucking love you. His words whispered through her mind again.

So it hadn't been a candlelit confession. No roses and fancy dinner and sweet words.

It had just been—Gage. Heat of the moment. In the middle of the fight. Rough. Hard.

Her wolf.

"Let's get out of here," Jonah told her. "The wolves—they should just be left alone."

Her eyes were on Gage. "I don't want to leave them alone."

Jonah stiffened. "Uh, what?"

Gage stalked toward her. He was wearing jeans now. Someone in the pack had brought backup clothing for everyone.

Prepared pack.

"I'm not going back," Kayla said. She'd always feared a wolf's claws. Hated the power of the beast.

But Gage was different. His beast made her feel safe.

He made her feel loved.

"Kayla, it was just a job!" Jonah sounded more than a little desperate. "Just a mission gone bad!"

"No." Gage was almost on them. Her words weren't really for Jonah anymore. They were for Gage. It was time for him to understand. "It wasn't just a mission for me."

"Aw, hell. " Jonah stepped back in surprise. "You did fall for the wolf."

Gage's gaze swept over Jonah. "You're . . . healing."

"Yes, well, a slash to the arm can take some—"

"You're lucky I didn't kill you." Gage flashed his fangs. "You ever shoot at her again and I'll—"

"I'll be damned." Jonah's jaw dropped. He shook his head, and took a minute to recover before he said, "You love my sister."

Kayla frowned at him. Did he have to sound so shocked?

Gage blinked and looked annoyed. Just the way she felt. Gage said, "I married her, didn't I?"

It really was that simple. But she'd been too blind—too scared and desperate—to see the truth from the beginning. It wasn't about packs.

About mates.

About hunters.

It was just about them. Man and woman.

Need. Lust. Desire.

Love.

"But the real question is . . ." Gage's voice had deepened and his focus was on her. Totally. "Just why the hell did she marry me?"

The wolves were watching. Her brother stared with wide eyes.

Kayla didn't speak.

Jonah cleared her throat. "Um, see, man, there was this mission . . ."

Gage shoved her brother away. Shamus grabbed Jonah's arm before he could charge back at him.

"Was it just the mission?" Gage wanted to know. "Tell me."

Kayla shook her head. He had to hear the mad galloping of her heart. The drumbeat filled her ears. So loud.

"Then why?"

So many eyes on them. *So many.* She knew how important this moment was. To the wolves. To her.

To Gage.

She lifted her right hand—and realized she was still holding the gun. Jonah's backup weapon. The one he kept loaded with silver.

She tucked it into her waistband and lifted her hand again.

"Why?" Gage demanded.

She smiled at him. The pain and horror of the past were slipping away. Her hand touched Gage's strong chest. "Because you're mine, wolf."

She heard the growls of approval from the pack.

Mine.

"And I don't plan to ever let you go." The pack would need to get used to that fact. *Deal with it.* They'd have a hunter in their midst from now on.

She wasn't afraid of the big, kick-ass wolf. She loved him too much for fear.

Kayla pulled her wolf closer. Stood on her toes. And kissed him.

She'd promised forever at that little chapel, and forever was exactly what she'd give him.

Wolves weren't the only ones who mated for life. Humans could sure as hell do that, too.

Forever.

Gage's arms closed around her, and she knew . . . she was just where she was supposed to be. With the man who loved her.

She was home. At last.

EPILOGUE

The bride took slow, deliberate steps down the aisle. The minister smiled at her, but he was sweating.

Hmmm . . . wonder if the guy knew he was in a room full of wolf shifters and hunters?

The hunters were on her side of the chapel. Looking fairly nice and presentable. No black ski masks. No weapons. They'd *better* not have brought weapons to her wedding.

The wolves were on the groom's side. Again . . . fairly nice and presentable. As long as you didn't look too closely. If you did, you might see the flash of some fangs. Maybe a few claws.

The groom waited at the end of the aisle. He wasn't smiling. He'd smiled before. On her first walk down the aisle. Back then, he'd looked so casual and open, but that cool appearance had been a lie.

There weren't going to be any more lies between them. Not now.

That was why they were starting over. This time, they were getting things right.

"You okay?" her brother whispered. Kayla turned her head and found Jonah watching her with worried eyes.

What? Did he think she was going to break and run? She was already married to the wolf.

But Gage had insisted on another ceremony. One in front of the pack. One without any kind of deceit.

One to tell their kids about.

Whatever. I'm telling the kiddos about the first marriage. And the wild ride of fighting and running that followed.

Because she never wanted to lose those memories.

"Kayla?" Now Jonah was paling. Probably because he was afraid he'd have to tangle with a little chapel full of big old wolves.

She smiled at him. "Everything's gonna be all right."

He exhaled on a slow breath. Then nodded.

Poor guy. He was getting used to the wolves now, slowly. The Vegas wolves had started working with the group of hunters that were left. They were all rescuing those unjustly imprisoned under Lyle's psychotic reign. And stopping the real supernatural threats that were still out there.

Having a wolf on your side could be a very, very good thing.

Kayla stopped walking and stood just in front of Gage. So strong. So dangerous.

So hers.

A very good thing.

The minister/preacher guy started talking. She was supposed to be listening. This was all important.

She couldn't hear anything but her own heartbeat.

She couldn't look away from Gage's eyes.

Had wolves really haunted her nightmares for years? Because she couldn't imagine her life without this one wolf.

Then Jonah placed her hand on top of Gage's. She repeated vows—for the second time. She pretty much had no idea what she said, but that didn't matter.

Because soon Gage was kissing her and she was kissing him back. She had her forever, and it was the best thing in the world.

The best.

The wolves howled and the hunters cheered . . . and Kayla got her happy ending.

★ ★ ★

Gage carried her over the threshold. Not some too-pink honeymoon suite this time. But into his home. His bed.

Not that they were gonna make it that far . . .

Kayla was already stripping him.

He tried to slow her down. "Sweetheart, let's go slow, let's . . ."

Her hand was on his cock. He shuddered. Okay. Screw slow. They could do that one next time. They had nothing but time now.

They made it to the couch. He pulled off her dress—she'd been so beautiful in it—then stared at her white garter belt with desperate eyes.

"Um, Kayla?" His hand tightened on her thigh. "You weren't wearing any panties." Just that sexy as hell garter and thigh-high stockings. Hot enough to make a man drool.

She smiled. "I figured I'd save us a step."

And even though lust was freaking eating him alive, laughter burst from him.

Kayla. She'd gotten to him from the very first moment. Wrapped him around her little, lethal fingers.

He spread her legs. "Well, if it saves us a step . . ." He put his mouth on her. Licked and kissed that delicate flesh and grew even more frantic for her.

Love her taste.

Her hips arched against him. She was wet. Ready. But he wasn't done tasting.

His tongue slid into her. His thumb pushed over her clit.

She shivered beneath him. Her nails dug into his back, marking him. For a human, the woman sure had some strong she-wolf tendencies.

He stroked her again. Licked.

And felt the tightening of her muscles around him. That was it. Just a little more . . .

Kayla came against his mouth.

It was gonna be one hell of a night.

Gage used his teeth to pull down her stockings. He took his time licking and kissing her skin.

"*Gage!*"

Definite she-wolf tendencies.

He thrust into her. Sank as deep as he could go. It still wasn't deep enough. Would anything with her ever be enough?

He kissed her. Withdrew. Thrust. Her legs wrapped around him. Her arms held him tight.

Nothing else was this good. This perfect.

The beast inside was snarling. Wild for his mate, and his mate was wild for him.

Kayla's nails scratched down his back.

When she came again, he erupted within her seconds later. *Just the start.*

He'd make sure that the woman screamed with pleasure every day of her life. Every. Single. Day.

Gage wrapped his arms around her. After a while, he finally managed to get them to the bedroom. This time, he wouldn't have to worry about a silver knife being shoved at his heart in the middle of the night.

Kayla already had his heart. She didn't need to try and take it again. It was hers to keep, for the rest of their lives.

He lowered her onto the bed and stared down at the hunter who'd come for him. His wife.

No, there would be no silver knives this time. They *would* get a real honeymoon. And if they didn't . . .

He just might have to kill someone.

Gage climbed into bed with her and pressed a kiss to Kayla's lips.

Forever had never tasted so good.

Can't get enough Shelly Laurenston?

Get to know her arrogantly sexy dragon shapeshifters, whom she writes about as G. A. Aiken.

An excerpt of this month's release, *How to Drive a Dragon Crazy*, follows. . . .

"Iz!"

Izzy heard her dragon cousin's screamed warning and was able to move her body out of the way in time to avoid the ogre attacking from behind, but the blade of his flint axe cut across her arm. The wound began to bleed almost immediately and she knew she'd have to get it sewn up. But she refused to worry about that now. Not with the ogre leader in her sights at last. She could see him about thirty feet away. So very close.

Izzy spun, swung the club, and slammed it into the neck of the bastard behind her as he tried to run away. He went down face first and Izzy pulled out her sword and rammed it into the back of the beast's head.

"Izzy."

She heard her name called again, this time by a much different voice than her cousin Branwen, but she had to ignore it as she was being attacked again. *Gods, the ogres just keep coming.*

She blocked the flint mace aimed for her face by using the club she still held in her left hand and cut the thick arteries inside the ogre's thighs with her sword. She spun and slashed her sword again, cutting a throat, spun again and swung, but her blade was stopped by an obscenely large battle axe. She knew the weapon was not an ogre's. They only used flint weapons and although deadly were often crudely made. This was a well-made weapon forged by a true blacksmith.

So Izzy struck at the knees with the club she still held. The heavy flint made contact and there was an angry snarl from beneath the heavy fur cape that covered the face and body of the axe wielder.

"Izzy! Stop!"

She ignored the command and swung the blade again. A big gloved hand reached out and shoved her back.

"Gods-dammit, Izzy! It's me!" He yanked the hood of his cape back, revealing his handsome face and dark blue hair. Some of it in braids with leather strips, feathers, and small animal bones tied throughout. "It's Éibhear."

"Yeah," Izzy answered honestly. "I know."

Then she pulled back her arm and threw the sword she held directly at his head.

Éibhear knew that because of his size, it was believed he was quite slow. Lumbering was a word he'd often heard used from those seeing him doing nothing more than standing. Yet at that moment when he saw the short sword coming right at him, thrown by a woman who clearly knew what she was doing, Éibhear would say he'd never been so grateful that everyone was wrong. He was fast. Very fast. And it was that speed, being able to drop to the ground in seconds, that really saved his life.

Once he hit the ground, he looked up and saw that Izzy was running right at him. He wasn't sure if she was coming to finish him off or just kick the shit from him, but the thought of batting her away or blasting her with his flame— stupidly—never entered his head.

He would never know why.

When Izzy reached him, she snatched his short sword from his belt and leaped up, one foot landing on his shoulder. She used that foot to launch herself, lifting her body, and spinning in the air. Éibhear turned over and watched as Izzy raised the sword that most human males couldn't lift and shove it into the nine-foot ogre that had stood behind Éibhear. He'd been so focused on Izzy, he hadn't even been aware of the big bastard wearing a human skull on a chain around his neck.

But even with the sword buried in the top of his head, the ogre wasn't dead yet. He was snarling and snapping at Izzy as she hung there, and that's when she spoke to the green bastard. Éibhear had no idea what she said, but he was positive the ogre did. And the words were so guttural, so vile sounding that he knew she was speaking the ancient language of the ogres.

When Izzy finished, she released her hold on the sword and dropped to the ground. With one good kick to the ogre's stomach, she knocked him on his back and walked around until she was able to look him in the eye. Gripping in both hands the club she still held, she raised it above her head and brought it down once, smashing the ogre's face in.

It was then that Éibhear realized this must be the ogre leader because all the surviving ogres stopped fighting and began to turn and run back toward the mountains in the distance, probably to choose another leader and regroup. Izzy seemed to know that as she yanked Éibhear's blade from the dead leader's head.

"All of you!" Izzy called out while walking back toward Éibhear. "Don't let them reach the caves. Kill them all! *Now move!*"

Izzy stopped by Éibhear's side, looked him over. "Why are you here?" she asked.

"To bring you home."

"Can't." She dropped the blade on his stomach, Éibhear barely catching it before the blade possibly cut something vital. "Not done."

She turned away from him, dismissing him without a backward glance. "Lieutenant Alistair." A full-human male rode up to her.

"General!"

"Rally the men. Pull several to get the wounded to healers. We'll deal with the dead later. I want those ogres meeting their green-skinned ancestors before the moon's high in the sky. Do you understand?"

"Aye, General."

"Go."

He rode off and another female rode to Izzy's side.

"Fionn. How are we looking?"

"Good, Iz. But there's still some fight left in the South Valley."

"Take a contingent and strike them down."

"Your arm, General," the woman Fionn pushed.

"Yeah, yeah. I know, Colonel. I'll deal with it." She laughed, waved the woman away.

Then, without even looking at him again, Izzy walked off, leaving him lying there.

"I don't know why you look so shocked," a voice said from beside him and he looked up into the face of his cousin Branwen. "What did you expect from her? To drop to her knees and suck your cock right here?"

Well . . . it had crossed his mind.

If you liked this book, try these other anthologies available from Brava . . .

When He Was Bad

Two of paranormal romance's bestselling authors combine their extraordinary talents and set the pages on fire with an after-dark anthology featuring Alpha males so hot, so wild, and so bad, they may just be the best you've ever had . . .

Miss Congeniality
Shelly Laurenston

It's those damn stockings that get me every time. They have this sexy little line down the back and I can't help but stare at her legs . . . constantly. And you'd think she'd be all over me like every other female in the Seattle area. I'm young, good looking, and one day I'll be Alpha Male of my family's Pack. But Professor Irene Conridge acts like I don't even exist. How is that possible? Now she's got enemies coming out of the woodwork and I have to protect her. Why? Because that's the kind of man I am. Yes, I am that amazing. Of course, it doesn't hurt that while I work to secure her safety, she'll be hanging out at my house. That's hours . . . days even that I've got Irene Conridge right where I want her.

Wicked Ways
Cynthia Eden

I'm too dangerous for her. I know it, but I can't get my sexy new neighbor out of my head. When I hear her scream one night, the absolute last thing I expect to see is Miranda Shaw—star of my hottest fantasies—being attacked by a vampire. Now the undead jerk is after her, and I'm the only thing standing between the beautiful lady and a killer who just won't stop. Well, too bad for him, because that vamp has just made the worst mistake of his afterlife—he's tangled with a shifter. And Miranda, well, she's so busy watching out for him that she won't see me closing in on her—not until it's too late—and I'm about to show her just how wild I can get . . .

Everlasting Bad Boys

They're bad boys—with that little something extra. Sexy, wild, out-of-this-world talents that can leave any woman feeling weak at the knees (among other body parts), they're the ones to call when you want pleasure that lasts . . . and lasts . . .

Can't Get Enough
Shelly Laurenston

Even for a dragon, Ailean the Wicked has a bad reputation. For 150 years he's been renowned for his fighting prowess, but now he's got a new conquest in mind—a gorgeous dragoness known as Shalin the Innocent. Ailean suspects she's anything but. And while he's saving her from her enemies, he plans to prove that, even in human form, a bad-boy dragon can show a girl a good time that's truly off the scale . . .

Spellbound
Cynthia Eden

No witch in her right mind would summon an immortal soul-hunter to her aid, but Serena Tyme needs Luis D'Amil's help to destroy the warlock who's stalking her coven. And she's willing to pay any price he names . . . especially when the tall, dark, sexy-as-hell assassin shows her he can work some sensual magic of his own . . .

Turn Me On
Noelle Mack

Finally, Beth Danforth has found a man who can flip her switch. That's because supersexy Justin Watts, CEO of SpectraSign, is literally made of light. His dazzling, custom-built body can't ever wear out. And talk about energy—Beth can't get enough of the guy. The sex is electrifying. The love will never fade away . . .

Belong to the Night

The Wolf, the Witch, and Her Lack of Wardrobe
Shelly Laurenston

Jamie Meacham has enough trouble controlling her supernatural abilities. There's no time for lust, or for Tully Smith, even with his smoldering amber eyes. But Tully's grappling with his own animal instincts as a powerful shifter-wolf, trying to protect all his territory . . .

In the Dark
Cynthia Eden

FBI agent and leopard shifter Sadie James' undead ex, Liam, still arouses her deepest desires. By teaming up with Liam, Sadie has a better chance of tracking the brutal rogue shifter who is terrorizing Miami, but as passion consumes them, she stands to lose more than just her heart.

City of the Dead
Sherrill Quinn

Dori Falcon is a witch with a plan: get to New Orleans, locate her missing brother, and recover a mysterious and powerful amulet. Her plan never included falling for sexy Cajun cop Jake Boudreau; but without his help, she may never find the key to her family's survival.